# MY SUNSHINE LOVE

## MONIKA CHOUDHURY

**First published in 2018 by**

**Becomeshakespeare.com**

Wordit Content Design & Editing Services Pvt Ltd
Unit- 26, Building A-1, Nr Wadala RTO,
Wadala (East), Mumbai 400037, India
T: +918080226699

Wordit Art Fund helps deserving authors publish their work by
providing monetary support. To apply for funding, please visit us
at www.BecomeShakespear.com

ISBN - 978-93-87649-29-3

# About Author

Monika Choudhury, is an Indian author, a simple person, loves to hone her expressions into words, and to live the life, the way it is. Has Masters Degree in Political Science and Advertising.

# Contents

# Prologue: A Little About Me

It is one of the early day of January month. The cold and bitter windis enough to stagger me. Even pulling of my woolen cardigan closer to wrap my body in the much needed warmth seems to be my futile attempt to shield me against that. Moreover the unruly wind is making my long, dark curly hair disheveled, which is framing my face while protecting my ears from getting numb. But now my mass of curls, are a complete mess. Luckily, I spotted a Café, to take shelter from this bone chilling weather. All I need, is a nice cup of hot tea to collect my thoughts, which are frozen in brain by now. It will melt my life's dankness somehow too. Oh! What a world's good it will do to me. I said this, though getting skeptical about the mere cup's power, which is going to do that Herculean task for me. Quickly I crossed the foggy street with a caution, to dash inside the shop. Tracing my finger on the brim of the cup, and through the hot steam, which is coming out of the cup, I contemplated further... About me, and my current predicament.

My company has been downsized, and I'm out of work! The merge savings and the money from my last paycheck, are all that is left in my name, in this world. And the amusing thing moreover is, this month is my birth month. If simply put, my birthday is coming soon. It's not that I'm being enthusiastic over it, to celebrate the day, anyhow. But my simple reason in remembering is only because I will not survive to see that day, and it will be my hoping against the hope then. Even the blind can see that, if my pathetic plight goes on like this... Yet I will be a dishonest person, if I do not reveal my one and only precious asset, which I have along with me all the time, which I will never even imagine to be parted away with, even if I die of hunger or be out in the streets lying cold! It's my mother's sole remembrance which she gave to me, at my last birthday, before she was alive... and that day was the last jubilation of my life, and my last birthday celebration too! It's nothing grand to boast about, a solitaire diamond pendant in size of a dot which I wear with a gold chain on my neck as my lucky charm as my benediction. For me, this is the most priceless thing, the most valuable thing on this earth!

All of a sudden amid my ponders, a horror of reality gripped me! "I don't want to die of hunger, I don't want to be out in the streets to die there, like a street dog!"

It's only me, who knows, how I have gritted my teeth, to endure all the wickedness of life, for years, just to live on, while thinking, that from the next year everything will be alright, but on the contrary everything has become worse and worse, day by day! I'm twenty three, and soon going to be twenty four, if I survive to see that birthday anyhow.I have a graduation and a short duration advertising degree in my hand.

But my career didn't spiral up the ladder, the way it should have. Even though I was efficient in my work, but most probably I must have lacked in worldly qualifications...I have nothing to boast about my recent milieu either, neither I have been to any kind of relationship, nor there is any prospect of settling down in near future. So getting a life like any other normal girl, is a far fetched idea for me. Although I know, I'm somewhat smart, attractive, pretty, with my moderate slender figure, and is blessed with a good height. I have my charming beauties, my pair of large dark sparkling eyes in almond shape and my long curtain of soft curls, silky hair... But still I can envision, that I will die, remaining a chaste and single girl, and so finding someone of my heart's own is ruled out, from the book of my hapless life...I have also been agonized with the brevity, my parents had died in a severe car crash, and it's more than four years now, that I'm living without them. Neither I have any siblings nor any living relations even. It is an evident fact that I'm all alone in this crowded world, with only me as my company, with no home of my own, no support, and practically nowhere to turn to, not even a sympathetic shoulder to cry on to... No miracle is going to happen for me. I know my real predicament. And I know, it's absolutely not the right time to think about all this also...My body quivered in a dread of survival. "No! I must act fast now, to find something to earn, before it's going to be too late to act upon, it's a 'do or die' situation for me!"

Amid my self-talk, I spotted something there, a newspaper, which someone must have left in a hurry. I glanced around to make sure that no one is noticing me. Then my certitude discovered that the coast is clear. I quickly picked it up, that stranded paper from the adjoining table. "Ah! Good, it's today's newspaper." I exclaimed inwardly. And without wasting any more of my precious time, my Raptor eyes hunted over the printed adverts of the job classifieds column. "Wanted a...no...an efficient, oh no! Not that... Um." After crisscrossing several options, my eyes suddenly fixed on something. And that something is going to be the real life-saver opportunity for me... I can bet my life on!

# Chapter One: An Unknown Step

I packed up all my belongings in a couple of suitcases and in a few of my duffle bags. I stuffed my entire world, my every single memory of life, in bags and baggage, just like that. And whilst doing this, I cleared up all my rent and pending dues too, to clear away my every trace of debts of which I'm incurring to, and that includes my every little emotional attachment which I have in my hometown, for my birth city, before leaving it forever to relocate myself to another one, to commence a new phase of life! And I did all those obligatory duties, before boarding my morning train...

That placement agency which I've contacted through the newspaper advert, the lady-in-charge there had confirmed me several times that the job is all mine without any doubt, and someone definitely would be there at the station to pick me up. So in a way after relying on her word of mouth completely, I took up this unknown step of my life! Nobody forced me to take this decision I admit, but despite of that, a sudden intense tension is started building up inside. And by each passing minute, it is increasing even more, especially when my destination is getting nearer and nearer...

By now my unsteady nerves are unsettling me immensely, and is getting beyond my control, and besides this I started having second thoughts on the outcome of my step!

But quickly brushing aside any doubt, I evaluated my future position of work, to fork out a brighter side of this… from how I have to take the position of a personal assistant, and also have to act as live-in-housekeeper, to a ready-made Garment manufacturer. Although I'm assigned to do a double job with single salary, yet I'm not complaining, as the sum which has been offered to me is tidy enough to cover my moderate expenses and when it includes my accommodation and provision too. In this way, I'm not only be saving my rent, but the ration money out there besides. And in a few months, my worst financial situation might get over by this. Yes! Everything will turn out well for me. My nodding head nodded in an approval after calculating the gains. Now I'm hoping with a fervor for all that goodness to come. And apart from that I know the naked sooth, that I can't be a choosy one now, not in my present plight…And I pondered on those during my entire journey. Finally the wheels of the train, the wheels of my fate, screeched at the station platform, to inform me, that my long journey have been culminated, and it's my time now to step into my new world…I huddled outside with my long trail of suitcases and baggage, with a difficulty. The platform of the city named 'Kalyanpur' looked rather deserted to me, and the day is once again windy and nippy, to heighten my shiver of fear, and it have not been lessened even after the good vibes I've felt post stepping out here, of being in my second home? Nothing is helping me to make my tremulous nerves still…

My anticipated wait awaited on desperately for that man to show up soon, who is supposed to meet me up here. It must be after quite a bit of time that, I spotted someone…a man, who approached to my direction…a debonair man, with handsomeness dripping all over his body. A man of lofty height, and a man in…(the age, I tried to estimate then) must be in his early thirties or less, it is so hard to gauge even that, simply by looking at his imposing look and well maintained appearance, his boyish looks is rather mystifying me. And his flamboyance is mystifying me even more, from his hairstyle, his cladding of a very expensive suit, custom-designed one, in a rather exquisite style, to his wearing of a very luxurious brand of watch. And those diamonds set in a platinum bracelet, that exceptional design, must be from some famous and pricey company, they must've cost him more than his fortune, I'm sure of that! For a few moments his dazzle blinded me, confounded me, that whether I had mistaken him as my expected escort or not?! Yet, his advancing footsteps which sprung towards me, assured me that I'm not in any way. His apparent striking sight filled my entire vision to astound me profoundly…*Man!* This is the most handsome and hottest man, I ever laid my eyes on. What a perfect shaped physique, he must be a regular member of his gym, the tautness of his muscles lurking out from his clothes is answering me there. He has such a well defined, clean-shaven aquiline features, such luxuriant dark hair, neatly styled, that my mouth gaped in an admiration! And those pairs of eyes, he got, the most marvelous pair of eyes anyone can have, midnight dark, deep and soulful, and on top of it, the most captivating ones. Yes, they have captivated me. And they're enough to pierce through my heart, enough to dive into their charm, enough to mesmerize my soul. If I want to compare him with anyone, then I can undoubtedly say, he is just a replica of some Greek God!

*"Oh dear God! Please have mercy on me!"* I whispered intensified for this work of art of the maker, and absolutely amazed at my

girly part's sudden tingling, in such incredulous way, by the effect of his demeanor! I pinched myself too, to check whether I'm dreaming or not? And I wonder, why his presence afflicted me so much, when I never have even had cared to look at some man? But the billion dollar question still remains.

*"Who is he?!"* I mumbled, through my gaping mouth, which is still gaping, in his enchantment…He is not a chauffeur, nor looked like someone from working staff of my new employer's office. Absolutely not, not after seeing his classy taste in clothes and everything. And not after seeing his donning of such expensive clothes and adornments which are vouching something else. Then who is He really? Amid my sea of self-confusion a mellowed voice, with a touch of drawl addressed me, to introduce him along with his penetrating gaze to abate my confusion.

"Miss Minisha Ganguli, I presume? I'm Debobroto Mukherjee!"

So! He came here himself, my employer, armed, fully to kill me, first with his killer looks, now with an enchanting voice, together with that alluring gaze, so he can slay me mercilessly! On top of it, his height paired with his broad shoulders is towering over me, to make me breathless, and to make my heart race wildly, specifically, when he is at such close quarters. But he is totally unaware of his fatal impact on me, and simply waited for my reply…I stood there stupefied with my parted lips, firstly on account of such unbelievable fact that my employer have actually come here to pick me up, when he can easily send one of his servants, and secondly in the blazing fascination for his presence, and for his provocative tantalizing masculine scent, which my nostrils are getting filled with. It must be of some expensive cologne or something grand, I'm certain of that imported brand…but it has a sensuality as if being melded with his raw masculinity. Somehow I managed to utter by steadying myself hard. "Sir??!"

He must've sensed my disposal of confusion in my eyes, and alarming flushes on my face because of his unexpected arrival. He tilted his dark head to scrutinize me thoroughly. "I have come to fetch you, because my driver is indisposed, so unable to find anyone at such short notice to welcome you in, moreover, it'll remain in my conscience if I leave a lonely lady stranded like this in some unknown Place." He explained himself in a restrained manner, yet in an urbane way... And then without waiting for my response or without waiting for any ceremony, his chivalry suddenly started lifting up my suitcases to carry them up with his hands. That action simply flabbergasted me, as I didn't even dreamed that my rich employer is going to lift up my suitcases like a porter, and I couldn't allow such an elite person to do such a thing, for his underling... and when he is my boss! With an alarm in my eyes and voice, altogether, I cried aloud in my protest.

"Please Sir, don't do that, it's not necessary at all, I will manage myself perfectly, thank you so much for all the same."

And listening to my earnest protest, he just shrugged off his shoulder nonchalantly at my disapproval. "Fine then, suit yourself. "

He strode his steps forward while leaving me in the middle, to struggle with my array of bags and baggage... But patience ran out for him after my, several unsuccessful attempts in doing that. He signaled a 'coolie' then to carry out my load into the car. Once again, the car flaunted richness of his own, it's a very expensive one indeed, I can smell leather and money from it.

I know it's a swanky one, not by speculating at its exterior and interior, or by the posh name, but on account of my familiarization with this type of car, in my lifetime! I opened the back door gingerly, after my belongings have been loaded in the car trunk, but suddenly he objected my opening of that door... And he simply closed the car door back to my utter surprise.

"Please sit on the front seat beside me, I insist on it, please." His eager request rather commanded me. That very idea disturbed me so much so, that I rooted my stubborn feet just there, without making any slightest effort even to move. He saw how obstinate I'm getting at it, so he remarked in his convincing tone to convince his gesture.

"Please Miss Ganguli, don't think me as a rude person, it's that, I have to inquire about something on my way along, and I might get distracted, and can meet up with some accident, if every time I have to look at the car mirror or turn my back to talk with you. Don't you think, it is unwise of me? As you know very well, how we have corresponded only through the placement agency, and the emails sent to me, and when few points have to be cleared up soon, before you start working for me. I'm a very busy man, so I hardly will have time for this in the future, it will save up my time too, while we talk through driving." He finished in one go, of what he was saying, and the stern look he gave, is enough to make me understand, that his insistence is not in a habit of hearing a 'No'! Especially after what he imposed on the people. What else I can do then, when he is my boss? Moreover, his request seems to be legit and sensible one, when I know how my Parents had died. Besides, I don't want to give him a bad impression about me either, not on my first day, when I haven't secured the job yet?

Who knows, he might have his personal reasons too, he didn't want to look like my chauffeur, who's chauffeuring me around while I sit back behind like some haughty owner. And when he behaved in such a gentlemanly way all along, so without refusing or retracting his request further, I nodded in an agreement...I quietly rode in the front seat beside the driver's seat to discover more riches, the car is loaded with expensive gadgets as well. I remained stolid while compressing my mouth, when the engine is ignited to move ahead.

He remained silent for a quiet while and is entirely concentrated on the steering wheel and the road and that awkward silence and my sitting beside such a charmer, is making me more nervous. I lowered my lush lashes to veil my eyes completely from the moving view as my way to compose myself. When suddenly I heard him say, in a very pleasant tone. "Well, if you keep diverting your vision like that, you'll miss the beautiful scenery around here. Don't you think, its one of the most beautiful city?! I don't have any intention to compare this with the big city, from where you came from, but yet this is the place of which I always take pride of!" His cheery voice persuaded me to lift and direct my glances at his proud and glowing face..."So just relax and enjoy the rest of the drive. It's still an hour or so to reach my home." He added in his convivial tone while throwing at me, his quick, attentive glances. Then, suddenly, he threw something else too, his one lopsided, dimpled smile at me!

And that smile simply caught my breath in my lungs, and my heart started throbbing wildly, beyond my control! And stupidly I blushed, blushed very deeply... and it made me wonder in return, about his rather friendly and charming behavior to me all of a sudden! Or is it in his nature to behave like this to all of his paid employees? As far as I knew, he is married, and have one girl child of six or seven years old, and he lived with an army of servants in a palatial Bungalow. That's all the information I have collated from the agency. I re-checked about his company, it's reputable too... But nothing else I can scout about his personal life even after delving so much on the internet. Only this much I have learned that he is a fellow Bengali like me, that too because his surname suggests it. My mulling came to a conclusion, that he might be doing this just to cheer me up or to motivate me to work diligently, or to make me familiarize with the alien environment I'm going to be in, soon. Yes, that seems to be the plausible reason.

"Yes, Sir! " I just managed to murmur that, only as my reply. Judging my communicative self, he carried on once again.

"Frankly, I'm very curious to know about you? Why you're here, out of the hubbub of a metro city!? And why you've agreed to do this job?! You've quit your last job? Right? Pardon me, but you're an orphan, and your parents had passed away? Yet leaving your hometown like this, is compelling me to question you! As the agency people gave me so little information about you and it's so scant that before I permit you to employ, I must hear this straight from the horse's mouth. Pardon my phrase. You haven't been interviewed by me, properly. So that placement agency's backing, holds no water!"

He questioned me with a sudden change in his tone, by replacing his earlier amicable mode, veering his subject of the conversation to shift it into a more businesslike mannerism. It seems to me, that he is somewhat lamenting on his mistake of not investigating on my background before appointing me, which may be his ground rule for employing any off comer? "Well, sir, I lost my parents in a mishap and it's been almost five years now that they had died..." I controlled my brimming emotions here, before continuing in my calm and frank tone. "And as for my previous company, where I used to work, it was on the verge of fold, so they had sacked each and every employee out from last month. I simply turned in here just to earn my livelihood, and people do move away to a new place in search of a job…I promise you that I will work hard and try my level best to do justice to my designated position… and all the testimonials are with you to back up my education, even my word of mouth… and the description of my past job presumably you've received by now, along with my resume?"

I reasoned myself in a dignified way, in hope to satisfy his curious queries, to ace his test, and to abate his subtle suspicions which he has been hurled at me in a polite way. But I concealed something to him in spite of my candidness, my desperation, in seeking this job! I can't display my impecunious plight so soon to him. I didn't want him to look down upon me, no matter how worse my situation is. I have my share of pride as well.

And he seemed to lend his patient ears to my explanation, and after keenly listening to everything, he remarked. " Hmm… So that's the case, I'm so sorry about your parents. Yes, I got all the necessary papers…but you have to work very hard, slacking off in my work, I will not allow at all. Do remember that. And I have very observant eyes, nothing escapes from it." Here, he threatened me coldly, in the form of warning, before resuming with his says… "Let me throw some light on the list of duties you're assigned with them. First of all, you've to be my full time personal assistant to my home office. Whenever I will return from my office you will check all my appointments, manage and plan my office schedules which have been capped off or pending, or what to carry on the next day, and have to go through with a few of my personal paper works also. However, in the meantime, you will supervise the upkeep of my house, there are two maids, a driver, and the gardener who also does all the odd jobs, besides there are two guards; so it's not that you've to do the ground work there. Just keep a firm and an alert eye on their regular ongoing, particularly my daughter very well, she is only seven, and in the first standard and is being taken care of by the maids all this while, but still as you know..." He hesitated a little in saying this. "My wife had died almost five years ago, and I'm a widower... So you can understand, I need someone to watch her over all the time, as I hardly have time to spare.. And of late the maids are finding it rather difficult to look after her, after managing the entire house."

His voice sounded so bereft, then most probably due to the heavy emotions I guessed, attached to his late wife, and for his daughter, who is deprived of her mother's care and affection and for the sorrow, on his lack of attention to her, due to his time constraint. And those simply touched my heart, because my bereft can be connected to their melancholy. I can relate with their dearth of love and care in life, even when paid helps are around the house to take care of them. Meanwhile, his hoarse emotional voice somewhat steadied itself quickly, he must be wondering why an austere person opening up, before a stranger...and he continued once more, in his restricted tone. "Anyways, you will have to report me back, time to time...And you will be paid suitably of course for all your duties. And I already have ordered my servants to ready a room for you. I hope everything you will find there, will be according to your liking..."

Though he implied all his list of commands rather abruptly to me, yet he chose his words carefully, so I don't take any umbrage to them. I'm glad for his courteous behavior. And after learning that nature, and his sole aim to get my efforts towards the work only, made me sigh in a respite, so to steady my unsteady self, which was getting vulnerable earlier about the nature of my employer, when the world is full of wolves for a lonely girl! Anyhow, in this way, he sketched a rough draft of his household scene side by side, so it could not frustrate me further, while I will be at my load of work, which I have been prescribed for, before I actually begun performing them. I nodded at him to understand my enlisted duties, which are inevitable, and nodded again at his sole concern which is only for my work and not on the other way round... Yet honestly, this seems to me a lot of work, still I cannot retract, as I'm here for work, and not for vacation. And when this is my sole hope of survival, I have to slog, without slipping it from my hand, with all my might, no matter what! I made up my mind to take my new life in a new perspective, even when my current position of job is a menial one, compared to my earlier pink collar job. And regarding my liking as he quoted just now, I wonder who will think about that for a subordinate to whom they're paying, who have such broad mindset, who have such humanity in today's world? This intrigued me, his generous reason behind my hiring, and that puzzled me so much?

Why he did that because of pity, or for some other unknown reason? I drew in and out, a deep breath to brace myself up for the challenging future ahead! Our long drive ended finally and the uniformed guard opened a huge gate for us whilst we entered through it, for a very beautiful and elegant bungalow! A bewitching beauty is this house, which sat in the middle, while it's equally bewitching sides enchanted me, from it's carpeted lush lawn, surrounded with soothing greenery, to its beautiful blossoms which are adding animation of color and infusing the so much essence of warmth, while making the house much more extravagantly attractive and serene. It is one of the finest and the most enchanting house I've ever seen, as if a fairy picture house has come straight out of an interior magazine, but without marring the essence of homeliness in any way even in its grandeur. And I felt this house as akin as my paternal home, so much so that it seems to me, that I've come to my home at last, after being away from it for so long!

That feeling comforted me so much, that I looked on and on, right after alighting out from the car. I can conclude that it's a good start so far for my new taken steps, my liking of the house, my liking of my workplace.

Even though I didn't even have glimpsed it yet from the inside, or have met up with the people who belongs with it.

And the thought of an opulent interior and the sophistication residing inside, persuaded me to straighten up my tousled curls with one hand, and with another, my disheveled dress. Due to the long journey my clothes have been creased in several places. I put all those efforts to make myself a little more agreeable and to boost up some self-confidence within.

My this gesture on the contrary, has attracted his attention, he halted his proceeding steps to stare intensely at my face, and those intensified stares made me conscious, my heart skipped a beat. For that I gave him a surprised look in return, by lifting up my one brow slightly as a way to shield myself from his uncomfortable penetrating gazes.

And he must have seen the discomfort which peaked out from my face, and that made him opine in a crisp tone. "You will like the house I'm sure, come inside, and freshen up a bit, then let one of my servants to show you around, and to introduce yourself *with everything and everyone.*"

I know why he used that tone suddenly, just to subdue my startle, which I have faced up with due to his stare. And then to prove his point, he flashed a faint smile at me but no matter how faint it was, it has the same charm like his earlier lopsided one, and it caught up my breath once again! He must be innocent about its effect on me, his probable intention this time too is just to ease up my tension. So I also smiled slightly back at him, in courtesy and for his considerations... Yet I remained simply on an edge, for everything from then on, *without easing up at all!*

*************************

# Chapter Two : Getting Acquainted

Inside the house is as beautiful as it is from the outside, the way I've imagined it would be. It has such soothing and pleasing atmosphere, despite of its lavish and extravagant decorations. And this feeling possibly can't be ignored, even though it's similar to one of those interiors, who gives you the idea of actually been stepping into some grand hotel. Just then a maid came to my rescue, to break my daze of wonder about this house, and its owner's as well. I'm surprised at myself for not realizing that he left me there? But when did he leave? He sure can walk with his lithe steps, without making any sound...She introduced me to everyone of the staff around there, and each one of us exchanged our cordiality, but there is no sign of the child. And then the maid showed me to my room. And it seems to me, that only the female staff stays in their rooms downstairs within the house, and the members of the family upstairs, and the rest of the male staff, quartered to the separate outer wing, which is outside the bungalow...And the room which is allotted to me is directly under the flight of the ascending stairs.

It is small, neat, but comfortable enough to live your entire life in, in spite of the jaded furnishings, but at least I have them. There is one sofa, chair, who is going to play the double role of my writing cum sitting chair, and it sat beside the narrow writing table with a drawer. In the middle of the room, is a cozy bed, furnished well, with bedding, pillows, comforters and linen, and there is a bedside table next to it too, and on it, a bunch of keys, those keys are reminder of my new responsibilities…I saw a glass and a carafe of water placed on it also, and that proved, they are considerate enough for midnight parches. I don't have to go all through the way into the kitchen, for that purpose at night. And above all, I'm the fortunate one, who don't have to share the bathroom with others, when I have my own attached one, to my room…Oh! There is a closet with a full length mirror, on one of its side as well, how thoughtful of them! And that, must be my single window, but at least, it's wide one, and curtained, and when it is overlooking the garden, so my choking life will not be suffocated in the breathlessness, and even the rays of the sun will come to me in my sunless life. "Oh! This is the right wing of the building… Hmm." I surveyed my most convenient refuge from every angle, like some shrewd real estate agent, which have come to me as a my blessing. An obvious homely feeling suffused the room, and not a cheesy feeling at all, like you have while staying in a guest house… I left the idea of an elaborate unpacking for the night, and simply picked up a decent dress from my hold-all. I slipped into a warm pair of leggings, a tunic dress, and a thick warm woolen jacket over it. Despite of well air-conditioned house. The warmth is still not reaching properly to my parts of the room. I felt a bit chilly for that or rather more for my new standing…After freshening up a bit and brushing up my hair, I came out to start my doable jobs, according to the latest set of instructions… Again, that polite help came out from the kitchen for me, and her name is *Mira*. She told me to go directly to her master's home-office cum library cum den, and a tray of coffee is already placed there, as he wanted to have a cup of coffee with me. That came as a real surprise to me! As who would want to have a coffee with a hired servant? Neither I'm his acquaintance, nor a white collar staff of his office, but only an off comer, who is his housekeeper, no matter how much I camouflage, but that's the real truth. The personal assistant rank is just being added by him as a consideration for me, to revere my prestige. I know he is a courteous gentleman, yet this seems to me as one of his oddities. I said nothing to her, but hastened myself there, to see what others are waiting for me instead…The room is situated in the extreme corner of the entrance door downstairs. I knocked at the thick Mahogany door, and a faint sound of *Come in* floated into my ear. Gathering some courage, I pushed the door to open, and saw him leaning against one of the windows with his back turned before me. I noticed, he had changed into a fresh set of clothing. He wore a pair of slim brown trousers and a dark green cashmere pullover over it. Slowly he turned his back after hearing my footsteps, and gestured me to sit down, in one of the leather couch, with his hand. Then he requested me to bring up a cup of coffee to him. By this time, he sat against the gigantic teak wooden desk, in his revolving leather chair. He is looking more charismatic in his casual clothing, than his earlier formal attire, quickly evening, my breathing, due to its aftereffects. I placed the cup carefully on the edge of the table, as it is littered so much, with the number of stray files, papers and stationery, besides housing a desktop computer, his laptop, Tablet, and so on, that there is, hardly any space left for the cup, to reside there. "Thank you. You can have your cup now, you must have been tired. We will talk after that."

His consideration suggested me in his soft voice. Why he used this strange tone, so much different from his earlier tone? That made me wonder, whether he wants to know me better, completely in a different light or not? I thought about it, in my baffled state, while perching on the edge of the sofa. I'm sipping my coffee silently, but before I can finish up my cup, he ordered me once again. "Miss Ganguli, can you pour me down another cup?" This is rather strange, why he sloshed down his hot coffee hurriedly, so he can order me again, and how easily he has forgotten, that I haven't finished mine yet. But I'm his paid employee and this is my job, so I got up to obey what he asked for, and poured down the hot coffee from thermostat coffee flask into his cup... and he simply extended his hand nonchalantly, to lift up the cup without lifting his eyes, as his eyes is rather glued deeply on the laptop screen.

Post serving the order once again, I sat on the sofa, to almost gulp down my coffee, to finish that cup in a one go, as I'm afraid that he will summon me again with his orders. At least I must have a cup of coffee by now, as since morning I haven't eaten much, and it's near about six in the evening…Amid this, I waited and waited for that talk, but he looked completely detached with the real reason, beside my presence, and it's getting so late by now, and besides my rumbling stomach is making so much din for hunger that I wished that he doesn't notice my this embarrassment through his workaholic self. Then I thought of popping the question myself, to stir a conversation.

"Sir? Where is your daughter? She is not at home, I gather?"

"Huh? Oh! Miss Ganguli, why you are still here? Why so? " He drifted his eyes at least from his work to me, to inquire about my untimely presence. And that inquiry made my patience impatient, so I muttered to myself.

*"Is something wrong with this man? He called me himself to have*

*a talk, and I waited for that for the past half hour. And now he is asking me, why I'm here? Or did he completely forgotten that he hired me? When I need my instructions to work on from tomorrow."* Aloud I said in my calm tone to him. "Sir! You told me, that you wanted to have a word with me, so I...."

"Really? Oh yes! We can do that tomorrow. Be here at seven-thirty in the morning, sharp...And remember, I'm very punctual with time. Now go back to your room, it's getting rather late." He retorted.

And once again, I muttered to myself (and it's becoming habitual now)."*What? What's the meaning of this? Did he do that to test my patience, or just to pester me? Is this some kind of ragging? Yes, he can do that, when he is my superior. But I have a news for you, I'm neither going to be flared up, nor going to yield, for your attitude. Do remember that!*" My patient silky voice replied aloud to him, before closing the office door. "Very well Sir, I will do that. Goodnight then."

"This man seriously. What's wrong with him?" And me and my mumbles made a way to the kitchen to inquire, whether they eat dinner or not, or at all? When everything around here is so bizarre except this house, that it is possible for them to refrain themselves from eating as well...

And this time I'm welcomed by the other help, named Shefali, who also work as a cook. I thanked my lucky stars, *if there is any*, after learning that they actually eat. And the female and male staff have that right here, at the kitchen breakfast table. I sighed a huge relief. But before settling in the chair, I ordered Mira (a sense of duty came to me naturally) to clear away the coffee tray from the office, and to make sure, that Debobroto Sir has his dinner served properly and promptly too. I don't think he will mind or object, of my calling him that in front of his servants. Well! I must start from today, if I have to keep up my position... And nodding politely, she obeyed. And latter served his dinner in the dining hall, where he usually eats with his daughter... And we all had ours in the coziest nook of the kitchen, and it felt so pleasant, eating and talking cheerfully along like that, during our dinner time. Such a happy feeling I felt then, after all those years of my lonely nibble times... Amid that good dinner, which I have eaten since long time, I learnt that little Missy's name is Tia, who went for a visit to her Maternal Grandmother's place, and will return next week or so! The staff here seems to be a nice bunch of people to me. And they are getting rather sweet to me, as I'm going to supervise them from now on. But I didn't mind on the contrary, instead, that gave me a feeling of being someone important, for once in my lifetime too.

In the later part of the night, I entered into the kitchen, to refill my water carafe, but a startle is waiting for me, to ambush, in form of Debobroto Sir?

He is sitting on one of the chairs, while on the table, a glass of hot cocoa and a plate of choco-chip cookies are placed. The crumbs of the cookies are stuck on the sides of his mouth, and even an apparent chocolate milk mustache is on his upper lip, and those suggested me, that this fastidious man must be having them like some child. And suppressing a giggle I observed how he looked akin to a cute kid in his night suit and gown, with his ruffled hair. But he looked nonchalant of my presence. My bashfulness stammered while waving my carafe in the air, in a hope that at least I will not be accused of prying!

"I... I... came for the water! Can I help you with anything else Sir...?! " I added that further in civility.

"No, It's alright!" He replied in his withdrawn voice. I nodded in obeisance before greeting him Goodnight, once again, before filling up my carafe in a rush. I dashed out from there as quickly as possible as I didn't want to display my flimsy nightgown to him any longer either. Still, it seems so weird, his this nocturnal activity.

I rambled while I'm on my way to the room. *"He had his dinner, or did he completely forgotten about that too? The way he was devouring the cookies. Ah! Everything is so strange about him, so his handsome exterior and suave nature, has some quirkiness added to. And yes, some rich people are known to be eccentric, in their way. Don't they? Thank God! My Parents were not like them in anyway!"*

To my another utter surprise I slept well in my unfamiliar place to my foreign bed, without having any nightmares. And this my delicious pandiculation next morning has vouched!

*****************************

# Chapter Three: New Challenges

I woke up early when it's my first day at the work. I went to the kitchen to espy Shefali's prepared breakfast, instead whetted with an enlightenment. "He (Debobroto Sir) usually has his black coffee with plain toasts at breakfast, and hardly ever comes to the lunch, he even dines here occasionally. Sometimes he goes out to eat...so it's hard to tell exactly, whether he will eat at home or not? It all depends on his mood, *Didi* (Calling me elder sister, as away of her respect here)!" That made me wonder and prodded me as well, to know all the habits and regularities of the members, about the house, as fast as I can manage the house deftly. And for that, I must jot down all these pointers as soon as possible, so that I can plan well. "Shefali, that means he is available at the time of the breakfast, and it's the only important meal he eats at home. And when he works so hard, these irregularities in the meal won't do, and having only toast and coffee as breakfast won't do. So let's make it a hearty and streamlined one. Shall we?"

Her enthused self nodded at my infatuated idea, before I queried further. She like others have deep reverence for their master. " But tell me one thing.

Does he eat eggs... and cheese?? I mean, he is not a picky eater."

"Yes *Didi*, he does. But whether he is picky or not, I don't know, he never have complained."

"Oh! Alright then. I will prepare something today, you leave the dish quietly on the table. Let him decide, whether he will eat that or not, besides his toast and coffee. We will observe for the time being and then careen with our future meal plan...We can do this much for him." I lifted up my thumb to become victorious, and to make her my confidant into this. She giggled at my audacity and secretive venture!

For that something, I with an aplomb whisked together half a dozen of eggs, lots of cheese, strawberry preserve, and evaporated milk for a delicious-*'Dairy Double Omelet'*...and then baked it in a Microwave, it's better this way for the nutrients to remain intact. Though I'm totally unaware of his preference, yet I can't bargain his healthy diet. I stepped into his private world of taste with my chin up, for a palatable change for his sake. I told Shefali to cut that omelet dish into generous slices, and instead of one or two toast, to place an entire toast rack, a butter dish with dollops of low fat butter, feta cheese spread, bits of roasted almond, peanut butter, beside them. In this way he, on his own accord and taste, with whatever assorted items he wants will spread his toasts. Wish I have enough time to put more things on the table. I can't help it, when we are out of fruits, veggies and so many things, the Green grocery and other grocery deliveries are still due, this I learnt from Mira. I must act on those things instantly, after he finishes his breakfast...Serving good food should be my first priority, my determination encouraged me. In the meantime Shefali served him the way I instructed her to, post that I urged. "Okay, you worked hard, thank you, now go on, see that you and everyone else have their breakfast right away. I will join later..." After she went away, I quietly stood there outside the dining room's doorstep. I want to ascertain his actions and reactions, *as luckily*, his back is turned away from me, so he didn't notice my watchful eyes over him. At first, he only nibbled his toast with coffee, but later on, his intense agog persuaded him, to reach out for that Omelet dish...He picked up one slice, then second, third, and in this way polished off all the omelet slices from the platter. I smiled at his back warmly, as this is my first success. Yet I can't retract myself, not to mull. "He must be real hungry..." I saw how his hand extended to reach out for more toasts & the way he started dressing them with those accompaniments, one by one. "So he usually, remains half-starved, *Poor Rich man!* Yet he didn't bother to complain about them to his servants, in spite of being the owner of this house, not for once! How docile of him!" His pitiable plight, his earlier melancholy about his bereavement, and daughter, made me tenacious, made me sentimental. *"No! There will be a new set of terms, and new course of meals around here, when I'm the housekeeper. And when this is my home."* I promised myself, while shaking off my head at those negligence, at mismanagement.*"Yes, from next time, there will be more fruit baskets, more salads and soup bowls, beside the full four course of a meal on this table.*

*I will see to that..."* And promising this to myself, I quietly left the area with a content in my heart, that he have breakfasted well. I felt as if my stomach have been filled, even when it has been empty.

It has been eight thirty in the morning already, I rushed to the office for his orders. But finding no one there, I sat on the couch, when suddenly my mobile beeped and I checked out the SMS message.

"Happy Birthday dear customer!" A birthday wish from my bank flashed on my mobile. Oh! Today is my birthday, how remiss of me! It had completely slipped out of my mind. At least someone remembered. I smiled warmly on the phone screen, when that very moment he entered into the room, and the smile I exhibited to the mobile screen astonished him, so before he thinks me of some weirdo. I greeted him with a warm voice. "Good morning Sir!"

"Morning, Miss Ganguli! And we need to talk, before I head out to my work."

"Of course, Sir!" I murmured to him, and then murmured again to my inner self. *"Don't I want that too, to know what exactly I have to do here?"* And I remained attentive, lest I miss out something important of his say…

Sitting on his revolving leather chair, he decided to talk at length in his deep voice. "As you know, my company is a maker of ready-made garments, we have our online site to sell it, and we do supply it to our other partnered online stores and two other big department stores as well. All my things, though, are managed by my professional staff at the office, but still I need my personal planner, on which day I have appointed do what. So you have to prepare that, my manager will furnish you with the list shortly, alright? Although my finances are in an expert's hands, but still I need a personal portfolio. Make that! Will you? Despite paying the salary myself to the domestic staff here, yet the house runs every month by the money provided to the maids. I want you to be amenable of those household expenses, as well. Do that! Assemble this place, and all my files of home-office, while marking and sorting out properly, as quickly as you can. I don't trust my servants for this, they will mess up the things further. There's a separate PC for your work. See to that! And besides looking after entire servants and this house, you have to give special attention to my daughter's needs. When Tia returns... Her studies, her schoolwork, and whether she is eating well, or sleeping and playing properly, or not? I want you to take full responsibility for her! Report me, if there is anything. Don't bother me with everyday niggly issues but every fortnight, a gist of important things will do. Apart from that, I like everyone to be prim and proper, disciplined and punctual, in every way, and want my surroundings to be exactly like that...Spic and span, well-managed, neat and tidy...You can call me a finicky and detailed person both at personal, and work level, if you like. Devotion and perfection towards work, I always want. Do I make myself clear here?!"

He suddenly emphasized on the last part of his sentence, after gushing out methodically. He thought, that I will be able to grasp all that at one go, he wants me to make an astute person like him. But without showing any confusion on my part, I replied with confidence. "Sir, I understood very well, and will work on it. But if I may, can I have a planner to jot down all this?" He cut my sentence in middle to question me with his quizzical expression of face. "Why, you know computers?!"

I nodded at him before making my point clear. "Yes Sir, I do, but still I will be comfortable if I write down everything to remind me later, while I'm at the work...call me an analog person, digitally." My bizarre jest to cheer up the grave environment, didn't put humor to him as expected. Instead, snubbing off my attempt, he continued on..."Hmm...You can find that on this table." He pointed out his finger to that scattered table with heap of files on it. I nodded once again..."And that will be all!" He finally announced his final command abruptly. I got up on account of the adjourned meeting, and is about to seek the door handle, when I heard him say in his raspy voice. "*Many happy returns of the day, Miss Ganguli!*"

That warm wish astounded me so much, that my footing stumbled, while I turned my head. By now the look of his eyes has been softened, like his voice. Oh God! So he knows! Then it triggered in my mind, that he must have read that on my resume profile obviously, how stupid of me! But my exhilaration knows no bounds because he remembered, a non-significant thing of a nobody, like me. When he is somebody of significance. Almost a whisper escaped from my throat, which he listened, like glancing at my radiated face for his tender gesture with attention. *He noticed me!?* "Thanks so much...Sir."

I closed the door softly while leaning on it. I took a moment's breath. My happiness beamed, as someone else remembered my birthday, someone else wished. But his remembrance of this day particularly, his wish besides, is the warmest of them. This gesture simply *touched my heart and moved soul!*

After he left for the office, I went straight to the kitchen, to make certain what more I have to deal with. They gave me full account, from the laundry to cleaning chores, everyday shopping agendas, and so on...I memorized all of them, while instructing them side by side strictly, that we will divide and allot each day for doing some particular chores, along with our routine ones. This will help us to finish the workload, thoroughly and systematically. Thereby, we have decided, that Monday will be our cleaning day, Tuesday, the assembling and ironing day, Wednesday and Thursday, the grocery and laundry day, Friday and Saturday, recipe and kitchen day, finally Sunday will be the Vacuum cleaning day. But we will go through with these schedules from tomorrow on, not today, and they should carry on with their duty normally. It's so amusing, as how my sudden household management skills are surfacing out in an open, out from nowhere, but before I lost against time, I quickly re-ordered the deliveries...A little stern voice is all I needed, to make the store owner deliver all the groceries, at our doorstep fast. While Mira and I, cleaned the cupboard, and stocked the groceries, I told her to wash the veggies and fruits thoroughly side by side, then directed Shefali to prepare lunch for the staff, and chop veggies for the dinner beforehand, and store all that on the airtight containers and refrigerate them properly after that. And all this, they obeyed with patience, while I labeled the containers, the cupboard sections and sub-sections, with sticky notes, with written instructions on them, to manage well. This will help me a lot while I will go through with the work around here, while I will make grocery lists, while I will check the availabilities of provisions, while I will watch the expiry dates, and so on... During that course of time, I contemplated on my plight, while dovetailing with all my tasks, how I have been transformed into some efficient housekeeper, all of a sudden like the one I often read about in Victorian era dated stories. And who knows, most likely going to spend the rest of my life, roaming around these cupboards, while imposing the directions to my subordinates. And if it is going to be my permanent writings of the fate, then I really need to dig out that Diary from there, to become an efficient house manager... After giving a quick glance to the smooth operation there, and when it is already twelve thirty in the afternoon, I dashed to the office, with a belief in my heart, that I will be able to sort out the office entirely, in a day or two...

Placing my two hands on my waist, I evaluated the mess accurately. With a determination, I buried myself deep, to sort out the files from the table, while dusting and assembling them side by side...I sifted out that bulky leather diary from that messy heap even, at last, when suddenly I noticed, that underneath the table and the chair, a dynasty of dust bunnies have been built up. Sighing and mumbling... *How Gross!* I ran to the kitchen closet for the vacuum cleaner.

Preparing myself for this new challenge, I knotted my hair, and covering my head with a kitchen towel, I wore an apron to tango around with the vacuum, to clean the cupboard, carpet, floor, ceiling, chairs, and the table. After much hard work, I succeeded in my mission. But still there is more cleaning to be done underneath, so I stooped down to vacuum the area, and to do that, I have to crawl on my knees, so I can crouch under the heavy teak wood table. I switched on the vacuum cleaner button once again… 'Vroom-Vroom-Vroom' is the only sound resonated around my ears then, while I engrossed myself in the capturing of all those monstrous dust, and dust bunnies. Post conquering my long victorious battle, I crawled out from there. I removed the kitchen towel from my head, then the apron, before straightening out my hair through jerk of my head, to dust off the residual dirt from there, and this loosened my knot of hair on the other hand, and my cascading curls spread to my shoulders. A few stray locks came forward to my face as well, but pushing those behind my ears quickly, I whispered to myself…"*Well, that will do!*" while arching a triumphant smile on my face. But some intuition persuaded me to give a sideways glance at the door, and the sight is enough to beat me! Sir is standing there at the doorway to witness my cleanliness drive, with his penetrating deep dark eyes, staring hard right at me, they almost bore to my face to redden my face in an inhibition. And he must have seen it all, right from the beginning, and perhaps even my effort of tidying myself up. How embarrassing!

*"But when did he arrive? He sure knows how to walk like a cat, or maybe I'm unaware of his arrival, because it was camouflaged by the sound of the vacuum. Possible! But what time is it? And why he is here?"* All those questions hovered over my mind, and my foolish mouth simply stammered a silly remark to make

the matter worse. Why I'm wordless before him, only God knows. " I...I.. Sir, I was cleaning here."

He gazed coolly at my face, and then to the surrounding, before saying in his cool voice too.

"*Hoon,* I can see that, tell Mira I'm here for the lunch!" He dictated his verdict just like that, to make me panic!

*"What? Lunch?! Oh dear God! But I didn't order Shefali to do anything special today. Really, he does like to test my capability! Why all of a sudden, he came for the lunch? What will I do now?"* Mumbling to myself I controlled my mounting tension somehow. And pulling my wit together, I replied patiently in my steady voice. "If this is not too much to ask Sir, then will you kindly give Mira, twenty to twenty five minutes of time, for that?"

And that allotted time actually, I need for myself. And his considerate head nodded at my request knowing that sooth too.

"Thank you Sir, for being so understanding." I managed to say that as a response. And placing the vacuum there, I literally ran to the kitchen to break the shocking tidings, and in a breathing time, I explained everything to Shefali and Mira what to cap-off. Like me they looked baffled too at his *unannounced ambush!*

I requested former to knead *Atta* with *Ajwain* in a food processor, and without wasting any more time to make light and fluffy *chapattis* fast. "Mira, I will be back in a jiffy. Please gather ingredients for salad, and soup making.' I announced hurriedly, before dashing to my room to change my cardigan, in a fear, that it must be still dusty. I knotted my hair again, and scrubbed my face well, and washed my hands and arms thoroughly, once again in a fear, that I'm getting callous regarding the cleanliness issue, which I ought to maintain, his earlier orders to be neat and tidy, are ingrained in me. *How I'm becoming like him?*

I returned to the kitchen donning a fresh apron to commence my kitchen work, to win another battle! Whilst Shefali is busy in making *chapattis* and putting them side by side in the thermostat casserole. Mira steamed the vegetables in the Microwave, while I made a thick tomato soup, to that I added those steamed veggies, and then transferred that to a hot casserole. Time is running short for me, and I don't have four hands to finish my job, yet I blanched a selection of grated cabbage, radish, stems of celery, spring onions, lettuce, chives, and baby corns, slightly to retain their crispness and color, and after that, poured over them a dressing of whisked warm olive oil, plum vinegar, pepper, and dried mint leaves...I got reminded of my promise to ply him a nutritious meal every time, and that imprinted image in my mind of his devouring cookies in pangs of hunger, made me work in a lightning speed. I thanked God, for my presence of mind for buying fresh vegetables and groceries in the morning, and for the preparations into the airtight containers, as they came so handy now. I sighed a relaxed breath when the lunch is all ready, and is waiting to be served. I begged Mira to inform him immediately about that, and to place the trays of food one by one, but not in one go. She understood everything, even the total emergency, we are in. First, I let her take away the first tray, on which I placed the thick *vegetable, mushroom, tomato soup*, and that *Crunchy mix vegetable salad*, and instructed her to remain there until he finishes. Those dishes will create a wall to his stomach, to digest the main course well. My caring heart mulled. Then after a while, learning that he is soon going to finish his first course, I gave her the second course on the tray, on that I placed the *chapattis,* bowls of *Dal, Mixed Vegetable,* prepared by Shefali, *as our lunch.* I put only one serving of steamed rice in a bowl, too much of carbohydrate will make him doze off in his work. I became his dietitian, my fetish for healthy diet might be the cause. Subconsciously, I fretted for his health concern & that became my obligation...Like before I told Mira to stay there, till he finishes his meal properly, and to inform me if he needs anything...I breathed deeply a respite, when Mira signaled an 'Okay' with her hand, this means his lunch is finished. Whether he liked this simple lunch, or gave a nod of approval on our prepared simplicity, nobody knows about that...when he just ate his lunch without uttering one word and left for his work quietly. But now it's time for my curiosity, to turn to Shefali, to ask her in a serious tone, to double check whether she has been lying to me earlier or not, as her way to bully a newcomer?

"Shefali, you have said that he never comes for lunch and detest taking home-cooked Tiffin? Then why he lunched at home, today?"

"Believe me *Didi,* even I don't know why? It's so strange after all those years?" As innocence reflected out from her eyes evidently, so I believed her words. "He is testing your worth, *Didi!*" Quipped Mira. Then both of them started laughing. *For some hidden remark?*

"Really?!" I cried in an utter surprise. I could not agree more, it's possible, he wanted to test my prudence at time of crisis? But what a queer way to learn that, seriously?

During those past days which have been flown away, after his lunch visit (surprisingly, he never came for it again or went for his dine-outs which Shefali informed me of) In due course of time, I was able to manage and sort out the files in a proper way, of which I have been instructed for. I cleaned and rejigged the office once again. The leather, the wood, the ceiling, the floor, the furniture, the glass cabinets with wide shelves, everything simply gleamed in perfection and pride. I worked zealously for those, and slaved for my job. Yet, there is still one thing left attend, in my assigned duty list, that is, his schedule making, it remained unattended because *his manager didn't turn up* with his timely arrival, to provide me with those list of appointments?

In one dun of the evening, after surmounting my tiresome long list of duties, and when the dinner is all ready, waiting for his beck and call, I settled into my room, to take few leisure moments for myself. Belatedly, I didn't get enough time to take care of myself. My legs and arms are getting chapped rather badly, due to the harsh winter season. As I always seemed to be dog-tired every night. And sleep possesses me instantly whenever I plop on my bed. So I intended today, that I will not stir an inch, until I moisturize my skin with milk, almond lotion, and then with calamine lotion, with my two luxuries, which I have with me, besides my toiletries. In this fraction of allocated time, I have to finish that time consuming tasks. I bolted my room's door, and went to the washroom, to strip off my clothes, but remained in my undergarments in case. Quickly with swift hands I applied a generous amount of lotion on my chapped legs, arms, and shoulders, and on my dry face, and then I started applying the calamine lotion. Amid this, when it must be a few minutes to nine in the night, I heard a tapping on my door…my eyes rounded in an alarm, I literally hollered. "Who is it?!" To my utter relief, it's Mira's voice, and she came here to inform me that, I have been summoned by Debobroto Sir, as he has an important visitor!

I drew a sharp breath on the fact, that it is getting problematic now...his knack to order me around, whenever he wishes for, at real odd hours? "Alright! I'm coming right away, thank you Mira... And listen, make sure to put the coffee kettle on." I shouted again, still from there.

The deftness I have shown during my lotion application, the same amount of speed, I used during my washing of hands, slipping into my slim jeans, thermal T-Shirt and in my Cowl necked sweater. I brushed my curls, the time consumers with rapid hands. I know, Sir wants everyone to be neat and tidy all the time, and especially, when he has a guest in his reclusive life. I can't possibly go there looking untidy to stake his reputation. I took a quick glance at the mirror, not to preen, but to worry over my cheeks, which are now in deep pink hue, due to the frictions of my lotion application. I hope this will not going to startle Sir, *and won't be mistaken as blushes for glimpsing him?* I didn't have enough time to cool them off either...

*His office door is ajar, good.* I entered there easily while balancing the heavy tray full of cold sandwiches, coffee mugs, and a thermostat flask of hot coffee. Indeed there is someone with him. They are chatting on the sofa when they shifted their attention to the direction of my entranced steps...But I didn't like the look on his guest's face at all. "May I come in, Sir?!" I directed this to Sir. He nodded absent-minded.

"Yes, Miss Ganguli!" He said that only.

I placed the tray on the coffee table quietly...But I noticed, that once again his guest's eyes are wandering over my face, then all over me, from top to bottom with a salacious tease.

"Oho! So you are that pretty little thing, who have come from the big city, for Debobroto only..." His vulgar tone flung an innuendo at me, before smiling slyly, which curved his wicked mouth. I stood there stone faced without answering him back…Then Debobroto Sir, introduced that man as Prabhat Sanyal, his manager, and his childhood friend, to me. I bowed my head slightly for a half-hearted greeting, even in my dislike for that man, simply for the sake of Sir's prestige.

"You want anything else, Sir?" I said to my employer in my placid voice.

"No, that will do. And take that file with you, study it, you can find my schedules and so on, and then record them in the planner accordingly. And that's all for the time being, and tell Mira to set the dinner table for two."

Sir replied sternly, his face looked somewhat disturbed. Is it for my discomfort I faced, on account of his friend? Who knows?

"Very well Sir, as you wish. Dinner is almost ready…" I said softly.

I'm about to pick up that file from the table, and about to leave the room also, when I saw from the corner of my eyes, his friend's indecent gaze is all focused on me, they roamed around me to support staunchly his blatant misbehavior. "Tell me sweetie, do you like this place? And your work here, day and night at a stretch? " Finishing his insinuation, he winked knowingly at Sir, as if conveying some deciphered Code to him, and that seems to evaporate my patience.

"Let me correct you here, Mr. Sanyal, my name is Minisha Ganguli, if you please. And yes, I do like this place of work, and thanks for your concern." I opened my unhesitant mouth to reply in my ice-cold tone, but he chuckled simply at me, without paying any heed. "I will call Minisha sweetie, then."

And disregarding his friend's reaction, I went away from there, what else can I do, when Sir simply remained passive in all of this? I left the door ajar, so Mira can bring back the tray easily. I didn't have any intention to go through with his friend's immoral gazes and insulting talks once again! I stood at the corner of the door for just few moments, to settle down my shaky nerves, when I overheard his friend talking once again to Sir. I can sense perfectly well, for whom this has been referred to.

"Debo! You are such a lucky man, I really envy you. From where you have picked this girl? Give me that agency's name quickly. Seven days in a week in the same roof, with her. I'm impressed with the progress of my saint Debo, really, it's a good start, *yaar*!...So you've noticed, how hot she is, from those seductive eyes, that luscious curly hair, that bee stung inviting mouth, to those soft cheeks. And have you seen such...her those front assets...Such healthy ones...and the shapely legs and the tight...hidden in her pair of jeans besides...Oh my God! She is a ravishing beauty, from front and behind. So this is the real reason, why you have felt the need of a housekeeper suddenly, you were waiting to pick this flower bud, while she is fresh and untouched, and ready to bloom through an experienced hand, like yours...have you kissed her yet?... when you would be done playing with her, pass her to me for our long friendship's sake...What you say?!"

Those vulgar barking of his mouth, those loathsome chortles intermittently along, made me mortified, made me petrified, they hurt me immensely, that I clutched the file into my chest with my arm, to still my shaky body, and clenched my other hand into a fist, in a wrath!

*"What vile things he is saying?"* I hissed at myself, through my uneven breathing. But before I could hear what Sir has

to say about his obscene remarks. I thought it would be wise of me to finish my ordeal hastily here, so I can go back to my room's security. Without giving them the suspicion of what I have heard so far. I went to the kitchen with my feeble steps, to see, what they have done about the dinner. And they informed me that they are ready to serve the dinner, but there is nothing in the name of the dessert. I sighed heavily, because I've to think of something fruitful, despite of my troubled mind...I made a steamed *Gajar Halwa* in a microwave with sugar free sugar, almonds, and evaporated milk powder, making it as delicious and as nutritious as possible. I didn't want Sir's health to deteriorate, while he indulge himself in his sweet tooth. Though I'm still in an emotional turmoil, yet I can still recall his gorging on those chocolate cookies. *That night's memory doesn't seem to fade away from my mind, or from my heart. I wonder why?*

Back to my room, the recent horrible incident haunted me! The still of the night unable to still my nerves. I didn't like that horrid man, but more than that, I didn't like the way Sir has reacted? That shocked me, his silence on this matter. Why he allowed his friend to vomit rubbish? Where his earlier shown chivalry has gone? My unsteady mind pondered upon, while my plaintive cry, cried its heart out. *"Why, why, why? Why didn't he say something in protest? Why didn't he interrupt his friend's corruptive talks, which was polluting his mind? Why this world makes it difficult for a lonely girl, to earn her decent and honest livelihood? It's not my fault, if I'm alone, or the way I look. Who gave him the authority to demean me? I might be paid by them, but I'm not their bought slave, that they will humiliate me, whenever they will feel up to it? What should I do now? Well, as long as Sir is behaving in a decent and dignified manner, I will tolerate, but otherwise I will go away somewhere else.*

*But where will I go?Dear God! Who knows, perhaps the same thing is going to be repeated in my new place of employment too?*

*Whatever...I will not tolerate sexual harassment at any cost! And when that secretive defensive trait, is right under my sleeve, no one would dare to touch me!"*

I wiped off my tears and my residual dread as well, which is languishing my courage. And this I always do whenever I'm attacked with appalling distress or threat...Day culminated like a nightmare. Impertinence made me indignant but not sluggish to my arduous duty. *I should retire to my bed now, my haggard self advised, before another dawn!*

The next morning I've been called to his office, like usual he stood facing at the window in his silent mode. Even when he had heard my tap at the open door, even when he've heard my footsteps right behind him, still he didn't make any effort to stir his stance. After quite a while he reasoned in his husky voice, his sheepish face turned to me then, his honest stares stared at me then. "Miss Ganguli, hope you are not offended by my friend's way of talking last night?" My inner cry whispered. *"Which one he is indicating at, the heard one or the overheard one? When he remained mute without defending me for once..."*

And once again, I caught up with his apologetic says are saying. "I'm sorry about my guest's conduct, but he is always so impudent in his behavior, and that makes him like a rash fellow, but he is a decent fellow at heart. I know him well... and I can assure you, that there will be no repetition like this, in the future too, nothing is going to happen which will offend you in any way. I'm giving you my word of honor!" He clarified his assured words, to defend on behalf of his friend's defiance.

After taking a deep breath, I opened my candid mouth. "Sir! I will work as long as the place is decent enough for me, too, but if something does offend me, then no matter what, no matter how much I need the job, still I will leave my services instantaneously. And I want to assure you that I don't want to encourage any insolent behavior either, it's not in my book of conduct... I value my self-respect and morals more than anything else. Thank you so much for your words of assurance. For that I will work hard to make it up to you. You can count on me..Good morning Sir." I made my straight forward statement, loud and clear by lifting up my determined head, a little higher, by showing my subtle anger. And what he did as a response, he smiled sweetly at me, for my candor and courageous eyes, for flushed face which stared straight at his face, and for my little rebel!

His smile made me realize that I didn't offend him in any way, so my relief readied myself to go outside the room, but he interrupted my move. "Just a moment before you go. Tia & her grandparents are coming to this Sunday, I mean tomorrow. So be prepared!" He sallied his teasing remark at me, as if forewarning me with a smirk, plastered on his face...

He waited to test my reaction on that, with his communicative eyes."*Now how are you going to fight against this tricky situation, Miss Smarty?*"

"Alright Sir, I will be!" I took his challenge bravely to conquer over it, and went away silently, casting down my eyes....*Prick!* I muttered inaudibly.

But my bravery shown earlier has been ebbed, my heart raced wildly for my outspokenness (*and for his that charming smile*)! What will be the outcome of this open frankness? Clueless! I simply twisted and untwisted my fingers in anxiety...

When I suddenly remembered about Tia & her maternal Grandparents home coming...I've to deal with that situation? Once again I turned to Shefali, to my mentor for assistance, to know the secret traits to win over their hearts...

To my utter horror, the *grandmother*, is the worst kind, and loaded with fussiness for everything under the Sun! Shockingly she never acknowledges the management of Debobroto Sir's household! Another hurdle to jump? What am I going to do with this hard to please person? God, can you please help your puerile daughter out?

# Chapter Four: All In The Family

They arrived punctually in the Sunday morning, I mean Tia and her Grandparents; getting busy for their refreshments prodded me not to take a glimpse of them even, while they lounged in the living area...My tension to be efficient directed Shefali to fry *Samosas* quickly, while I stuff the mixture prepared by me earlier into its empty shells. The filling is nothing grand, compared to what they usually eat... I thought. My simple innovation of a home cooked mixture of Cashews, raisins, *Mawa* (dried thickened milk) dried Mango-Pomegranate seeds powder, with boiled Potatoes and Peas for the *Samosas*, is making me iffy, about their choice of fare. But at least I have famous *Makha Sandesh* of this city's posh shop. I placed heaps of those on a large bowl. Former already have made both ginger lemon Tea and coffee, as ordered by me. When it is wintry still, so I ruled out the idea of giving fruit juice to Tia, on a second thought I realized the fact, that she might hate to have her chocolate milk after a journey. So I placed a large steamy mug of tangy Orange and Tomato clear soup, on the tray. After giving a scrutinized glance on the food tray filled with those delicacies, the beverage tray, on the food trolley, I signaled Mira to place them on the living area's coffee table. Even made it clear what beverage she should serve, to whom, and for their convenience have sent a tray with spare plates and four tongs, so they can help themselves out as much as they want…I didn't know yet, whether they are going to approve my placed preferences or not, and how their actual appetite are, and my nerves are getting very jittery at the thought of it!

After quite a bit of time I'm being called by Debobroto Sir to the living area. I dragged my feet, by taking feeble steps to reach there. It's hard to walk even, when I'm floundering in tension. But before I can enter, I heard Tia's Grandmother's high pitched voice scorning at something. "Well Debobrato, what a transformation?! Earlier, it was only biscuit and tea, and now *Shingara* (Samosa)and *Sandesh*. Mira and Shefali must be improving by now, with my influence!"

"*Aarrey*! It's because of that *'notun meye'* (new girl), it's all her doing. Can't you see for yourself? When it's apparent here. Tell me, who will put tongs for the *Sandesh* and *Shingara,* and prepare the coffee and tea, both, and will send a mug of soup for Tia, who will show such consideration?"

This has been interceded by Tia's Grandfather heartily on my behalf. He has suspected my hand behind the food arrangement. But to divert everyone from her husband's talk, she has begun again, this time with a grave tone.

"Why don't you settle down Debobroto, with your father-in law's friend's daughter, Mitali Majumdar? You met her several times. She is a fashion designer… beautiful, smart, and the highly-sociable girl of twenty nine. And when both of you share the same line of work, and her father besides, is rich enough to back you up, whenever you will face trouble financially. She will be Tia's real mother, trust me she has a tender heart, and you don't need to hire a nanny anymore for Tia, when your wife will be around to take care of your daughter. Besides its high time you need a wife too, after my daughter...*Not the servants*..." Her grave tone turned into an emotional outburst. I can hear her loud sobs by now!

I'm in such a tricky situation, that whether this is the right time to barge in or not, when they are in the middle, of their important private family talk.

I waited for the silence to take reins over the situation, then at the right moment I tapped at the door.

"Oh! Here she is, Miss Minisha Ganguli!" Sir looked rather elated for my presence, *it seems he wants to dodge the emotions of his mother-in-law somehow*, and with a relief in his eyes he continued. "Miss Ganguli meet Tia's grandparents...Mr. Abhay Banerjee, and Mrs. Charulata Banerjee, and this is our Tia!" Nodding my head, I greeted them in obeisance, then folded my hands together to form a *Namaste* gesture. "*Namoskar* Sir and Ma'am." Mr. Banerjee smiled warmly but Mrs. Banerjee just stared at me hard with her cold eyes, without responding to my warm greeting at all. Just then, little Tia jumped out of nowhere, and clasped her hands, around my right leg to hold that firmly. She just clung on to my leg, and that mischief of hers made her titter. "I'm Tia! *Masimoni* (Aunty)!" She said joyfully!

My heart simply touched by her way of showing affinity to a paid help, to a stranger...she must have inherited this sweet nature, from her father.

"Oh really!" I grinned with joy too while stroking her little head. Our exchange of grins could tell, that we liked each other at our first meeting, somehow we felt being connected also. She is the cutest and prettiest little one with large dark and deep eyes, from where naughtiness is sneaking out... and she inherited once again this same pair of beautiful eyes from her father. She continued tugging at my leg to test my skill of walking and patience, with that restricted leg. "Ah Tia! What you are doing? Stop that this instant, you naughty monkey!" Mrs. Banerjee scolded her sharply, that sudden hollering startled the little child very badly, her tiny arms left my leg quickly...her beaming smile which was spreading all over the face, vanished right then. Ashen faced, she obediently sat beside her Grandmother quietly. My inner self protested, my deep frowns came in for the behavior of the latter. I simply detested the way Tia has been treated. I saw the same frustrated reaction on Sir's and Mr. Banerjee's face also. This convinced me that they are upset at Mrs. Banerjee's behavior as well. Suddenly to break the monotony of her domineering behavior, or probably to change the mood of the atmosphere Sir requested me.

"Well, Miss Ganguli. Tell Mira to take Tia's bags, and please tell her to set the table for the lunch also."

"Alright Sir, but I will take the bags and Tia to her room, and going to see to the lunch this instant as well.

Anything else Sir?" I said in my sincere tone, as I didn't want to disappoint him at all, especially not in front of Mrs. Banerjee. And then at that very moment, I have been targeted by her.

"*Aijey meye!* (Hey girl)... just a minute, you are a Bengali like us, right?

Do you know, what '*Shukto*' (a Bengali curry of bitter gourd and other vegetables) is?!"

I nodded my head. "Well then tell Shefali to include that in our lunch menu." She interposed her request sternly. I nodded again before quietly carrying up all the bags, while holding the Tia's hand. And I'm about to go, when I remembered something rather important, so I addressed to Sir meekly, as

I'm unsure about his reaction to my intrusion in his family time.

"Sir, can you please spare me fifteen to twenty minutes after the lunch?

I've prepared your business planner, from tomorrow on you ought to know your schedules. As by morning it will be late, as I'm going to be busy for *'all cleaning's day'*. Tomorrow is allotted for that Sir." I explained myself, my side of disciplined management, to his disciplinarian self.

"Yes, yes, I think I can spare that duration of time." He agreed readily while glancing around, it seems to me that he had found out this as a good excuse, to escape from the clutches of his mother-in-law once again? "Come Tia!" I said softly. Holding each others hand together we happily marched past from there, but not before my ears could hear, these drifting words! "All cleaning's day indeed! Do you trust that *chit of a girl*, an unmarried one, with her face value only as her skill, for your entire house hold and Tia?!" An apparent sneer of Mrs. Banerjee's judged me then.

"I have full confidence in my judgment." That's all I could hear from Sir's lips. And those few words, I treasured to my heart, more than anything else, because *that is my first compliment from him, although indirectly placed, but enough to make me exultant!*

For the first time I ascended upstairs to walk past Debobroto Sir's room. I went along with Tia to her room, at the left hand side corner of the corridor. Its for the first time too, when I have been introduced to her prettiest room.

I thought how Tia's Mother must have decorated this, for her darling, with love and care. I could realize how each & everything there, are expressing & interpreting just the word 'love and love'! That reminded me of my happiest days spent with my Parents...*Oh! How I missed them, so so much*...A choking grief while remembering them I felt right then. But this is not the right time to think about those, so I employed my thoughts once again on what I came here for. To veer that emotion, I assisted Tia with her washing, to put her into fresh clothes. I opened her bags to take out the contents while carefully arranging each and every article to the closet, giving her a teddy bear to play with, I instructed her to remain in the room.

"Tia listen, please stay here sweetheart while I'm sending Mira right away, as you know *Masimoni* have to help Shefali *Didi*...play with your teddy dear, just for now before the lunch.

Alright?" I delivered each & every word softly, so she could understand me & my situation.

"Alright!" Her chirpy voice agreed to my suggestion. To my respite, I found her already getting involved in a tête-à-tête, with her teddy.

"That's my good girl!" I kissed her little head. While picking up the dirty laundry, I went past the bed, *when my eyes caught the attention* of a large silver photo frame, where I saw a snap of baby Tia in the middle of her father and mother, all together in one frame, looking happy and bright with their sunny smiles! That framed happiness, caught up my breath in a deep melancholy, because the picture of late Mrs. Mukherjee is simply breathtaking. *She was one of the beautiful woman I ever have seen in my life!* My heart cried out for Tia, for her deprivation of mother's affection, for their family's once cheerful smiles, and above all, for Tia's mother, a beautiful lady who had died so young! I sighed heavily before running downstairs...Mira has been told about

Tia and about bringing her along during the lunch time...
It felt strange, as how I never have delved into the things
related to late Mrs. Mukherjee or even showed any curiosity
at the cause of her death or even in her name, only for a fear
of becoming an insensitive and prying self!? And for another
thing, the repercussion of my insensibility, might hurt Sir
and Tia immensely on the other hand...My heart is somewhat
getting more considerate towards their feelings.

With a great hurry Shefali prepared the *Shukto*, while
I prepared the two fish dishes, *Doi Mach* with *Rohu*,
and *Hilsa curry* with *Posto*. Thank God, I have ordered
grocery beforehand, and Babulal, the gardener, have
bought the fresh fish from the market also...But at
present, I'm simply afraid, whether I'm going to
pass this new test or not? Whether my cooking will
be up to their satiable taste bud or not? What to do, when
former never have tried her hand in the fish recipes before?
She told me how whenever her master or his wife, or Tia,
or any of their guests wanted to have that dish, they simply
would order them from any posh caterer, or from some
famous Chef! This vital piece of information is enough to
put me into an edge, as my way of cooking is far, far away
from any skilled Chef, of which they are used to? I shrugged
off my shoulder in helplessness, and simply concentrated on
my new way of making a salad, then decided that it will be
better if I make *Mitha Pullow*, along with the steamed *Biryani*.
Tia might like the former variation, so I rushed towards the
microwave to aid me, and for dessert I have already made
reservations on *Mishti Doi* and *Rajbhog*.

During the lunch time I have been called again. This is for
the first time, I had set a foot in the dining area. I stood there
lowering my lashes, waiting to hear about what I'm subjected
to for now. It is Mrs. Banerjee, who spoke cynically to me.

"So, it was you all the time, behind everything? Now this lunch is cooked and supervised by you also, that's what I have been informed about!?"

"Oh my God! Who could have revealed this secret, that too in front of Sir?!" I wondered, while directing my glances at Mira. Her sheepish look confirmed me of my suspicion, so she has spilled the beans?

My undermining of being an incompetent cook made my face drab, I stuttered. "I...I... Well, ma'am, is anything wrong?!" My body shook in tension, whether the food is suitable in taste or not? It's hard to tell, when Sir is eating silently, with no expression on his face. I bit my bottom lip to steady myself. But luckily, once again her husband, who came to mediate on behalf of me. "*Aarrey!* It's just superb in taste. I can guarantee you that Minisha, isn't that's your name? " I nodded gently at him, he called my moniker with an affinity for being an elderly that elated me. He has finished his sentence, now directing this to his wife. "After such a long time, I have tasted such '*Doi Mach* and *Illish Posto*' Charulata, you know, it tastes just the same, the way my mother used to cook!" Mr. Banerjee is getting overwhelmed, emotional, nostalgic, all together about my cooking of those fish recipes. "What do you mean by that? Don't I cook those for you without taking any servant's help??" His wife snapped at him.

"You do, but something is always amiss in the taste, but not this cooking, it tastes exactly the same, the way my mother's loving hand used to prepare. Bless you, my child! You have worked very hard for our tasteful mouthfuls." Mr. Banerjee keeps on showering his blessing and lauding for me, in between his relishes. Yet in spite of feeling proud and happy, I'm entangled into a whirlwind of very difficult position, because my appreciation is angering his wife very much. I decided to search some way to skid off from this mess. Then saw Tia and her struggle with the fish bones. That intimidated me, lest she stuck some of fish bones in her throat. "Tia do you need my help, in picking up bones from the fish? Do you want me to do that dear?" I asked her tenderly.

"No! Mira will do that. Now you tell me, from where did you learn to cook?" Her flustered Grandmother's commanding tone interrupted me.

"I...I think, I have rather taught myself!" I managed to squeak out a stammer, when that's the simple truth. For years I had to cook for myself to save money, even if I'm still a novice in the art of cooking. Treating myself in the restaurants or ordering palatable food from the caterers were beyond my means, so whenever I had found the time and chance, I had experimented with different types of recipes and items. Sometimes I even had invented my own fusion recipes as well.

"What about your mother? What is she doing? Doesn't that's her duty to teach her daughter? How callous nature she is? Even sent her pretty and unmarried daughter to stay with a single man simply for the lust of money?" Those sudden remarks are enough to flare me up, because now the matter is going too far! What my dead mother have to do with this? Why she is dragging her poor soul into my unknown faults? Why forming such misconceptions about her before learning the truth? Yet I just kept quiet, though I intended to reply back at her tart remark. My deference due to her age, made me silent. Seeing my distress Sir's silence broke, his considerate tone said politely. "You can go now Miss Ganguli, okay?

I will be right there at the office after finishing my lunch." To oblige his that consideration, I went away from there as being told, and waited in the office in an anticipation, for his arrival.

Finally he came to sit behind the desk mechanically. I just stood beside his chair to explain him, my making of different folders for him. What I created, what I downloaded, how many of personalized planners, date-wise, week-wise, month-wise I have made, what I have typed on them...From the dates to the nature of work, as the details provided by his manager on the designated spaces, in an explicit way... and how they can be connected online and offline, whenever he wishes to check them, from whatever device he wants to. I told him how I have saved those folders in his email drives, so it can be available in his laptop, Tab, or iPhone always, with one touch of finger. And if by any chance his computer crashes, still his planner will be safe and sound, for this feature. Further, I illuminated on my making of other folders too, as I took the liberty to make an inventory list of all of his files, while highlighting what the file is for, what contents of documents it has, and where it has been stored, what to be done for future prospects, and if he wants, how he can simply print it out, that particular paper. I've finished my explanations at one go like a Bot without taking a break. I must have wanted to finish the ordeal soon, as I have to lean forward over his chair. To be in such close proximity with him is making me awkward, shy, giddy. Beside rapid pounding of the heart with some unknown tension. It is getting too much for me to bear that feeling. Moreover tingling sensations are running all over my body to my astound? I've to deal with so much, just to control a havoc of my feelings, on top of it, my curls are conspiring against me. If not, then why they are coming forward to my shoulders, time and again. I thrust out a kerchief from my jeans pocket, to tie my unruly mass of (mischief) curls into a pony tail, to tame their tease, which my heart is provoking...This act of mine on the contrary, made him swivel around his chair sideways, so he can flip his side to my facing side. And our sensory feelings faced each other. He gave his intense midnight dark gazes on my face, without leaving my face at all, and that made me more, and more tense!

*"Sir?!"* I whispered aloud promptly, to shield myself from those menacing gazes, to plead him for not to entice me. And I blushed stupidly when I realized how he have no intention of sweeping away his intent, adoring gazes, from my face. I blushed even more...but soon he came to his senses, from his off-guard. His eyes looked apologetic as well for taking me along, *in his journey of adoration.*

"Miss Ganguli, you have done very well, thank you. And... I'm so sorry about what happened earlier. Please forgive my mother-in-law, that was really inconsiderate of her, about your mother. But she didn't know about your Parents earlier, as soon as I told her, she sent her sincere apologies right back to you. Will you forgive her?" With his barely audible voice he entreated me, to ask for my forgiveness, how tender his voice sounded, so different from his usual one. And it is evident that Mrs. Banerjee never have sent her apology to me in the first place, it is his heartfelt concern, his twinge of guilt for me, which are asking on behalf of her, just like the way he did, for his friend before. I felt so sorry for him, that my heart moved. His earnestness I can't defy, I can't ignore, when I can feel his soft nature too, I'm surprised with my realizations for him!

I responded to him, with my earnestness also. "I think, I can Sir. Tell her, that I have accepted her apology, but don't thank me please, when it's my part of job."

He must have seen my saddened face, he must have listened to my heart's modesty, that's why, he suddenly switched his track of conversation to another subject, probably to lighten the tension. "Have you eaten?!"

I shook my head slightly at him. This is for the first he inquired about me, and that made me really glad, and my heart smiled in exuberance.

"What? You haven't tasted yet, what you've cooked before serving us?!" His sudden squib astonished me, his flashing of a fascinating grin even more. I have seen his naughty smirk before, when he informed me about his family's arrival. Yet unfurling more in front of me, from his earlier austere nature, that is period!

"I'm going to eat in a while, Sir."I relaxed into his satire, my broad smile automatically flashed for him too. This is for the first time he shared a jest with me. Is it a guilt for ignoring my earlier teeny-weeny one's?

*But what was that? Why did he roved his audacious stares at me for so long? Wasn't that too much of him, when it tensed me, for that, I had to burn my face with crimson blushes in front of him & my heart wavered like a fool?*

# Chapter Five: Unjustified

A month have been elapsed after that day of Tia's grandparents' visit. Today is laundry day, so I'm helping Mira, while Shefali is busy with other household chores. Amidst the churning of clothes and linen, round and round into a soapy solution, through the conspicuous front door of the washing machine, I watched an interplay of foam and rotating of clothes, that inspired me to ride on a similar rotating merry-go-round of the last month, to glimpse conspicuously the interplay of events, which have taken place in my life! I mulled how I slogged away, oscillated around non-stop to devote myself to maintain my job and to care for this family, so that I could feed and shelter myself. So that I can keep my body and soul together... And honestly, my heart-felt gratitude makes me feel serene, whenever I do something for Debobroto Sir, and Tia, most probably, I'm getting attached to them. Why not? The dreadful memory of that day's of my dying in the street like a dog, the tremulous feeling for it, when is still haunting my mind, my gratitude know how Sir's job came to rescue me!

Just then the clock ticked to inform me about the time of Tia's return from school. The car halted in front of the house to answer my query...After lunch I have to request a rather emphatic Tia to take a noon nap as there is a lot to study in the evening, when her final exams are going on. I know I'm working hard with her, the way I used to do for my own exams. I want her to fare well in her Class, no matter what! She does need some energy despite of what she is always been burst of with. She concurred like a good girl of what I advised, because of my promise that I will bake a chocolate walnut cake for her, with loads of chocolate icings. Her constant liking of dainties prodded me to sometime bake apple, banana, plum or carrot cakes, instead of sugar, I use honey or dates, while baking or icing them. I don't want the sugar to harm her, or her teeth while she binges on the sugary treats. Although I know I'm bribing her in this way, but when it is very trying either for me, Shefali or Mira, to feed her properly, as often she screws up her nose, especially when it comes to vegetables, fruits, or milk. I have to devise so many innovative ways for her, so she can at least get her daily supply of minerals, vitamins, protein and calcium, needed for a growing child, and for that, even if I have to poach or bake fruits, I will do that. Amidst this, I always keep aside I always keep aside similar chunks of delicacies for Debobrato Sir, every time I bake those, as it's impossible to erase that resonating image of him of attacking on the cookies. So he and Tia, are somehow my inspiration, behind my cooking and trying of newer things. It's amusing how he behaves like Tia when it comes to food, he is more like a kid, than a grown up man. A warm smile played on my face for that and for my busy hands, who seems to be always full, to satisfy their taste buds. *Sometimes I wonder why I never have caught him up with his midnight feast again?..* Mira without fail put delectable goodies beside his evening coffee, variety of stuffed sandwiches and fruit salad every time, according to my strictest of advising. I don't want him to drink coffee in an empty stomach, or gorge only sweets at any cost… It seems I've boarded a long train of ponders, because recalling of what I've done so far are not leaving me that easily? From my regularity of sending of emails to his various important clients & associates, to those emails I've sent to Sir stating all my household accounts & reports of the house of this month's (as he was very busy of late, even for talking for a fraction of a moment) Why one such morning I've even placed an envelope with a wad of currency notes inside, on his desk! My first balance amount of the household expenses, out of what he has given to me. But my smug in an efficient financial management soon dampened, on account of his reticent self! Whether I've done well or worse? I'm clueless, as he simply had put that envelope into his locked drawer then, without griping or suggesting anything to me. I knew this was coming & my expectant heart was *not expecting any appreciation from him either.*

On my accord, I categorized all his books in the library into a Catalogue system which I've downloaded from the web, in my snippets of time. I usually do all my computer work from the spare desktop PC on the other desk, I never dare to go near his computer, laptop, or his any belongings, touched them solely for the cleaning purposes. I'm still keeping a watch on his schedules before he forgets to acknowledge them. Side by side, I've paid attention to this house's management & its cleanliness, my insistence to the maids, to keep it neat and tidy, particularly has engaged me and my entailment daily. I don't want to boast here, but I didn't show any slacking on Tia also while looking after her every need, her studies, her school projects, her health, her exercise. Each evening I make sure she has taken plenty of fresh air in the garden. My attachment with her emotionally is growing deeply day by day…Ah! The garden reminded me, how I've coaxed Babulal tactfully, so he could take proper care of the lawns & the garden, so no weeds, insects, or withers, could breathe into our greenery, and for that I bribed him sometimes with my special dishes. It is one onerous job for me to keep everyone happy, *except the house*. The house seems to be pleased with my efforts! I tried my level best to achieve those with perseverance, for the last month. I wonder how time must have settled me, that without any pangs of guilt or nostalgia for my hometown, an entire month has already been spent by me, in this new city satisfactorily. And when the talk of getting acquainted with this city is coming, then how could I forget to mention, that I took few car rides along with Babulal's marketing trips, while our driver Ramon*da* used the other small car, reserved for the servants for their use. Those car trips were inevitable, because I had to clear some formalities in my bank, and to check the transfer of my account here to it's new branch. I've to be vigilant about it, when my merge savings are in that...Another time I went out to deposit my first paycheck there, and on my way back, I glimpsed at the market places, even checked the location of Tia's school as well to familiarize myself with its route, if necessity prevails in the future. And I admit those drives had practically enabled me to map the surroundings, and the roads leading to it, aptly on my mind!

Tia's final exams are over...Today is her sports day, also the last day of the current semester, before the closure of her school. And it will re-open once again after a fortnight or so for the commencement of a new session. Those anticipated holidays excited her so much, that since the morning I nearly had to struggle with her to get her ready for the school... Later, I waved at her happy self for the school while the car drove her away.

It's during her school hour, near about one in the noon, when the home phone rang to convey a very bad tidings! I had a premonition from earlier that something bad is going to happen, yet I didn't take that seriously. This odd hour phone call from her school proved my intuition right, a mishap happened. She had hurt her leg during a race, the shocking news terrified me! I inquired them whether they've called her father or not, but they mentioned his unavailability! Total panic gripped me to numb my senses in crisis! For fleeting moments I simply stayed immobilized before acting further, on what to do next. Unfortunately the driver is not even at home.

He hadn't returned yet, he must be with Sir. I informed all this to Shefali & Mira immediately, but both of them didn't know how to drive. Thereby I didn't wait for the cab, which will waste my precious time further, or for the arrival of the public transport as well, which seems to be a futile, when I don't know what route number of the bus goes there, or where the bus stand is? I decided to take a plunge in this emergency. I'm sure, I will remember my driving lessons, so instructing Shefali and Mira to stay at home and to keep trying to contact Debobrato Sir...I drove the servant's car like a maniac, while heading towards the school. I might be out of practice but I still can remember how to drive a car!!

Thank God! I reached there in time, I thanked God once again, as it is a slight bruise on her knee, and she looked absolutely fine! I heaved a sigh of respite, my warm tears of relief rolled down from my eyes. The school authorities are apologizing to me profoundly. The school clinic doctor already have taken care of the wound, and bandaged her leg, but I couldn't pay heed to them, as my attentive eyes are on my brave Tia, who is smiling despite of her pain, as she have won the second prize. If she was not being hurt, the first prize was going to be hers, she chattered on. I just hugged the child and kissed her both cheeks.

"*Masimoni* is here, Tia. That's alright, if you got the second prize, next time I'm sure you are going to win the first prize! Are you in lots of pain? Is it aching very badly? Tell me sweetheart, tell me?" I queried her, what is troubling me in the first place, *her pain!*

"No, I'm alright, let's go home, let's show this trophy to *Baba*." She still chirped on with her glowing eyes full of pride. *They glowed my eyes tooin pride, because her victory is mine, the way her pain is mine.*

"Yes, sweetheart, let's go, he will be so proud of my Tia!" I crooned, while joining in her happiness.How I'm getting used to it, in calling her *my Tia*.

The School authorities allowed me to take her, as they saw no objection from Tia's side, when I seem to be her acquaintance. When it was me who picked up that phone call. So we set off for the home, on the way back home, first, I called to their family doctor, (the number which I've saved on my phone in case of any emergency) then to home, informing Mira that Tia is safe and well, and we are coming home right away. I learnt from her that Sir also have arrived at home too.

Half an hour later. I saw him waiting at house's entrance steps looking harrowed! He lifted her up from my arms, to carry her. Quickly I closed the car doors & locked it, & followed him with my hurried steps. "Did the doctor arrived yet, Sir?!" My anxiousness and moistened eyes asked him. He turned to nod at me silently, before entering to her room.

I paced back and forth outside the corridor, while the doctor examined her inside. Then after he went away, I peaked into the room to hear on what he had said. Sir informed me that everything is alright, it's only a scratch on her knee, but still he gave her a tetanus injection as a precautionary measure, and that might make her feverish. He pointed his finger at some prescribed medicines which are to be given to her at intervals. I nodded and readied myself to bring the refreshments for Tia, before she will swallow those dreadful medicines, and for him a cup of coffee to strengthen his shaky nerves. But before doing that, I put the trophy quietly at the bedside table, and stroked simply, the sleeping Tia's head. But the gush of emotions made me sit beside her bedside for a while, I wept silently, recalling how her brave smile shined, in spite of the pain, which tried to obscure her happiness. Then I smiled looking at the trophy, which she earned...I became totally unaware of his presence, as for a few minutes I went to my own world thinking only about Tia! But now, I'm ashamed of my exhibition of raw emotions, in front of his eyes. And yes, he is astounded by that view. He must be thinking me of being a hysteric type. I thought, it's better to explain myself before he jumps to any conclusion."You must be in a real surprise Sir! Well, I cried because Tia is in so much pain due to her fall and injection, and I smiled because in spite of that, she had won, not only her trophy, but over her pain as well! Regardless of undergoing with so much torment, she put a brave smile, Sir. She is one brave girl!" I poured down my frank blurts straight from my heart before him, and without waiting for his reaction I stepped downstairs to rush down to the kitchen...

I was there with Tia, the entire late noon and early night. I decided to stay there till her temperature becomes normal, also for the medicines which are to be given at regular intervals…Mira came with a tray of food to press me hard to eat something, but I refused down right, as worry have robbed off my hunger. But I requested her to look after Sir, who must be worried sick, and is tired to the core too. I checked Tia's temperature from digital thermometer time to time, and to my great respite, its moving towards normalcy… Around midnight, I must have been dozing off to the sofa chair beside her bed. When I felt someone is tapping on my shoulder with fingers, and calling out my name as well. I blinked my blurry, sleepy eyes, and…through the gap of my narrowed glance, I saw a shape, just like Sir, who is trying to wake me up. My sleepy daze broke in a shock, and I rubbed my eyes real hard, I jerked myself out from my sleeping posture to sit bolt upright.

"Nothing to be alarmed of, Tia is alright, it is five-thirty in the morning. I will watch her from now. Go catch your rest of the sleep." He said in his soothing tone, to subtle my shock caused by him. So he guessed my alarm.

"Shall I call Mira or Shefali? You must be tired also Sir." He shook his head.

"No! let them sleep, now go on."He said calmly while motioning his hand off at me, to go to my room.

I nodded in an agreement. While moving towards the doorway, my yawns ambushed me. I tried to hide them in one hand. I can't be manner-less in front of his disciplinarian self. Then I noticed how tousled my curls are while making me a barbarian, so with the help of both of my arms I tried to gather my unmanageable cascade into a knot, but just then. I felt something scorching my back. I snatched a quick glance from behind my back, to scout the culprit! I found out, its Debobrato Sir's pair of dark eyes, which are right behind me! And those turned into amber color by now. He kept his intense gazes on my face passionately. I shamelessly looked at them too, to peer into his deep midnight dark eyes, to decipher what they are saying to me, as whenever our eyes met, they try to say something, they try to mesmerize me! Surprisingly, some unknown force cohered our gazes for so long, so our heart beats can be in sync. It became impossible for both of us to sweep away our glances from one another. A surge of sensation danced into my whole body, making my mouth parch dry, making my erogenous zones tingle with desires. I saw how his jaw tightened? Is he controlling his sensory feelings as well? I wonder at my *wild* guess. Yet his resolute stares on my face kept alluring me, kept luring me to snare my heart & soul, so I can surrender myself to him! But in time a woman's instinct encouraged me to retract from his over-powering stares. I volunteered to cast down my eyes, to shun my every emotion, before darting out from there.

*"Now what was that?! Why he stared at me like that, again? And today, I was his partner in crime too!"* I chastised myself.

I didn't like the way my body was burnt by his provocative gazes. I didn't like his appealing eyes to me. What they are appealing to me, about what? Wish I can admit the answer of my inner voice. Moreover I didn't like my shoulder's reminder of that tingling sensation, which it has felt, as if being electrocuted, when his gentle fingers tapped on it. I didn't like anything there, at all!

In the morning I prepared the breakfast with a will, that I will concentrate on my work solely from now on, without getting distracted by anyone's stray gazes. Tia's fever has subsided, her health is back to normalcy, so I decided to make a special brunch for her, something which is nutritious and tasty. Suddenly, amid this I heard a car screeching outside our house, and the loud ringing of the door bell. Mira dashed out to open it. It seems like a commotion of noises to me. A baffled Shefali and I, ran out of the kitchen in the direction of that ruckus of noise. While we assembled in the foyer. I saw Sir along with Mr. and Mrs. Banerjee standing there. After seeing me there, the latter almost hustled into my face. There's immense vexation, hatred and suppressed rage in her flaring eyes. Then hurled out loud, ruthless, insulting words, her baseless allegations one by one to me, just like that, while pointing her sharp finger at my face! "You, you, the new girl! What have you done to my grandchild?! Tell me? This never happened before, but why it has happened during your presence, answer me? What *Jaadu tona* (black magic) you are casting upon her? She was so healthy earlier while with us, but now she is ill and in extreme pain, just after she started staying with you. With Tia out of the way, you have schemed to trap Debobroto, with your virgin beauty, and then to lay your hands on his money. That's why, you have entered into this house, that's why your cooking is so delicious? What potion you are putting into the food to hypnotize people? Answer me? How could you answer, when each and every word is true? Let me clear one thing, Debobroto will never set his eyes on a street wench, on a character-less girl like you, with all the noxious blood running down your veins...Never at you hussy! You witch! You didn't see the last of me. I will see for how many days, you will remain here. I will make sure of that!"

Her series of derogatory remarks, cold threats went on & on, till my ears are pounded, till my face became blood red in humiliation, till my body covered in pain, for all the inequities instilled upon me one by one without any reason, without any faults of mine! I stood there still & immobilized, only clenching my hands, only curling my toes, only staying tongue-tied, without saying or doing anything, because my noxious blooded parents as she called them just now, didn't implanted me with the idea, that you should insult your elders in return, when they behave harshly to you in any way. So I kept quiet, because of the deference towards the elders, which is ingrained in me, because I have a deep respect for Sir, and have a deep affection for Tia! My eyes brimmed with hurt, with emotions, they became dewy, welled up to stung me, but the proud tears of reserved emotions, are not going to show up, not in front of them, they don't not want to mortify me, they don't want me, to display my deep hurt, my poignancy, in front of their ruthless hearts. They don't want me to make a worthless person, in front of the distinguished worthy people!

At that time, a nonplussed looking Sir intervened, and it's about time too, as I saw how Mr. Banerjee is paralyzed with shame, helplessness, and loss of words, for his wife. "Why it's been the fault of Miss Ganguli? When it happened in the school, it's their fault at the first place! And she is from a good family, and is an honest, hard working girl. She has taken good care of Tia and us, believe me. Please don't be so angry at her like that…Please control your emotions, for your heart's sake, for us *Mamoni*." Sir pacified her. And despite of all the false accusations flung at me moments ago, I still felt my heart getting overwhelmed, because for the first time he defended for me, on my behalf!

"Alright! I will. I'm from a reputable family not from the streets, like someone here. But I'm going to take Tia with me, to my home. She will be there till her summer holidays, then we will decide about everything else. Debobroto, send her things later, hope you don't have any objection, when she is the only one left, of my blood now!" She moaned loudly after her outburst of words.

What happened after that, everything just whizzed past me like a cyclone. I could not remember what have passed, but all I know, that Tia and Banerjee's are gone! Yet amid this, I can remember a murmured apology of Mr. Banerjee to me.

As expected I've been called to present myself in the court of Sir, for his judgment! And he's sitting there behind his desk, head bowed down, thumbs entwined, dismayed brows drawn together, eyes closed, and he is in his total state of consternation. I knocked my presence at the door, which is open anyhow.

*"Miss Ganguli!"* He sprang up from his seat abruptly. Ashen-faced with Doleful expression, he came closer to me, to where I'm standing..."Will you forget the whole incident which has passed, just now? Can you forget the whole episode? Could you forgive her for, once again, and me, could you? Please? You must not get offended by this! I know, you are very upset and hurt, but please try to forget the whole thing, please try to forgive her!"

I never knew he can dramatize himself, so well, each phrase of his words, each expression of his face, looked so theatrical to me, at that time, even when he looked so perturbed. Because I can't forget the whole incident as he have commanded me to. When this is his house, he is accountable for all of his guests and their behavior. People just come here from nowhere, simply to humiliate me, to insult me, to hurt me, without any reason, right under his nose, and what he does, he simply resigns himself in those situations. But I'm not going to resign myself like him, when my innocent dead parents are dragged into this, twice, whom they never knew in their life. Something just surfaced out from inside then, a sudden reposed self-respect of mine, I guess, a sudden awakening, that I'm also from a respected Ganguli family, my drab face reddened for its glory, just like their much bragged blue blood!

"What you expect me to say? Alright Sir, I'm going to forget everything, when it is just a trivial matter, I'm going to forgive her also, because she was joking, do you want me to say that?? Tell me? You have assured me, that there will be no offending repetition...Your smart brain's memory is not that short-lived I presume, please condone me by saying so. Yet, you are unable to keep that word Sir! So it's entirely your fault that I have suffered today too. Forget about me, and those false accusations imposed on me, even when Tia is taken away from me. But what about my dead parents? What wrong, they have done to her? Tell me, Sir? And regarding my being upset, I don't know myself...I'm just a paid servant here, what will I gain, if I say, we servants are human beings too? May be, we are restrained in our manners because of our positions, but we can talk back Sir. But as my parents, no matter how lowly they were, taught me one thing, that you should respect your elders, no matter what. So there you are Sir... And do you know one thing, to get respect you have to earn for it. Isn't that true? Now...Please excuse me, as I have loads to do. Mira will fetch your breakfast right away. Good day to you, Sir!" I slammed a blunt precision at his face!

My repressed words simply came out in open, my simpleton heart full of candor was unable to keep quiet to that moment, was unable to cope out with the pressure, through calmness and golden silence, when it doesn't have that much worldly wit? I revolted in front of him, along with my daring soul, without caring a thing in this world, or considering what he is going to think of me, or how hurt, he is going to be, or how he is going to punish me for my impudence, or how he is going to take revenge on me?! Even if this might jeopardize my job! I simply didn't care at all!

I flounced away from there along with my flushes & rebelled self, leaving him nonplussed…so to start vacuuming the entire living area with a pure vengeance! This is for the first time I argued with him, even showed him a fiery side of Minisha, who loves honesty and justice above all!

*****************************

# Chapter Six: The Party

The days have simply flown away monotonously in stony silence of the house! In all those radio silenced days, I worked like an automated machine without emotion. Even if I ran across Sir, I tried my level best to answer him as civilly as possible. Surprisingly, he also have decided to give me his cold shoulders. In between this, sometimes have taken a pause from my daily routine to think about Tia, to wonder how she's been doing with her Grandparents? Soon her exam results will be out, hope she performs well in them. For her, I pray to God often, to make her happy, healthy, to protect her from evil, to bless her in every moment. I really miss my little cherub, especially whenever I make some dainties. One Saturday I cried so much over icing on the chocolate cake, which I was making for Sir, that poor Shefali had to pacify me with greatest difficulty!

*"It's past two months now, that I have been working here."* I thought of that in one end of the evening, before immersing deeply into filling his planner with engagements, sending of emails. Meanwhile the hammering sound of the keyboard, beguiled my ears with the word 'work'. With each clicking sound of keys, I determined to live my life through work only, till my death, no more emotion I will spare to anyone, to make me feeble or tentative. I must be meditating

on what I'm doing, that my ears missed out the sound of his soft lithe footsteps, even after when he stooped over my desk. Even when he called me in his lazy voice, it must be the second time of call which have broken my trance…My heart skipped a beat to the way his handsome deportment hunched over my desk. I stared at him in an astound, as if seen some surreal person? It is so unexpected of him to lean over like that, to whisper like that…My strange facial expression amused him. He gave me his signature dashing smile, to charm his way to my heart. *Is this some kind of repentance for his earlier nonchalant behavior to me, despite of my being right?!* But before that smile could melt my heart, I made my heart very rigid, devoid of any emotions.

"Sir! You are back early. Is anything the matter?" I tried to conceal my startle, but that is in vain, he caught me.

"I startled you, didn't I? I apologize for that. Well, I've something very urgent to apprise beforehand!" Suddenly he pulled himself together to become serious and business like.

"There is going to be a cocktail party.

A sort of get-together with my closest friends and associates. Can you able to arrange that in this coming Saturday?"

So for a clamor he acted that way. I should have known. He really does have a knack to pester me. He announced such an important party with such a short notice, I hardly have two days in my hand, and all in my life, I never have arranged a cocktail party? But I didn't want to face the defeat either, right before his important guests with my incompetence. After all, I'm the housekeeper of this house!"

This Saturday, but that is not in the list of your engagement? Which caterer I should contact for this, you have to suggest your preference Sir?" My tensed voice queried him.

"Yes, this is a short call, today is Wednesday already! But can you able to manage? I'm sorry for informing you so late. I don't want any caterer or event maker to attend that. I want you to handle that all alone, to make them feel homely!" No matter how much desperate he sounded, but he acceded his already planned decision in the form of a request to me! I conflicted with my self-thoughts for that. *"Indeed, how cute of you. While pushing me into a mess to deal alone, you are asking can you able to manage? Seriously, this man, his demands, his imposing attitude towards people to abide them... And don't give me those soulful gazes, to show your mellowing heart, when you threw a challenge at me. I accept your challenge, I will show you, of what I'm made of for sure. I will outsmart your astute self. I'm not going to be moved by those gazes anymore. Do you understand?! "*

But aloud I said. "I will try my best Sir. But how many of them are going to come, do we have to send them invitations of any sort?"

"Yes, that would be splendid then, though have told them casually. I will give you their numbers, call them tomorrow definitely, and there will be only ten to fifteen people, alright? So it's not much of a crowd."

*"Only? He got to be kidding me? It's an army of people with such a short notice. I never have seen such a rich miser, why thrusting me into this Herculean task, instead of hiring a Chef, to entertain his guest's gastronomy?"* I muttered again to myself.

"Yes Sir, I will see to that. But do you trust me, I mean for the party and in my doing all that?" I reasoned this to him simply, to know my boundary of freedom while arranging that, and also to forewarn him for the future, if somehow that party turns into a fiasco, then he doesn't have any right to put the blame entirely upon my shoulders.

"Yes, of course! I trust you. But are you in any way...?" He didn't finish his sentence & left the riddle for me to unravel.

"Very well then, Sir. I will send Mira with the coffee tray." But my move is disrupted by him, through his deep concerned tone he asked.

"Miss Ganguli, are you ill?" His remarkable quality of jumping into another line of conversation always confuse me. He is such an enigma to me. "No Sir. Why?!"

"You look so pale... By the way, do you know something? Tia stood first in her exams!"

"Really!!" This made me so exhilarated, that my heart somersaulted in joy. "So the results are out. Congratulations, Sir for Tia! How is she? I really miss her... Oh! This is such a great news! Thank you." My happy tears started spilling, right in front of him, despite of my determination not to show any emotion. And when I have barred my heart specially for him. Seeing my heart-felt emotion, he gave me one of his sincere looks, as if he is touched... I didn't have the answer right then, as why he is looking so touched? "Shouldn't I be the one, who should congratulate you? She never has been so bright. And she is fine, don't worry. Miss Ganguli...thank you very much for everything!" He crooned, cognizing the real truth, my immense love for Tia. He threw me a meaningful glance to make me realize that he meant each and every word.

My modesty simply replied to him, even after his honest eulogy. "No, Tia has worked hard, and anytime Sir, when you pay me for my work. I must get going then, Good night."

*"Coward!"* I scolded myself inwardly while picking up my diary, to run for cover from there, as fast as I could. It

is getting real hard for me, to remain frigid in front of his warm presence. It is getting very difficult for me to take my eyes off from his adorable face.This simple truth he knows as well, *because his gregarious eyes smiled mischievously at me!*

From the early morning to comply with Debobroto Sir's orders, in a lightning speed I started my mission of inviting guests. I called each and every one of the invitees with my message.

*'Hello! Conviviality of Debobroto Mukherjee's is requesting you to honor his cocktail social, over few bites & drinks by your esteemed presence on this Saturday evening at his home. So please be there.'*

Somehow I got stuck with one particular number, that of Prabhat Sanyal! My fingers shook while I tapped the number, my call to him is unavoidable. Luckily I'm relieved from such horrid duty. I left a text on his unreachable Mobile call.

It triggered in my mind that I have to think of some music, the soul of any party, to keep up with the liveliness needed, in enjoying the food, the company and to set the mood of entertainment. Sir hasn't permitted me to contact any caterer or event planner for that purpose, or for any other purpose. So I have such limited options. What else I can do? So giving it a thought, I decided to download some exotic collection of soul & chilled lounge music from the internet, few selected songs from the Retro mixes and trance. That will cover an entire duration of five to six hours at least. I hope this must be the estimated length of time of the party. In fact, I downloaded all the music, after a lot of research, then mixing and blending well like a DJ, I finally saved it to a pen drive. My very own assorted grooving album, ready for the people to give or to take a drive through their acoustic. If I'm not wrong, that home theater and tower speakers are enough to take care of the music playing problem in the living area, which is decided venue for the event. I got stuck again with the idea of serving alcoholic beverages, people have freedom to choose their preference, but being from a family of teetotaler, my lack of knowledge in this field, might come as an offend, who prefer this kind of drinks or wine, even if I ignore the sinister reason of my shudder at the word *Alcohol* or at the sight which is akin to *Blood* for me? Yet my trauma can't make me unfaithful to Sir's wishes. My faithfulness to him made me pliable, to go through with this duty.

This time again, I turned to Shefali for help, what she used to do with such similar parties. She told me, how her late mistress used to arrange that, but after her death, master always invited his guests to a hotel, whenever he wanted to throw any party! Anyhow, she dug out the contact details of the caterer, which late Mrs. Mukherjee used to contact during her time. I'm so irked by Sir's indifference to me. He could easily entertain his guests to a hotel, then why he imposed this impossible thing on me? I wonder. Moreover, why he overruled me to contact any outside help? Ah! To evaluate my par at excellence as a housekeeper, to judge my standard of knowledge about a Posh party? Alright then, I will show him my *Gyan* (knowledge)! I decided to hire one or two waiters from the caterer (He doesn't have mentioned of not to hire helps so I outsmarted him here!) who have expertise knowledge in the mixing of cocktails, serving the drinks to the guests properly, although, this is going to be a buffet system, it will further help me, Shefali, and Mira too to have a handyman around...I have to run to the market now with the allotted money, he gave it to me for the party expenses in the morning, along with the call list. I'm really in a jam now with this tight budget, as with this small amount of money I have to choose a variety of ingredients which are required to prepare the recipes.

I have already prepared a mental list about what to include in the menu when, I have to pay the waiter for their services including the price of the drinks too, so many things with so little money! How I'm supposed to do those with such a meagre sum? In dilemma? After this not a single penny is going to be left, and if I fall short of money somehow, only heaven knows from where I will ask for a loan, for the surplus? I didn't dare to ask Sir with more money. Only good thing out of this, is that, at least I have saved money on the music part by striking the right chord, similar canniness, I have to show to other areas. That's why I must avoid mistakes in the arrangement of the party. Crossing my optimistic fingers, I contemplated. In the afternoon the driver was available, so I requested him to drop me off to the market. Before that I went to the bank to deposit my second monthly paycheck. I'm totally aware that I haven't touched my two months salary, my tiny nest of savings yet. And I didn't have any intention of doing it either, in the near future. Who knows on what circumstances I will be in, if they kick me out from the house, without giving any notice? Yet amidst my wariness of my finances, I got bit by a reality, that I have no dress to wear, only few shabby jeans, leggings, and a few of my dresses as my wardrobe, or even I don't have a thing called 'make-up', besides my toiletries, a calamine lotion, that big bottle of lotion, the only things of luxury which I owned for now. I needed something to make my appearance presentable, but I harnessed my impulse, bought one smudge-free Mascara, an eye-kohl, a colored lip balm, even if I have a flawless complexion yet to enhance it more, I bought a Face powder cum foundation compact, a face primer with Sunscreen, to serve the dual purpose of make-up and skin protection. I have to be smart with my necessities while splurging. Those luxuries I bought with the currency notes left in my purse from my previous job, after I cleared out my rent, dues, paid for the travel fare. I really don't want to look disagreeable at Sir's distinguished party. I don't want to do something, that will put him to a shame either! Why I'm so concerned about his prestige and social circle, I don't know? Am I behaving more like a friend than a housekeeper, I wonder? But I'm back to square one, the problem regarding my dress. What should I wear? I don't have the money to buy a new dress for myself. All those, which I have, are not suitable for this party at all. When suddenly, I remembered that a dress is there after all, which *Ma* bought for me, for my last college function. It's a *Tussar* silk bottle green colored *Churidaar*, with a combination of rust red and magenta colored *Angarakhka Kurti* full sleeved, of the same material. And it's fresh from the dry cleaners. I crossed my finger in anticipation for the outfit to fit me in, and not to get tattered in front of the guests, as it's almost five year old dress…

The driver waited patiently, for my each trip, which I have taken to the party. He have lots of respect for me, for my food particularly, which I cook for the staff; and he always call me *Bodo Didimoni* (elder sister) even though he is ten years older than me…Meanwhile I've contacted that trusted caterer of the household, managed to get a concession as well, they promised me to provide with finest of drinks and best waiters with moderate charges. I guessed their strategy of showing such liberal concern suddenly, because in some way or another they want to renew their services again, after the gap of all those years, when their services are ceased post late Mrs. Mukherjee's parties. I simply rushed to the kitchen with my hands and shoulder full of those array of shopping bags which I brought from my market trip. I landed them on the kitchen table. I bought the munificent amount of things, with a fear that I might be ambushed by some unexpected and unwelcome guest, if he or she decides to tag along in the party unannounced. Or might be with someone of sumptuous appetite to guzzle everything from the table. I viewed this as being the most practical decision I have ever had made, on my buying of surplus things. I self-congratulated myself on my acumen.

With a wise nod I checked again, my menu on - *Paneer Tikkas; Crisp Cheese curls; Baked Jacket Baby Potatoes with nutty, tangy fillings; Spicy Tangy Cocktail Samosas; Marinated fish cutlets; Crisp Chicken Croquettes; Vegetable Crispies; Rainbow Finger Sandwiches; Canapés topped with spicy whipped cheese, crunchy vegetables, and orange marmalade...* I thought this would take care of both Veg and Non-Veg taste buds sufficiently for the dessert, I have finalized my specialty...

*Honey Roasted Almond and Walnut Chololate Balls, and Cassata Ice-cream*...It's wise enough to place this latter sweet variation, as the warm weather is approaching and the winter is on the brim to exit. For the accompaniment, various varieties of dips are going to be to choose from. There is -*Tahini, Cream Cheese Pepper Dips, and Sweet Tamarind Chutney* and so on...I decided to add two additions in the drink list, besides mineral water bottles, it's '*Mochaccino* and *Fruit Juice Mocktail*' despite of the catered alcoholic cocktails, for someone who is a teetotaler like me and Sir! (Funny, how to gather this piece of information, I contrived my way, without giving any second thoughts that I'm prying into his personal life, which I detest. I wonder why I want his tastes to be compatible with me?) The more, the time of the party is nearing, the more I'm becoming high-strung. I simply prayed to my Parents and God, to help me and guide me in this haute cuisine making challenge, for the monied people, who are coming here, when it is completely in contrast from what my home cooked food is going to be, which I have served to the members of this family informally, up till now. I can't take any chances, or risk either at my job, in any way. I have to perform well with all my might.

"I will fight!" I cried aloud, my slogan of battle, while throwing up my hands in the air, to connect with the higher authorities.

In the evening I informed Sir, that I have called everyone from the list, yet was compelled to text his friend. When suddenly beyond my imagination something happened! He crackled out loud in his rib-tickling laughs!

"Don't worry, each and everyone has received their party invitation messages, my mobile was flooded with their returned calls all day. They seemed to be so enchanted by your voice, that they pressurized me all day long, to tell them from where I have found this husky, sweet voice for my calls, they wanted to meet the owner of that voice, so they can hear it for numerous times!" Again he cackled in his fit of laughs on his own engineered pun, but something must have guarded him, not to reveal any more of his good-humored side to me. He became suddenly serious.

"Don't take this too hard on you, and don't worry too much, you will pass the test with flying colors." Through his serious console he directed a very mischievous grin at me. And if I count that earlier waggish grin of his eyes, then this is his second impish grin, he gave to me officially!

That piqued me, even when his humor and consoling words tickled my troubled mind to take it easy. But somehow for me, his being in a jolly mood is not looking good on him, when he trapped me in such a difficult situation (and this is for the first time, I saw his this much happiness, during my entire stay here). Yes! He can have all the world's rich laughs, when he can afford that, when I feel like crying due to putting me into such distraught. I simply said nothing, but went away, before informing him, that Mira will give him his evening fare.

It's Saturday, the 'D' day of the party! Thousands of butterflies fluttered in my stomach for the day. All day Debobroto Sir intended to be out in his club, to relax before the party, but that luxurious word is not for me! For how many times I entered and re-entered into the kitchen, for how many times I checked and re-checked the menu of the prepared food, for which I toiled so hard, only I, Shefali and Mira know, they've helped me a lot to assist & calm down my distressed nerves. The caterer boys arrived precisely at early evening. One by one, they & the helps placed the delicacies on the hot casseroles on the buffet table, in the living area. I took that on rent for the party from caterers. I thought it wise enough to place printed note cards alongside, to every section of Veg and Non-Veg cuisines, to distinguish them for the guest's benefit. Mira and Shefali are directed to take out the desserts only from the refrigerator when they will be on the brink of their finishing point of the meal, to retain firmness and the coolness of the sweet course. At the moment of their arrival, I left the waiters, Mira, and Shefali in the living hall, so I could rush into my room to change for the party.

I know Sir will call me at an unexpected time without any prior notice, thereby before barging like a complete mess, to humiliate him, its better that I pat my civilized looks for his sake quickly.

With a little difficulty, I slipped into my thick *Tussar* silk *Churidaar* and my full sleeved *Angarakha Kurti*...my ethnic dress is elegant enough for the glitz of the party, to protect my dignity, and thick enough to shield me from the nippy weather. It fitted me proportionately around my curves, I thanked my regular aerobic exercises for maintaining my S-line figure. I brushed my curls till they shone, tying a few front curly strands at the back of my head with a snap clip, I left the rest of my hair loose. Now it's time to contour my features. I applied foundation cum compact powder with swift hands, for a seamless base. With a careful hand, I drew a slight line with eye-khol to outline my well-defined eyes to add sparkle in their effervesce for the soiree. Then slightly stroked my shapely eyebrows with a mascara brush before applying mascara to my lush lashes, to make my eyes more dramatic. After those highlighting, I put my subtle colored lippie on my lips to improve their suppleness and rosiness. To my surprise they trembled a little, for the aftereffects of a pigmentation. *For whose anticipated caress, they have reacted like that, I wonder?* I wonder at my naive lip's boldness! But now my appearance puts me into a dilemma. Whether I looked too garish or pert? But my enthused mirror assured my reflection to be of a very subtle, natural, and a very graceful looking, pretty girl, who is smiling right back at me from there. So finishing with a mist of lavender deodorant spray…I hurried to the living area, as the crowd has already started gathering…

I found Sir nowhere to be seen. Remembering for what I've come. I inserted my music album to play on softly, at a moderate volume in the background. I also put the remote beside it if they prefer to quiet down the melody, and not their percussion. And post a few of my directions to Shefali, Mira, and those boys, to trim out any excess callousness left on my part, I'm all set to go to the kitchen where I have decided to stay, until Sir sends for me. When suddenly to my utter shock, I collided with my worst nightmare!

A slimy snake Prabhat Sanyal appeared right before me! "Ah Minisha! There you are, my sweetie-pie. I was searching for you. Where you are running off to, after adding color and spice to this bland party? Don't leave your Daddy alone here?" He said sleazily, while putting a wicked smile on his face, and this time his gaze is full of flirtatious lust. My eyes, searched desperately for Sir to come to my rescue, to save me from this man's clutch, but he is still nowhere to be seen...And former grasped my hopeless efforts to seek my rescuer. "Don't worry, Debo will be soon here, have patience. Otherwise, if he finds out, that you are looking like a bombshell, then it will be *hard* for him to keep his calm, he will forget everything out here, the entire party, his guests, everything...I know him very well, he hardly will be able to resist your tempting self, that will be very regrettable. Isn't it? So play safe with me for the time being. I'm a good player too."

He jeered his crude vulgarity to me, though I trembled but steady enough to batter his wicked face with my slaps, to teach him a lesson for his verbal sexual abuse, but God must have been there at my side, when someone called him for a chat. Taking that golden opportunity in my favor, I escaped from there as fast as I could!

That offensive encounter was upsetting, but the delight expressed in the party, where the guests relished almost all the items on the menu, that compensated my distress! Their revelry are loaded and re-loaded with more food and drink, again and again... The desserts are devoured with the licking of fingers. All those succeeding news relayed to me by Shefali and Mira, time to time, when they took trips round in the kitchen to refill the empty vessels. They also stated that, how the guests have enjoyed to the fullest, have been congratulating and complementing Sir profusely, for the smashing success of the social, for the enjoyment given by the delicious and exquisite cuisines. They never have tasted such delectable like this before, not even in the best of the hotel in this city can provide this, as it could not be compared with what they have tasted today... And above all, for the thoughtfulness in including veg and non-veg recipes in the menu, and alcoholic and non-alcoholic beverages as well. After hearing that trumpet of triumph and song of praises, I invoked God in my little prayer in thankfulness, and to my parents for their blessings to me!

I realized that guests are departing from the party as one after another, all the headlights of the cars, trailed ahead through the main gate of the house. It's late in the night already, the clock's hands showed the time a little after Ten thirty. I waited impatiently in the kitchen for other guests (if there is any) to leave too, so I could clear away the after-mess. I have to pay the caterer boys. Just then Mira informed me that Sir is looking for me, and the waiters are going away, and demanding the payment. I went along with her and paid them. I made sure that they have given me a signed receipt. Whilst my deep engrossment, I haven't even noticed who are around, after she and the boys left me there. I turned my head slowly to look around, for the whereabouts of my employer. And I placed Debobrato Sir then, after my long desperate search in the early parts of the evening. He is looking much more handsome, much more debonair tonight, matched with his sensuousness, in his elegant tuxedo suit, and the breathtaking sight of his, simply caught my breath in the throat. He spotted me along with his affixed eyes on my face, they just held me captive there for so long, until my two red spots of color, could mount on my cheeks. At last he jerked himself away from ours mesmerized trance, to advance towards me, his husky voice simply requested me to bring along those two folders which he has put on the desk, to show something to someone. So one guest is still there, and that someone is sitting with his friend Mr. Sanyal! I must be so lost in the world , Sir, that I didn't notice that both of them have the same pair of sordid looks for me, and they advanced to, where we are standing. That someone's hawk eyes dug for me for scrutiny, likewise his friend's lustful ones repeated the same survey.

"Debobroto*Ji*! Where this pretty thing was hiding? Have you engaged her for our entertainment?" That man spoke lewdly while referring to me, to whom Sir was eager to show files, rubbing his hands in glee. His boorish words petrified me, all my colors washed out from my face! I looked white as a sheet. This is for the second time I'm attacked with vulgarity! Sir looked in utter shock and stiffened after hearing this, in anger, even in discerning my every inch of discomfort faced by this lurid insult.

He with an alarming voice, sternly to him remarked. "No! No! Mr. Oberoi, you are mistaken, she is my respected employee here, is from a decent family, please show her, and also to the woman of society, some respect!" Debobroto Sir backed up my and my fellow gender's position with tact, so not to encourage this chaff mouthed associate any further.

"Oh really?! Sorry, my mistake then, Miss, but still... What a waste?? Mr. Mukherjee at least let her fetch me a peg or two to swig down my disappointment!" This associate seemed to me, a very thick skinned man, he still continued his line of misconduct to me, even though he have been warned by Sir just now And former's talk, Prabhat Sanyal is relishing, as he is also from one of his clan. I lowered my head as it is getting under my skin...

Then suddenly Sir in order to transport me out from this obscene environment, directed me with a very strict tone before them, toward me from the vice. "Miss Ganguli go to the office, I will come myself to take the files from you in a moment, and after that, please go back to your room, it's getting late... go right now!"

A look of sincere concern he gave to me then, and this is all I need, his earnest concern for me. Although, I can protect myself from these types of perverts very well, can bark at them till they eat their own words, but still I would love to have my very own knight in the shining armor too, to rescue me in a distress for once in my lifetime...I dashed out from there, with my hastened steps, almost ran away from those two wolves, like a red riding hood.

During my picking up of the files Prabhat Sanyal came in the doorway of Sir's office to lean against it. I tried to pass through the door, but he deliberately blocked my way, even smirked at my futile attempt. I snarled at him. "Please excuse me, and let me pass through!"

But he didn't stir, instead talked in a distasteful way, so that he can space out each of his words to stress his sick say. "You will be excused, when you promise to entertain me and my guests, to some night party. You left me 'high and dry' today!" He flashed an obnoxious smirk for his latest innuendo, smirked more when he guessed that I understood his dirty and foul meanings hidden behind those words...And that is the last straw for me to take action against this verbal harassment, to show my last resort, to protect myself. I raised my leg to kick his shin...Boss's friend or no friend, I will not tolerate this implicit vulgarism, but before I could act, suddenly I heard Sir from behind, thundering at his friend. "Prabhat?? What's going on here? What is the meaning of blocking Miss Ganguli's way like that?!"

Then he addressed me. "Let me have those files..." And he must have heard those lewd remarks of his friend, must have noticed my raised leg's attempt of kicking him, and that deep frown which my dismayed face showed, those can't be missed by him.

But his friend interfered our conversation. "*Aarrey* Debo! I was asking her to arrange a similar party for me, but for that it seems she needs your permission."

"Miss Ganguli is indispensable and this is my house so you will need permission for everything here, and she is my employee... so you have to hire someone else for that. We need to talk later...you must be late for your home, when it's a long drive from here." An undertone cold threat he threw at him. His friend, simply ignored him, his taunt chuckled at him. "Yes, sure we will talk when you will be sober enough." Then, before exiting from the entrance door, he winked at me salaciously!

I simply pursed my lips hard and dug my fingernails on my palm, everything affected me so much, that my feet glued to the very spot. Earlier I thought of commemorating my first success of putting up a party, but all those atrocities, insults, and being the cause of creating a rift between his friend and associate (although, it's not my fault) made me devastated! Even though I have put so much effort, and input for this social, but what I have earned, just bitterness and humiliations subjected to me. My misplaced self-respect felt a nauseating feeling, so disgusting feeling, that my stomach churned. Further it pursued me to be on the verge of tears. And one such disobedient tear already have escaped from my eye, flowed down my cheek, after that, they didn't need my permission at all...the streams of pathetic tears just flowed down from my eyes continuously. Sir witnessed every felt emotion of mine from his naked eyes... my position appalled him. How it affected me he saw that, he saw my tears, read each and every painful emotion imprinted on my body gestures, in my eyes, on my face, he had seen it all!

He crooned to abate my agitation. "Go to your room, everything is alright now. And it will remain so in the future. I'm here to see to that! You can rely on me! Aren't you going to do that? You must be tired, please take some proper rest, and have faith in me. I'm here for you for always!"

I never thought he will say those tender words to me. I never thought an employer will vow to protect the dignity of his mere paid employee, and fight for her. Though he did not lay his caressing hands on me, but I felt the touch of his tenderness through his tender gazes, through his tender heart. I felt so close to him, though we both stood so far...I nodded quietly with a teary smile. And through my eyes, I talked to him, to make him realize that. *"Yes, I'm relying on you, on you only, this time too, like I was earlier."*

His eyes replied back to me, and I could decipher them clearly, what they are saying. *"I have the warmth, the faith and the respect for you..."* and something else his eyes said, those unbelievable words...

*" I have deep affection for you!"* I must have misread that part, no it can't be possible. I lowered my lashes in inhibition, till they touched my cheeks.

I veiled my blushing face under the shade of my lush eyelashes. Quickly I garnered enough energy into my legs so that I can run to my room fast. He also paced his footsteps to step into the living area. Too much of the emotion is getting beyond our endurance...I bolted my door as my whole body is in a tremor, the interplay of emotions is too much for me to handle, especially after what I have discovered recently into his eyes! I shook my head in denial, it's not so easy for me to admit what he have actually felt, for me. I must have exaggerated my skill of reading his eyes. Yet a deep sense of respect aroused in my heart, for the way he fought for me, I must have earned my respect. The way I told him before, to get respect you must earn it. But still I wonder, about the obscenity present in the air of this city? Why every man here wants to pounce on me? But it's only Sir, who is so gentlemanly, so different from the rest of the crowd. Yes, he is the special one indeed, a man with a rare kind of beautiful heart!

\*\*\*\*\*\*\*\*\*\*\*\*\*\*\*\*\*\*\*\*\*\*\*\*\*\*\*\*

# Chapter Seven: Blast from the past

Today is Sunday, the morning post Saturday night's party *fiasco*! The very word of which I was so afraid earlier, and to avoid that how I worked with my sweat and blood, how I planned so meticulously, but perhaps something is inevitable. That is so true in my case, the disaster did come to fondle me. After yesterday, my energy seems to be draining out from my body, due to the harshness of party night. Still like an automated robot, I'm working at my job, to vacuum and clean Tia's bedroom. Besides this room, the guest room, and the second bedroom. I usually carried on with my cleaning and arranging things in regular routine like this, except for one room, the master bedroom, the Debobroto Sir's room, to which I have never been inclined to trespass, as it seems to me, the private world of him (saving that information of him being a teetotaler, I never have pried into his world again) so Mira has taken the responsibility of cleaning that, but I do assist her as much as possible from the outside with all my will and might.

In the middle of my work Mira reported that, Sir refused to have his breakfast, and is called to present myself to his home-office immediately. This is what I was afraid of. What I could possibly do? I'm mentally prepared for any worse. My life made me go through with this time and again, it taught me that wrongness and injustice are the meed I will get, no matter how diligent and honest I'm for the survival! I trotted into the room, knocked at the open door. As usual, his back is turned, to look outside from the window. His deep silence swayed my body, but I managed to speak out in my poised tone.

"Sir! Please have your breakfast. Don't do this please, I admit of being lousy in the party. I admit, that my lousiness had ruined your party, had put a damper on your enjoyment and everything. I'm sorry for the rift caused between you and your friend, also for putting you in a very awkward position, in front of your associate. All those must have been exasperated you. I'm prepared to take the entire responsibility, if you would be kind enough to give me a one week's time, so I can quit this job, Sir!?" I swallowed hard on this part. I found a noticeable difference in my nature, earlier on that day of the outburst, I didn't care about my job or about him. Now I'm groveling for it, is being apologetic to him & feeling distressed for losing my livelihood. Getting exceptionally sad to be away from Tia, and *him!* Does he have a guilty hand behind my transition & stirring emotions? Wiping off my sentiments, I slowly resumed again. "I will go away from here, but don't punish yourself, Sir, like that, when breakfast is the most important meal of the day... Have something, please." He must have listened to my each and every word, I have uttered so far with an attentive ear. But he didn't seem to budge at my roller coaster ride of emotions...Suddenly he swung around to face me. To my sheer surprise, he's smiling like anything. That puzzled me, his recent displayed cheerful attitude.

An equally cheerful voice remarked. Who will believe, that this person used to be an austere man? "You have finished. Who told you to quit?!" He looked around to hunt down that guilty person, who must have insisted on that, then he began with a sincere tone, in his mellowed voice. "Who've put that idea into your head, huh, that I'm being vexed, that you put a damper on my party? Did I say something to you? Doesn't the final decision of firing you, lies with me solely? I'm the one here who will decide, whether you will quit or stay, do you understand?!" He waited for my reply while cocking one of his eyebrows to me in impishness.

"But I thought…" His lukewarm attitude amazed me! I tried my best to say something meaningful, but I desisted.

"What you thought? You are the lousy one. Yes, you are indeed, that!"

"I'm Sir? How?" Now I wanted to know how, after putting the very word into his mouth.

"Where's my breakfast?!" He questioned my competency.

My amaze readily replied to learn about the conspiracy of that vanished breakfast. "How can that be possible, when I have made stuffed vegetable omelet, creamed fruit salad with oats, toasted open sandwiches and coffee, besides Muesli, pomegranate and grape juice are for you, Sir?"

"Did you really? And you think, I will love to have those?"

"I thought this is what you prefer Sir. Would you like to have something else? Please let me know so I could prepare them in a jiffy."

"Hmm…What happened to last night's food? Is there anything, left?"

"Yes Sir! There is some."

"Go bring those for my breakfast, it's my order! I want to

taste all those. Eating your preferred breakfast is not eating at all!" It's so strange seeing him, demanding his whims in a puerile way, throwing tantrums like a spoiled boy all of a sudden!

"But Sir, is it wise to have those, first thing in the morning? I mean all those fried things...Instead you should have something nutritious. Please re-consider this, and have them later in the brunch." He took a deep breath for my advice, the patience is running out for him.

"Listen Miss Ganguli, it's my Sunday, my house, my food, and I will eat what I love. I have enough of your nutritious food all the time. I don't like being nagged either. " He made a firm statement regarding his legit demands.

He was right. I was so into his welfare, that I've forgotten of crossing my line. I blushed hard in shame. "I'm sorry for nagging Sir... But I thought, then I must be, I'm so sorry."

"You think too much. Is philosophy your favorite subject, by any chance?"

My baffled face and puzzled head shook to deny that, for that he gave me, one of his heartiest boyish laughs, to charm me? And he succeeded, my heart is smitten by them! Mirth seems to be his guest of honor today!

"Now go on...what are you waiting for? Do what I told you, I'm starving seriously here? And don't ever thought..." He stressed here. "...Leaving of your job without my permission. It's my acquaintances who disrespected you under my roof, right in front of me, I know how to deal with them. Now go on..."

"Alright Sir, I will stay. You are so kind. And I'm going to include all those things which you want in the breakfast too now, but only if you will have them with a fruit salad." And nodding, he smiled at my stubborn resolution, of coaxing him for his healthy diet. "...And thank you Sir, very much for everything!" My heart said softly, that honest sooth.

His sweet nature made me speechless for what he had said to me, what he thought of me, which I didn't care to know earlier. A load of weight indeed lifted off from my chest, my job is secure, Sir is not angry with me. And it's all his doing, for that I'm thankful and grateful. My brightest smiles welcomed his warm heart, they spread to my sparkling eyes, so with a sunny smile on my face, a sun in my eyes, I looked at his bright face without lowering my eyes in inhibition this time. And he became fascinated with my sunny face, he warmed his heart and soul through their rays of sunniness!

"Miss Ganguli...thank you, that was a lovely party indeed. We really had enjoyed it to the fullest. Believe me, it's been a long time, that I've enjoyed this much. It was simply perfect, you made me so proud before my guests. Thank you for putting up with me and my circumstances." His sincere appreciation overwhelmed my heart. *What he's talking about? When I'm indebted to him in gratitude.* Seriously, this man is so modest, when he has done so much for me. I wonder how my tone differed here, earlier whenever I used that particular word *seriously* to address him, I used only to express my vex, but now I'm using it to express my tenderness.

I turned to see to his requested breakfast, when I realized that today is after all a lovely day, but he interrupted my move and my deep thought. "Before you go, here is your music album, Miss DJ!" Piercing a naughty smile on his face, he teased me while handing the USB drive. I laughed a little... Then we shared our grins, once our informal interaction culminated. Our sparkling ones, irresistible ones, whole-hearted ones. I tilted my head a little to capture the image of his fascinating smiling face, his splendid breathtaking eyes, into my eyes and heart *forever*. I pushed back my thick strands of front hair idly behind my one ear. The very thing that flickered his heart once again, the play of my curly hair! His eyes turned into something else, they tried to entice me with something. Something which is beautiful and mesmerizing. They did not let me go, until I surrender to them. They dragged my eyes into an appeal, to be in sync in a rhythm of some magnetic enchantment, in a rhythm of most beautiful feeling which has a very lovely name. We both contradicted that sweet feeling which we felt, our inhibition is the impediment in the path of our confession that moment, and somebody else also played a gooseberry into this...His mobile device, to hamper our honest realizations. It gave such a shrilling rang that we both have to come down to the earth, as being a couple of earthlings. I quickly turned my face and went away from there, to treasure the moment in my cache of heart. *Our first banter, our first moment of shared smiles!* A week has been passed away after ours that Sunday morning's sunny banter. I still miss Tia...and today, the emptiness of the house are infusing more emptiness in my heart. So to divert myself from the gloom, I decided to take a saunter in the garden, to breath some fresh air to my dejected heart. It is one of the evening of March month, and though the air is crisp yet balmy enough to walk on the beautiful, soft, green grass with my bare feet to feel the soothing blades...it is yet to get dark, despite of its dusky sky, so until then I'm going to enjoy this splendid and refreshing feeling. With a dangling pair of shoes in my hand, I sang in my subtle melody, a song of reminiscence along, because rendition is so akin to my heart's present condition.

*You are my sunshine, my only sunshine*
*You make me happy when skies are gray*

*You'll never know, dear, how much I love you,*
*Please don't take my sunshine away.*
*The other night, dear, As I lay sleeping,*
*I dreamed, I held you in my arms.....*
*You are my sunshine, my only sunshine...*

I just ambled there without paying any attention to hither and thither, not even in the noise of a car entering the house, passing by the garage door... Or even when someone approached me. I'm in my own secluded world. Amid my reclusive state, I stumbled across to Sir and to his midnight dark perceiving eyes! They looked so different, while observing me... my bare feet, my blowing of hair softly in the breeze, even my blushes on my cheeks, as they are pink with the startle, which he just gave me. I halted my act of dangling shoes while saddled them on my shoulders. I stifled my euphony too.

"Miss Ganguli? What are you doing here?" His voice sounded so strange, a bit gruff, as if having a cold. I didn't notice that before in the morning, he's catching up of cold? How his gazes have become kind of drowsy too? Like kind of being feverish? Everything is so unfathomable from his throaty voice to those sedated eyes...as he stayed there to wait for my answer.

I primly replied to him. "Sir, you are back early. It's that, I was feeling very stuffy inside, so just came here to feel the grass, that's all..."

But it seems to me, that he is no mood to leave the place so early, and wants to pass the time with me somehow, if I have not guessed it wrong. He asked me then, while emulating my earlier frank tone.

"Then tell me, what song you are singing just now?" He looked so amused, and his eyes twinkled in an amusement.

So he heard, how embarrassing! Why I always find myself in a hot bowl of soup, before him? I just staggered with my words. " I...I didn't, honest Sir." It is an obvious white lie I knew, but I'm ashamed to admit my crooning.

"Hmm... Really? Then why it sounded like something on- *Sunshine*- to me, when the Sun has already gone down?!"

If I can hide myself anywhere at that moment, I would sure do that. And it looked to me, that he is in his one of the mischievous mood, his impish eyes danced before me. I just clawed my feet on the ground, and lowering my head, I blushed harder than ever. It is really an awkward situation, his sudden informal way of talking to me like that, his intent to spend time with me like that, when the night guard is watching us from the gate. He tried to peak into my lowered head, to my reluctant mouth, and then gave his cute chortles to awe me.

"Alright, alright! That's enough of my teasing. Come inside. I need a cup of coffee and something to eat as well. Didn't you hear a growling stomach just now?" To my astonish, he exposed his jest and candor to tickle my snicker! He chortled again at my hilarity.

My turtle steps of shyness followed him inside the house. Like always, he becomes a very different persona, a more dashing, a more cute, a most adoring one, whenever he smiles, humors, and breathes out his tenderness for me especially!

This was my first fraction of the evening which has been spent to have a friendly conversation, for a word or two, for a laugh or two with him. And to my utter surprise once again, I want more and more of this to happen, my spending of time with him. Is my respect for him is somehow turning into liking him too? I shook my confused head, for my sudden deep feels for him. *I must be dreaming with my eyes open?!*

In the night I went inside Tia's room, to stroke her pillow, her concern hovered over my head, and a weariness tiptoed into my eyes...

I dozed off on the sofa chair beside her bed, unaware, while hugging that soft pillow. Thinking that she is personified into a pillow...In the early morning, my mobile phone's morning alarm broke my slumber, then I recollected where I'm? But what's this? As far as I could remember, I didn't wrap myself with this comforter then how on earth it landed up here? Why of course, Mira? She must have done that, after seeing the light coming through this room. Anyways, it's time to start my work...

Sir is ready to leave for his office when he saw me standing at the home office doorway, twirling my finger on the surface of the door, with some hesitation. "Do you want to say something to me, Miss Ganguli?" He perceived my hesitancy in addressing him.

"Good morning Sir! It's that... it... I want to know how Tia is? It's been a long, long time, since I heard her voice. And you know I might upset her grandmother if I try to contact her. So, I'm wondering, whether she is doing well or not? I know, you are missing her so much, and asking you this, will make you even more upset...but believe me, I don't have any intention to make you upset with this. Please don't think me as being careless, and if I have acted like one, then I'm so sorry Sir. It's that, it's almost time to start her new session in school... And I..." I almost stuttered with sadness, and discomfort.

For a few fleeting seconds he just stared at my face, as if I have spoken in some foreign lingo, then he replied very gently in a drawling voice. " Yes, she is very well, and misses you just the same. She will be home very soon. Don't be so upset, and do take some rest, you look haggard. And Miss Ganguli, I don't think your compassionate heart can upset anybody ever.

Bye." He ended his reply like that, before heading for work, while leaving me with a company of my awe, deep respect and endless likeness for him.

What he had said just now about me wavered my heart and soul so much, that it impelled me, to just 'lo...him so much, no I must be wrong here, it's not that coined word, it's not that... it's so soon, so soon Minisha! I chided myself severely further for my wrongdoing of loving him.

*"What you have done silly girl? Why you giving your heart? What if he doesn't reciprocate? What if he toss your heart away like a mere plaything, what about that then? Will you endure a heartbreak, after finding a heart of your own? Can you live in a sunless life after finding your sunshine? Witless fool, you have committed a gravest mistake of your life! You have ignited such a feeling which is going to burn you alive, just wait and watch!"* All my chastise on myself, simply darkened my face in repentance! Meanwhile I asked Mira whether last night she have covered me with that comforter, or not? But she looked baffled! That's confusing? I squeezed my witless brain to find an answer. Then who else could? Was it by any chance, *him*? Nah! It's not possible. I'm just being imaginary due to my change of heart, it's Mira's doing all along. She must have forgotten. I wonder, why today Sir's voice sounded so normal, not a bit of hoarseness is there? *Did I imagine that as well, his feelings for me?!*

I could sense that, this month, is the month of, the resurrection of my reposed past, of my remembrances...

One such evening someone paid visit to Debobroto Sir...his maternal uncle and my father's ex-partner in the business, Mr. Badal Chatterjee!! A pang of deep heartache for my parents, I felt right then, after finding the wrong-doer at the same threshold of this house!! It's his uncle, who, while stepping in, shrieked loudly, at my presence, as if, he has gotten one of the fright of his life! He didn't intimidate me, as my conscience is as clear as a mirror unlike him. *"Khuki tui ekhane?! (Child you are here?)*What are you doing here??" Sir, looked absolutely bewildered, after discovering our acquaintance! I just ran to the kitchen with an excuse of bringing up the refreshments for them, after dragging my obeisance to greet his uncle in a cordiality. What an irony of fate? Who would imagine that this man who robbed my father's money (I'm certain of that, after my parents' death!) will come here, moreover is a kindred of Sir? What a stark contrast between them even when they are related, like day and night? This Badal Chatterjee can change his color so fast, even faster than a chameleon...But yet I really got scared to death as his sinister existence near my surroundings can make my life hell! Although I didn't have any concrete proof, but some intuition, some sixth sense of mine, always have told me that this man had cheated all my father's money by forging some false loan papers, claiming that the company they both used to own, was drowning in a deep sea of debts. I didn't think my *Baba* would have had taken so much loan, that my house, his hard earned life savings, had gone away from that, to pay some unimaginable imaginary figures, to clear some enormous amounts of debt and loans!? What this life wants from me? Why it tests, my endurance?!

Bracing myself fast, I thought, when I'm not the wrong one, have been honest and truthful always like my parents, then I will not going to be afraid, or shrink back anyhow. Instead, his uncle should do that. Perhaps, if Sir suspects something fishy in his uncle's dealings, when he learnt now that I was his uncle's business partner's daughter, the scenario of my position might change, my job might get jeopardize!? *Why this family's relations are always after me, armed with their wrongness?*

I steadied myself somehow to carry the tray of snacks and tea in the living area...when his uncle started creating a scene. It's apparent his gloat, for my wretched state, still acting all innocent, in front of his nephew, lest I spill the beans about his embezzlement. His feigned voice croaked. "Who would think, that Ganguli *Dada's* girl, will work here as a *Jhee* (called me maid, in a derogatory way) here? What doom has fallen? But Debo, *Ma*..." He addressed both of us simultaneously, for a minute, then shifted his remark to me to put a veil over his crime. "My hands were then, and now, are tied, you know that. Your father was not made for business, it's for him, we suffered so many heavy losses, there were heaps of loans piled up, which I had to clear up all those one by one, and had to pay the due salaries of employees too, and so on... All alone. And for that, I almost lost all my money, and in this whatever Ganguli *Dada* had left for you, went away too. Minisha *Ma's* inherited money and belongings, were all gone! Poor child! She was not only been deprived of her parents, but bereft of her house, and her inheritance! All had to be sold, so money could be acquired from it, so could be used to pay the loans. Don't you remember how truly I wanted to help you? But you had been always a high spirited and a self-reliant girl, and you refused my earnest offer downright!"

I bit my lip lest my bad mouthing displays, yet in front of

Sir, in the light of the world, I want to expose his sinister character, but kept quiet because of my parents upbringing to show respect to the elders, for reverence of Sir! Does Debobroto Sir will believe me, if I confide the sooth? Does an outsider's mouth will be considered  against his uncle's fake distress and conclusive lies? I'm not sure of his reactions, so my dilemma persuaded me to keep my silence. Yet I'm unable to silence my inner voice, unable to stifle my inner soul, who is bleeding for justice.

" *Help!*" I hooted inward."*You promised, just promised to give me only a mere five thousand rupees, which was not enough to last for two weeks to survive, especially when the existential cost of living has been skyrocketing! Even if I was given the money, which you didn't have given me anyhow, what would I do then after that?! JUST DIE! I was in the streets literally... If I hadn't secured that job in the college job fair, only God knows what would happen to me then? And what you did, when I appealed that this meagre amount, won't last for my survival, you said, you haven't opened a charity, so nothing else for me from future on. And it would be better, if I don't pester you or try to contact you for anything... I had seen you rolling in cash, that was my Baba's money... For days, for months, for years, I waited for the bus in soaking rain, cold wind, scorching heat, and you drove by in your expensive AC car, that was my Baba's money! You were warm and comfortable in your bungalow, while I was on the charitable lodge, into tattered sheets shivering in cold and anguish, famished for food and care! I knew how I starved myself, so to scrimp money to rent a tiny room of my own. I knew what torments, struggles, I had faced, but I never sold my pious body, or my pure soul to immorality or to the devil, never. I'm as pure as an angel, I'm not afraid to boast that! I struggled hard, to retain this position, and will continue doing so in the near future. What help you are talking about? You are pretending to be hurt, but you are in a revelry because you swindled and confiscated, all what was mine! As power and money were both of your mistresses then, so nobody dared to catch you red-handed, on the contrary, had forgotten about the existence of a Ganguli business, and it's heiress, the daughter of Ganguli's!''*

A muted heart to heart with my melancholic heart conversed, without uttering any complains to Sir, or without insulting his uncle. Once again I buried my deplorable pain inside, which is there for so long, even when this man today tried his level best to rip them off wide open, all my forlorn memories of the past, all my raw wounds which are not healed yet!

After quite a bit of time Badal Chatterjee and his evil self darted away on a false pretense, that staying here, seeing me face to face will remind him of Ganguli *Dada* and *Boudi,* my plight will torment him even more! He showed his crocodile tears to us before leaving. "I'm going child. Do your work honestly here, don't disappoint me, do not let my nose cut in front of Debo. *Bhogobaner ki Lila* (God and his strange tricks).'' He muttered those latter words to sicken me more I was already made sick by his abominable sight!

Past that, I simply stood there with my paralyzed body, ashen-faced, perturbed eyes and numb senses! I felt as I have been into some horror filled, dangerous roller coaster ride! Sir perceived the gravity of thesituation. He called out Mira immediately to give me a glass of water, and pleaded me to settle down on the sofa. For the first time, I didn't feel annoyed for his commands, on the other hand it felt so good. I obeyed. I collapsed on the seat, and then placed my sagging head on my palms, just to compose myself...I know, Sir is soon going to fire away his curious questions, and one thing more, I'm dreading of, his announcement to fire me from my job! His pensive self kept on sitting on the opposite sofa, and waited patiently for the proper moment of my composure,

before asking gently, to enlighten him with the briefings…
After he saw my earlier state of dismay has been improved.
So without snubbing his kind request, I told him without
any reluctance what I know so far. Ironically I had heard
those from his uncle. But I concealed my suspicions on his
uncle's dubiousness, while detailing him as I'm not positive
on how far he would believe me in this. Besides my dearth of
concrete evidences to point out, his crime, and his swindles,
all retracted me to reveal my suspicion. Moreover one way or
another, I always have come between his acquaintances, to
cause a rift between him. I don't want to repeat this again. My
parent's money is not going to come back, even if I do so. But
my candor, my restless outrage, perhaps for the inequities,
forced me to slip out from my mouth, the naked and harsh
truth. Why I'm confiding my soul to a complete stranger? I
don't know. But why I'm considering him as a stranger even
after giving him my precious thing, my heart? I don't know
that either. Plausibly my bottled up emotions has suffocated
me so much, for so long inside, that they want to gush out in
front of his compassion…or his non-confession of feelings for
me is dwindling my trust, by thinking him as a stranger still.

"Sir! If I would have any means or access to some concrete
proof, I would certainly have investigated the root cause,
and would have gone to the bottom of it too. I don't think,
my *Baba* had run his business so callously. Besides, what his
equal responsible partner was doing, when the company was
on the edge of ruin? *Baba* had given him the power of attorney
for everything, even the access of his bank account to him,
that's all I know. Your uncle was right, Sir, *Baba* was never
been a materialistic type, and he trusted blindly his close
friend, which resulted in having no investments in my name.
To raise money for starting up the business, my father sold
all the *Ma*'s jewelry and the property, he had on his name. So

each and every penny of my inheritance and my wealth, were spent in the company. I was left with some amount, which I had on my Bank account, but with that, I paid for my studies, the bills for household expenses, salary of the servants and rendered services, what was due after my parents' death, and the rest of funeral services, and to support me, in housing and food for months. After that I was practically penniless, and homeless too. But luckily, I got a job in the job fair, and from then on, a nineteen year old Minisha started her struggle real hard, to save salary to house her in, and for living expenses... And I stood up on my feet with my own merit Sir, I didn't beg or did something dishonorable at all. I just worked hard to survive, and to keep my good morals intact, as I value them the most!"

His astound is really taken aback by the time I have finished my piteous saga of my past days, with my bold frankness, yet he is so pleased with my honest implications towards the matter altogether, which surprised me too, his proud feeling for my honesty.

It's an unstirred atmosphere, nobody spoke after that, but remained still. Finally, Sir while breaking the quiet silence inquired about my decision for the present circumstance. Whether I would like to remain here after this? So that's it. I was hoping this noxious thing to come out, he doesn't want a once a rich girl, his uncle's ex-business partner's daughter to work around here as a housekeeper, it will affect his superiority, it will put him into rather a preposterous position, it will level him up against me. Besides his uncle's point of view, must have some influence on him too. But I'm not deceitful like their whole lot. I reasoned with him what my straight forward heart thinks. "What do you suggest Sir, you want to fire me? Tell me honestly. Though I don't know where I will go, this is my only job for now, and *my only home...*" I whispered on the latter part. I took a glimpse of him to read his eyes, of which I have first rate knowledge by now but instead of reading them, my pathetic eyes, my shameless eyes, displayed my hurt, my miseries for him to read in return… For repeated wrongs of my fate, I must have suspected his high-mightiness about me earlier, but his softened eyes for my agony, his understanding attitude for my each emotion, for my poor plight, made me remorseful then. He cried out in deep angst. "No! Never! Don't even think of that. I never will sack you! No matter what the storm will knock at my door. I will never let you go, never…Do you understand? Never! You are always welcome here, and are going to stay here with me, it's my request!" (Strange how contrary of his frequent words like 'it's my order', he has used 'it's my request' now. How tender his feelings have become for me, his statements not rhetoric anymore…) I breathed pleasantly when it feels so good, before listening to him more…

"Go to your room now please, and forgive me please, on behalf of my uncle, I'm asking for your forgiveness. Mira will do everything from now. It's been a very long and difficult memory lane you have journeyed, take a good rest Mini…!" He stopped here abruptly while pronouncing out my name, instead he guarded himself quickly to call. " Miss Ganguli…"

I simply nodded to agree with him. That was such a kind and gentle voice of his, such tendered emotions he has expressed to me, for that, my one warm, captive tear escaped from my prison, which I tried hard to uphold. I never knew he is such a sensitive man, with all emotions, so different from his austere and commanding self. But why he has said that he would never let me go, and wanted me to stay with him? Why?! Did he somewhat likes me too, his heart has started developing some feelings for me, like me for him? Or it is just his sympathy for a pitiable condition of mine, which is consoling me instead? But my 'Love' for him has captivated my heart, and my admiration for his being a sweet nature man in reality, lured me to commit a sin. And that sin is, I simply have fallen in love for him! Yes, it did not remain only up to my liking him, I started loving him. I really, really, love him so much!!

After that evening's horror and Sir's compassion...a couple of more days passed away. Today is the last of the March month, to culminate. I entered inside his office in the early morning to attend one of his summoned calls.

He seems to be in no mood to leave for the work somehow. I wonder why? As usual I stood beside his desk and leather chair, to get ready for my bidding. He just lifted his eyes slowly while guessing my presence, that is what he always does. "Oh! Miss Ganguli... here is your paycheck." He handed me that. It's his considerate habit of paying my salary before the end of the month, he looked so impatient about something, to impart, as soon as possible. I waited for his further say patiently. "Do you know, Mini...?!"

It started to slip once again bluntly from his tongue, my name again, this must be for some excitement, but he checked his off-guard once again quickly. "Tia is coming today in the evening for a visit, so I want to inform you that, you looked so worried about her on that day."

So he remembered my dejected face of earlier. Well! If there is something which have a power to lighten my saddening world, then this is the very news which did the work. I grinned widely like a village bumpkin, and so did he. "Oh! Thank you, Sir! You have made my day, thank you. But for that, can I be excused in the afternoon for a short market trip just for an hour or two? I will finish my work here, before going out there."

He nodded his head in approval, but somehow that disappointed him, as well. I know why, I'm going to be busy more than usual today, due to my outing...so to whom he will order around, to whom he will command his impositions during my absence. Anyway, I turned to go to my work, leaving him in his deep thinking. When I have lots to do for my Tia's homecoming celebration.

"Where are you going now? It's not afternoon yet." He disrupted my move, with a surprise in his tone.

"To work Sir, and I must be keeping you away from your work too. You are already late for the office for me. I'm sorry."

"Yes, you are doing that, keeping me away from my work, but I don't mind it at all, in fact, I'm enjoying it." He relaxed at his leisured remark, while placing his both crossed hands behind his nape, and stretched his legs forward under the desk more. He lounged at his reverie.

"Pardon me, Sir, but I don't get it." His sudden gibberish talk puzzled me, his insensitive say perplexed my look, for that he pitched a simple boyish grin at me. My heart somersaulted in deep affection, which I feel, whenever he grins at me like that. Then he veered his previous subject of conversation, (this is his usual habit).

"Tell me one thing, I presume you have no siblings or living relations?"

"Yes. None Sir."

"Friends? "

"Yes few, but had lost contact with them." My candid blurt

broke out to make me more vulnerable, as if my earlier remark for his query, was somehow didn't do the justice.

"Hmm...alright, you can go now. And don't worry, I took a leave from the work today for Tia's arrival. You know how I miss her too." His emotions spoke out.

" Yes, I know that Sir, how you miss her terribly. Alright, I'm going then."

I replied softly with a soft smile, for his candor now. Though his giving me a reason for his idle way, wasn't necessary, he could have ignored that answer easily, when I'm just his paid help, but by doing so, he proved that's how he values my position here, and my acumen. And that given respect, heightened my affection and respect for him even more! Further, when I know it's his doing, persuading Tia's grandmother for their visit, for my sake only!

I prepared an early lunch after finishing my other chores with an earnest instruction to Mira and Shefali to attend Sir well, and also to make sure that he eats everything at the right time. Then, I dashed for my market trip, despite of having ample time on my hands, before the approaching evening. I thought not to disturb the driver even in his rare holiday, and brushed off the idea to touch the servant's car either. Instead, I hunted in the deserted road, a way of conveyance. Luckily, I spotted a hired cab, which came to that locality, to drop off the kids to their way back home from their school. I requested the cab driver, if he will be kind enough to take me to the main market, and he readily agreed to. I hurried down there, to buy a few things of grocery from the household expenses amount, and also to deposit my salary money in the bank...but on a second thought, I withdrew some of my salary to buy Tia, some presents... And my wandering feet must have reached in the middle of the market, when through the narrow lane of the market, in the opposite side of it, I noticed something else too... A government owned reputable, and an exclusive working women hostel building... a little away from the hubbub of the market. I don't know why, or on what basis of premonition, I have headed to the hostel gate with my dallied and curious steps, to inquire about the requirements needed to lodge anyone there? As it is a Government backed institution, so the charges seems to me minimal, further more, it is for the working women only, and no one is allowed there beside the staff and the lodgers, and they have some rather strict rules regarding the late night arrival, and about male visitors, even male relatives are not allowed here... Why this procedure made me happy, and relieved for such rules, besides being such trustworthy ones, that is my utter surprise, when I'm not planning to board here someday, by any chance?!

I'm back to my home, yes, I can call that now, when it sheltered me from my destitute fate. It is still early in the evening, and I know Tia has arrived. How? Mrs. Banerjee's car is parked right outside the entrance, and her famed grumblings floated into my ears from the living room itself.

"Where is that new girl? How reckless of her, only cooked your lunch, so she can vanish off, to who knows where?!"

I ignored her, as I'm too tired even to listen, and after washing my hands and face quickly. I filled the trays with savories and sweetmeats, prepared by me earlier, then put cups, and a warm tea pot of citrus tea, and a tall glass of pineapple juice for Tia, (it is summer time already).

Pushing the food trolley, full of those contents, I darted my feet in the living area, while slinging a shopping bag to one of my shoulders, which contained gifts for Tia. I started envisioning, that latter is going to jump in joy, while seeing me, and will exclaim in thrill, when she will see her gifts! What delightful sight it will be?

I will once again going to hear her tinkling effervesce, her lilting voice, I will once again see my darling daugh...if I can call her that! My eyes became dewy in emotions and heart heavy, I must have missed her so much!

Mrs. Banerjee's scowling face barked at my appearance. "So you are here now, *Maharani!* Finally, allotted your time for us from your frolic and dilly-dally! Where you were loitering around, and to whom you went to meet, your long lost boyfriend?!"

I'm prepared for this. I don't give two hoots of her unpleasant talks whatsoever. I'm not afraid of her even. Loving Sir, though secretly, that one-sided love of mine has given me enough strength, that I can remain stolid to anything. I replied to her with my patience. "Sorry madam, for being so late, I was marketing for Tia's gifts. Here are your tea and refreshments. But where is she?!" I looked around with anticipation. "What gifts? I won't allow it. From where you have found the money for that, answer me? It must be from Debobroto's pockets? Tia is not here and upstairs in her room, taking a nap." She sliced me with her ultimate height of vex.

"Yes, gifts for Tia, ma'am, and don't worry, they are not some voodoo dolls in any way." I remember how she accused me falsely of casting a black magic on them, called me a witch, a street wench too. I continued boldly. "Because these gifts can't be voodooed, they are read along story books, necessary for the kids of her age, to polish off their reading ability, and a Magnetic doodle board to practice her drawing, she has every potential of becoming a good artist, and all that I noticed during my slacking off days with my work." I taunted on that part, she accused me of that just now…" And yes, in a way, they came from Sir's pocket, because I bought them from my salary money. Regarding my boyfriend, you have guessed it right, he is indeed long-lost!" I finished my audacious reply with a slight conceited smile. As her talk flared me. And I'm tired of her browbeating to me. I'm tired of placating her foul questions and accusations all the while. I raised my one brow in irritation.

And boy! This angered her too, my justified straight faced answers, my bolder side. I can see clearly how fiery her red eyes are, how grim her mouth is, all ready to spurt out venom anytime. But I don't care at all what she thought of me. As neither I'm her bought slave, nor her chained dog. She can't put me under her thumb. As long as Sir is here as my boss, and Tia is there to love me…I don't care about a pack of snobbish villains around me. And to confirm my notion, I threw a quick glance at Sir, whether he is blown off by my sudden revolt?! But with my utter surprise and sheer joy, he is trying desperately to suppress an irrepressible laugh, from coming out from his mouth. And his eyes are so much amused in mirth, that he has to turn his head to the other direction so he can hide them from his mother-in-law's sharp and observant pair of eyes. That's all I need, a little backing from his side to prove my side of honesty, and dedication towards my work. But invincible Mrs. Banerjee is not leaving the field so easily when the word 'defeat' is not in her dictionary. She aimed at me once again with her deep rooted annoyance.

"*Aijeye Meye*, you love to notice around then why didn't you notice, that April month is coming?? Oh dear God! And on the fifth of April is my daughter's death anniversary! What have you done as preparations for my darling daughter Shamita? Shamita, died so young in a car accident, who would have thought, that some brute would squash my innocent daughter's car, I'm cursing the rest of their family who had killed my daughter!" Her howls increased together with her slapping on her chest, and it became so intolerable for Sir, that he ran to her side to calm her down.

For a fleeting second her crying words put me in a haze, but I jerked myself out into a reality soon, because those words which cracked out in the surface, are gruesome and intolerable for me to bear! My parents had died on that very day, on the fifth of April, that is their death anniversary date too! And what Shamita Mukherjee? Wait a minute? Why this name seems to me so familiar? She died in a car accident too? That can't be possible? It's too much of a coincidence? But it was not mentioned in the police records, that she was married to Sir or she was the daughter of the Banerjee's?! So it was a very schemed out matter, a total hush-hush to protect the identity and the reputation of her darling daughter! I got to know on which highway, it has taken place, I got to know at which time, because that day, at that time, only one sole car accident took place, I got to know all here! Pallid in horror and in trauma, my whole tremulous body shook like a trembling leaf...I screamed out loud, on top of my voice, my love for him did not help me in remaining stolid this time. "Which road it was? Which road?? It was Belroad highway, was it??! Six-thirty in the evening on fifth of April 20--??!! Tell me, answer me for God's sake?!! Was the car's Registration number was yyyyyy?!! Don't stare at me like a nincompoop, answer me God damn it, right now!" My outrage cussed at them with so much fury and repulsion! I'm getting hysterical in anger and sorrow, by now! Sir ran to me, he surmised my verge of prostration...Yes, when he is capable of reading my expressions, it is one of his traits. "What is it? Why you are asking that Minisha? Tell me?!"

I hooted inside! *"What Minisha, are you agitated too out of fear, Sir, as the heinous crime of your wife's have been revealed out, which you have toned down?! That's why you are calling a mere servant by her name to threaten her…"* My anticipated dread he revealed then, a poignant truth he spoke out, which have devastated and ransacked my entire happy life! "Yes, it was the exact location, and the exact time was six-thirty in the evening too, with same date and a same car number, and at the broad highway, it was! What is it? Was it there, where your parents were killed? Did their Car hit by…? " He assumed it accurately. Why not? He is always so good at suppositions. I swooned in grief, in anger, and in injustice, because of my fate, because of this horrid family! My nostrils filled with such disgust present in the air, and my vision with such abhor, due to the sight of that lady, due to this man (who I love so much)! My nauseating stomach churned in. I just crushed that shopping bag filled with the gifts for Tia, which I bought just now. Which I bought with so much enthusiasm, love and excitement. I crushed that into a pulp, and they slipped from my hands on the floor, because something much more powerful overpowered me! Gripped me! I staggered into a state of shock, as if somebody shook the earth underneath my feet. Then beyond my imagination, I tossed my head a little back, and laughed like a madwoman, while crying profusely side by side! "BINGO! You have guessed it right, Sir! You are always a good guesser! Aren't you going to boast around about that Sir?!" I clapped my hands to applaud him, for his geniuses! By now I must have reached into a state of insanity. A towering rage quaked my whole body, in entirety, I heaved with irregular breathing. I hissed at them, both, at Sir and at Mrs. Banerjee. I pointed out my shaky forefinger at them. "Sir, your beloved wife, and you, madam, your precious daughter had murdered my parents mercilessly! She was a drunk driver! A maniac drunken driver!

A swamping and reeking alcoholic she was! She was so soaked in the spirit that she didn't realize whose life she had been robbing; whoseparents she had been robbing; whose happiness she had been robbing?! Now what bad blood and recklessness persuaded her to do that heinous crime, answer me?? This hussy right here is a teetotaler, and your goody one was a blood thirsty drunkard! What you have to say now, about her debauchery? You all were accomplices of her crime, your hands are covered with my Parents' blood, the very bad blood you named madam, that day, was in your hands!! And you, madam, just now cursed my parents' rest of the family, you cursed at me, just now! You are so good at cursing. Aren't you? I wish, I could curse you back too, but I simply adore Tia so much, that I could not do so. God Bless her dear heart! It's not my parents who squashed her car, but she crushed my parents bodies ruthlessly; she rammed her car into them, and trampled on the bodies of my *Baba*, and of my *Ma*, mercilessly! I have the evidence with me, it was in the police records, and it was reported in the newspaper; an unnoticeable small newspaper report, but noticeable enough to prove your crime! I have that newspaper cutting, and the copy of the police record with me. I still have an evidence to hang you all! This mere servant still has that power against your powerful influences, which had corrupted the police department and the media, to hush down the crime. Do you hear? I have the evidence of the brutality, against a whole lot of you, of what you all are famous for… You people are so expert in your brutalities, that from your *Mamoni*, from your friend, from your uncle, to your dead wife, all of them, one by one, thought of me as some lifeless commodity without any heart or soul, who is simply branded to project their brutal torments, time and again. Your wife, Your daughter is the murderess, yes, she was the murderer of my parents, and this is a murderess's house!!!"

For the first time I saw Mrs. Banerjee listening to me stupefied, a nonplussed Sir with a guilty feeling looked on, due to my hatred and hostility to them...I shook with an acute rage! I stifled my mouth with my fist, to stop my moaning outcry. In fact my present turbulent emotion is way too much to handle, for my body, because all of my energy is washed out...After that...I collapsed on the floor like some dead leaf! Somebody patted on my cheeks with a hand, while trying to wake up my sleeping consciousness! "Minisha, Minisha! Wake up, please wake up!" I heard a very faint sound of someone who is calling my name. I know who it is, the same one who dared to call my name, a little earlier... And that's all I can remember in my state of senselessness...and it's getting dark again in front of my eyes, I must have fainted once again!!

# Chapter Eight: Declarations

I blinked my blurry eyes slowly to find out I'm in my room? My sagging body and my weak nerves did seem to have enough strength to recollect the earlier events, one by one, even conscious of my surroundings that I'm still staying in the house of a blood thirsty mistress?! All of a sudden the remembrance of that made me gather some strength, so I can run away from this house as soon as possible. I tried to lift my head for that purpose, but it sagged back to the pillows. "*Oh dear God!*" I sighed a moan.

My that feeble moan stirred Mira. She leaned over me to support me into a sitting position. "Thank God *Didi*! You have gained consciousness. We all were worried sick about you. Just rest your head against the headboard and pillows, like that. I'm going to fetch the doctor and something to eat. It's been a day now, that you are being like that." Her haggard face wiped off her tears in a relief, after seeing my stable side.

"Oh! What date is today?! Please tell me...how is Tia and... *Sir*?? " I bit my lower lip before inquiring about him further. "Please fetch me the newspaper, will you, please?" I didn't knew my voice is so feeble, that it sounded like a thin shrill.

"It's second of April *Didi*, now you stay in the bed like a good girl, alright?But don't tell a soul, about what I'm going to say now. Otherwise, I will be in a deep trouble…Tia is fine and is with her Grandmother…but latter told her, that if she stays here with her *Masimoni*, with you, then you will be more sick… and master, I don't know whether I should tell you about this or not, but he was so agitated and worried with your condition, since the day he carried your collapsed body in your room. He hardly ate or slept, or went for his work! All he has done, was sitting on the stairs, fixing his alert gazes at your door!" She confided a heart wrenching truth, under a shadow of fear. That heart-felt concern of his, that deep worry for me, I'm not prepared to learn, as after hearing this, my foolish heart might want to renew affections for him. And that is not in my mind right now. All my preoccupied mind is thinking, is of finding ways to escape from this house!

After a while the doctor arrived along with Mira and Shefali in my room, he is that very family doctor who came for Tia that day. He examined me, and reasoned me with something else too. "Now you seem to be much better, it was due to over-excitement that's why you have fainted, so to overcome this fatigue, you must eat and drink heartily to gain your lost vigor. And then again, your cheeks will be back in their rosy color. Otherwise you have to remain in the confines of this bed, for one whole month. I don't want a pretty and young girl like you to waste away like that!"

"One whole month…that can't be possible!" I cried at him to protest, with as much vigor as I have left with, in my limp body. A whole month in this house, I have to hatch a plan to get away from here immediately. All I need is some strength in my listless body for that. It is better to die than to breath in this poisonous air! My determination deep inside, somehow compromised with my present predicament. "Alright doctor,

I will listen." I said to him in a soft whisper. Nodding his head for my obedience, he replied gently then. "Now my dear, I will give you an injection...Mira and Shefali please close the door, will you?" The doctor ordered them, and they did as being told. The jab of the injection is not that painful, compared to what I have endured till now. It made my eyes heavy, a deep slumber dunk me into it. My half-awake state heard someone knocking at the door, for a fraction of moment my emotion tingled, by thinking, that Sir has come for me, but it is Mira again, now with a laden tray of food, and a glass of juice. My deep shock thrusts me into a dilemma, whether to eat this sinful food and drink or not? But still I gulped down the morsels of food, while stuffing them into my mouth like a mad, my tears of agony cried as well...As *sin* and *blood*, all those words pounded my ears constantly. My sanity even decided to leave me helpless, when I sloshed down the juice, with my trembling hands, in this process all the fluid trickled down from the sides of my mouth, soaking me wet with a poignancy. Yet I finished my tray of punishment, just to gain strength in my feet, so I can slip by from this criminal environment, so I can fade away into thin air, away from Sir's world, so I can wipe off my inherent love for him from my heart, forever! Mira seems to be in great agitation after seeing my insane state, she rushed to call the doctor again, and with him, now Sir came. And as soon as Debobroto Sir, entered into the room, an essence of serenity pervaded around to lull me.

The doctor inquired me in great concern. "Well! What is it? Are youalright dear? Don't over-exert yourself in your condition, your heart beat, blood pressure, and pulse beat, will get excited by it, it would be very difficult for you to cope with it, take lot's of food, liquid and rest, and no anxiety, if you want to be up and healthy again!" His advice and sincere tone directed then, to Sir. "Debobroto tell her that, and make sure she listens, to what I'm suggesting her." His shouldered concern Sir took happily, as his head nodded sincerely, my frail vision can see, how he wants me to become rosier in health too. "Alright, I will listen to what you have said…" I weakly assured the doctor, my awkwardness regarding this, or my eagerness to release my troubles off from Sir's shoulder, made me to do that.

"*Arrey* Debo, isn't this girl is the same, who phoned me earlier at the time of Tia? I remember now, her sweet voice. What a lovely girl she is? Does she by any chance an aspiring model of your fashion house?!" To lighten the gloom, I thought he must have said that. Then he aimed his remark at me. "Please don't mind me *beta*, think of me, as an elderly uncle of yours, but you are a very beautiful child!" I laughed a little to astonish him.

"Why did you laugh?" He looked worried for my sudden humor. "It's in the ear doctor, this flattery. I didn't mind at all, even when it keeps torturing me. And now I'm used to it so much so, that it seems to be my oxygen." And with that delirious sarcasm, I closed my drooping eyes…I know somehow, both of them have left me, to be on my own, in my delirium.

After a while I slowly opened my eyes to act fast, but nevertheless my staggered and swooning body made it impossible to lift myself up, but with a support of the headboard of the bed, I tried to stand up…slowly, slowly, little by little, I reached at the footboard. Then, holding that, as my life support, I took tiny, feeble steps to the writing table on the other side of the wall, to pick the mobile up, which lay there, while balancing my arms to balance my body…but my oppressing destiny informed Sir deliberately, so he could catch me red-handed. He emerged suddenly from behind, to discipline my puerile act.

"What are you doing here? You are not even fit to stand up yet, go to your bed right now!" His authoritative scolding scolded me, with such an affinity, that I fell in love with him again! Even if I romanced with his scolding, yet disregarding him altogether, I held the edge of the table to grab my mobile, when he picked it up from the table instead!

"You want your mobile, alright here you are." He handed me that, while unaware of my hidden scheme. I almost snatched the device from his hand like my lifeline, to quickly slip it into my night robe's pocket, he extended his hand to succor my swaying shoulder.

"Don't touch me please, don't do that." I screamed out my resistance. I knew my senseless body was caressed by his concern, when he carried me out here...but my awakened senses now, wants to resist his deep concern, as it did not want to accord with my deep down emotions, which I have for him, not in my present vulnerable condition. That will languish my heart. But my weak body betrayed me and stumbled upon his kind arms, to surrender my heart, to build a sand castle of my love, before the tide of my cruel fate can wash it away! He sighed heavily at my rebelled self, gripped my shoulder with his arm around to support, and with the other arm, held my hand firmly, to aid me to my bed.

This is for the first time, I can feel his passionate touch. That touch infused a rapture into my body, which helped me to regain my lost vigor, to recuperate the sickness, and something else, a beautiful desire to be loved by him! I slumped on the bed, then he covered me with the comforter carefully, while making sure that his long fingers *are not touching me at all.*

He walked away to keep a distance, to stand near that faraway window, of my room's. His back turned, while he kept his arms behind his back, hands clasped together. I can surmise his, that gesture, he is deep in his anxiety for me. That wrenched my heart, because of being the reason. It's ironical how that little distance of ours from the bed, seems to be being miles apart from each other...His mellow voice broke the stiff silence to begin, in order to confide to me with something...perhaps his confession to me? I can sniff the essence of his heart!

"Please forgive me, I know, this is not the right time, but still I can't help it. I took the doctor's advice, he said you are much better now, so on the basis of that I'm intruding in your weak condition. Please forgive me, but it is my rightful duty to enlighten you, of what had happened exactly in the past, it's necessary to illuminate your disillusionment. I'm not outraged with your anger, hatred, or accusations either, because deep in my heart, I know that you are being treated in an unjustified way by each of us, one way or another... Shamita, with Tia's mother, I had an arranged marriage, her father used to be a friend of my late father. I didn't knew her problem of alcoholism earlier, she must be addicted to that in her wild parties, in her frivolous college days. She was the only child of the Banerjee's, so they had spoilt her ultimately, with their indulgent upbringing. They doted her with money and blinded love, and were completely negligent about her ongoing. That heavy drinking habit of hers permanently resided with her, even after her marriage. When I learnt about that, I went along with her for the therapy. I initiated with it, she improved also. But during my busy days, somehow when I didn't have enough time to spare, during that time, she must have had renewed her friendship with alcoholism furtively! Without my knowledge, she was enticed by the craving again, and started drinking! And she hid it so well, that nobody had suspected anything...That day, when she had died, she was in her friend's party. She nicked her friend's car keys to go to a bar. There she drank her favorites...Vodka, cognac, whisky, schnapps, scotch... She swigged them down one by one, to satisfy her parch, to satiate the temptation! That craving urge was so strong that it exhorted her to do something fatal. She forgot what she was doing actually...in her haze, drove ahead in her friend's car, to one end road!! And the rest you know, what happened after that...You know what was the repercussion of that... I know she did the crime, had sinned, yet was young at the time of her death, and paid a price too for her sin, through her death, and by making Tia motherless, me a widower! She was never been a filial daughter to *Mamoni* and *Babai,* so making them issueless was not surprising! She killed herself to wreck three families. So we all paid the price along with her! No matter how much I condole you, no matter how I console you with copious amount of consoling words, but it's the truth, that I can never console your anguish. Your parents are not going to come back to you, with those mere words! They are not. And directly or indirectly, we are connected by this crime and sin. We played the part of the antagonists in your life…But before all this heinous revelation was unveiled, right before you. Before all of this...

When you came here, when I saw you for the first time, near that stranded station, I was smitten by the beautiful you! I was smitten by your lovely face, blowing curls, enchanting pair of eyes, your pert nose, soft beautiful mouth! I was smitten by the splendor of yours. You were standing there, with your cowered down shoulders, due to cold, fatigue and loneliness...As if waiting  for me, to hold you close, to give you warmth to your heart and soul. You looked like an angel to me, a being which came from another part of the world, something God have made specially for me, then sent to me, and for me only...Post my wife's death, in all those dark years of life...I worked, like an automated machine, work was the only life for me. I was alive for the work only. I hardly came home or had eaten with an appetite, that was long gone for me, it was for Tia, that I lived...All the pain and wrongness, all the hardships, sorrow, hopelessness, I locked, barred, and bottled up inside my heart, it was like living in a deep, dark tunnel with no way for a tiny fickle of light to come through, with no way out...Until you came! And from then, everything changed. I'm so glad that you came into my life! I'm so glad that I came for you. You are like my Sunshine too, (the song you've crooned that evening, it's relatable) in my sunless life, who just came to brighten up my dark world, to warm up my cold world...You are so beautiful, kind, caring, understanding with a smart wit, that I have fallen for you, and started loving you. I love you so much...a whole lot. I never have loved anyone, the way I love you. My love for you is not my momentary infatuation, or a short-lived crush, but an ingrained feeling which neither is going to fade away, nor going to pass over just like that, when you are my everlasting love, when I'm fated to love you! This is for the first time I have loved someone with such a passion...I realized this, that without your love, my life is lifeless, I might die even without it...

When Prabhat behaved with you badly. I kept quiet in helplessness. My dilemma thought, my intervention would offend you, as I'm just an outsider for you. I was so unsure about you then. I didn't know your feelings are as honest as mine, it was not conspicuous in front of me. Because for the first time, I might be feeling the sensations of love. I found out your true feelings step by step, when you started unfolding before me, through your surprises, your puzzled expressions, your bright and sparkling gazes, especially those curious ones, which always peers into mine, to read my true emotions. And my desire to compliment you grew along with my love for you…Your cascade of soft curls I so long to touch, and your turns, tilts, tosses off your head, whenever you outwit us, I so long to admire. Your soft parted lips when you become vehement, your blushed soft cheeks in the startles, inhibitions and flares, I so long to caress. Your painful tears, I so long to wipe off, and for your happy ones, I so long to kiss your eyes. Your tender, beautiful curving smiles, little laughs in triumph, in humor, in love, in care, I so want to make mine. I loved all your courageous frankness, your honest fights against agonies and unjust, your outsmart, whenever challenges are thrown at you…your clever argument, your banters, and your lovely being, all those simply beckoned me to love you, tenderly and very deeply…I was lulled, even more by your that enchanting song, to make me aware of your euphony…Above all, do you know, what touched me? Your beautiful and immaculate heart and soul! You are like my bright, happy sunshine, whose beautiful, loving, caring and warm rays simply spread its wings just to light my dark tunnel, so my whole world can sparkle by your sparkling existence…You thought of me as some arrogant boss, who orders you around. But no, my dear (if I can call you that). I did that only to see and only to feel, you every inch of existence, as your absence suffocated my existence. I was so curious at first, after going through with your resume, that's why a bright eyed and lovely faced uptown girl, wanted to do this job?...I was so curious to know you, that's why I hired you, that's why I also came to pick you up, just to get acquainted with you first! But on the contrary by doing all those, what happened to me? You stole my heart at the very first sight… After that, you proved me wrong, that you are not just a beautiful uptown girl, for whom I have fallen for, but you are as efficient as my other employees at the office. And one thing more, I have discovered to my utter disbelief, that you are a naive and unblemished soul! When those men behaved impudently on that party day to you, I was so in my dread that I didn't sleep that night. I was thinking of ways to protect my adorable, innocent lamb from the clutches of the wolves. And that day, for another reason I didn't wink asleep, because you looked so stunning in your ethnic wear, the image just lingered in my eyes...I have never seen such an enthralling beauty in my whole life...And for that, my worries became never ending, due to the atrocities of the world towards you...I didn't know about my uncle's dealings with your late father before, and I didn't know why he kept quiet about my wife's involvement in your parents' accident also?

Why he had conspired in this?! Why he didn't reveal that, when he came here? I don't know... But I have talked to him about this, but he simply washed his hands off it, even after my threatening. So I simply had to sever my ties with him forever...I know, how you care for Tia whole heartedly with your unconditional love, how you love her, and us, and in return you never have asked for anything. You are like a real mother to Tia, more than her birth mother! You must be wondering why I kept quiet, when *Mamoni* abused you. Because she has a complicated heart problem, after her daughter's death, so I kept quiet, like you, I respect my elders too! So I was helpless once again, my beautiful bloom, yes, you are that to me Minisha...and that evening when you were strolling in the garden, you looked like a nymph of the woods to me. I was so awestruck with that hypnotic effect, that I was drawn towards you in some magnetic force...so you could see a reserved person's garrulous side. My withdrawn self, that's long gone only because of you…How can I forget, that you made me laugh as well, I laughed heartily, I laughed a lot…Mirth came to my grim life. Every distress which were obscuring my smiles is chased by you. I smiled, I smiled a lot. For once again, I have re-lived my life…I felt the hunger for the food for the first time also, after so many days, your hand must have weaved some magic, the way *Mamoni* has said… '' He chortled during this, because humor is clung with him, due to my entrance to his world, before continuing again…"So the taste to my tongue is still left in my mouth, I thought, and to check, whether that omelet was cooked by you, whether the breakfast was served so tastefully by you, (I'm aware of the *cordon bleu* of my helps)…I re-visited again at home to clarify my suspicion, and that's why I came for the lunch that day, after all those years… And the food whetted my conclusion and suspicion, as well. The soup tasted the same, the salad was prepared with a same tasteful way. I loved your, that impermissible authority taken from me…I liked the very idea so much, as nobody shown such affinity before, nobody cared for me so tenderly, except my late *Ma*! You are much more than an assistant and a housekeeper to me, you are like a true friend, and like a… *lover to me!*'' His hesitant dilemma about my feelings for him, whispered the later part. "…And your sincerity always moves my heart. And I always love, how you flare subtly… But that day, you completely bowled me over, I never had seen such a fiery temper, yet despite your angered and hostile words, I loved each and every tempered moment of yours! Oh! How I have fallen in love with you again, then! Now, I want to re-confess… I love you, I love you, I love you, and if you agree, I want to marry you! I want you to become mine, to be my wife, because not a moment I ever think of living without you. I want to share your pains, joys, sorrows, victories, fights, happiness, cheers, smiles, laugh, your nuances, your love and your touch with me! Everything about your sweet and pure existence…I want to be by your side, for always, to grow old together! Will you be my love by my side, Minisha? Tell me your honest answer? Will you love me?! Will you marry me?!" And his that lengthy beseech ended like this, his appeal to accept his proclaim of love, his proposal of marriage waited for my reciprocated nod, in a great anticipation!

His those beautiful words, his soul-stirring confess, made me soporific in his enchantment! I accused him of being a theatrical man at one time, how wrong I was! He is the most poetic, romantic, and splendid person inside out. I never have read or heard such words of love. The way his declaration of love has touched me, nothing can move me in this world, the way his words have done. His proposal to me is one of the wonderful, sweetest thing, that ever have occurred to me, in my life! I didn't know he loves me so much too, he has so many repressed, beautiful emotions, thousands of them for me, and his tender heart has reserved them for me, it was kept hidden inside, as my keepsake. And for that, I thanked my unfortunate destiny for once! It is such an emotional moment for me, that my whole being tingled... But what I said in return, so his dear heart can be broken into pieces. And for that, I'm not going to forgive myself! I deliberately became cruel all of a sudden, to justify my parents death. I shrilled aloud, shaking my head up…"It can't be, it can't be! I don't believe any of your words."

After that, every ounce of energy seems to be washing away from me before saying something more. I sighed heavily, and fell back on my pillows, with a loud thud! He turned his back to hasten his feet towards me. He became agitated with fear and an alarm, that he made me sick again!

Quickly scooting the sofa chair to sit, he faced my side. "I'm so sorry Minisha! My timing was wrong!" He gently stroked my curls, then my forehead.

I slanted a faint glance at him. To my utter horror, I saw his raddled look, his face has shrunk to half its size, in my worry! He looked at me with his careworn, hollow eyes. His sunken face is getting beyond my recognition. How I wish to erase his weary looks with my magical touch, which he mentioned that I have one, how I want to touch his face, to rejuvenate him! How I want to do all those things. But I could not! His predicament is noticeable, because his face (like his heart) is reflected by the lamplight, or probably I'm fully awake now, because of his drawled voice, for that splendid touch of his? I shut my eyes while vowing never to open them again, I shut my eyes to curtain his sight.

"Please don't touch me, please don't do that!" I cried. A sensation to love him has started arousing within me. I know by facing him, I will melt, and will be averted from my determination. But I re-opened them because what he have said in a response, goaded me.

"Why? Because you feel the same, the way I do?!" He simply said softly, while realizing my heart's true feelings, for him.

"How do you know, how I feel?!" I saw in my faint vision, how he is laughing at my innocence.

"Oh come on! I know you love me too, you are so transparent that I can read you like an open book! Your every action, movement, reactions, apparently spoke to me, to claim your love for me. You know how we feel when our eyes meet, they ignite such passions, you know how we feel, when we share our smiles and laughs, the cheerfulness creeps all over our body. Neither you can deny, nor you can ignore that true fact. Still, you don't want to confess your love to me?" I just pressed my lips tightly, and seeing my adamant, he said once again to instigate me, in confessing my truth. "So my strong willed Minisha will not confess to her Sir? I didn't know, that she is such a coward, when she is a torchbearer of truth?

What happened to her candor, which used to come straight from her heart? That Minisha will lie? She will lie to her Sir... Why she is so afraid to be happy, to be loved?!"

Those words did provoke me, like a fool I yielded right before him, to admit everything! I murmured. "I'm not a liar, nor made of stone, I too have a heart that is still beating fast. I'm not deceitful like a whole bunch of you. Yes, I love you a lot, a whole lot! And without your love, I will die too! Now here you are, you have heard my candor, I obeyed you once again to listen to your command, you have won Sir! I have confessed, you won Sire. This is what, you wanted to hear, yes, your slave has been defeated! Happy now? But despite of your victory, I can't accept your love or your marriage proposal at all! I can't stay here as well. No one on the earth, has the power to stop me from getting away from all this. No one! What your wife did, I can't forgive or forget, but for Tia and you...I'm saying this, I want your permission to let me go...Please, and for the first time, I'm asking you for something. You and Tia, and this house too, haven't sinned, I know that from the bottom of my heart. It gave me shelter, food, and my salary during my dreadful, destitute days... And I'm glad you came, and that I came across to you Sir. I'm so glad, that words fall short. Because you are my Sunshine from the start, in my life, that song of evening, that's why it came out in open, you know, how direct my heart is? You lit up my world. For the past four years, I struggled hard to survive. I was living in a deep, dark cold tunnel too. I used to pray to God and my parents everyday so hard, that in answer to that prayer, they have sent you and Tia, and this job! You came to me just like a ray of hope. You are a sunlight to me, will remain so forever. But still I cannot forget, what your wife, *Mama, Mamoni,* and your friend has done to me, the way they robbed what was mine...Oh! I can deal well with them, as I have dealt with the bullies of the world before. But still I kept quiet, doing nothing, just for your sake Sir. I didn't want to create any rift between you and them. Now you know, how your uncle conspired for his greed, that's why he kept quiet. I don't want money, but I want justice...And that day, was too much for me to bear. I burst out with my pain, which was hidden like a hot volcano deep inside my heart, it erupted outside suddenly.

I was young when my parents had died. I was all alone, destitute, nobody was there to love me, care for me, or to hold my hand to guide me, to live the life on...Do you understand? What I meant Sir? I was young, too! I was just nineteen! I didn't knew, that Tia's mother, your wife, had killed my parents...then I would never have come here...I admit, I have acted very badly that day but I was out of my mind. I have my obligations as a daughter to my parents, Sir. Please believe me. Fate has always mocked at me, no matter how much I tried or worked hard. It mocked me, and robbed me, even when I have found the love, which I never think of even parting! But the recent circumstances, and the write-ups of the destiny, are forcing me to take this step now, just to be away from all this...You accused me of stealing your heart and peace, but you have robbed mine too. So we both are partners of the crime!" (And at this point, I heard his famous little laughs). But without getting attracted to them, I finished my heart's says. "Thank you, Sir, for loving me so much. And also thinking of me being eligible enough to be your life partner, and Tia's mother too! Thank you, it is a great honor for me, believe me. I promise you, I will always treasure this, in the bottom of my heart forever..." My murmurs ended, to put an end to the tortures of my heart, and how I did that, by exposing all of my concealed feelings out.

"Minisha, please forgive me, I'm asking for the forgiveness of what my related people, had done to you. I admit you have endured from such a delicate age, but that's why I'm begging you not to deny my love. Don't close the door on what your heart feels for me, don't ruin our lives, let us relive, let us love, let us marry, let us rejoice in our intimacy, let us live together forever till eternity...I don't want to lose my Sunshine again! You again! When you are my harbinger of happiness and luck, your coming into my life have released me from my chain of malediction. Can't you see your rejection is killing me, it will be like living in the dark, in the cold world all over again! I beg of you to re-consider!" He entreated me with his heart-rending pleas once again. But I remained unyielding like a stone to his pleas, moreover became sullen because of his being remorseful self again on behalf of the sinners, that I fought for him on his behalf now.

"Why you always feel sorry and apologetic for your relations? You haven't done anything wrong, it's their sin, let God decide their punishment, and their crime. Please stop feeling sorry, stop your apology, it's not your fault, but theirs. I don't want to live in a dark and cold and in my aimless life too, but still I can't accept neither your marriage proposal, nor your love. Love and happiness are two luxuries of my life, which I cannot possibly afford right now. I must go away from here, if possible on the day after tomorrow. I will do that definitely!"

And by the time I finished my sayings of the heart, my recent demonstrated vigil has also thawed which I have shown little earlier. My body quavered in pangs of sentiments. My afflicted body at once fell into a deep sleep... Through my slumber I hearkened to his rustling sound of soul, due to a stir caused by my obstinate resolution, that made me realize, that Sir has quietly left me, *all alone*!

The morning of the next day came, the day, post that beautiful day of our confessions. To my surprise I felt a bit energetic, it's nature's given gift, I suppose...it is happening due to the survival of the fittest or by learning that his heart is actually beating for me? I still fidgeted about the newspaper's job offer advert, fumbled with my mobile too. Ironically, this mobile was handed to me by Sir, so indirectly he led me into this...The people who have adverted are of some reputable advertising agency. They are seeking for the interns, through conducting a telephonic interview to make a shortlist of interviewees. So I decided to plunge into it. I tapped their number, luckily the interview went well. They have accepted me, but will offer me the job after the final interview! Somehow I felt their acceptance of me is not because of my caliber, but for the reference of my previous job, because of Sir's reputation? But I was impelled to give my last job description and my current address also. I haven't spoken with the lodge yet, for a room arrangement, before the interview. I was unsure about my securing of a new job, and when the lodge people will allow me only after my permanent proof of work. But now I can do that by showing the SMS of the company, where I got the job in a way, and from the next week, all the job formalities will be cleared too. I called the Lodge from my obtained contact details during my last visit there. They agreed upon boarding me only if I show them the text message received by my prospective employer. The day they will board me is...

Fifth of the April! So the fatal day, the fifth of April it is, so it is fated again then! Destiny dictated all this. Alright, I will go away to avenge my parent's death on that day!

These past two days I don't know how I have passed, as the sanctity of the house echoed once more, the intolerable, cruel words of *'Sin'*, *'Blood'*, *'Revenge'* around my ears non-stop. But somehow, I have stabilized myself to stand up on my feet, to keep my head sane and with rapid hands have packed up my all belongings to prep-up, for my escapade…

It is fifth of April, the day of my new journey…I got up very early, as I had a fitful sleep. I tossed and turned all night till the crack of the dawn. I swaggered with the bulging bags and heavy suitcases, to come outside of my room. I closed my room's door, the room which sheltered me, day and night, during all those months, where I had shared mine, all those gamut of emotions, time and again, and where, something very beautiful happened to me…both Sir and I, confessed our love! I closed the door of my beautiful days, of my that beautiful chapter just like that.

I tapped at the door of the office. I knew, Sir will be there, he is an early riser. Even though it is too painful to bid him a final goodbye! Still I gambled with my emotions, just for the last glimpse of him, for my brimming eye's keepsake. He was sitting in his leather chair behind the desk, just what he does always, one of his elbows rested on the handle of his chair, his forehead propped on the palm, his eyes closed…Today, he is in a different attire, rather than his usual one, he is in his *Kurta* and *Chost Pajama*, ready for the *Puja* in the temple, arranged for his wife's death anniversary, the day which is my father and mother's death anniversary too! He is looking absolutely very dashing, despite of his anxiety, which is caused by me. I never have seen him in his ethnic wear before, so my eyes to adore him, kept on staring without any intention to sweep away the gazes. Like always, he hypothesized my presence. He knew I was standing there looking at him. I simply placed the diary, the balance money, left after the household expenses, and my resignation letter on the table quietly. He stared at me very hard, with his blank face, devoid of any emotions for a few moments, before his doleful expression of the eyes came out in open. He failed to conceal his inner feelings, failed to suppress his apprehension for me. I braced myself, and in a placid voice, I said, so that all my emotions and tears can remain submissive. "Sir, I'm leaving today. Thank you very much for what you have done for me, these past months. Please believe me, I will never forget what you mean for me. And Tia also. I will not forget her ever! It's a beautiful feeling knowing you, and loving you and Tia, and to be loved by both of you. But I must leave, I must now, otherwise it will be very difficult for me to leave this place…and *you*. Please don't think I'm doing this because of you or Tia, or for your *Mama*'s avarice and conspiracies, or for your *Mamoni*'s hidden grudge against me, or for your friend's designs on me. I'm doing all this for my Parents, because of their death. I'm indebted towards them as a daughter. I'm weighed down in their love. I'm obligated to perform my duty! That's why I'm sacrificing my love!" I poured down my heart, but he remained silent, and that killed me!

Moments later he surfaced out from his submerged immobilization, he said passively. "Alright, I think I have no right to stop you. It's a beautiful feeling knowing you and loving you too! I will not forget you, MY SUNSHINE GIRL, as long as I live!" His calling me that, felt like an oasis in my dessert like fate. His soft voice added further…"You are a beautiful being inside out, and you are my first and my last love also! And it is such a wonderful feeling to be loved by you..." Suddenly he speculated to stir my rigid decision, he became berserk to pursue his insist. "What I will say to Tia, tell me? Won't you give me the address, where you are going to, Minisha? Aren't you going to tell me? Ohh Minisha! Don't go...pl-ease, don't...for God's sake, don't leave me, I love you!" He cried out his pain aloud, looked so poignant, that my heart tore apart, but my helplessness said, what I have to say.

"No! Then you will get excited to meet me, and that will renew again our affections for one and another, and I don't want that to happen...but I'm so sorry for doing this to Tia, please forgive me. Take care of yourself and Tia, Sir, Goodbye!"

"But Minisha, a goodbye is not a farewell...you never know." His ray of hope quipped, even when I crushed his heart.

My muted heart turned its back, while saying nothing on his Wordsmith without relenting to that fostered hope of his... not a sound of my plaintive cry can be heard. I choked them inside, my every emotion. My steps lurched ahead as my clouded eyes are filled with pathos. It is much more harder than I thought it would be, of saying a goodbye to Sir, even if he thinks it's not my final farewell, but that is for me. I simply closed the door of that very office, where my love have been blossomed, where the spring has sprung on me, which was absent all those years in my life.

I shut my feelings, by shutting that door, just like that!

I trod outside while pulling out the baggage one by one. The guards came to my rescue to carry them and to place at the threshold of the Gate. By that time, Mira, Shefali, Romonda, Babulal, Guards, all of them, gathered around, crying their heart's out. "*Didi* don't leave us, don't go please."

They cried in unison."I must, I must, and I will never forget how good you all were to me, never. I know, I don't have to say this, but please take good care of Debobroto Sir and Tia, please for my sake! Goodbye all!" I replied in my quietest of voice, while biting my tremulous bottom lip, so it did not quiver again in weeping pain.

I mouthed a "Goodbye" a final one, a deserving one, to the house. I'm not that dishonest or ingratitude who is going to forgot, how under it's kind wings, I took a shelter in my dire needs. And this I mumbled to my inner voice to solace myself…"*I must sacrifice my love for him, my affection to Tia, I must sacrifice all my love, to wash her sin and mine too. As I have unknowingly stayed here, and have sinned also. My sacrifices shall avenge my parent's death this way!* "

It is the time for that cab which comes here every day to drop the school kids, fortunately that came today again. I signaled at the cab driver. While he is loading the luggage into the trunk when Babulal interposed his help to do that in between. I cannot object him, as this is his gesture out of respect for me, his way of bidding a farewell to me. All are loaded into the cab trunk, my entire world, one by one…Without glancing backward for once I drove along with the cab, to set off for a new destination of mine…During my car ride I opened my purse to check my worldly possession of few bucks, which are left in my purse to pay the driver, after I paid for Tia's presents that day. Tia, my lovely darling! I breathed heavily, I didn't even get the opportunity to get a glimpse of her! Then I gave a faint smile to myself about my foresight, from the withdrawal of money, to my taking down that lodge address…I carried on with my journey to the gate of the lodge has appeared. After alighting out from the cab, I stepped inside, and they boarded me…

I paid the advance charges of the boarding by my Debit card. I laughed a sardonic laugh here, as I paid through the salary money given by Sir and of that house. My wretched situation how made me helpless by leaving no other options either.

It is still the late afternoon, and evening is yet to approach, so I withdrew some cash from the ATM, and headed for my Parents' death anniversary *Puja* in the temple. After culminating that ritual, I'm compelled to ask the temple *Purohit's* advice, I didn't know why I'm bothered to do that? When there is no guilt on my conscience! "If somebody does some heinous crime, but before he or she can actually be legally punished, he or she dies, and an injustice is inflicted on the victim's family during that time, due to that...What that afflicted family should do for justice, do they have to forgive that deceased criminal and his crime?!"

"Yes, if he is dead, and beyond the hands of law, then they should. And you can't impose judgment on him, which is not in your hands, you must leave that purely to God, it's in His hands. You must forgive that person, as he had left the world together with his bodily sin, and gone to Him, you don't have the authority to judge or punish, as it's God domain, surrender to Him, the decision of that punishment. Besides, a soul is pious after death, devoid of any sin. All this feeling of hatred and revenge will further victimize the families on both sides, who are innocent, and living. So resenting the departed person is not advisable, that is a sin too. Hate the sin not the sinner *beta*!"

I could not believe what I have heard from the *Purohit's* mouth even it is his wise advice, yet so incredulous for me to listen, it seems to be full of inequity and hollowness! I must be blinded with so much agony that I'm unable to decide what is righteous or what is for my own good perhaps. I said to myself while spurning his sagacity, the way I spurned Sir's imploring to love him. *"How could I forgive her? Even if it is written in the scriptures, how could I?"* I wept and just wept while invoking God, while seeking for my parents help, to guide my bottomless dark path, with a light, of a right decision, so that unlike other sinners, I do not sin, or do something wrong to innocent people. I don't want to be a part of a crime. Then I remembered what I advised to Sir, on our confession day. Didn't I tell him the similar thing, about letting God decide the punishment of sin? My restless heart and indecisive mind made me tread cautiously from there, to the lodge. I felt as if I'm walking barefoot on a bed of scorching ember, while taking a new deviation of life!

# Chapter Nine: Detour

I danced with an immense joy in spite of my trauma, a person's Biorythm, no matter what, must have hand behind this? "I got the job! It's my payback time now. I will pay back to each and every one of their crimes." I threw up my hands in the air with extreme happiness. I cried out to the world to chastise it. "Yes, I got the job! I will take the detour of my life, I will live on. I will get on with it with my head up!" Although only after the lapse of six months, my job will be permanent, till then I have to work as an intern here. Whatever, at least I got the job, I got my wings through which I can fly away, from my miseries. I got my own seat, my own table, my own divided cubicle, no matter how paper thin, it's partition is, but for me, it's a solid ground to start my new life. I have my colleagues, my teammates, very soon will have my own regular salary. I got a place of my own in this world, even if it's in a size of a palm…Our team is headed under Mrs. Shyamali Guha, our team leader. A stern and patronizing type of person, but I'm not bothered about this, as I have come here to work, not to associate.

It's one of my busy day when Mrs. Guha called me at her office. And she remarked plainly, in her commanding tone, after I stepped inside her cabin and stood near her desk. "Minisha, Look who is here? I presume you don't need any formal introduction as you know each other very well. And he came to us as a client!"

I spun my heels to see who that anticipated visitor is, who is known to me as well? And the sight of that visitor is enough to stumble my steady feet, and to squirm my whole being! Debobroto Sir, is sitting there on the sofa aside the corner, looking smug, with his dark midnight gazes, which are penetrating at me! My face became pallid, my mouth dry at his sight, amid that my ears are getting clogged as well, with all those words of my boss, which her stern mouth is spouting out. "He needs us in his business to advertise well, that's why he chose us. So for you and your team, this is the first job, work hard without slacking off. Understand? I don't want my client to complain on the basis of this. I'm leaving two of you here, talk it over Minisha!" Her silky voice stressed my name, and besides throwing a stern look at me. I understood what that look meant. *"Or else you are out of job girlie, if you don't snare this client for me."* She just took her outward steps from the office to leave two of us alone, in the cabin.

My heart raced, while Sir gave me one of his mocked smirks, he reacted as if he has snared me instead, with a bait. And how I confronted that,I just floundered. It's getting hard to find the words, even to speak. My speechless self, stumbled out few blurts but to chide him. "How do you know, I work here?! Tell me fast. Why did you come here? Why not one of your staff, approached us? When I told you specifically not to follow me around? Does it so hard to grasp, all those plain words, you aren't that obtuse?!"

"Easy, Miss Ganguli, easy! Remember I'm your client, and came here with every intention to remain that. You don't have to take this hard on you!" He said drily, to my castigation.

So it's Miss Ganguli again? Why not? When he doesn't want to mix his business with personal matters. He is back again in his old self. Welcome back Sir! Though love doesn't listen to logic, yet I didn't want to mix my business even with my personal matters like him. I addressed. "Mr. Mukherjee (instead of Sir)...How are you?" My that address instead of ruffling him up, twinkled his eyes in the glint of amuse. Yes, that much I have expected from his sweet nature, when he had scouted me for the sake of his love. Although I said that with a voice filled with icicle, yet my eyes filled with warmth, on account of his pleasant vision! I missed his sight so much, his whole self so much, that a lump of emotion stuck in my throat. I thought I'm going to forgot how he used to look even...We sat with such close proximity in the sofa, with only few papers acting as a bridge, to distance us, for that my stomach knotted in a sensory sensation, my breath caught in my lungs, my heart throbbed wildly. Today he didn't look that much haggard, the way he looked earlier that day. He appeared like a debonair man, the way he loves to, with his sleek hairstyle, matched with his poised manner and chic accessories. Well, it looks like, he has harnessed his situation, well, it's good for him and especially for Tia!

"Well Mr. Mukherjee, I'm just an intern, before you will go through with the contract with us, you must see the presentation, what we, and our seniors as a team, are going to prepare?! After seeing our output you should finalize anything. All I can say that for now. I will try my level best to make it up to the mark. And even though our agency has a reputation, still don't believe my word of mouth, to proceed further, agree after our presentation only. Please do that!" Amidst my portray of actual position in this office and summing them honestly. Like a friend, my undertone warned. Nothing beyond that, I've said.

My intertwined emotions of happiness, love, sorrow, worry and depression, are hampering me in doing that.

He kept his silence all this while allowing only me to talk? Or want to hear my voice again for long? After a quite bit of time, he said tersely with a hint of satire, rolled into one. "Alright, Miss Ganguli, I will do that, after evaluating your presentation, scrutinizing the input of your team, then will decide whether to carry forward or not?!" Then again fostered his old way, so he could move his theme of talking to another track. "By the way Tia has sent her *love*." He stressed on the word *Love* specifically. I emulated him.

"Say to Tia that I *love* her too." I stressed on the word *Love* also. After that, he simply dashed away from there to desert me, in my whirlwind of feelings, without giving me a backward glance, even for once, just they way I had done earlier, despite his poignant pleads!

That brief encounter prodded me to peep outside the office door, to see his splendid demeanor once more. But to my utter horror I saw him speaking to Mrs. Guha, about something rather serious. That made me restless for a fleeting moment, on the nature of his talk. Does he want to take a revenge on me? Or does he, by any chance is revealing our failure in making a relationship? Later, I became ashamed of myself, for suspecting a pure and loving soul like him, that my red face quietly returned to my seat, to my regular office job, after making a great blunder. I concentrated on my computer typing of market research data of other clients...When again I have been called by Mrs. Guha. This time she is not so stern, but looked rather pleased.

"Well Minisha, though Mr. Mukherjee didn't give a nod to the contract yet, but has agreed to give it a thought after the presentation, so we have to do our best.

Tell your other friends to work hard and to learn the entire process, about how a successful presentation is actually being carried out. And it's good to know the upper hand people in this business, that's a smart move of yours. I hope he will trust us, as he trusts you...Now go to your work, and remember this contract is entirely relying on your moves." She targeted at me, a permanent misunderstood, cold threat, to a temporary intern!

This is what I have been dreading of. I became spiritless once again, only because of a worry for him. I knew this is going to happen, the minute my acquaintance with him is going to get revealed. I'm going to be pressurized not only by my boss, but by team mates also to influence him, in this negotiation. I don't want him to trap in this foul web of business dealings, when I love him so dearly. *"Dear God, when will everything in my job, in my life, is going to work out well? Why did he come back to my life, seriously?!"*

The presentation turned out well. It was an arduous day! I worked hard as much as I could. I can't afford a failure when my survival is at stake, otherwise only calamities I have to face in my life.

We have been informed that Mr. Mukerjee will give his final nod of decision after quite an elapse of a period...It's my lunch time, so along with others I went to our office cafeteria. Somehow I found a very deserted nook to place my tray of salad, and a glass of apple juice on the table. I munched my food slowly without tasting it even, when I'm worried sick with my life and scared to hell with that, so my hunger has gone.

Amid my deepest of troubles, someone ambushed me, and it is Sir! He pulled out a chair, to sit beside me. His first reaction? Chortling hard at my scant lunch! "So Minisha is again at her nutritious salads?"

"Sir?! What are you doing here? You are supposed to be with the 'crème da le crème' people. Please spend your lunch time there. Go away from here, people will misunderstand. I'm just an intern here, you know that." I glanced around seemingly, for that undignified fear.

"Let them. I don't care. I rather prefer to sit with this pretty intern, during my lunch time. Please Minisha, *don't take my Sunshine away*." His resolute mischievously said, to spend an unfettered time.

"But I work here Sir, please!" I insisted.

"Don't worry. They will be *pleased* (he stressed on it) as my decision for the contract, is still pending."

This is what I was afraid of, so I forewarned. "Please Sir, consider the decision only by the real facts and figures, don't by listening to your heart."

"I've been in the business for so long, that I know what to do. I never mix work with emotions either. But what if it jeopardizes our Minisha, then?

What should I do? Should I re-consider?" His head turned sideways at me for my valuable expertise, then he propped his face on the palm while placing the elbow of that hand on the table, to support it, with his slanted teasing glances, he waited for my enlightenment...I'm accustomed to his attitude and jest, so without getting irked with this recent demonstrated charades to mock me, I carried on. "Yes, still. Be on your guard and don't worry about me...it will be then 'Que Sera Sera'. And why you are calling me Minisha all of a sudden? When I'm Miss Ganguli for you?"

"Ohh! That's the case, that's why you are glum? But you've called me Mr. Mukherjee too, now calling me Sir again?!" He reasoned his action, and reaction, while etching a lopsided smile on his face. So his coldness is melting away, his warm self returned again, that is my respite!

"That was tit for a tat, which we both gave each other, Sir."

"Is it?! I *thought* of something else. But tell me how are you?" His placid expression suddenly inquired about my well being.

"*I'm fine Sir.*" I crooned a lie.

Seeing his tender side. I mustered up some courage, to query a thing which is eating up my brain, his scrounging around? "But how do you know, that I work here?!"

"From the lodge."

"Lodge? How do you know, that I'm staying there?!"

"From my sources."

"What sources?!"

"The particulars of the cab Babulal had noted, during your desertion of me.I contacted the cab agency, then at the Lodge, & they told me about your job designation. Nobody dared to say *No* to me, except you, who threw refusal at my face? And I allowed that, *dare of yours*! Besides the smart Minisha left so many loop holes, perhaps for me?"

"So that's the case?" I got infected by his usual phrase of words, so imitating them? I replied with wit. "Yes, I knew, this is going to happen! Babulal is good at observing and memorizing things. And I'm a dunce! But what you expect me to say?! When you, yourself, has allowed ME, *that dare*!?"

"My witty Minisha is in action, it's good to see that! But the matter for which I'm here, is Tia. It's not my personal insistence, but she is getting desperate to meet you. So how about this Saturday?" His firm command imposed. I responded simply. "This Saturday? But that's my work day, that's our field market research day!"

"Don't lie, you work for half-day on Saturdays. We still shall have the rest of the evening to enjoy. Come, when you finish. Call me then. When we know one another mobile number?!" He smiled at my astound! Because I'm a felon. I changed my old number, so I could disconnect everything even the vibration of my love, which sends telepathic messages to him, oft.

"Yes, even when you did that to hinder my attempt to trace you, yet I gathered your current one. Mrs. Guha enthusiastically updated on her own accord. So I'm not guilty as charged? Or are you really afraid of...?!" His unfinished sentence challenged me, in his drawl voice, lifting his one brow slightly at me.

"I'm not afraid and that includes your knack of gathering my information.

You can go to any length. You tricked me for this outing. I can say that with certitude. Aren't you a good schemer?" My brave front blamed him. "But my relation with Tia are not shallow that I will disappoint her. I will come certainly, please tell her that." My affection for her, apprised.

"Alright! Think whatever you like! But our outing is a deal Minisha?! I will come to your place, to pick you up?"

"You can't Sir! Male visitors aren't allowed there."

"So, Minisha not only eats green leaves, but also lives in

the Nunnery, like a reclusive hermit?" His heartiest laughs ragged me.

"Don't tease me?" I collected myself before speaking again.

"Tell me, honestly, how are you? How is Tia? Does she still with her *Didai*? Are you eating well? Are you taking care of yourself and Tia? Please cut back your coffee intakes, have lot of juices, soups and water...Oh! For God's sake drive safely. Instead let the driver to drive your car. Please remember all that! Have you eaten yet? Let me buy you something?" I smothered him down with my deep buried concerns of eons, at one go.

My re-established frets touched his feels, but camouflaging that quickly, he became a *no feelings man.* "Why?! Why you are asking this? When you have left us, at your own will? You have no right to know! Tia is alright and is with her *Didai* still...Tell me on what assurance, I will call her back in an empty house? When there is nobody there? Do you know, how much we miss you...How we suffered, suffering?? Do you know that honestly? And I don't want your salad either! Why I should eat, when your love doesn't cook for me and Tia anymore?! When we remained famished for your caring hand?!"

He grumbled in an indignation and aggravation at me! Yet not one uttered word, is false! I know how wrongfully I have treated him and Tia, in my helplessness, how I have deprived them from my affection!

His belligerent and sullen mood, made me unquiet! To pacify him, I down-poured whatever came to my mind. "I know you are infuriated and feeling aggrieved! You have every right to feel that way! When I pained you so much. But please calm down, have faith in time, it will take care of everything." My words to comfort him turned inconsolable. To alleviate his agitation, I chimed cheerfully & used reverse psychology. "Okay, let me save the day and the time of our outing here then!" I switched on my mobile to do that, and is about to save...When to my utter surprise, he simply snatched it from my hands?!

"What are you doing?!" I shouted at his sudden waggishness. "I'm drooling on a pretty and fascinating youngish girl!" His eyes scintillated on my mobile wallpaper. It's my picture when I was nineteen. A close face picture with *Baba* and *Ma*, side by side along; clicked during my birthday celebration; my last celebrated happy faces! Brushing aside my grief for the sake of his happiness, I feigned a pout. "But that pretty lady is me?! Why you are all eyes on her? Look,

I'm sitting here in person, right in front of you?"

"Oho! So you are jealous of girlish looking Minisha!?"

"Why should I, I'm still young? I'm just twenty four?"

"No you are not, you are just going on, in Granny's age. And right now I'm so intrigued, that I'm going to drool over more of those snaps of this irresistible dame's!"

He tapped the gallery button for that purpose, and to hinder him in doing this, I tried to snatch back the mobile from his hand. I know there are many more of my snaps stored on that mobile, foolishly with an unlocked screen. That piece of information he read in my transparent eyes, that's why he is in his playful mood! He lifted it up with one of his hands, while dangling it up, into the air to tease me. I raised my hand to grab it. "Please return my mobile back! It's my private thing?"

But he lifted his hand much higher, beyond my reach, while waving it in the mid air. He is at his total height of mischief. I don't have any choice left, but to pinch his insistence or other arm.

*"Ouch!"* He wailed in wincing pain, that helped to loosen up his grip on my mobile! I simply snatched it back. "What you have done to me just now, Minisha?? Do you know, abusing your client in the premises of your office and in front of your colleagues, can land you in a grave trouble?" He poked a satirical threat to me, and glanced at me, with a fake seriousness, soaked eyes.

"Client or not client, I will not allow anybody to manhandle me, Sir! Mrs. Guha is approaching here, so it's better if we split up right now, and tell Tia, I will come. Bye then." I quipped at him fearlessly.Then got up abruptly from my chair, but in between this, my leg got hit by the leg of the chair! I wobbled my step and stumbled forward.

"Steady Minisha, steady, don't be swayed by my presence. It's the chair who has given you, a tit for a tat, not me?" He pointed out his innocence in his impish tone. I gave him a glare, and he, his dashing grin.

That was our second banter. Our first casual interaction filled with teases. Eventually my recent woes has been chased away, by my *Sunshine Boy*!

It's that anticipated, Saturday! My special day out, with my Tia and Sir, compared to my days of doldrums! It's only half-past two in the afternoon. Yet his punctuality, already has been waiting for me at the appointed meeting place at the bus station where I told him to. He was leaning against his car, when I reached there...Boy! My inner self blew a teasing whistle at his imposing sight! How breathtakingly, awesome he looked, dazzling in his awesomeness, sizzling in his sensuousness! Awesomeness also became aware of this (like me) that how his boyish charisma, is more awesome than it! He wore a biscuit colored slim corduroy trousers, with black full sleeved Henley T-shirt, and every taut muscles of his are exhibiting out from it. The sleeves cropped up, hands thrust in his trouser pockets, that dark shades on his eyes, and those idle locks of hair, leisured on his forehead simply, to charm him. But his signature bracelet is missing? How different his hairstyle is today from what his usual sleek neat one? Did he styled them differently on purpose? To woo me!?...Goosebumps ran all over me after seeing his tempting demeanor, which is waiting to lure me! A terrible fear I felt for this, as this will thrust me into something rueful, this might reclaim my love I have for him! I blushed, while recalling Mrs. Banerjee's vulgar taunt, about my long lost boyfriend. How that has become true! There he is, my boyfriend, my fascinating one!

*My Boy!*

Something tickled my senses, that I haven't been notched up to match his par. This surprised me. At how I never have given consideration, as how I looked before him, but now getting conscious over my looks? I simply grunted at my dress, it is of bottle green color, crop up harem styled slim pants, as my bottom wear, and my plush purple hued full sleeved cowl T-shirt as my top. My high heeled, light strapped sandals are keeping my feet firmly on the ground, so his handsome bearing doesn't melt my knees. Ah! Why he have to look so handsome all of a sudden?! Somehow bucking up my poise, I approached there. I brushed past him to open the back door of the car, where I assume Tia must be. I showed him my faint ignorance of his presence, because I know how he and his masculine scent are afflicting me. Probably his eyes are covered with the shades, that's why his fascinating lips are highlighting his face, and I do not intend to focus on them as well, as my lips trembled in anticipation. What's happening to me? Why I'm egging myself to fall into a temptation of love? Nervousness made me bite my bottom lip, and twirl my stray curls with my fingers, and the curls clung to them to attract his attention... And he did get attracted, slowly he took off his dark shades, to fling his menacing gazes at me, they just clung to my face too. I cast down my eyes, as I can read the meaning behind his gaze. My heart fluttered, and untamed sensations started cultivating something fiery. Controlling them fast, I simply extended my hand, to open up the car door...

My darling Tia was sitting there. Happy and excited to see me. She chirped. "*Masimoni, Masimoni*, where have you been? Why don't you stay in our home anymore? Why?" It is so serene seeing Tia once again, her cheerful face and her effervescent voice. My eyes moistened in brimming emotion. I kissed her cheek and forehead tenderly. "I'm here sweetheart. I'm here now. How are you? Are you doing well?"

"Yes, I'm, but I'm angry, very angry at you." She pretended to be in anger.

"Yes, I can see that, and it's sitting right now on my Tia's cute nose. Shoo! Scram! Tia's anger!" To chase it away from there, I flicked gently at her nose with a slight touch of my fingertip. She giggled. I smiled beatifically at her. "Alright! It has gone now. Let's enjoy our outing, then." She nodded happily. "Yes, let's go."

I'm about to ride my seat beside her at the back when Sir peeked in from our rolled down car window. "Minisha, sit at the front with me, I need to talk."

"No, Sir! It's my Saturday, my day out, and it's my Tia, so I will do whatever I feel like. I will sit right here with her. I'm not your employee anymore, so you can't order me as well."I emulated him what he said earlier while refusing to have his breakfast, that day , after the party.

Grasping that, he smirked, while shrugging off his shoulders. He walked quietly to the front of the car, to sit at his car's driver seat. But to have his way anyhow, he slanted the front mirror forward, so he can focus all his glances on us, and our doings. Then he remarked in his teasing tone. "Yes, I'm at your mercy today." Igniting the engine on, he drove the car ahead to the road.

I must be immersed in the idea of having a fun-filled outing with Sir and Tia, that it has slipped from my mind, the location of our excursion? I inquired. "Where we are supposedly going to, Sir? How remiss of me, not asking this before? I simply forgot!"

"It's because you always stay in your own world. You don't have enough time for the mortals like us. Isn't it obvious enough that we are going to an amusement park, when Tia is coming along?! Unless I elaborate you, you can't seem to fathom what I'm directing at? You aren't that, obtuse?!" Suddenly his soft-spoken self, threw a sarcastic remark at me, while mincing the words, mingling the feels of the past!

How right he is? A nymph, a dunce like me, how could glance and fathom, the high-profiled mortals? His hurtful sarcasm is aimed because he is deeply hurt by my doings. But he is such a fool! I'm equally being hurt as much as he has been. Wish I can rip my heart wide open to let him see, whose name is etched on it, how much love it has stashed for him. No woman could love a man, the way I do. I intentionally acted in indifference, remained innocent of his taunt, bitter words.

For him, Tia, for mine's sake! I don't want to ruin this God-sent chance of being together and happy, by being overly sensitive!..."Amusement park?! Is there's one here? I didn't know that?"

"Yes, there is. Didn't I tell you before? This city is my pride, besides being one of the beautiful city? You forgot in your forgetfulness! You only stayed with us for a short duration, before I can even show you around! Come down to the earth, Minisha Ma'am!"

So his cross mood is armed with cruel words to make me cry..."I haven't forgotten Sir. I didn't have the courage to ask you. Circumstances entailed me, not to stay long there. You know that?" I mumbled.

We are hankering to prove our sides so much so, that we completely forgot that Tia is listening us with keen! Suddenly with directness, she quizzed me (bluntly like her father) "*Masimoni, Masimoni*, why you scolded *Baba* and *Didai* so much that day?! I never have seen you being so querulous??"

"Did I?! Oh! I must have done that for being sick." I reasoned. Regretted, for my behavior terribly. I howled so much that I must have had waken up Tia? All those hurtful things I hollered to accuse her mother, she must have had heard it all! Dear God! What I have done?

"What's the name of that sickness of which you were ailing?!" Her agog wants to know my baffling illness where the affected person barks at people?

"I had a *temper* as my sickness dear." I replied meekly.

"Temper?! What a funny name, *Masimoni*! Why *Didai* always calls you, *Badmaish Dustu Meye* (bad and sly girl)?"

Her curiosity's level has risen. I panicked on it's getting beyond its limit, and with its possibility of making her aware in return, that how heartless her relations were to me! I cannot allow that? I should not allow Tia to hate her grandmother. So I stroked her head gently and said tenderly.

"Isn't that so good about her? She loves me so much, that she has given me a lovely pet name.''

Tia laughed hard as she didn't know earlier what a great amusement was hiding in it, all this while, and she had missed that enjoyment?! Whenever, her grandmother must have called me by that name?

I sighed a breather. *"Thank God! She is unsuspicious still, it didn't polluted her mind yet.''* So to encourage her humor further, I joined in her laughs too.

*"Masimoni,* you are a funny girl, you had a temper as a sickness and *badmaish dustu meye* as a pet name?'' She chortled.

"Yes, I'm really a funny girl, and have lots of funny things to laugh about!'' I laughed once again amid my weeping heart, and this time Sir joined us also, to encourage our hilarity. I know to sweep away my bleakness and his guilt for being bitter to me, as well!

It seems that it's my turn in Sir's questionnaire round now. His concerns chastised instead, than his retorts of earlier suppressed anger. "Minisha, how are you? Tell me honestly? Is your job satisfactory? Is your accommodation comfortable and secure enough? Does someone has shown overbearing attitude to you? Are you eating and resting well? Please detail me without hiding anything?!''

"Easy, Sir easy! Yes, I'm fine, and my job is satisfactory, so is the lodge. Don't worry Sir, it's a reputable place with lots of working girls like me, staying there. They have settled down there like being in a home, while leaving their family, so did I. And nobody is bullying me either. I can deal with the bullies in my own way. They way I have done for the past. I try to keep myself well. So Sir, you can rest assured."

"That's so good to hear, now I can rest assuredly. You don't know for how many days and nights I have been tortured by the worry of your welfare and of your whereabouts? I lived in a hell, spending sleepless nights thinking only about you! Minisha, you didn't have to be so cruel to us? How could you leave us, like that? Why you are being so cruel?!" His heartache, anxiety, and raw emotions has an outburst!

"You know very well, I'm not cruel or heartless?! What you would have done, if the same thing would have happened to you? Didn't I underwent with the same pain like you? Please Sir, don't push me so hard, that I land on the edge, please." Hot words melted my repressed sorrow so to flow down in the form of warm tears, which I tried to suppress. Quickly wiping them off, I tried again to compose myself, but a notorious droplet of an exposed tear remained there to nudge his attention. And from then on, he just started giving me his quick, attentive glances, in between his driving, and all those burning gazes made my heart squirm.

Meanwhile Tia again fired questions, at me. "Why you left us *Masimoni*? What wrong *Baba* and I, have done to you?" I stroked her head once again, sighing deeply for my helplessness.

I crooned, so she could understand my plight. "Oh! Tia sweetheart, it's neither for your *Baba*'s or for your fault, believe me, it's only for my personal reasons and reservations, who are blameworthy! That's why, I left you and your home.

Over time, when my Tia will be a grown up girl, then she will learn and understand, why *Masimoni* did that?!"

After that, we both became silent...He drove his car silently too, but his pair of penetrating eyes remained active, to throw his secretive glances at me, throughout the entire drive.

After a while we arrived at our destination, the drive took near about thirty five to forty minutes of time. Presuming to cheer me up, his playful mood triggered to say this. "Minisha what dangerous ride you are going to try out first? How about that 360 degree spin ride? Huh?" He pointed out his finger at the most risky and dangerous ride up in the air, in his drawl voice. I could hear clearly all the riders howling screams and cries on top of their voices! Fear of danger and vertigo made me giddy. "I... I.. Sir..." I stammered hard.

"So our adventurous Minisha, is afraid of heights and dangerous rides? I can't believe a person who plunges in risks, is afraid of a mere plaything? Look at Tia, how she is going to choose one, of her favorite ones."

"Sir, is it safe for Tia to take such rides? That too unattended without any adult!?" My tremulous self queried in an anxiety.

"Don't be absurd, those are meant for children. Look, how many children of her age are going to try..." But seeing my washed out face in scare, he agreed to take a ride along with her. And they both took several rides safe for children, while waving at me. I looked on while inspecting their every move, just to take reins of any catastrophe into my hands...

When both finished their adventures, they came running to my side, flushed, happy, and excited. It is so beautiful to see both of them in an euphoria, to capture that pristine moment, my hands automatically saved their picture on my mobile.

"*Masimoni*, I had one of the wonderful time in my life! I enjoyed it so much. Doesn't spending time with your family is one of the joyous moment in life?" An exuberant Tia quipped. In someway knowingly and unknowingly, this little angel has included my name in their family tree too!

"Minisha I've seen what you've done just now, you've clicked our pictures without our permission? You know that's a crime and..." Listening to Tia and her joy made him effervescent, so his eyes twinkled with humor at my misdemeanor. "So I have done a crime, a grave one too, by clicking happy faces of my known friends. I haven't clicked the picture of any unknown strangers, still I'm ready for any kind of punishment!" I challenged him tossing my courageous head back.

His impish self contemplated, to tease my immense health-consciousness. "Hmm...a punishment for a grave crime? Let's see, what that can be?! OK!

We will have some junk food then! Hamburgers, pizzas, colas, to our heart's fill!"

"But there is juice and fruit salad joint, right here, then why?!" I exclaimed in horror! Yet not a minute ago, I was all up for the punishment, & when he declared his way to discipline me? I'm retracting like a coward.

"So you don't want to be punished?! We will have hamburgers like everyone else, that's my order! Enough of your juice, fruit, and salad. We will enjoy life and our hamburgers, and the giant ones too."

He placed orders as has been decided, of hamburgers, foot longs, wraps, fries and what not...Practically the entire shop. Then Ice-creams, tall glasses of Colas. I sighed in disappointment, and picked up my fork and knife to cut the burger mechanically, while obeying him. When he objected at my queer way to show off, my refined food etiquette.

"I have never seen anybody having their burgers, with the cutlery before?"

"Well, Sir, what's the point of stuffing large chunks of food, straight into your mouth? Am I a Hippo?! It's unladylike."

To annoy him further more, I started cutting tiny pieces, deliberately, before popping the bite into the mouth. That instigated his good humor. So to annoy me, he gobbled up the whole burger to emulate a Hippo! Fascinated with this fun. Tia imitated her father, the same way. Both of them continued their ultimate annoyance throughout, while eating the food. I remained calm while suppressing my laughter. I wonder how could a gym freak like him, crave for junk food, and where all those greasy junk goes? His taut and flat belly perplexed me!? Amid our junk noshing. I can't ignore the nicest time of our life has been spent, the warmest smile has been smiled, like Tia has mentioned earlier. My first eat out with them became my momentous moment of life!

After a while we sat on the amusement park's lawn. While we slouched our tired bodies. Tia still bursting with energy capered around, clutching her soft toys her father has bought, with her cherished bubble of happiness, along which our presence have created in her heart. I filled my vision with the image of dancing Tia, whom in the future, I will never have a chance to be with! When suddenly Sir queried me to exhort out something.

"Minisha, how you were at nineteen?! What made you so nutritious food fetish, it must be hard on you, living all alone, all those years?!" I simply smiled at his inquisitiveness, about my food habit. His curiosity is justified when that tormented him, with my constant nags.

"On the contrary Sir, I used to like junk food, like any other normal teen. But my Parents death augured an intense scare! The death and the name of alcohol, made me adhere to veggies, fruits, nuts, to juices, to survive. It's a hollow and lonely feeling when nobody is around to help you, if you got sick! Only that's why Sir. I know I tried to implant on you and Tia the same thing, but old habits die hard. I'm sorry, for me you have internalized that Sir!"

"No, I should be sorry. I will not tease you on this from now on." His remorse for his lively teases made me sad, when after all those years of somber, he once again learned to laugh, learned to know the real meaning to be happy. So my soft words diverted him. "Don't be absurd, why you've to be so sorry? Look at Tia. Doesn't she is the most lovely and the cutest girl in this whole world?"

Then we glanced at each other with our love-filled gazes, gave our sweetest of smiles. We are lost in our reverie…our glittering hearts, fostered his hope, he implied to me. "Minisha, you are not my employee anymore. I'm not your client here either, and when you, yourself have called me a friend, just now. So is it right to hurt a friend's feeling? Will you keep your word, if I ask a favor from you, a friendly request?"

His eager request through a riddle, baffled me. "Yes Sir! I will, if it's within my means. What is it?" His eyes sparkled with joy after hearing my promise. "Really? You will call me 'Debobroto' then, from now on?!"

That shocked me, his snatching of my consent without my knowledge, his proposition to call his name! What insanity possessed him? I pursed my lips together adamantly.

"Say it!" Seeing my rigidness, his insistent self, elbowed me at my arm.

"*Aah!* Why did you do that?! Do you have any idea, how your well-toned elbow hurt me?" I winced while rubbing my affected arm.

"It's tit for tat for hurting me for long, now say it! So you are a coward and a promise-breaker too?" He is getting importunate at this!

To succeed in his mission, he called out his sweet auxiliary. "Tia! Tia! Come here, help your *Masimoni* to pronounce my name. She is not good at it!"

An amused Tia rushed to us, leaving her fun-filled play to polish my lack of knowledge, (when this is going to be more fun) to assist me in this lesson of pronouncing her father's name perfectly. She stretched the letters, carefully putting a gap to each of words, to form it for my ease.

"*Masimoni,* say...De-bo-bro-to like this." It's mortifying to me, both father and daughter's insistence, on pronouncing the suggested word *Debobroto*!

It seems to me, that I'm not going to be excused from this until I finish the ordeal. I muttered under my breath, '*Debobroto*' just to please them. It is audible enough for him to hear, but his teasing pestered me.

"Tia, did you hear anything?! Something must be wrong with our ears?" Tia laughed with capital 'L', and he grinned ear to ear at my blushes for my inhibition, and flushes for my irritation.

His naughty grin irked me. I cried out aloud to call his name three times, in a row, to desist their further din. "Debobroto-Debobroto-Debobroto!!"

"Oh my God! Minisha! What you have done just now?" He covered his mouth with his hand, with a pretense to be in a great alarm! That shocked me too, my felony of what I have been guilty of!

"Minisha you know, now we are married, because you called my name three times!" He ragged me in a grave tone, concealing his waggishness well, to make his engineered ritual, official.

"Come again?! What a nonsensical talk is this? You are something, you know that seriously!" I hid my face to my knees to escape from his naughty mocking glares, and Tia's twinkling eyes of mischief...But to attack me with more annoyances, Tia and Debobroto rolled on the ground, snickering hard at me, while making funny noises.

"Please stop it, both of you, please, people will think you have gone crazy!" Completely ignoring my request, they continued on. I threatened them.

"Okay, I'm going to leave two of you here alone. Do you want that?!"

"Why? Have you upset your stomach so much with junk food, that you want to go there? The restroom is that way, by the way." He pointed out his finger in its direction, and both of them carried on, with their fits of laughter without taking a pause.

I became so vexed with him, that I swung my balled hand at him, and suspended it in the mid-air in false pretension of striking him, if he doesn't stop. He stopped laughing to look at my flared face for so long. I blushed even more. The redness spread to my ears, and with every intention to cool me off from my anger and blushes, he jumped up into a sitting position, and placing Tia between us, he simply clicked a picture of three of us, together with our sunny smiles, from his mobile camera!

"Why did you do that? You have committed a crime too." I teased him after masking my happy tone, in mock seriousness.

"Yes, old habits die hard, it's for my mobile wallpaper, but it looks like that I have to edit it, by some Photo editing App to enhance it?" I peered a glance on the saved pic, to see if it's really needed that much editing or not, but on the contrary it looked perfect to me. So I queried him in baffle knowing his habit of perfection. "It looks so perfect to me, why you want to do that?! "

"You are correct, we are perfect, but you are not...I wonder why we have not taken our snap with that younger Minisha, then that would make this photo simply perfect!" He started pulling my leg again.

"What?! You are editing because of me...Seriously, you are too much, then why don't you simply delete my wrinkly face?" I pouted in displease while crossing my arms across my chest.

"No, not in this world for anything Minisha, let's go now." He suddenly transformed into a grave man, his laughs and pranks all vanished, all of a sudden into thin air?!

Holding Tia's hand, he went near the car park. *This is one of the splendid time I had in my life* thinking that, I took a deep breath of that happy air to inhale all of it inside...I followed them.

We hit the road to set for a journey back to our separate homes, and to our separate lives! Inside the car his inseparable mischievous self possessed him. His car's USB music player, first played my song I sang in his garden... *You are my Sunshine... How I suppose to live without you... Sacrifice...Still loving you...Baby I'm your man...Uptown girl...Words don't come easy...You are beautiful...*so he made a Play list too, of his choicest songs, the way I had done earlier for the party? The melody played on and on, to keep the theme of love on reprise mode for my acoustic journey...Each and every song depicted our story of love, from the budding to blossoming part. The rendition of his feelings for me, then summarized and shrunk into four beautiful words-*I love you still!* I know why he opted this method, it's far more effective than expressing it through words...by this music, he is pursuing me once again with his love? He doesn't want his zealous passion to fade away so easily? So he is not giving up, is going to outsmart me with this challenge of seducing me, till I reciprocate back his love with equal zest!? All those carousel of emotions made me tizzy and dizzy, with the passage of time it is getting worse, and impossible for me, to keep still. To veer his impish method, I simply turned to Tia, to inquire about her school, her studies, her friends, and how she is living her life with *Didai*, and all that...Amid our deep chatters I found Tia dozing off with tiredness on my arms. I smiled back at her sleepy head. I cuddled her, and then put her sleeping head on my lap, lest she fall off from the seat. By this time his Play list is somewhat finished, and he is back again at his job of attracting me with his scorching gazes, to see how receptive I'm with his seduction devise? This time, I didn't feel abashed for his attention on me, so to make his task easier (I know he is still looking) I threw him a radiant smile of mine, the sparkle in my bright eyes while tilting my curly head a little, so that my sunny picture can retain in his eyes, and can be etched into his heart, a remembrance of Minisha, forever there, the girl he has loved for the first and the last time!

The car stopped, when we reached a little far away from the lodge Gate. I got off first, out of the car opening the door, then carefully carrying and placing the sleeping Tia on the front seat, with a large teddy behind & with a seat belt secured her body (Sir quietly watched, allowed, me to tend her, and keep under the scanner of him) I closed the door silently, then the back door as well. I simply peeped inside from the front side of the car window, my heavy emotional voice said to him. (parting with them like this, is getting very difficult for me).

"Look after Tia, will you? And don't let her fall, take care and...Please drive carefully, way back to your home. Have a safe drive and Good night! This has been one of the memorable day of my life! As we will never meet again in future, so Goodbye as well, Debobroto!"

Separating my nags and cares for them, is impossible, like his hope for my return to him...I called his name as a remembrance to his acoustic, emphasized on the fact that I have actually obeyed him the way he implored me to.

"Thanks for dropping by Minisha again in our life, it's been a memorable day for us too. But destiny is not written by us...events just happen, so we must try to give our best shot in life. Who knows, maybe one day we will meet again, it's neither in your hand to take the *detour*, nor it's on mine's. Remember, how your last goodbye was not a farewell to me, and see how we have met again. So be optimistic, don't give up on your love, so easily, let's give hope, a chance, even if it's only one percent! Okay? So just Goodnight for now. And, don't change your Mobile number, if not for me, do this, for Tia's sake!"

He crooned his sagacity, warns, in one of his sincere tone; when he has seen more life than me, when he has endured more pain than me, when he loves me more than his life, when he is still hoping against hope! With that, his car, he and Tia, whizzed past me from there, leaving me wistful, while I clutched the gate of the Lodge...

I wept at night very hard in the restroom, while sitting on the toilet seat, so not to disturb my room mate's sound sleep. I cried for so long, my tears obliged me, so I don't have to cry tomorrow...I cried for my stubbornness, for my obligations, for my dither, for my first and last outing together, with them!

# Chapter Ten: The Truce

It's Sunday. In spite of last night's grief, yet I'm over the moon! Though my sorrow is wilting me, my careening life making me slipshod, but the essence yesterday's beautiful moments has encouraged me to be agile and steer my life well! Post Debobroto's call, (he duped me in retaining the number in pretext of Tia) which has come in the morning, the residual traces of sadness, weariness have left me!

"Minisha, are okay? Are you tired still? Are you really okay? You are not sick for the junk food? Tell me? I'm sorry. I was wrong in forcing you, this way." His spontaneous concerns bombarded me, in his husky voice.

I can't help not to laugh at his cute queries. "Easy, Mr. Worry, easy. I'm okay. But how's Tia, and you?" My mirth, my informality still has that worry.

"We are alright in a way without you. But she's back to her *Didai's* place, first thing in the morning. You know after hearing our outing, her Grandmother has become skeptical of your presence in our life. And I miss…" He lamented, before finishing his sentence for me, to decipher it all by myself, like always.

"Who, me??" My anticipated heart blurted.

"No, your cooking!" Knowing that feeling, he teased. "Why didn't you bring any goodies, yesterday, for us?!" He complained, as he is bereft of my pampering to him, which he loves the most.

"I can't cook here, when it's our lodge's mess which provides the food and the kitchen is their domain solely."

"Why so many cant's there...can't cook, can't visit? Come here, stay with me, otherwise you will forget how to cook? Minisha, yours, mine, and Tia's, living is hard, isn't it? That's why asking you to marry me! Let's live together happily, let's grow old together till our last breath. Huh?" He found a tactic, to bring me back into his life. Through his adamant cajoling.

"I knew it, you will be at it again. If you want to visit, then at least wait, until I rent a flat. Okay?"

Averting that tiny bit of hope, he pouted. "What other choice do I have? But honestly, I miss you. I love you so much, Minisha, without you, every moment is killing me. Believe me. Don't you love me anymore? Am I not a good person to love? Is our age gap is putting you in a dilemma? Tell me, please?" His heart's candid worries awaited for my reciprocated responses, but finding an excuse quickly to avoid the topic of my life, I said in return. "Debobroto listen, can we talk later? Need to go to the restroom immediately, my stomach seems to be upset, as you have predicted. Bye!" I ended the call abruptly, to break his sweet heart again, but not before hearing a half-hearted laugh of his, which he gave for my timely wit and cordiality's sake. He is a good person, when!

One day of this new week's, Cheerful looking Mrs. Guha looked made us gather round her in curiosity, because we seldom have seen her happy! She informed us that Debobroto has agreed to sign the contract with the agency and to commemorate on this, they have decided to throw a party as an incentive to the employees! Yes, it is indeed a cheerful news to cheer on. The happiness pervaded to the entire office milieu, and my sunshine boy is responsible for this!

In a secluded corner, Mrs. Guha thanked me for my acquainted share, which must have influenced Debobroto, while signing on the dotted lines.

"Ma'am, I don't think that's the reason, because he is a thorough business man, you and our team's hard work is praiseworthy and our agency's name, trustworthy! That's the only thing which has persuaded him all along, to negotiate with this deal." I presented my judgment and honest opinion before her. She glowed for my dedication to work and loyalty towards them, as an employee. "Minisha! You are so correct here, that's the real thing behind, sorry if I mistook about you and Mr. Mukherjee. Kudos to my girl, keep up, the good work!"

Later in my cubicle I smirked like Debobroto, for coming party and the cynical things related to it. How I'm getting used to it, from calling his name to emulating his ways and words. I'm getting more and more like him, so I can be infused with him, whenever I will miss him! But my mind troubled me, over that posh party, about my career, which is at stake for impression. What should I wear? I can't duck under the kitchen counter this time, with my ancient ethnic wear, in this formal office party. I made up my mind to splurge, on this weekend, on a shopping spree, from my first and recent paycheck, as Monday is the party day! I planned simply to swish into a shop this Saturday, for an *escapade of girl's blues*, when it's my half-day. For once I will not act as a miser, when I have all the time and money of this world, for my very calculated impulse. I'm not that fool still, in my daze of happiness!

My Saturday's work has been capped off. It's time for my much awaited shopping! My canny brain checked off few extras from the checklist. First, I decided to buy a pair of Jeggings in black, when I have my coffee colored stilettos in perfect condition, so I ruled out buying any new shoes, but got stuck what to wear at top; then spotted a good bargain, a cross bodied tunic dress T-shirt, sleeveless, in turquoise blue, the neckline outlined by wide shimmers to add a dash of *Bling-bling*, which I want for my evening party. And as my long thick curls will fall over my shoulder, this will cover and take care of my sleeveless arms. I don't have to be skeptical about buying that top? Now for some make-up thingies to indulge in. I already have my previous party supply in my kitty, still decided to buy an eye shadow case, a nude pink blush to add a tinge of color to my blemish free complexion. Luckily I have my almost new wide flapped clutch in coffee color, wrapped in tissues. Few imitation jewelries left from my college days, which I have for years...So I opted out those from my buying list as well. I will choose later what will go by with what according to fashion trend. But I should buy a pair of dark shades I thought, to protect my eyes from the blinding sun's UV rays, and as for market research, when I have to take many field trips. I don't want to harm my precious part of the body. All those I coveted from a discount shop, and the amount which I have saved from the actual price, I spent that, on another mortal pleasure of mine...I trimmed a few of my front locks of curls in a hair salon, to look like a long fringe cut, while keeping its bulk and original length intact. My curls are now much more manageable than before. Those errands I have done in one go, and despite of spending my almost two weeks salary on that...I admired my latest confident, diva reflection on the shop window glass. I preened from my current wavy fringe cut, my new sunshade donned eyes, my tight blue denim Crop pants, my baby pink half-sleeved dress shirt, as my cladding, to my high heeled, black open wedges sandals who is making me stand tall in confidence. It's amazing to know, that my prepossessing sight elevated my under-confident, sagged posture of earlier, just with a few alterations. A new confident girl is now ready to fight any vexes of the world. Somehow Debobroto's dashing looks which undermined me that day, has some underhand in this spree?!... I must have been submerged into a new me, that I didn't notice who is behind. That person tapped my stooping shoulders, while exclaiming at my new *Avatar*!

"Minisha, isn't that you?? Can you spare me an autograph, please? You remember me, don't you?!" I thought my love for him, suffuses me with so much of him, that I must be hallucinating Debobroto's voice now, even with full of tease, out of nowhere. My quick turn bounced to face him, and his naughty grin startled me utmost! I looked as I have been caught, stealing the apples. Today once again, he is in his suited-booted-elegance, in a very striking self, far from his casual, and boyish looks, yet that intense sensuousness is there, which never varies, no matter what attire he prefers to adorn him.

"What are you doing here? And why you said that? Don't tell me you stalked me, it can't be a coincidence!?" I shot my confused questions at his impish comments, to hide my startle.

"Hey! Don't think me, as being one? I didn't do such a thing. And it's not a coincidence, but we are fated to meet like I always say...I stay here, or you have forgotten that too, come out of your world for a bit. And what else I could say, when you look like one of the famous, pretty model, ready to slay the onlookers? "

"I'm sorry, I didn't mean that, but I'm the oldest Minisha, look!" I took off my glasses, while tucking them behind my ears to prove my point, and jutted my face even a little forth, for him to recognize me.

With seriousness, he scrutinized my looks, & looked so sincere in his analysis, yet his immense amusement can't dupe me. "Hmm...you look like a genuine Minisha to me, but by whose permission you have cut your hair? Answer me that?!" His mocking chide made me guilt-stricken, his concern I value most, so in my defense I cried.

"What?! It's mine, why do I need anyone's permission for that?"

He looked hurt, felt so cheated as well, by my attitude. "You are cruel that's what you are! You deliberately have done that to punish me. Isn't that being your intention somehow?"

I know his fetish for my hair, but it looked like, that we are having a spousal quarrel in the middle of a shop pavement, and he has taken an impermissible authority too from me, without my permission! To quiet his discontentment, and to distract people's attraction, I murmured to him.

"Hush, Debobroto, please! Why are you creating such a serious scene for nothing? Look! I have just trimmed few traces at the sides, alright? The length and the bulk are the same, the way they were earlier. It's much more manageable now. Do you know, I was the only one there in my office, with my unruly barbarian hair?"

"It was not unruly, it was so beautiful, and you have ruined it now, you look just like a pert doll! "

"Does this supposed to mean a compliment?! Are you going to make me cry?"

"No, never! I don't want to be the cause for that, ever. I just exaggerated a bit. Please forgive me, but really, you are looking like a pretty model!" And for the first time, this didn't seem to me an obscene remark. Instead clinging to that compliment, I dazzled a broad smile for him, and he gave a dazzling one to me, in return.

"So now, I made you happy, well it looks like, I still have my sunshine charm left." He looked so boastful, and that word reminded me of something...I stomped my feet on the ground all of a sudden, and urged him eagerly.

"Debobroto, can you wait for me here? I have forgotten something. And if you are not in a rush, then will you wait for me, please?!" Though he eulogized my new effervescent self, yet he spoke in his mirth.

"Yes! I can wait for you, when I have all the world's time just for my Minisha. But where you are off to now, don't tell me, to the restroom? You are looking so desperate?"

"Seriously! Why you are stuck on that track? I wonder what happened to you lately? You were so lordly earlier, now, suddenly transformed into a naughty boy!?"

"So my Minisha thinks me as a boy, and a naughty one, too? Wonder will never cease, something really must be in the air...for this transformation."

He hinted the talk of *air* to emulate my earlier say to the doctor.

"Ah! Stop it." Deflecting my attention from his charming converse, I ran literally for that thing, while struggling hard to balance myself and my heavy bags. My bubbly enthusiasm over that thing has a beautiful reason, as it is a return gift for my Debobroto, a T-shirt which I have designed with such care, and gave it to a printer to print it. It is a graphic designed one, in a color black, with the word *Sunshine Boy* in the middle, written in calligraphy by glittering gold paint. His wearing of that black colored T-shirt is imprinted on my mind so much, that nothing seems to look better on him than this color…I almost snatched the packet from the shop, and with haphazard footsteps, I returned to him, to reach for him as soon as possible. As never in the world, I'm going to make him wait. I wish I can do the same in accepting his proposal, when he is still waiting for that, ardently.

"Ohh! You are still here…" Panting hard I huffed. " Thank you so much."

"And thank you for giving me those pretty blushes, which are only meant for me, I presume!" His eyes coruscated at my scintillating look, but I re-routed his poetic praises from what is factual.

"Don't be silly, those are flushes, due to my exertion, and don't make me talk, it's getting rather difficult for me to breath even."

"Why? You are wavered again by me?"

"Seriously, be serious for once. Now, here is your gift!"

"What an honor? But why all of a sudden, your kind eyes have befallen on me?!"

"It's a *thank you gift*, for that outing day! Earlier, thought of sending across by a courier, but due date fell on today, and I came across with you, so…But I have couriered Tia's gift already to your place, it might reach latest by today evening."

"But that outing was my present to celebrate your belated birthday?"

"Debobroto, please forgive me, but I have never celebrated that, after my Parents' death, and vowed that I will never re-thought of celebrating that again, so can we skip, that hurtful part, and talk of something else, please?"

"Minisha I'm so sorry, if I offended you. Alright then...What is this?"

"Well, open that in your leisure, when you will be back at home. But it's my time to return to Lodge. Bye for now, till your another fated coincidence?"

"Minisha, you meant that truly really? You made me so happy! So can I bother you with my calls too? I'm clueless whether you are on FB, or on WhatsApp? So I could chat at least, when I'm your Official friend!?"

He twinkled, so he could house shared feelings by technology's help, if not by fate's. His desperate methods to keep me close! I shook my head against his elation of meeting with me again or of calling, chatting me like a fanatic. But even if there is only one percent of chance, his happiness continued.

"Before you go, tell me why you are splashing so many things?!" Tilting his head, he sneaked into my eyes, to know the reason.

"Well, suddenly, I became rich..." I whispered my quip.

"Really?! How?" He whispered too, in his hushed tone, so that the news of my sudden richness, could not fall into some bypassing mugger.

"Through my paycheck, of course!" I replied simply against his twinkle.

"So how about sparing some coins on this fella, for a coffee?" He pleaded in mischief to refresh my elusive memory, which had urged of buying a lunch for him earlier, further, his lament of missing my culinary.

My time constraint made me say this. "I wish I could, when there are not 48 hours in a day? I have loads to do, but just wait a moment here."

I bought him his favorite Latte, and chicken croquettes takeaway, from a nearby coffee shop, in a haste.

And there he is, with his brilliant sweet smiles, simply waiting for his coffee to arrive. As if some expensive gourmet is being served to him, he looked like that, when I handed him those packs, carefully...

"Here you are, you do love to order me around Sire, when I'm your ex- employee now." Grabbing that as a last resort of his life, he took that as my responding love while he revealed the real reason behind his sudden request.

"I love to see, how your expressions emote in every fraction of varied shades of emotion, your nuances give me such delight, that my eyes want them to behold, time and again... But what's this, I asked for a sole coffee, not a friend to accompany it?"

He seemed to be pleased by my thoughtfulness and looked peckish. After hearing his reason behind the orders. I said in my pleasant tone. "Empty stomach of yours, doesn't know you are going to torture him with hot latte, have those, least this I can do, in place of my cooking."

He simply smiled his dimples at me, those fascinated me so much, that my teases flirted in open. "Debobroto! What impossible thing you have done, right now?" While his obstinate sipped his coffee first! I threw this at him. "You are a famous fashion house man, and you talked to an aspiring model for the last fifteen minutes in the street, in a broad daylight too. Just wait, till tomorrow's edition of tabloid newspaper. The front page is going to be flooded with the flashing photos of you and me, and with some juicy gossip story. Sometimes put your nose down to these gossip papers too, besides your usual financial times…" I cackled hard in my chortles, and he joined me too. But his quip is ready for me.

"Then, I will call a press conference by declaring my innocence, and let the world know, that I'm only talking to my fiancee and soon, we are going to be married."

"But that would be a white lie!"

"Is it Minisha?"

"I don't know." I bit my lip for that sooth. "And don't change the theme of conversation, like you always do, it's a bad habit of yours!"

"Yes. Old habits die hard!" He sighed once again, his exhilaration is obscured by the harsh reality. To divert him, the way he hopped from one topic to another, I did the same.

"Debobroto go home now, but drive safely, and beware of those Paparazzi."

I gave him a naughty smile, my eyes danced in mischief. He grinned. "So it's *Que sera sera* then Minisha, huh, until our coincidence will let us meet again!" This man is getting under my skin! Why imitating me? Why devising ways to manifest at every point, that he is my Alpha and Omega!? I waved at him before approaching to that cab with gliding steps. Despite my irk at his ways, I'm feeling exuberant, because I saw him, had our heart-filled repartee, and my secret yearn to be in touch with him, to nestle into his depth of love, to defy my harsh fate!!

It's Monday. My office party day! I don't have any anticipation for the fun, taking it as my mere duty of being an employee. Like a Mannequin, I slipped into my black Jeggings, tugged my cross bodied turquoise tunic dress. Then dug deep into the loot, of my chunky imitation jewelry. And found, a find, a flat-faced bracelet of paste stone in turquoise color, well bound by the brass, the perfect accessory for my same colored tunic top. I brushed my long curly fringes, till they bounced back with shine and luxuriousness. I then concentrated to enhance my face's features one by one. I applied foundation cum compact to pancake the surface of my face, with quick strokes applied the eye shadow of turquoise color over my eyelids, outlined them with eye *Khol*, brushing forward my lush eyelashes with mascara. I put every effort to dramatize my large sparkling eyes without making them droopy. I dabbed my lips with color gently… in the end, gave caressing strokes on the apple of my cheeks with the nude pink blush. They are tinted, but blended so well with my natural skin, yet contoured my cheeks perfectly. So this *Fashionista* hasn't forgotten how to give few make-up touches, it seems. I took a deep breath before slipping into my coffee colored stiletto sandals with metal pencil heels, and clutching my wide flapped coffee tinted flat purse, I'm all dressed up to hit the party! I looked at my reflection to assess my overall poise, the same thought came whether I look gaudy or garish, the way it came to Debobroto's party? But when a self-confident, smart, pretty, and subtle made up, looking girl smiled back at me from the mirror. I tossed my head back, to give my reflection an air kiss. This confidence to be a human being, of flesh and blood, and of someone, with a beating heart surfaced out, because of my romancer Debobroto's sweet romance. And this whiff of sweet romance reminded me, to spray myself with some Lavender. I can face the music of the world, when I'm ready to strike the right chord with my panache, and one thing more, I'm certain of today, that I will not give a damn about some fiasco! It's my pay back time. I will laugh and enjoy life to the fullest without any guilt. *Baby, I was afraid before but not anymore.* I said that, to bold me, and not to my meek me!

Taking a deep breath, keeping my confidence and poise, in tandem, I stepped into the party hall! I realized people are being thronged there already. From my superiors, colleagues to almost every businessman, businesswomen of the city have gathered down here. In the background, a DJ is mixing his groovy music…I noticed, that most of my female colleagues, have an expensive dress on, with exposed shoulders or back, few flaunting their shapely legs or cleavages. I dithered on my rather inexpensive one, and on my earlier ruckus on my makeup and decency for a sleeveless top?! I'm behaving like an old school? Are dress codes, labels people? This party atmosphere is one step ahead compared to what I had attended earlier? So, why I'm getting shocked? I must've been cut off from the world for too long?! Shrugging off, baseless thoughts. I chatted with a few of my office mates. But instead, they preferred to mingle with those distinguished business people out there, than with my less important personality. When making connections and acquaintances are in their mind, for favors, promotions, and social circle. I stood there lone in the crowd like some critter.

Some familiar voice called me from across my shoulder. I must be absorbed in the surrounding, that I didn't noted the voice before? That one person's voice which is the most significant to me, compared to the rest of the elite world! I turned my neck sideways to glance how my sun has come, to light my whole world by his arresting and dashing personality, by his adorableness! My sunshine boy, my Debobroto is wearing my designed T-shirt underneath his expensive blazer! Today he looked kind of cute, in addition to his extreme handsomeness and dapper looks! It's inevitable his coming here, when it is in his honor, he didn't stalk me, but arranged another fated meeting for me!

He whispered huskily into my ear, to commence our oft banter. "Minisha! Did your agency by any chance has arranged for an ambulance for the casualty's down here?" His satire on my appearance with his equally amused eyes made me an equal partner of our banter game. "Why? Oh! Sorry, should I call you Debobroto or you prefer Sir, in front of polished business people around here?"

"One at a time. I'm already swaying by your enchanted poise! Well, it looks like it will be on my shoulder, if people have their heart attacks due to someone here! What would be the outcome, then? If, one by one dropped down here before us? Doesn't that will make me an accomplice too? As the culprit is known to me, and I will be thrown into the jail for that?!"

"Well then, what about you?! When all those girls here are going to collapse on the floor, one by one, right in front of you? By your dashing sight? Doesn't that, make me an accomplice too, as the culprit is known to me? I will be landed in a jail, besides losing my job??"

"Why my uptown girl is so catty all of a sudden? Is it because of my designer wear?!" He targeted this quip to make me cognizant that he has acknowledged my designed T-shirt gift, and my love for him! For that I'm touched, as he could have wear, any of his elegant and expensive designer outfits, if he wanted to, but he showed his love and reverence at my efforts, and feelings. So I tickled his emotions with me, to revere our banter.

"Hmm...I don't think, it has a label of any fashion house, so it must be designed by someone special, at your honor?"

"Yes! This is designed by a pretty, witty, and lovely nineteen year old girl. By a very sweet teen!" He winked playfully at me while adding. "She's very sensuous one, so close to me that I always carry her snap in my mobile! Would you care to see that lovely lady?!" He hinted, how he has made our outing snap with Tia, as his Mobile Wallpaper!

But I let it pass, his amuse, his update. The impact of his flirtatious wink is disturbing me with some unknown sensation! "You win! But did Tia liked her present? Does she's doing well?!"

"Yes, she is and loved her *Masimoni's* gift very much! But hers is much lovelier than mine!?"

"Don't be so envious of your own daughter, when it is just a polka dotted, night pajama suit in Viscose? Are you going to try that out too?!"

He croaked a laugh at me. "Tell me? Did you design it?!"

"Where you have been Debobroto?! Didn't you read my resume, carefully? I used to be in the advertising field? I do have a degree, or you are so into drooling some pretty's snap, that you have partial amnesia now?"

"Now, you win!" He laughed at my transformation, my way of interaction of meekness to a sassy one. And he is loving it. His radiant face, his twinkle of eyes told me that.

"You bet! We are even, but it seems, that you are catching some attention and gossip here, before I look like a snob, who knows a Stellar, I'm dashing off." I hurriedly replied.

"Why you are deserting me? What I have done now? Am I boring you? Do I have some contagious disease?!" His disappointment pouted.

"Yes you have a disease, getting too sweet on lonely ladies. Go mingle with your friends around here, not with my boring self, and have a blast! Bye!" With a backward glance I threw a sparkling smile at his chuckling self, but his penetrating gazes traveled along, to give me my menacing goosebumps!

I went to have a chat with Mrs. Guha, to stamp my presence as an extrovert. After boring myself with *me* as a company for a while. I decided to join my colleagues even if they would ignore me, but I don't want to look rude by remaining detached, by sulking in our legitimate success! When it's our joint effort, besides it's against the office team's work ethics. It's my share of success also as much as of theirs? Needless to say I joined them, hit the dance floor. I jigged gaily in the lively jives with my office friends, to have a gala time, the way I used to have, with my girlfriends of the school and college...

But it's ephemeral, because suddenly I spotted a loathsome reptile of this earth's, who approached towards me! I skidded past from there when I caught up by my sunshine boy again! I felt relieved.

"Minisha! Whoa! Are you running from the crime scene after causing a massacre?!"

"Noo!! Debobroto, I'm running away from a very dangerous epidemic out there!" While hiding behind his back, I pointed out my finger at Prabhat Sanyal!

"Minisha listen, don't worry at all, let me handle this." I nodded to rely on my *Man*.

"Prabhat! don't you have something to say to Miss Ganguli? Now say it!" Debobroto thundered at him in a furious tone. I never have seen my sweet-nature sunshine boy so much angry. Even if he had shown anger and scolded me earlier, for my own good! Yet, he has a temper like mine too?

"Miss Ganguli! I was looking for you to ask for my forgiveness. I offended you rather rudely that night. Could you able to forgive me? All my past misbehavior? I can never think of losing Debobroto's friendship, and my job? Will you forgive me please?"

Its beyond my imagination hearing him getting apologetic, looking sheepish!

It's Debobroto's doing, so for the latter's sake only, I accepted the apology, even after his friend's vulgarity.

"I will, and I'm doing this because of Debobroto Sir, and for not to be a cause behind someone's lose of job and friendship! Okay then!" I flounced away from there, to deter this incident not to blight my party, and to eat something to subdue my pangs of miff!

It's been a while, my time to head to my lodge has come. Cutting past the buzz quickly, went outside, to wait for the cab I booked...When a totally different person, a shameless and a drunken one has emerged right before me...Prabhat Sanyal ambushed me! This is what I was dreading. I knew of his rotten character, a betrayer by heart, with lowly, lecherous mindset.

His slurring self, and his wicked grin attacked me. "Oh Minisha Darl! Where you are going? I apologized in front of Debo, did-n't I? My duty done. Now let's go to some discotheque at first, I want to press my carnal crave against your alluring body fast. After that we will make this night ours, and together, we will ride a feral ride of pleasure...Getting... uncontrolled, in heat! If you persist we will continue this, in my car, in any hotel, or where you want, till morning or for days. Come, let's go. I am going to explode!" Amid his stream of ear gagging lewd remarks, he grabbed my hand to drag me along with him, to his parked car, this brutish act of his, made me so ferocious, that I jerked off violently my hand from his filthy grip! Then without wasting any more time, I quickly lifted my leg, aiming a hard kick on his shin, which made him wobbled, he growled hard. And then I kicked him violently once again to his second shin, and dug my metal heel on a foot too... in this way I incapacitated both of his legs, by my kicks! He whined loudly in pain and by then Debobroto came to that area!

Seeing him Prabhat growled to clear his side. "Debo! I was so wrong about her, she is, no untouched bloom but a wild cat? Did you know what she did to me? She fractured both my legs?" He limped hard to show my crime!

But on the contrary, Debobroto flung his rage and snarls."It's good for you, because this wild tiger is going to punch your nose and break your every single bone in body, right now... just go away from here, if you don't want me to call the cops, or to get killed in my hands! I will deal with you later!"

I, allying with Deboroto yelled at him. "Yes. It's good, I only kicked you in my self-defense, because just one call to the authority is enough to land you into the jail, for sexual assault and kidnapping attempt! Make sure of that. You backstabbing sick bastard, lowly skunk of the drain!" Dumbstruck at our unified cussing and threatening at him, he ran away from there, as fast as he could, with his limping legs!

"Minisha?! Are you alright??!" A perturbed Debobroto for my plight looked akin to a white sheet! His voice trembled in utter fright!

"Yes, I'm fine, but I'm regretting as why I didn't dig my metal heels at his front asset of which he is so proud of?!" My recent conceited act, made me toss my head, to arch a smirk, of grimace, even when, I'm shaking in an intimidation, and feeling nauseated for loathsome words, of Prabhat Sanyal!

"So you heard everything, that day!!" He whispered an astound, surmising.

His disquiet about me persuaded my courage to reveal more of his friend's disgusting exploits.

"Yes, I did! But tonight was the extreme, a scathing proposition, he targeted at me. Do you know, what he did right now?! He dragged my hand to his car, so his arousal could spend the night with me there, or in a hotel! He wanted to press his lust close to my body while dancing! Besides his offensive sexual talk! And you hadn't heard what vulgar passes he made at me, to your house in the early part of that party night. He wanted me to play with him, and that you are all ready to be fresh with me? Sick pervert! He dared to touch my hand to drag me along with his slimy, filthy hand? Don't you think, he is so overconfident of himself and his capabilities? When this sex maniac is not worthy to spit even, on his face!?" My rage trembled me, fumes of fury came out from my nostrils. And this afflicted him further!

"Oh my God Minisha! You are really mad!! Why didn't you tell me all this, before?? I'm really sorry, that you had to go through with such harassment, and now this traumatic experience, and it's all my fault, please forgive me!!"

"Yes, I'm fuming! What should I do other than that?! Didn't he behave that way in front of you, twice? You had witnessed those on the day of his arrival for the file, and on the Party. So yes, partially it's your fault too, that I had to face this...And these perverts are everywhere, they need to teach a lesson, they've made a girl's life a hell! For them, they could not work without a tension of harassment, couldn't commute properly, or stay out late at night, freely?! Indeed you did nothing, stayed mute, passive? Why you are so docile? Why you support such bias, harassment? Because she is not your wife, girlfriend or sister? What's the use of your six packs or having a pack of morals?! When you can't protect the girls out here, so we girls, have to combat our own battle!"I accused him falsely without knowing his feminist male voice, without at least try to learn what he had said that day in response, to defend my honor, when I didn't wait to hear his side that evening!?

"So! It's my turn now Miss Ninja, for my callous acts?!" His meek voice still have a glint of humor, because he is pleased with my courage.

Brushing his humor aside, a concern now said, seeing his haggard look. "Why? Even though I admit that you have remained passive all this while, but still you didn't do anything disgraceful to me at all, till date? And yours is not a lust, but pure love! Bye then, take care of yourself...I'm going."

He disrupted my prancing feet to move forward for an earnest plea. "Now where are you going? Leaving me alone, when I thought to request a friend with something? I'm feeling very sick. Will my ninja will be kind enough to drive me home? My driver will then take you back to your lodge? Please?"

His plight must have made me simmer down my boiling rage. He looked so distressed that I gratified his wish.

"Ah! Why didn't you tell me that before?! And this is all doing of the junk food that you must have eaten at tonight's party, and because of that disgusting man, your blood pressure level has raised! God is going to punish him severely, just wait and watch!"

"Yes, God will help me, to do that for sure! And go easy with your level of blood pressure too, when you have to send me home safely? And what a transformation from my timid Minisha, into a Warrior Princess Xena?!"

"Don't be absurd, I have not changed? This is the real Minisha you are seeing! Didn't I tell you once that I can deal well with the bullies in my own way?"

"So? Are you going to drive this bully home, in your own way?"

"What else can I do? Sit inside...and Debobroto, thanks!"

"Why? I didn't fight your battle? You did with your lone ninja hand? I was just passive?"

"Oh come on! Don't look so innocent? I know everything about your sudden sickness! To protect me from his further ambush you pretended to be sick. Didn't you? You don't want me to take that cab alone in night, or to return to my lodge without anyone by my side? Didn't you? You are indeed a good schemer!"

He just grinned weakly at my remark, with his agonized eyes full of worry.

"But I need my protection too, from any ambush, so I need my ninja, right beside me..."

"Alright! Enough of this, now we shall hit the road. Although, I haven't driven a car at night, and please don't give me those stares, that makes me nervous, and conscious..." I blurted.

He grinned impishly. "Do they really?"

"Oh! Shut up! Do you want a chauffeur or not? I'm responsible for your safe drive, you just sit back and relax... let me see, seat belt, mirror, gear, clutch, brake, accelerator... check, and now insertion of the key to surge forward!" "Minisha, what are you doing? Suddenly are you the car instructor?"

"No! That's silly of me! Okay, let's go."

The engine purred. I drove along while slanting glances at his half-closed eyes, it is so unsettling to see him indisposed. "Debobroto, are you really feeling very sick? Let me stop at the doctor then?"

"No, I'm alright really, when you have caught me red-handed about my spruce, but Minisha thank you so much."

"Don't thank me, I know this will break my promise, while entering that house. But my parents would have never forgiven me, if I didn't listen to an earnest request of a friend, and when you meant so well. Don't worry, I'm in truce with my ill fate, my circumstances, and you know our fated meets, the way you call them, has made me do with that!"

"Minisha!! You are a very beautiful girl with a very beautiful heart. Do you know that?!" His overwhelmed heart crooned.

"*Hoon*. I know that, when this complement always, follows me around, and I wonder why?"

He snickered hard. "Tia was right, you are a funny girl indeed. And you are an excellent dancer too! "

"Well, I think I'm... Ah! Nothing escapes from your eyes." My face then filled with blushes.

His adoring gazes fondled them more. "Don't you know by this time how my eyes always watch at you, and search for you? "

"I know that, and don't brag about this habit!" He laughed.

"Were you a regular in disc, or a party-hard type girl?" His intrigue queried to know more about a girl called Minisha, my earlier demonstration of audacity must have astonished him. I tried my best to clear the mist, that I'm a homely girl, even if I'm labeled wild, once a rich girl!

"No, not a regular one, but I did go there, to celebrate my friend's birthday, once or twice. And being a good dancer doesn't mean a party-hard type girl?! But why do you ask? What are you insinuating at?"

"Well...Don't take me as wrong, but when you do look so naiveté, and that made me wonder then. How?"

"Seriously, if a girl doesn't have a boyfriend or she is a teetotaler, can't she have a simple untainted fun with her friends, even? Let me clear something.

I'm a head strong girl, who doesn't love being toyed around, that's out of my book."

"No, no! I didn't mean that because you danced like a Pro, that's why asked! It seems like Tia, your anger is also sitting on your nose, you look like a Rudolf, the red reindeer. Do you want me to shoo that anger away?"

His sweet temper humored, and his mirth made my angered self relax. He is right. I'm getting agitated at no fault of his at every point.

Seeing my composure he added. "About your second thought, I know that already, didn't my strong willed one, refused my love, and don't brag about that too?"

"Seriously, it's not to be bragged about. And regarding your first curiosity, it's to keep me fit, I learnt my Aerobic dancing! Where do you think my fat goes, then?"

"Really Minisha?! Hat's off to you, it seems, all the layers of your qualities are un-layering in front of me, one by one! But tell me one thing where is your *Sunshine Girl* T-shirt, or are you waiting for me to design one for you?!"

"You are again on your transposition to different theme? Are we a couple, that we will have to wear a similar T-shirt?!"

"Oho! So you are dying to become one?"

"You have put that word into my mouth. Keep quiet. But jokes apart, Debobroto. I'm serious now, it's not about me, believe me, but what if your friend, hires some goons to take revenge on you, he could hurt Tia or you?! I'm pretty sure, he can go to any length after displaying his true character! What will you do? It's all because of me, I'm really scared! Please don't laugh it off like some joke. Let Tia stay with her *Didai*. Do they have a trustworthy guard at the gate? Does the driver who takes Tia to the school is a reliable one? I'm so worried, and why all of a sudden you want to become a Car race driver?! Why don't your driver, drive your car anymore? For what, you have employed him, for then?! You should hire some Bodyguard soon!"

He is absolutely in his fit of mirth about my downpour of frets at one go, and for being under a shadow of terror, which are looming large, but on the other hand, his ears are elated, post listening my concern and love, I have still for him and Tia, deep down in my heart!

"Easy, Miss Worry, easy. Why there are so many question marks in your questioning remarks?! Nothing is going to happen either to Tia or me! Do you understand? So stop being a paranoid! Why you always think of others? What about you? You are all by yourself, without a conveyance!"

"Oh, that! Don't worry, I have God, my Parents are watching from above, and I'm Miss ninja even. Did you not see my brave act? And if something ghastly does occur, anyhow, then I will request a friend here, to help me. How about that?!"
"Oh! Thank you for that, to consider me as a 'friend in need' and don't think that you did something that to be guilty of, you did to protect your dignity and honor...people should take example of this, from my brave and sensible Minisha! I'm so proud of you, really!"

"Really? Well, I'm relieved then for your nod of approval. Alright, I will spam you, I will irk you...With untimely calls, till you will be on the verge to change your number!"

"Don't be absurd! I would love you to do that! I won't change my number ever, unlike Minisha!? Can you do something, if this friend request's you with something else? "

"Seriously! It's getting a habit now, what now?"

"When you reach home, can you call me just to inform me that, you are alright!"

"Yes, I will, it's a deal. Now rest a while, okay? You don't look good. We will reach home soon. Alright?"

"Minisha, can this Fella, ask you something more? Can we go somewhere to have an untainted dance of ours? "

"I don't have a choice, do I?! But I don't know, why you want to hit the floor? Are you a skilled one? Or you are planning to fracture my toes by your misstep dance steps?"

"No, you can count on me, just wait for me to float you up in the air."

"Really?! Wonder would never cease, looks like, your layers are un-layered too." And we both shared our hearty laughs.

For a while, we stared blankly at the road ahead then he sprouted his another request. "Minisha! I can't stand the silence any longer. It's killing me, sing a song for me instead."

"What? Why don't you switch your love Play list? I need to concentrate on the road."

"Don't worry, nothing will happen. Sing, please! "

"You are throwing tantrums again, you know. What should I sing? When I'm so nervous. Dear God! When I don't remember any of the lyrics."

"Then just hum, this would never have happened, if you stayed with us, then I don't have to be in desperation, or have to throw tantrums, for a mere sound of your voice, or for a glimpse of your sight!?"

"There you go again, *Accha*! "

I coughed to clear my throat, and to begin my euphony…" *Hush a little baby, don't say a word, papa will buy you a mocking bird…if that mocking bird doesn't sing, papa will buy you a diamond ring…*"

 "What's that?! A nursery rhyme?!" He shook in laughs!

"You wanted to hear a song, you didn't mention the genre, so I'm goingto sing this again…" I sang my reprise for the rest of my drive despite of his protests, and he had to relent.

"Debobroto, it seems you want to hear again, since you are not complaining. Doesn't this is an addictive song?" We both shook in our snickers and my banter-filled drive has ended like this…

Instantly, a deep melancholy and a shudder hit me, the minute I entered inside the gate of his house, for that resident abhorred happening related with it! Yet brushing aside that feeling with great difficulty, I left him to the entrance steps, with a promise to call him, when I will reach...I sat in his car once more, and the driver drove it to drop me off at my lodge. Latter remain outside my lodge gate as being instructed by his master, till I enter inside the Lodge porch...At last thanks to Debobroto, I'm safe and sound inside my refuge!

Before I could call, I received his. His voice sounded being in terror, in some quivering emotion! He must be crying in grief or in worry? My consoling words tried to alleviate him, as much as possible, possibly I'm alleviating myself by this way? The encounter with that house, the horrid experience of an escape from a sexual assault of not so long, his troubles for me, my petrify for his and Tia's well-being, has shaken me up immensely! His pacification is my solace too. When the filament of love has connected our heart and soul in oneness, tied us in an unbreakable bond!

"I'm okay!..Yes, reached at my place safely Debobroto, don't worry. But how are you feeling? Have you called yet at Tia's *Didai*'s place? Did Mira lock the door as well? The night guard is not dozing off, I suppose? Does your CCTV camera is working fine?" My patent nags strengthened him and he relaxed into his half-laughs.

"Everything is alright, otherwise I will become a Samurai too!" His amuse relaxed me too.

"Debobroto, can this friend ask a favor from you?"

"Yes. Shoot!"

"Will you be my 'BFF' for the rest of my life?"

His overwhelm cried. "Oh! Minisha!! You made me so happy! Didn't I want that?!"

"Why are you so excited, all of a sudden? You have misunderstood me, completely. It means -'Best Friend Forever' and not what your naughty mind is thinking of. It doesn't mean -'Boy Friend Forever' at all!"

He laughed harder at his deliberate ignorance. "Minisha, then will you be my GFF for life?"

"I'm not that naughty, seriously. No, I will remain your BFF only, now sleep tight like a good boy, when tomorrow you have to go to work!"

"So soon? When we just have talked for five minutes, it's me who is calling, so it's me, who is paying for the call too?"

"Really! You are too much. Don't you want me to have a beauty sleep too?"

"Why, so soon? Oh! You have a roommate, our talks woke her up?!"

"No! She's sound asleep. That's why, I'm at the balcony."

"Then, let's talk more when we are BFF's to each other, we should chat away the night...Minisha, when you will be on FB or on WhatsApp? How about it, so we can text each other with emojis too? Otherwise, heaven will punish you!"

"Saying No, for the time being! Let's settle with good old calls? And don't you think heaven punishes me intermittently, whenever it fancies?"

"Hey! Don't be so upset, Mini!"

Strange! After spending our time in a soiree, he wants to be more social through social media also, his heart is exuding his hidden desire to become more intimate. And now he's calling me Mini? His mouth has always slipped the first part of my name whenever he wanted to, whenever he became emotional, earlier. So he have coined that as my pet name without taking any permission as usual, while breaking every barrier of his hesitancy, or my dilemma? When he is so much in love with me, so he can dare? When he always says whatever he wants to say, when he always wants whatever he clamors for?

"What did you call me, just now?"

"Oh, that! That's your pet name given by me."

"But don't gather any hopes from me, to give you, one in return. I will call you, Debobroto only. That's plain and simple." I made my point clear. Probably my reservation or my awkwardness, in pertaining a relationship without any future? Or I'm doubtful on procuring a commitment?

His voice sounded dejected. "What? No pet names for me!"

"Well, don't you think, that will make it more unique? And this time, I'm going to the restroom. It's rather urgent. Bye!"

"Mini...Can I dare with something else?"

"Yes, when you are full of surprises. Somehow you know I love your dares now and then. Shoot!" My candor replied.

"Really? Alright! You ask for it. I love you very much Minisha, you are the only girl of my life. And how about your dare? "

Realizing that the warmth is returning to our relation eventually, he opened up his heart, once again to me. When he is so resolute in clearing away every impediment, every cob-webs of doubts, fears, from our path of love, then why he will retract from showing his true feelings once more!

I kept quiet for a while, before replying softly. "Then my dare is, that I adore my Debobroto just the same, and you are the only boy in my life. Happy now?"

My brimming emotions after confessing that, is getting beyond control, so camouflaging that with my frank humor, I added…"I need to go really, I'm hanging up for now. I can't hold it any longer, please. And besides, it's not the first one, but the second number, and on top of it, mosquitoes are feasting on me. Good night, for the final time. Alright?"

He must be on his laughing spree, because it's hard to hear him clearly through his laughs. "You are such a funny girl really, and I love our love banters so much. Goodnight, Mini then! Go to washroom right now, before you poop in the balcony!" He ragged me with his blatant amuse.

After our, that long and sweet phone conversation, I didn't get a wink of sleep in the night. Because another inevitable fiasco did happen after the party, no matter how much I have vowed not to care about it, this time, it's fatal, that it not only entangled me, but Debobroto and darling Tia, in it's nasty web!

In the morning, I feebly opened the lodge gate to begin my day. My heart is still pounding in a worry about Tia and Debobroto. A fitful yester night seems to be the cause of my weariness. I then spotted his car parked out there and he literally jumped out of it in an anxiety, seeing me feeble. "Mini, let me drop you at your office, please!"

"Oh! Debobroto, how are you? How's Tia? Thank goodness, you have listened to your BFF, you brought the driver. Regarding dropping me off to the office, that's not necessary at all. I will manage really. Now go to your work without any worry, alright? You must be getting late. Bye!" My coaxing crooned.

"Everyone is fine! But what's this? When I have listened to this BFF, then doesn't that BFF should listen to this BFF?"

I laughed hard for his maze of confused words, as to whom he is referring to actually. "You are talking in circles, I didn't get it? What you are talking about? And my office colleagues are the greatest gossiper of the world. What will happen, do have any idea, when I will reach there, in your car?"

"Then work for me." He stated a simple solution or rather his resolution.

"No! That's not possible either, now go please."

"Only on one condition, that you will answer my calls."

"*Achha*! I will, now bye!"

Even if I have said to him to go, yet my heart is saying to him, *'don't go, just stay with me'* and especially to hear 'Mini' one more time from his raspy voice...Sighing deeply, I signaled out an Auto-rickshaw for my work, after his car went past me.

Entire day at work, I remained spiritless, my mind jammed in fear. It's early evening, time for me to return to my home. I dreaded going outside from my secure office premises even, an apprehensive feeling of getting devoured by a lusty cannibal gripped me! Suddenly my phone rang, and it's my love who has called, to strengthen my ebbing courage. He kept his promise of the call! "Yes?" I simply pounced on it like my life savior.

"Mini, I'm waiting outside, come out from your office, this instant!"

"Alright, I'm coming right now!"

But there is no car waiting for me as I had expected, but far away in a cluster of bushes, someone is hiding, resembling like Debobroto? My curiosity and bother, approached his sudden urge to hide there, in this scorching Summer of May!?

"What are you doing here? Where is your car? Why you are hiding behind this bush?!"

"Well, Mini...Didn't you update me earlier, that your colleagues will gossip about my car and me? So I got rid of my car, but I don't know how to get rid of myself, so I'm hiding here."

For a long time, I tinkled in my laughs. "You are impossible.

A hopelessly naughty person, that's what you are? And still you will say that you are not sick. Why you have bunked off from your work like some college kid, just the way they do for watching a movie? Do you know, what else you are doing besides?"

He laughed at his deeds for a long time, and his curious eyes glittered in a humor too, for my further unravel of his adventures. "No! What I have done?"

"You are attracting attention by hiding behind the bush... Isn't that's obvious? And inside those bushes, do you know, is the kingdom of bumblebees, and who knows during the recess of your hiding, they might have gotten tempted with your bottom? Then repercussion?!" Once again I, in my fit of laughter, shook.

"Mini! You look nineteen when you laugh, just laugh like that more often, understand?"

"Okay! I will try to. But why you are here?"

"To spend some time with you!"

"What?! Are we not going to home then?!"

"No, I'm not, and you are not going to either. "

"So? What we are going to do on this highway, going to drool the road?!"

"No! We will walk. Later, will have our takeout food or whatever, we will just enjoy ourselves in each others company."...Then a startling thing happened, he held my hand while clasping it tightly! Small sparks of electrical currents started pacing back and forth into my body, to pull me off of his spark of touch, I chided at him, after being electrocuted. "Why you are touching me, all of a sudden?!"

"So to make you conscious. I'm simply holding a hand, nothing more or less, to walk along the road ahead..." He answered plainly or foretold our future? I kept quiet, while obeying his each word and action like my onus. I gave a sardonic laugh to myself, as earlier I didn't like ordering me around, yet now, what a transformation, I didn't hate it either! On the other hand, I'm loving his authoritative way of hand holding. He looked like someone who will guide me in my graveled paths of life. I didn't protest against his serene presence, in my havoc of turbulence. Whats happening to me?! I walked with him side by side, along the road, with our hand in hand, clasping them warmly and firmly in return. Then after a while he found a spot of his liking, and underneath a big shady tree, his down-to-earth nature like some commoner, sat on the grass against that tree, while pulling my hand, so I become compelled to sit there beside him...After quite a while, amid the cool and serene breeze, in the lap of nature, he broke his silence, while questioning me in his concerned tone. "Are you still upset for last night?!"

"No! I'm not. I'm fine." Lowering my head I murmured.

"Then why you look so listless?" He sounded unconvinced.

"Honestly, I don't know myself." I answered concealing panic for Prabhat's future foul play, against them.

"Hmm...Then you must be sick, let's go to a doctor then."

"No need for that. But there is something fishy about you today."

"What? By any chance, are you suspecting your BFF? "

"I'm not, but are you trying to say something to me? I could read it in your eyes. What is it, tell me please?"

"Could you indeed? Then why I'm suffering, why I'm in my miseries still? When just a YES from you, can sweep away all yours, mine, and Tia's despair, forever!"

"I wish you could read mine too, then you will know how I'm feeling? What happened to that trait of yours, by reading me like an open book?!" He painted a faint smile on his face to that remark.

Quickly switching his pathos, he said. "Well, for what I'm here, is to give you this!" He took out a photo print of our outing snap, where we three of us, together, were smiling, our happy sunshine smiles in one frame, the photo where along with us, Tia in between, have completed our perfect picture of happiness!

"Oh! It came out in print, so this is for my keepsake. Thanks!" That sweet gesture of his, the remembrance of our happy togetherness moved my heart, while stirring my soul. My eyes gleamed with love and joy. Instead seeing my emotion over it, he retorted. "Mini do you know, what this photograph means? Does my witty Mini know, what it stands for?"

"Yes, I know, the photograph, Tia has in her bedroom, was your past, and this recent photo of ours, being together, you want to make it, our present! Doesn't this photograph is the exact replica of what had been clicked with Tia, between her mother and yourself, when the former was alive?"

"Yes, bingo! You are a good guesser too!" He emulated my

earlier way of talking, and even mocked my act, by clapping his hands to praise me, the way I did for him!

His getting berserk time to time is evidently for wretchedness! The enormity of deep hurts by my guilty hand! Its apparent all over his eyes and face.

I broke down! My emotional baggage, I couldn't bear anymore! I unloaded it, by putting my sagging head over the edge of his shoulder. To expel my grief, my flowing foolish tears wept on...over my obstinacy! My one, NO, to him, is ruining three lives...Tia's, his, and mine's! My plaintive cry afflicted him.

"Mini! Please don't cry like that, I'm so sorry, I didn't mean to hurt you, honest! I was out of my mind with my hurt, minutes ago, it's my temper's doing? Please believe me!" Passably his strong arm came around my shoulder, to compose. But the touch stirred a fascinating, tingling sensation again...

I scolded myself sharply. *"Minisha, look how unwittingly you are depriving yourself from this beautiful sensations of love?"* The thought of it, made me cry even more with my heart out.

"Hush, Mini! Hush, I'm so sorry, what I should do?! You will make yourself sick this way...it's alright. Okay, cry on your BFF's shoulder as much as you like?"

Amid his desperate efforts to pacify me, I corrected him, drawing my sniffles in. "That's not a *shoulder*, that's a Side Hug!"

"Really, is that so?!" His innocent astonish intrigued him, he pulled me a little bit more closer. "What's this now?!"

"It's a Semi Hug!" I said wiping off my rest of the stream, through my gasping breath of sensory feeling.

"Really?!" By now he is in his extreme intrigue of passion! So to know the ultimate of our first sensations of love, he fastened his arms around me, to inch me even closer to his chest. My face nudged to his column of the neck, and my lips brushed gently on the skin. That friction sparked something tantalizing. He gulped down a passionate desire inside. It is enough for me, and him, to lose control of ourselves. He tightened his clasping arms more around me, to melt me in his scorching hug!

"Now what's this called?!" He gasped to query more from his heavy warm breathing. "A Full Hug!" I said in my barely manageable voice, through my havoc of sensations, which is quavering my body, yet I didn't retract from my enlightenment about my phrases of love.

His romancer hand fondled my back in the rapacity of swift strokes. I could feel his loud heart beat, his seductive warm breath caressed me, to become impetuous for that regrettable thing, which have such a sweet and rapt feeling. I perspired in the warmth, in a flame of rapture. My bosoms heaved hard, their peaks crushed against his. I realized how close I'm to him physically, for the first time...our long distance love, has made us succumb to our passion. Those irresistible sensory sparks, like electric shocks which is tingling us, due our engulfing embrace, that sensuous explicit touch felt so heavenly and breathtakingly serene as well. I just wish time to stall there, so I can remain forever in his warm arms...I moaned in a pleasure, which I never felt before. "Oh Debobroto! This feels so good! " I'm getting surprised at my newly found seductive voice, at my frank admittance of raw feelings, and at his equally seductive husky voice, confirming his set of sensations and desires, which are akin. He moaned in delight. "Oh Mini! Yes, it does feels so good!"We remained in each others arms, for such a long time...and into his ecstatic cocooning embrace, I must have slept off with a feeling of peace and an assurance, that my love is by my side.

Debobroto blew a few of his whispers to my ears, to wake my daze. Those caressed my senses. "Mini, O, Mini, wake up, wake up dear! You don't want the moral police to catch us like lovers!?" He lazily said yet his hands gently caressed my hair, my back to downward strokes, and by this time, the caresses are reaching into the lower part of my back...

This renewed my lingering fiery sensations back. It awakened me, making me realize, where I'm. But to remain lost in his world is my only desire, then, so I didn't like his wake-up call, or to be away from this beautiful hug so soon, not when it is our very first vehement embrace!

"What? Why you did that? When it's so wonderful to be like this? You are cruel Debobroto! And what moral police to edify us? I will turn Ninja to them, let me be like this in your delicious hug, just for a few minutes more, please." He chortled lightly at my frank remark. "Mini, you are impossible. You are one outspoken girl. I love my Mini for that so much. I love everything about her! Alright then..." He growled. Clasping his arms tighter around me once again, almost crushing, squeezing and suffocating my soft body, against his strong muscled one, he hugged me passionately to fulfill my wish. Even it suffocated me, but still I loved that suffocation, because I will love to die in it, anytime. For how long we remained like that, only the sands of time could tell. But something made him say sensibly for the sake of me. "Mini, it's getting late, I think we are spotted by bumble bees. Let's go from here."

"Yes, you are right, let's. And Debobroto, thank you for loving me this way."

"Anytime Mini, don't thank me for my mastered hugs, I'm at your service always."

"Oh! Don't be like that, don't pretend, as if you felt nothing. It's a very delightful and beautiful feeling to be hugged, and there is no need to hide what you have felt, when you felt that wonderful feeling of being in a hug. Didn't you? But the reason, I'm thanking you for, is what you have done for me so far! I know why you have come here, even after knowing that it will cause loss in your business, still you skived off from your work. And you have signed that contract for me. Didn't you? Now you have stranded your car, and stood in a street abandoned in this blazing summer heat for me, just to protect me...Just for my welfare...you held my hand not to touch it, but to assure me, that everything would be alright, because you are here to walk with me, to cross my hurdles along side. Didn't you? And you hugged me not for lust, even if I provoked your intrigue, but you hugged me only to love, to soothe my restless heart and my miseries of miserable life, to ease my tormenting pain, to chase away my bitter memories. You did all those to me, selflessly, without asking anything in return. You are a very good person, with a very good heart and soul, just like an angel. I'm so wrong earlier. Heaven loves me, that's why it has sent me, a very beautiful gift from above...The beautiful you!"

He is so touched by my gushed out emotions, that his eyes are on the brim of emotional tears, his welled up emotion, became tenuous for a moment, and he forgot what he is doing at the moment, only expressing his heart-felt feeling for me must be in his mind. So leaning forward over my face, he is about to touch my anticipated, trembling lips.

Our lips are just an inch away to culminate that feeling of lingering love, when I reclined my body back, and escaped from his embrace laughingly, by jerking off from his clasp, and got up on my feet abruptly. His adoring glances lingered on my face tenderly, for a while, but then with a sudden playfulness he smiled.

"Oh! I'm so honored, but don't worry of my being angelic, this compliment follows me around. And what BFF's are for, am I not a friend in need, a friend indeed?" He threw an innuendo and we both laughed at the underlying meaning hidden beneath it. How strange it is, his hints, his innuendos are so sweet, so pure, so heart touching? Neither they are boorish nor impudent unlike others. He is such a sweet natured person, and one of the most emotional one too... To reciprocate his sweetness, I became emotional, and held his hand, while entwining my fingers with his, so to fill the spaces between his fingers with mine, to fill the gap of our love, while making our love complete. I know now, why God has made gaps in the fingers, so your love can fill those with warmth of their hold. And for that I'm thankful, I didn't mind to touch him at all...I love to touch my man, my Sunshine boy!

Like two lovers, hand in hand, we stood there, while gazing at each other affectionate eyes, and while exchanging our sparkling bright smiles...

"Mini, thank you for loving me in this way, too." His mellowed voice whispered, but his ingrained intriguing nature asked then. "But tell me one thing, if you are comfortable in answering this. You didn't...You never have been K...d by someone!" He flung his earlier disappointment of unable to kiss me, bluntly like that.

"No-o-o!" I blurted out shamelessly, without shying away from this.

"And you are then... still?!" His intrigue wanted to know all.

"Yes, I'm a V... Still. Do you know, what talk we are having?

ER..., you have hypnotized me into this, that's why I'm talking so immorally?"

"Oh come on! Don't be silly! It's not what this is called, its heart to heart talk, between two innocent BFF's. Didn't we had our biology classes?"

Nodding my head, I said sheepishly. "Yes, we did!"

"Don't tell me you are...Queer!"

" No! I'm not a queer...What about you?"

"Me neither."

"Then, what we are doing? We should get going by now, straight ahead and straight to the road." He laughed his head off.

"Debobroto, I tickled your funny bone, that's why you are laughing like this, these days...*Haina*?!"

"I did yours too, you laughed so spontaneously, or suddenly the air is filled with laughing Gas?" We both started laughing again at his pun, at our gibberish talks.

"But Mini, what was the name of our last hug? After that full hug?" He is enjoying my coining of names of our hugs.

" Um... An Ultimate Hug! That's what it was!" He cracked again in mirth.

"But Debobroto tell me, did you change your brand of cologne recently?"

"Why? Have you all of a sudden become a scent sniffer? "

"Don't be ridiculous, I sniffed the scent while you are crushing me into a pulp that's all. I realized it's different from the one, you generally use."

"Yes I did! Why you want to snuff me? Alright a friend's request, coming up right now. Mini, you sniffed me around for my male scent. And I'm all yours to sniff me all over..." He leaned over my lips once again, to kiss me.

"Ah! Stop it...that was just an innocent remark... Don't pollute it!"

To divert his attention to another track, I started to tick off my checklist of our doings together. "We did lots of things together, we went out, we ate together, we had our love banters, we called each other, we became BFF's, we hugged, we tickled our bones, we nagged, we laughed and flirted, we..." And he cut my sentence in the midriff. " Yes, we did all that, my naughty one, but one thing, still remains to be done!"

"What's that?"

"Can I K...you, now?"

"Stop it...no, you don't, one of these days, you are going to get one from me!"

"Really! I'm waiting for that, in my baited breath. When will be the lucky day, tell me fast?"

"Stop it...I meant to strike you! "

And once again, he shook in his rib-tickling laughs. "Don't laugh, please stop, or I will desert you, or push you into the bumble bee's kingdom."

And we both laughed at that. "But why your outfit was slinky at the party? Are you by any chance were trying to seduce me?" He teased to continue our repartee.

"How did you know that? Yes, exactly that's was on my mind? To woo you!"

"You succeeded. I became vulnerable by your seductiveness!"
"Did you? Then don't you think, for that I need to improve more on my...You know what I mean? "

"Now...who's been naughty?"

And we chatted like this, in our puerile, garrulous, and gregarious way, by pulling each others legs, into the road together, while prancing our feet with our beaming happy faces, with our love-filled hearts, hand in hand like lovers, like soul mates, like romantic couple. I really wished then, for our happy times to never end, and I, to remain his for always! Because after my Parents, nobody has loved me like him, ever before, nobody have pushed away my poignancy so I can have hearty laughs too, nobody gave me meaning to live on in my life again, nobody, but his pure love for me! He loves me the way I'm, not who I'm, even when he is the most sought out man, even when he is among the who's who in the society. And I loved the serendipitous meets with him, with all my heart...as our heart connected once again for that!

He didn't abandon the car, but the driver, it's parked in the nearby parking lot. This time without waiting for his request, I opened the front door, and tied my seat belt of the front seat, much to his amazement, at my sudden change of attitude! So while driving, he started reading me like an open book, to read my interesting chapters of life.

"Are all your male colleagues in office, are married?"

"Married? Not really? Only few of them are. But why, you ask that?"

"What?! So there are many handsome bachelors, as co-workers, still around you then."

"Handsome bachelors? Yes, you can say that, but don't worry, you are the only one for me, I'm just a protective sister for all my male brothers out there, so relax, and don't raise your pressure, keep your calm, you have to drive safely. "

"Good to hear that, and especially when you think of me the handsome one, out of all them." My giggles popped out. "So I cured my Minisha's sickness, with my magical hugs. How about curing me now? "

"What sickness you have? "

"I'm love-sick, so doctor Minisha, what you would give me as love dose?"

"I will suggest a warm shower in the summers, and ice cold bath for the winters, and will prescribe box on the ears, and a good spanking on the bottom, for this naughty patient of mine, right now!"

"Really, I'm scared of my Ninja… But those treatments sounds exciting on the contrary…Well, let's go somewhere to eat, if you don't have any objection, to cool you off then!"

"Why not?! When it's you, who is buying, not me? "

"What? Aren't you going to pay for your share of food, then?"

"What? Why? I haven't seen such a stingy rich like you, before?"

"Stingy? Okay! I will show you, who is the real miser here, you will eat, till you burst. How about having a Pasta and an ice-cream treat, to improve your those, you know what I mean?"

"You are shameless! But on one condition, pasta should be of low-carb, and ice-cream has to be a sugar free and low-cal, only!"

"Not again, Mini! For once, enjoy your high-carbs and cals too."

"Alright, I will. When I always abide in you. Don't I?"

"Yes, except for one. Why you are not marrying me? Are you waiting for my hair, to turn gray?"

"Why you are being like this? Ah! Because you are going on in Grampa's age, already. Aren't you thirty four? And if I'm not mistaken, I can see a gray hair springing up right from your neat hair."

"Stop pulling my leg. I will not laugh this time, I'm serious, marry me, let's end this long train of tortures and sufferings, which we both are enduring for so long. We both understand and love each other, so much, and we are so compatible with each other, we are each others perfect match. So what's bothering you? Couldn't my kind-heart Minisha, will forgive her sinners, for once? Won't she will do that?" He entreated me, with his heartfelt pleas to make me pliable. And that miffed me.

"Don't pressurize me. Even though I have aggrieved you, even then. I need some time to think it over too. When it's a life time decision, commitment, for me. If you are in so much rush, then settle down with some other, pretty drooling lady. Stop being so inconsiderate, please."

"No Mini! Never! You are the only one for me, and don't you want me to be the protective brother to all my sisters out there? It's so good to hear that, you will reconsider about it, that relieved me. I think, from now on I should hug you more often, to motivate you!"

I thanked God, because he have lightened his mood, as his petulant mood always makes me so worried...to tease me, he went to an Italian restaurant to have a rustic dish of pasta, to have a stomach-full of homemade taste, with thick, rich sauce...I smiled, because his gourmand is guzzling the delish creamy sauce, more than the cuisine, the minute his ordered plate is put on the table. Poor soul, he waited in an empty stomach for me for so long there, he must be famished, or was craving for a good food. But I have to interrupt his 'bon Appetit' in a worry of choking himself or upsetting his stomach.

"Debobroto, can do well, everything, even eating...But please eat slowly, and chew well." My fear cajoled his food fetish self.

But instead my way of eating amused him in return. "Mini, why you are showing such refinement in eating. You must be conscious, in showing your heartiness while eating. I never have seen anyone twirling strands of pasta with a help of a spoon to fork, and you are also putting the spoon under your fork to support long strands and the dipping sauce, you don't have to impress me."

"Am I doing that? But at least spin the pasta on your facing side, then."

"Why?!" His twinkle of eyes asked, to unravel the mystery. "I heard it from somewhere, that, it will bring you good luck." I put my credulity, simply.

"Really? Then I will do that. Who knows you might agree to marry me?"

I smiled at him warmly, because he is fervently adapting this trivial myth, for the sake of my suggestion, and for the sake of marrying me. And from then on, he didn't forget to rotate the fork on the facing side, before putting his morsel into his mouth. Then to tease me more, so he can burst my stomach, he ordered every flavor of ice-cream from a famous Ice-cream parlor of high calories, and for that, I had to remain in the restroom for a while, and this further stoked up his humor even more.

We are back to the road once again, and this time, we are headed to our respective homes. Again, when he became inquisitive about me and my passions. "Do you love shopping? "

"Yes, like every girl, I think it's harmless to be Shopaholic. And doesn't this helps to boost your profit, this shop-o-maniac nature of the girls? "

"Yes, yes, you are always clever with words and genius in humor, I love you for this. "

"Thank you my lord, this humble servant is aware of that."

"Were you popular in your teen years? I'm curious why nobody noticed you before?"

"Popular, I don't know. I was in my own world all the time, that they might have thought me as an ice queen. How do I know?! May be I'm waiting for my dream man. 'You' to come along in my life, or there was something amiss in the air there."

"Yes, that must be the case, I'm sure. Don't worry, your latest exhibition in reciprocation of love, ruled out you as an Ice Queen... And Mini, do you know something else? Although, you look so enthralling in the western wear, but I could never ever going to forget or erase the memory, the way you looked in your *Churidaar Kurti* that party night. Why you are so into the western things tell me? "

"Ah! I'm not so into that, I'm proud of my ethnic wears also. It's that, I wear whatever I'm comfortable in, I don't bother about what suits me, or in which I would look lovely, that's all. "

"So you won't object, wearing a Sari?"

"No, why should I? It's that, I'm not used to it, my *Ma* used to help me when she was alive, whenever I need to wear that for any cultural functions, and I don't know whether I should tell you this or not? "

" Shoot. Why so much inhibition? We are BFF's after all. "

" Well, I don't know how to make Sari pleats!"

" Oh! I'm so sorry. Yes, there was no one there to aid you, I understand how hard it's been to you, fighting for survival since your teenage year, all alone, for so long. Please forgive me, for being so lousy. "

"Hey! Don't be so sentimental on this place, it's not your fault. I will try to wear a Sari! Okay? "

"How?? You want Mira or *Mamoni* to help you!"

"Are you out of your mind? Mira, I can understand, but not your *Mamoni,* in anyway! Who knows, with what fit of rage, she will shred my Sari into tiny pieces, instead of helping me out?! "

He chuckled hard imagining that. "Then how?!"

"I have my sources too. "

"Really! Who? I'm so intrigued to know! "

"Well, you are a cave-man then, when you own an online store particularly."

"What are you talking about my cave-lady?"

"I'm not a cave-lady. I meant Youtube, there's lot of videos uploaded alone, on 'How to wear a Sari' those will help me, and with a little practice of hand, I will clothe my Sari in no time!"

"Really? Then allow this online store owner to present you with one. How about that, my sunshine girl? "

"No way! I'm not that type of girl, who will love to pamper themselves with someone's shower of sweet gifts. I will buy one for myself, don't worry."

"Then, I'm waiting with baited breath, to see you into that attire soon, Mini! But on the contrary, I love someone to shower me with sweet gifts. How about a return gift, for the recent treat? You love to give return gifts. Don't you?"

"What do you want, as a gift? But I'm warning you, beforehand, no, hanky-panky business? I'm a naive one."

"What words Mini? From where you've learnt those? I meant, my pending song request!"

"Oh, that! Alright! I don't want to be in a debt. Well, let's see…"

"Mini, but no nursery rhyme. I'm warning you." I gave a beatific smile before singing, the song *Power of love* to glisten him with my kaleidoscopic colors of love, with my power of love!

*The whispers in the morning of lovers sleeping tight.*
*Are rolling by like thunder now as I look in your eyes.*
*I hold on to your body and feel each move you make.*
*Your voice is warm and tender,*
*a love that I could not forsake.*

*Cause I am your lady and you are my man.*
*Whenever you reach for me I will do all that I can.*
*Lost is how I'm feeling lying in your arms.*
*When the world outside's too much to take*
*That all ends when I'm with you.*
*Even though there may be times it seems I'm far away.*
*But never wonder where I am,*
*cause I am always by your side…*

My mellifluous voice sang that melody from depth of heart, for the rendition of my side of true feelings for him! I vocalized my feelings through music, that like him, I love him beyond words as well. I re-confessed my love, I reciprocated his unrequited love for me! For the first time, I saw, how his brimming emotions flowed down from his cheeks, which he has to jerk off immediately, so not to blur his vision for the sake of driving…Later I learnt something else amid this…his soulful eyes, his greatest love for me confided, that Prabhat has been suspended from his managerial post by him, further Debobroto has decided to put a lawsuit against him, for an inexcusable misconduct and a breach of trust! I'm so glad that I boarded that train, that destination train of mine, so that I could get off to my destined station named Debobroto!!!

# Chapter Eleven: Our Rapture for being in bliss

Heaven must've listened to our conversation, on our that sweet *Hug day*! That, for an office seminar, which is going to be held soon, all female staff are requested to wear a Sari! At first I thought of buying a ready-to-wear Sari, but after giving a second thought, decided to buy a normal one instead, to carry on with the genuine charm of draping a Sari. I bought two silk Saris of affordable prices. A *Jamawar* Sari in plush red for some special occasion, and another one in beige color for that seminar, or to use it, for any such similar purposes. My thorough lessons from learner videos has helped me a lot, to have an idea of how I'm going to drape it. After going through for few times more, I became quite an expert, even is ready to adapt myself in a Sari cladding for every day!

It's Friday. Pivotal day of the office seminar! I'm in my neat, and pleated Sari. This traditional outfit not only gave me a poise, but a feeling of gaining some power as well. As if, I have achieved something on my reliance!

During this due course of time, it has been decided among the office group, that they should consider an outing, when they have worked so hard in the past few days for the agency, without taking a break. So this Saturday after the seminar, they will certainly go for it. Luckily, it's an optional choice, even if I don't opt for this, still I will get a deserving day of holiday! I want to adhere to my decision of not going with them, as I need my much awaited, overdue leisure by all means, after getting through with many rough days of my work and life. Further, it will benefit my present state of emotional mind, to take a back seat too. But it seems, peace and leisure, are not in my dole, they are not meant for me at all! After a bone breaking tiresome day of the seminar, I'm about to reach for my place, to give a consolation, to my aching body, to my unsettling nerves, when I received a call from Debobroto's number!

That one call, beamed me, as that came as a solace to me, and hearing his, mellowed, sweet voice is just I want then, to chase away my blues and my fatigue. My anticipated self, tapped the call receive button with a simper...

Instead, it's Mira, who've called in her distressed voice to inform me about Debobroto's illness! "*Didi* come quickly, he must be calling your name, *Mini, Mini*, in his whimpering, high fever!"

I became frenzy in a panic, after receiving such dreadful news. Though according to her it's just a heat exhaustion, and the doctor has advised him to take a complete bed rest for a couple of days, yet my tremulous voice assured her. "I will be there in an instant, don't worry anymore. I'm coming right now, okay?" I wish to have my pair of wings, so I can fly to my love, but I'm just an ordinary, wingless, powerless mortal, who can only worry and sigh, then again worry and sigh.

First, I dashed to my lodge to pick up a few of my personal things, who knows if I have to stay there for an overnight, or more, I might need those. Somehow, I determined to stay there, till he is going to recuperate. I'm clueless, if Tia has been informed about this or not. Sweeping my feet as fast as I could, I rushed to his house disregarding the sinister reasons behind my leaving. My drab face, my agony, only knows that my life will be on the verge of ending, if my love has to endure pain. "Wait for your Sunshine girl Debobroto, I'm coming!"

I wailed out, while reaching there.

Running to the upstairs while missing my footsteps, a soft rap at his master bedroom without any hesitation I gave, where earlier I never have even dreamed of trespassing? All are gathered there, the doctor, Shefali, Mira.

And my Debobroto, who is reduced in size zero due to his ailment, with ashen, drawn out face, his limp body sagging against the pillows. The only bright thing in this, is my entrance, which brighten Mira and Shefali's face with a ray of hope.

And relaxed the doctor, utmost, as if, he has found a caring nurse all of a sudden in form of me! His jovial tone said. "Well, my dear, it's so good of you to come. Look, there's nothing to get alarmed of, it happens in summer times. But make him rest as much as possible, in a day or two, he will be fine and ready to work out in a gym too. All those medicines are to be given at regular intervals of time, lot's of fluids and light food, and if possible, a cold pad on his forehead for his temperature to run down... I will be tomorrow again, don't worry, it's not that serious at all!" And he went away, shouldering me a grave responsibility of which I love to be responsible for any time!

Taking the reins of my presence of mind, I ordered Shefali to bring the mineral water and *Electrol* diluted in it, as his energy drink, his dehydrated body through this will not be devoid of minerals and salts. Then I requested Mira to stay for a while beside him, till I change into some fresh clothing. After getting her nod of agreement upon it. I entered into my old room!

The door, I closed earlier with a promise to never set a foot in it again, I opened that sighing deeply. A quickness of my hand scrubbed my face, my arms, my feet, thoroughly, and to cheer him up, donned into my new red *Jamawar* Sari before rushing to him once again…

Mira looked astonished at my outfit, which is so different from what I used to wear, but she kept quiet, as Shefali have already placed that tepid energy drink I requested for, so I told former on her way back to bring Oats porridge with crushed plum, grated apple, and few slices of banana, after thawing down at the room temperature, and a tall glass of moderately cold pineapple juice to add on the tray. I'm done with my instructions for now, while I simply waited there, for the nourishment to come by. In between this my dilemma squirmed, on how to persuade him to drink this, whether to touch him or not, or to wake him up?

He guessed my presence, the way he always does. Slowly his weak and heavy eyes opened. It's saddening to see, how much luster of his shiny black eyes have lost. In a hardly audible voice he spoke. *"Who is it? Who's here?!"*

"Debobroto, it's me, your Mini! Can't you recognize me at all? Are you having any difficulty in seeing me?! Then rest your eyes for a while?" I crooned to pacify his agitation and my anxiety.

"Is it you Mini?! Am I in some kind of illusion? Why are you in a red Sari, and looking like a bride? Please tell me? Am I hallucinating due to my sickness, due to my deep desire to marry you?!"

"No, dear! You are not disillusioned at all. I'm really wearing that colored Sari! Didn't you ask for this favor, from me?

That's why, I have come here to show you this. Now tell me how do I look?"

His eyes for few moments caressed me affectionately, after that gave a calm reflection of his heart. "Mini, you looked like an enchantress who've come to mesmerize me! And if I could I would then have called a *Mandir Purohit* right away to solemnize our marriage, right here, right now!" He to culminate that ritual tried to get up!

"Listen please don't get excited! I'm so sorry, for being the cause? I didn't do it on purpose. But before resting again, please have a sip of this drink. Will you please?"

"So my Mini at last came here, to cure me of my sickness."

"Yes, the sickness doesn't look good on my effervescent and emphatic Debobroto at all! So I came up with my love cure. Now be a good boy, and lift your head a little, please drink this."

"I'm unable to up my head on my own. Will you help me please?"

"Why of course! Here, let me hold the glass like this, no-no, don't swig it down, sip it slowly...yes, like that, and see, it's finished..." Without any hesitation, I touched his shoulders to support him, to aid him to finish the contents of the glass.

"Now, you will go away!" His dismay grumbled.

"Who told you that? I'm not leaving you so easily. I'm going to be your house guest till you are ready to scheme out a scheme, to kick me out of here!"

My mirth, relaxed him in his feeble smiles. "Thanks. But does, Tia know yet?"

"No, not yet. As news of your illness has to break for her rather tactfully, she is still a child, this might agitate her. But I'm going to call her grandmother right now, and from tomorrow, Tia will be with us *forever*." I intended to do something, a beautiful plan involving our happiness, which is going to break my past convictions.

"Mini, that's so thoughtful of you. But how you will call her *Didai*, despite her hatred for you?!"

"Don't be silly. She is not going to chew my head off! And you are above of everything!"

"Am I?!"

I nodded at him. He smiled. "Alright Mini, do, what you think appropriate, then. But you have come straight from the office, rest a bit!"

"I will, when my patient will have something to eat, and then some magical medicines to get well soon...Oh! Here is Shefali with the tray."

In the meantime when she placed the tray near the bedside, I requested her to make some light supper for him. Nodding her head to accord with me, she left for the chore. But he doesn't seem to be in accord with me of having his nourishment, no mood to even put a bit of morsel into his mouth, so the problem of persuading him to eat something became one onerous job for me...I coaxed him fervently while sitting on the edge of bed to put slowly, bit by bit the spoonfuls of porridge. Soon the bowl became empty due to my cajoling. I gave him the pineapple juice before giving him the prescribed medicines. To gratify me, he has obliged to all my requests, like an obedient person. To put the tray back to the kitchen, and to check his dinner preparations, I'm about to go, when he called me.

"Mini, now you are going away." He moaned out a plaintive cry.

"No, I'm not, I'm here to stay."

"Are you real Mini, in person?"

"Yes! I'm!" But unconvinced he suddenly started making an effort to rise up from his bed, without believing my words or my actual presence there.

His swaying body to assure himself, tried to reach for me, that alarmed me so much, that I have to rush out there, to his bedside.

"What are you doing Debobroto? See, I'm real...alright, now give me your hand." I clasped his hot, feverish hand in mine to place that on my soft cool cheek, to convince my real existence. Further his burning temperature like hell, is worrying me immensely, the way his overexcited state of delirium!

"Yes, you are real in person, and this felt so good, when you touched me." His pleased self said convincingly.

"Does it, my naughty one? Then I still have my sunshine touch left!"

A feeble grin of his assured me that his excited emotion of earlier has been abated. I supported him back to his pillows... Soon, he fell into a sleep like a baby, with an assurance of my presence. An hour or so later he complied to have his dinner and his medicines once again. I checked the temperature and to my utter shock, it's a hundred and one! Worry is eating me out, and on top of it, his opening of eyes at regular intervals to check my presence! So to assure him again, I stroked his head gently, and he smiled faintly at me with his fever glistening eyes. I smiled back. While he slept again peacefully, I pressed his forehead during this with the cold pad, all through the night, as been suggested by the doctor…

It must be during the dawn, I dozed off in my chair, which I have pulled beside his bed, in my cold compression session.

In the early morning somehow few strands of my curls blew over to his face, when he flipped to turn his side on my facing side. Those must have tickled his slumber and his wakeful eyes, must have adored my dozing unaware head, which is swinging back and forth from the chair. Some instinct told me, to become wakeful at that moment! "Oh! You are awake, good. How you are feeling now, tell me?"

"Mini! You were up and awake for me all night. Didn't you?

Why you are so good, and lovely as well?"

Suppressing a yawn, I replied to his guilt-ridden query in my mirth. "Oh, that! To claim a title in popularity pageant!"

My light-heart remark made him laugh, that relieved me, his progress towards betterment. I turned to call Mira, but his shrilling voice in weakness, protested. "Why are you deserting me?"

"Oh! No, not so fast. As you know this heavy sari is making me so itchy, so just to change that. I will be back in a minute."

"Mini, wait before that please, just give me my mobile."

Ah! Now he wants his mobile, I never have seen such a

workaholic man, in my entire life before. "Alright, here you are." I handed him, the sought out gadget.

"Stand still, come a little bit closer. Yes... Beside my side like that, yes, that's it!" After giving instructions like some fashion photographer to click my portfolio, he clicked a snap of me wearing the red *Jamawar* sari in his shaky hand, before I decide to change into something else.

"Why did you do that? Clicking a photograph without my permission. Do you know it's a crime, Mr. Ace photographer?"

"I'm a patient, so I do have my whims, besides, I have clicked this, for a comparison. Who is more alluring, my western Mini, or my ethnic one?"

I threw my head back to laugh. "You are something, still in your mischief, when you are so sick? Okay, let me put it back, your work of art, where it was before."

"No leave it here, or else you will delete it!"

"Don't you trust this BFF of yours? Nothing will happen to this drooling lady, she is safe in your mobile. But now you have to excuse me for a while, due to this brocade some rashes have appeared."

He smiled, but before going away, I checked his temperature once again, and it is ninety nine degree Celsius. That gave me greatest respite, his progress towards normalcy.

Last evening when I have called Tia's *Didai* amidst her rant of abuses and accusations to me, she fixed her time of arrival with Tia, of this very afternoon's! So I have to prepare a separate lunch too...

After his breakfast doctor arrived. All of sudden blessed me, on account of Debobroto's care taken by me. "*Beta,* you will make your man, and everyone happy, when you will go to your in laws. You have a compassionate heart."

I smiled faintly at this, as this is never going to happen, yet respecting the blessing of an elderly, I kept my silence. He went away after giving strict orders of rest, to him...

I prepped up myself to set my steps out, to finish my pending tasks, when Debobroto called me in whispers. "Mini come here please..." Agitated on his health, I catered to his request.

I stooped a little over to hear him out, standing beside his bed, but he simply raised his arms to encircle me around in an embrace. I ducked my head in a nick of time and escaped from his attempted hug! The doctor's implications about me and my man, has enticed him.

"Don't overdo yourself Debobroto, it has severe after effects! You will be sick again?" I chided his mischievous self. He looked so cute in his impishness somewhat like Tia, that to punish him for his naughty act. I twisted the tip of his nose slightly and called him besides, a *Dusto chhele* (Naughty Boy).

His mock chide tried to correct my impudence. "Why did you do that?! Where is your honorific? Do you know we have over ten years of age gap between us?"

"Oh really! Then elders should earn their respect too? How about that?"

"I want to earn too, give me a magical hug, just the way I gave it to you, when you were sick?"

"Alright! I will. But only in front of your *Mamoni*, when she will be here in a while." He looked shocked after hearing the news. "She is coming now!?"

"So that scared my lover boy? Huh?" He grinned sheepishly

at me. "No Debobroto! I'm serious, please rest a lot, do that for Tia's sake. It's you, she has got now, as a parent!"

"Why you say so? Aren't you here for her? Won't you look after her Mini, in my absence, tell me honestly?"

"I'm so sorry. I didn't mean that way. Please forgive me. Of course, I will be for her always, till my last breath with whatever might I have."

"Thanks! I know, I could count on you. But where you are off to now, and why you are again in your leggings and tunic shirt? Where's that Red Sari?"

"Debobroto...If I wear that Sari once again, supposedly if have to go out, either I will be attacked by a mad charging bull, or people of this house, will connote, that an anticipated future is making me salivate?!"

"Stop your jokes Mini! I didn't know that a disconsolate girl who came to us, have such a funny side? Where your laugh was hiding? And salivate as much you like, because I'm with you for that luscious future." His jolly self exhibited grins for my squib on refusal in wearing a Sari, on my deflated hope.

"For the past four years, when I couldn't afford to smile, so how could I afford a luxury like a laugh. Probably all those submerged and subsided humors, are surfacing out suddenly in light, due to someone here. And our future, Que sera sera?"

He gazed at me with so much understanding, that I simply stood there static in awe, while affixing my affectionate gazes at him. His curiosity queried. "But where you are off too, tell me that at least?"

"Oh, that! This lovely nurse is going to give this naughty boy, an Eau-de-toilette sponge bath, for the body temperature to soothe. So to prepare that..."

"Really? I'm salivating for that! It seems I should make myself sick, more often."

"Oh no! Don't look so happy, you are not so blessed, it's only your neck and arm's area, understand? Or if you are resolute in having a thorough sponge bath. I will request your *Mamoni* to do that?"

He put his hands together to beg for a mercy! "No! Please for God's sake Mini, I'm sorry, don't be so naughty." An exhilarated laugh danced all over his face then. "Debobroto be happy like that always, no matter what. Oh! You are looking so super cute now, that I'm tempted to k...you! "

"Go ahead, be my house guest." Once again, I provoked his passion like earlier, in our hug's day...And as if I'm bound to oblige him, tip toeing on my feet, I bent a little over his face, and slightly kissed him on his right cheek! The friction of my lips aroused some unruly desires into him, and his eyes expressed them. But he remained in his controlled self just for my honor and sake. To ease up the tensed environment, he took a refuge to his friend...he teases. "Only this much. Are you some kind of bird who is pecking on a seed? You are a real miser! Do you know that?"

"I have to be frugal. This much only your BFF can afford for now. All right, I will come after a while then?" I murmured.

I scolded myself for my rueful act. *"Foolish girl! Get a hold to your temptation!"* I stride past from there quietly with a beautiful feeling inside, as this is my first peck of my un-kissed life!

A gust of chaos and anger came along with Mrs. Banerjee in the noon, but as Tia is the only one who have filled my vision and senses, so I didn't pay much heed to her

*Didai's* lambasting projected at me! Instead settling latter in the living area with refreshments and Mira by her side, to attend her needs. I scooped my Tia into arms, and together, we went to Debobroto's room...

She jumped out of my arms and ran to her *Baba.* Both of them are hugging and talking to each other at the same time. Effervesce is only one, who is present there. I'm drawn to this warm and loving moment of these two, so much of the persons, I love the most, after my *Baba* and *Ma,* that I forgot to foresee a cyclone is waiting for me to ambush, in the form of Tia's *Didai*! She rushed in there with a trail of her accusations to my imaginary crimes, to barge into my pleasant moment, into the sanity of the household, with a resolution to ruin it, in every possible way! I have to cover Tia's ears with both of my hands as I don't want her innocent and sensitive mind to poison further! It was my futile attempt, Tia's *Didai* is hell-bent to go on with her angry rants, even in front of her granddaughter. As it will not be wise for the little child to remain there any longer, so I crooned at the latter. "Dear, go to your room. *Masimoni* will be there after a while. Okay, sweetie! When Tia and I have lotta to talk about. Yes, go on, that's my girl." When I made myself sure that she is out of that disturbing arena. I closed the door of Debobroto's room silently...

Mrs. Banerjee prated. "*Aijey meye,* sending Tia will not stop me! Why you are here? Why you have come back to torture us? Where is your self-pride for your parents, now? Why you are in this murderess's house? Why making Debobroto and Tia's life hell? Why don't you just die, like your parents? Why don't you??" She fumed in an uncontrollable rage!

Debobroto tried to intervene but due to his weak body, he fell back into his pillows, that is enough for me to act, before it will go out of my hand!

When an elderly lady did not have enough tact or thoughtfulness, on how to behave in front of a patient, in front of a little child, then I, decades younger than her, have to prevent the calamity as my utmost duty, before it crosses it's extreme! I stood at his side aggressively, in front of her, to stroke his head gently, and to say tenderly. "Debobroto don't get so agitated, please, for my sake dear! She meant no harm, let me handle it. Trust your Mini for this time, please. Will you do this!?" He gave a gentle nod of approval.

I directed to Mrs. Banerjee then, as politely, as softly as possible, without ignoring my reverence to her, without pushing aside my patience. "Mrs. Banerjee for sake of Debobroto and Tia's happiness, please lower your voice down. Please think, how Tia's reactions will be, after seeing you like this, and please don't agitate him any further, he is very ill. Please, don't be so inhumane to Tia and to him, please, I beg of you! Scold me as much as you want, but not here, out of this room, please!"

"You don't have to beg, or to direct, where I should go, to say my says, when this is my late daughter's house too, and Debobroto is my son-in-law still, Tia, my grand daughter! But who you are to me? Nobody, nothing to me! I will go when you will answer my questions. Do you understand me?? You sly girl! What sudden fake love, you are showing to my Debo? What treacherous intention is hidden inside your heart, while you have come here again? Answer me, right now!"

Answering her regurgitation seems to be my last resort, to clear the matter, and I'm doing this only for the sake of my love, for him and Tia. I put before her my honest assessment about me, my heart's sooth, and my candor.

"Mrs. Banerjee, you want my answers. I will try to give them one by one. I will answer about all my intentions. First, about my dying, I wish I can die, but I can't. It seems, God, has other plans for me. I'm here for Debobroto and Tia, and I admit, I love them the most, from my heart and soul, and I can't live without them either. Please, forgive this *badmaish, dusto meye*, for that… That day, I was blinded with so much grief, that I forgot that you had lost your dear daughter too. *But I have forgiven her*. I'm forgiving Shamita for all her sins, please believe me, it's as true as the rays of the Sun. I have forgiven her from the bottom of my heart, and it's possible only because of my *Baba* and *Ma*'s upbringing and teachings of good values. They would never want me to hate the sinner for his sins, but they would want me to condemn sin! I realized something that's how by loving Tia, I love her mother in a way also. Tia is her part of flesh and blood too. If I keep stoking the fire of hatred like this, then a criminal and I will be in a same frame, in a same footing. I don't want to sin or do any wrong to anyone. I don't want to become an avenger, not any more. I know, it's your house, and will remain so, even God can't take that authority from you. I'm here only to love Debobroto and Tia unconditionally, this much greed I have hidden inside my heart. Please believe me, and now I'm going to see Tia, please consider about my forgiveness, and from now on, please try to think this sly girl, as your other daughter too…"

And before I can go to Tia, she just pushed me very rudely to march past me, while banging the door wide open. She went away outside. Only my sad face and a deep sigh remained there, in that room as a reward for my honest heart, for my selfless motive, along with my love, along with my Debobroto's ailing body. I went to his side quickly to keep my hand on his forehead, when I saw his silent tears of pathos rolling down from his cheeks. I composed him with my consoling words.

"Hush, hush…What are you doing? Like this you will be more sick! I'm so sorry, this has happened at the time of your sickness! I don't know why, I could not able to held back any longer, any of my true emotions? I exploded once again with my mind and heart's candor before her!"

"If for once Mini, I can touch your feet!"

"Hey! Don't be like that please. Why you will touch my feet? When you are older than me. It's a bad omen. It will affect your longevity. Please don't cry. You need to keep that stamina of yours for your wellness, and for Tia's sake…Oh dear! Okay, do you want to cry on my shoulder?" He shook his head in denial but pleaded for something else, which he longed for earlier. "How about giving me a BFF's hug at least?"

"Sure, why not? But this big hug is not from your BFF, but from your would be wife!"

I hugged his sagging body generously, without being miserly of which I have been accused of…For my bountiful hug. I screwed my warm arms around him, so he can beam to that liberal hug. My declaration of becoming his wife, glowed his face, his tears couldn't able to obscure his immense elation!

"Thank you…thank you so much, my angel Mini, for loving me, and Tia this much! I love you so much Mini, you are one tender hearted girl, besides my brave, kind, and one of a kind Sunshine girl! So without any delay let's get married!"

I said in my cheerful tone to support his wedding cheer. "Yes, let's marry."

"Oh Mini! Really? You made my day! Then ask me three times. To make it official!"

"Alright! Will you marry me? Will you marry me? Will you marry me?"

"Yes! Yes! Yes!" His effervesce bubbled out, while accepting the proposal.

"So now, we are Man and Wife!" I concluded while making our ceremony official!

We both laughed at our own puerile invention of this ritual. I wiped off the rest of his tears from the face, and very gently stroked his head for a couple of moments more. Then remembering something, he said excitedly. "Mini, that twirling of pasta to facing side, did the magic, I will eat pasta daily from now on!" I laughed at his cuteness but something abashed me, and made me restless. I poured out my heart to him, to my congenial Debobroto.

"But I have angered your *Mamoni*...I'm worried on my audaciousness in front of her. I did that wrong. Do you think, she will forgive me in future for that?! Please don't stare blankly at me, scold me if you want to, box my ears sharply, for my wrong doings, if you want to...I know I have messed up with my mouth again!"

"Scold you Mini! You! Then, that would be like castigating our dear God! And you did, what I should have done in the first place. It's my house still, and the insults hurled against you, were totally unjust and uncalled for, and by doing this, she insulted me indirectly.

Just remember that. She was insulting you since long, knowing my weakness due to the reverence and fear for her heart ailment. That's her emotional blackmail! You fought an honest fight, for me and for Tia's welfare. Now, how about giving me a K...then Mini, for messing up my heart, or I will box your ears for certain!"

I winked waggishly at him, and to revere to his fervent request I threw him a flying kiss, he caught it instantly, my blowing kiss, while winking me back with same zest. "Okay! enough of this. Tia is all alone in her room, and we can have our heart to heart, later. How about that?" He simply nodded his head slightly to concord on this…

At Tia's room, I smiled softly at that framed picture of her with her mother and father, without having any spite for Shamita. While I stroked at former's little, resting head on the bed. In between that, she asked me.

"Why *Didai* has scolded you?!"

"Oh! You heard then. Tia, she didn't scold me, but as she loves me, that's why to make me realize my mistakes, she did that! It was for my own good, dear!"

"*Masimoni*? Can I tell you something then?"

"Yes sweetheart, certainly. Listen sweetie, never ever hide anything either to me, or to your *Baba*. Please remember that dear!"

"Okay!" And we shook our hands to form an unbreakable pact.

She queried further. "You love *Baba*. Don't you?!"

"How do you know that?!" Bewildered I asked, because I know she has very observant eyes. "*Baba* told me!"

"Did he?? When??!"

"When on that day, you left us, that night *Baba* was crying in his room. I peaked in to ask him about the reason of his crying and he said to me…*Tia, my sweet daughter, I love your Masimoni so much, and your Masimoni, me too, yet she doesn't want to marry me, and refused either to become my wife or your Ma!* After learning this, I wept along with my *Baba*, all that night!"

Those simple words of an innocent child, have such heart-rending power to move me, that my sadden heart wept blood tears for her, for her *Baba*, for their heart-felt love for me. I hugged that sweet child tightly, in an apology, for hurting her, and smothered down her cheeks with my kisses, and she giggled hard in response to that. "*Masimoni*...you are tickling me so much!"

"Tia, cutie? Can I ask you a favor? Think about it, then tell me something? Do you really want your *Masimoni* to become your *Ma*, tell me honestly dear? Without any fear of scolding. Your honest answer is life or death to me!"

"Yes, I want you to be my *Ma*...as I don't have any, when my other friends have their mothers. I want you really to be my mother, when I love you, so so much!"

"Thank you dear, I love you too too much as well, bless your dear heart!

Thank you sweetie, then let me become your *Ma*. But for that Tia has to say *Ma* three times!" We both laughed heartily at the idea. So re-commencing our ritual of making our relationship solemn, she called me three times in a sweeter name of this entire universe. "*Ma...Ma...Ma!*"

"I'm officially Tia's *Ma!*" Our overwhelm danced, and to jubilate more, we decided to surprise her *Baba* with something at the dinner time! She twinkled at the idea, and we both giggled hard for our secret plan!

I served Debobroto, his lunch and afterwards gave his medicines, but sadly, the vanity of Tia's *Didai* on accepting my forgiveness, forbade her to eat my cooked lunch, and she headed for her home, leaving the prepared food untouched, which I made with such care while including all her favorite items. But sometimes you can't win everyone's heart...

After that, I checked his fever, and the thermometer showed normal temperature, to my utter relief and delight! "Oh! Thank you God, *Baba* and *Ma!* I'm so happy!" Whispering my thankfulness through my upturned face, I stretched my hands up in the air.

"Oh Debobroto! It's normal, your temperature, your fever has gone, dear!"

I spun my legs and jigged in my joyous enjoyment for a while, for him. Awed at my effervescent sight, he tried to be up too.

But I chided him in my strictest tone to remain in his bed. "NO! Not yet...it will be fatal then, take your rest. You need more rest and nourishment now, and only after the doctor's nodding of a *Yes*, you can finally be up from here. Now just sleep. And don't worry, I will check you in the evening, and now I must go to Tia. Here's your mobile, give me a miscall. I'm just my lover's call away!"

I winked at him and placed his mobile beside his bedside. He winked back at me, and while grinning he threw me a flying kiss. I simply pounced on it, to catch. Then we both grinned at each other for a while, then seeing his happy yet exhausted eyes, falling into a sleep, I closed the door quietly...

I went for Tia's lunch, and we had a quiet lunch together. Finishing that, I tucked and kissed her for the afternoon nap, after that I peeked inside her *Baba*'s room. A serene smile played on my face, for both Tia, and her *Baba*'s peaceful, sleeping heads...

I busied myself for the evening fare and dinner. In the evening, I sent Tia out to play with Mira in the garden, to have a fresh evening air. For moments I watched them, then went to finish my pending chores...During that time Debobroto's miscall came. I glided up, past the flight of stairs to his room in a hurry. "Yes? Are you alright dear? Please tell me? What is it?"

His hesitant self said in a reluctance. "Mini... it's that, I need to go to the restroom. I think it's enough of my using those urine pots and bed pan, that you have carried to and forth. "

"Oh that! I will help you to go there, just slip your arms around my waist from behind, for the support, Okay? And together we will trot along there, and then I will close the door, and wait for you to call me with my baited breath. I promise, a no peek-a-boo from my side." His agreeing laugh laughed, crooning he asked. "Mini..." While we waddled in our tiny little steps, while his arms are around my waist, my back against his chest. "But, what's this been called?!" His intrigue is still there in his infirmity, in knowing the name of our sensational touch! He wants to learn....

what her love, thinks about her first experience? "Oh, this! It's called a Behind Hug!" I tried my level best to satisfy his intrigue, while phrasing an apt name, the way I have coined for those earlier ones.

"Is it?!" His breath is getting heavier due to our sensory touch, and for exhaustion of his swooning body. He whispered passionately. "Thank you so much sweetheart. Thank you for coming into my life."

"*Hoon!*" One mere word only escaped, as my brimming emotions has witnessed his tear-jerking emotions then, thereby they stuck into my throat to answer further.

I know, he is finished as I heard the noise of his flush button, from outside the door, I just called out. "Debobroto! Are you decent enough? Can I come in, to put you back to your bed. Can I?!"

"Yes Mini, come in." I heard his hush-toned murmur. He leaned against the tiled wall beside the wash basin counter. That agitated me. "What is it?! Are you feeling giddy?"

"No, just a little weak. Can you help me out, to wash off my hands?"

"Why not, sure? Just grab this edge of the counter of the basin, yes, like that. And now give me that right hand...yes... and then the left one... yes. Let me rub them a little, now, let me rinse off the soapy foam from them...yes, that's it... And now how about patting them dry with a hand towel and...how about leaning on my shoulder a little again, while I scrub your face and neck with this face-wash...yes, there you are. Now a rinse, let me pat it dry too. Voila! Wow! Who is this majestic looking refreshing handsome man?! Is it you Debobroto?" I smiled sweetly at his reflection of the mirror, he clutched me from behind more, to hug me passionately. "Thank you Mini, thank you my God-sent angel. Thank you." His few pouring tears dropped on my shoulder to soak my T-shirt wet, to soak my heart with his pouring love. It is heart wrenching enough to see him like this. My heart simply crumpled into a ball.

"Hush there, now don't cry. Alright? So much emotion is not good for your present washed out body. Tell me are you feeling much better now?"

I looked at his nod of agreement from the mirror, so I added further my suggestion. "Then let's go, and change into some fresh clothes, while sitting on the chair, inside your walk-in-closet. How about that? I don't want you to be in your stale clothes. I will gather your things out of the closet for your convenience. And will be waiting right outside with a promise that I won't look in, no matter how tempted I will be! Do you trust me?" I saw his flashing grin. I turned my back for him to do what I have suggested...

"Mini, I have changed my clothes. I'm decent enough. You can turn around."

Then supporting him I put my one arm behind his waist, and he put one on mine's, this way I helped him to lie down there on the couch, covered his supine body with a warm comforter, while placing his head in a comfortable position on the cushions. Whilst he rested there. I rushed to strip off his stale and musty bed sheet, pillow covers and duvet cover. After changing all of them into fresh ones. I whispered to his ears, that I will be in a jiffy after putting all those dirty linens and clothes in the laundry room…

My content and attentive eyes during this, can see from the window, how cheerful Mira and Tia are at their Catch-a-Ball play, while I washed my hands from the kitchen tap.

In the meantime, I thought this is the right time for his evening tray and medicines before turning to Tia…I darted from the kitchen to his room while holding a tray full of nosh. I placed the tray on the table, and insisted him to have something for the medicines sake, he obliged. He nibbled on fruit and veg sandwiches, then tasted slices of date, plum, and walnut cake, and drowning them with a tall glass of pomegranate juice, he has finished his fare. When he is about to lie down once again, when I gurgled a laugh at his pomegranate tinted red mustache, which has been crafted on his upper lip, while sipping the juice. His astonish at my sudden humor, queried.

"What is it Mini? What happened? Am I not handsome, any more?!"

"You are still, but now you have a grown funny mustache, and is looking like a kid!" My unstoppable humor replied while bending close to his face, to wipe off his mustache with the napkin. "There, it's much better now."

When suddenly amid my act, he grabbed both of my hands, to stroke their backs rapidly with his thumbs. My stomach knotted because of the tingling friction generated by his strokes, a riot of wild sensations broke loose due to that, his akin feelings made his eyes turn into a different color, to reflect his untamed desire. My throaty voice requested him fervently. "Oh Debobroto!

Please stop this, my nerves are getting unsteady, for that unfamiliar feeling of passion." I blushed hard in inhibition, and my emotions heaved heavily along. "Mini! You are very frank, nothing escapes from your straightforward mouth?" He, and his not so long expression of desire, relaxed into a smile then, leaving my hands, his sincere tone begin again, to say something, to initiate a life-long promise to love, rely, and trust each other, on our decision to commit ourselves whole-heartedly, to respect our sacred relationship. "You have full faith on me, Mini? Don't you?"

"Yes silly, more than myself!"

"Thank you so much. Then, let's get married next week, there must be some auspicious date. I'm sure of that!"

"Coming week?! But for that you have to be well again. Don't rush, wait a little more for such things. Don't we need some time, for the arrangements?"

"How about next to next week, then?"

"Alright! Suits me fine. Consult someone for the auspicious date. What I'm going to lose, all I have to do is, marry you? As every burden of the ceremony will be on your sole strong shoulders, my Hercules!"

"Yes, for the love of Xena I will manage! But are you very scared of all this, Mini?"

"Yes a little bit, but don't worry. I don't have a commitment denial syndrome, that includes our pre and post nuptial commitments, so I'm not going to retract from either marrying you, or from my duties of making our relationship strong!"

"That's such a relief to know. I'm overwhelmed to find you as my love Mini. I know you will be honest with your relationships. Don't be so scared, I'm here to guide you, to love you, in good and bad times...when we belong to each other. But if simply put, to make our body and soul into one, we need a legal and social stamp in form of marriage. Alright?"

"Yes, I know that, and understood what you are conveying to me, that's why I'm relying on my love for everything."

"Then, it's a pact now. How about shaking our hands in sealing, this deal?!"

"No way! I don't want to fall into your biology tutorials, once again."

"Mini, you are something. Okay, let me have my medicines, and go then."

I did. We exchanged our happy grins before I succor him to the bed back again. Once again placing the mobile on the bedside table, I wrapped him well with the comforter...My fluttering heart stepped outside the room after that. Once outside, I skipped my happy feet a little, for my prospect of the coming marriage. With that exhilarated feeling, I went out in the garden to call a flushed Tia and Mira by the exercise... Former cooled her off with the both juice glasses of black grape and pomegranate, and her famished self noshed the chunks of cake and sandwiches at her heart's content. I felt my stomach being full without eating anything at all, because of her content smile, because of Debobroto's recuperation, because I'm being with him and her!

It's near about dinner time, the time to give him a surprise, as being planned by Tia and me. Thereby to set a dining arrangement in Debobroto's room, I requested Mira and Shefali to give their kind assistance. They, along with me, pulled the coffee table and two leather poufs alongside his bedside, so that while he have his, at the folding table on the bed, we can have ours to this recently arranged placement. The setting looked snug and lovely as well, that my eyes glowed in a fascination.

He caught both the re-furbished setting of his room, and the afterglow of my eyes, he asked through his usual intrigue. "What's this all of a sudden, Mini?!" My sheepish looks and meek voice, evaded a bit, as I have not taken the permission, before invading his privacy. "Ah, this! It's a surprise for us. We are so bored, and is dying to have some dashing person's company, to brighten up our dreary meal times. So to have that. So my lord, will you dine with two bright eyed ladies here?…Oh! You are annoyed with this arrangement of intrusion in your solitary? I can tell by the look of your eyes. Are you really? Tell me honestly. I thought, Tia stayed away from you for so long, you hardly have seen her. I know, how you must have been missing her, like she must have missed you. So just to celebrate this bonding, I thought of this. Of course this will be a discomfit to you, as I'm joining too, but I'm helpless, because I have to struggle with Tia, she always screws up her nose, the minute the veggies are placed on her plate, so just to accompany her for that purpose. If you tell me, straight faced, I will not be around here. I will amend my mistakes right now, I will not bother you, and will leave both of you in your conviviality. Please tell me, honestly." I finished my rambles in one go, and his patience listened, even contemplated on each of my utterances, before replying in his mellowed voice.

"Ah! Don't be so absurd, I will simply love you to join us, and when you are going to be my wife, so to maintain the decorum of this house, the need to learn about the real ways of an etiquette, about having a dinner with this lord, my lady!" His mirth took my intrusion lightly, to relieve me. So I quipped. "Thou art so kind Sir. Oh! You are making me really nervous. What should I do, now?"

"Why? Do you eat like a wild boar?"

"Are you kidding me? On the contrary, I even use fork and knife for *Gulab jamuns*, and chopsticks for *Sandesh*!" My metaphor humored him. But this time I'm not in my mirth, instead my serious side illuminated a stark truth of myself and my finesse. If I can boast of something which I seldom do, then it will be the dexterity in my eating habits. Nobody can beat me in this. "Really?!" His incredulous looked amused. "I never knew that you are so temperamental about this!?"

"I'm serious about this time, it's not my humor, you have never seen me, how I had dined before, did you? I was the real Queenie in my days, I used to turn my nose, if something unladylike, or brutish ever happened before me!"

An astonished Debobroto exclaimed. "Oh my God! Is that so? How your parents and friends, put up with you then? Mini, now you are making me real scared! Oh! That's why you were eating your Pasta like that? So using knife and fork for a Burger was not a tease, in that amusement park café!?"

His light reply for this grave fact somehow tickled my subdued lava of my poignant emotions, they erupted right before him, before his congeniality, before his compassionate heart…"Didn't God has punished me enough for my parent's cosseted nature towards me? Their pamper towards me?! For that, I lived in a haze of a bliss! When that was cleared away. I found myself all alone, my dearest parents were gone for life, leaving me as an ignorant, about the hardships and harsh cruelties of the reality!? I alone know how scary my days were?! All those years, this once a rich girl, who was surrounded by luxuries and gadgets had to wash her things with her hand, had to scrub vessels, and her rented flat's floor! In the beginning, I simply cried for days as I didn't know how to do all those things, which my maid used to do that for me...I cried while nibbling my sole sandwich, while walking past by all those fancy restaurants where I, with my parents, used to spend their gaiety times together...Do you understand, how hard it was for this Queenie to mold into a destitute girl? I, who threw my clothes to rubbish bin after wearing them once or twice, scrimped monies from my earnings, to buy an outfit from a discount sale, for making myself decent, and agreeable? Do you understand? What I'm talking about? Oh Debobroto! That was really hard... You know something, I was so intimidated by being alone in the city as a girl that, I used to fix the railings of the chair to the door knob in my flat, in a fear that somebody would break into, for... You know, what I'm talking about, while I sleep. I was so scared to death, while returning home from office in the dun of the evening! I, who used Christion-Dior is using a deodorant spray! Do you have any idea, how it felt for a brand conscious, Fashionista, teen girl, not to touch, one bit of make-up? I walked in the streets miles, got squeezed in public transports, when I never had been out without my car with a driver. I, who slept in my air-conditioned room, slept in my hot, burning, airless suffocating room...I cried for my tormented hardships, but I never begged for help, nor get trapped into a lure of indecency for those bit of comforts. I continued with zeal, my constant fight for survival, while keeping my body and soul pious, to retain honesty and truth intact, to be a good girl, what my *Baba* and *Ma* always wanted me to be! And for that, yes, I worked hard and remained an honest, healthy, hardworking, and a very good girl, all those years, with my tenaciousness. I'm really proud of my accomplishments, as nobody came to my rescue, to teach me, or guide me. I taught myself all extravagant lessons of adaptability in life. I tried to create a niche of my own, in this overcrowded world by using my gray cells...It might sound silly, but do you know, during my angry days, how I used to dance for hours like a crazy? I skidded, glided, slid and skipped, with my own choreographed dance movements, while remembering my learnt steps, till I collapse on the floor, so that all my pain could flow out to evaporate...That day, when I was out of my last job, with my last paycheck in my hand, I shivered in the bitter wind while standing in the road, when I saw a dead dog, due to starvation, freezing cold, and that horrid sight...was enough to tremble me in horror! My petrified self thought, perhaps that would soon going to happen to me, as well. I would be dead like that, out in the street, but just then...God must have pitied me. He answered my prayer, and a ray of hope was sent, in the form of a stranded newspaper, and with an advert on it! Your advert! And that paper, I'm sure was left by God Himself for me. Oh! Believe me, you are my answer to my prayer! I just wished, if you could come earlier for that younger Minisha, when she was just turning eighteen. Then I wouldn't have to be all alone and scared, being naive about the world in my nineteenth year. Why didn't you search for me?! Why didn't you combed for your Mini?! Your timely search could have saved me from the torments, which I had faced. Tell me, where have you been hiding?! I would think could become your teen bride? Why didn't you come to seek for me? Tell me? Oh! What's the use, crying over the spilt milk now...Well, it's long gone now, I'm happy with you and Tia. Let's enjoy the present, and our future! Right?" Once again my downpour of ramblings are finished, but this time through my withered down heart, through plaintive cry, for my dreadful memories. And to find solace, to my piteous state, I hugged him fiercely, to melt him in my crumbling hug. He stroked my head gently to pacify me. It seems my poignancy have afflicted him so much, that he mourned in my melancholy too. Then slowly, his holding arms came around me, and they pulled my legs on the bed, so that, I can rest well, against his slouching body, and without any inhibition, I rested over him, to snuggle my grief-stricken body. And my nose after sniffing his familiar potent masculine scent, from his crook of the neck revived, my frail energy...We both lay there simply into one another arms, with our nestling bodies as consolations. His soothing voice crooned. "Hush, hush Mini, I know how traumatic your situations were! But now everything will be alright once again, you don't have to endure any more pain from now on, when I'm here for you, for always! Please don't cry...believe me, I didn't know, you were there for me, otherwise I would have married you then, when you were eighteen, even if, for that, I would have to elope with my would-be teen bride!?"

"What? How could you do that? You were married by then, how could you marry me?? Seriously! That could have made you an adulterous, bigamist! Do you know that?" I tried to find some humor into my pain, a rainbow through tears, my dazzling smile succeeded, because he chortled too.

"Yes! Mini, it was real difficult for you to become an indigent one all of a sudden from a rich girl. And then striving along to brush up with the elite milieu."

My response sighed deeply to agree with his word to word.

"Alright, Mini...about the song you sang during our drive. Where you have learnt to sing like that?"

His trait of diversion from one topic to another, reflected again, but this time I'm not annoyed as he did it, for my benevolence. I need to be gladdened up. "From a very reputable teacher, who is very close to me." My twinkles whispered.

"Who?! Whom you are so close, all of a sudden?? Who taught you to sing like an opera singer?" His possessiveness made him unquiet. "Relax, this drooling lady of yours has taught herself. I practiced for days to get a perfect pitch."

In his drawling voice, he complimented me, his heart oozed out so much love, that I drenched in it, besides treasuring each of his beautiful words in my heart. "Really?! You taught yourself then so many things, from cooking, singing, struggling, earning money...you dance superbly, you can drive, although it needs a bit of polishing, you can design so well...you fight like a prosecutor, you have a temper to match your combat...you are lovely, smart, honest, thoughtful, a kind girl, with a heart of gold, and with an immense power of strong willingness, and you have a great taste of style, coupled with a great sense of humor...I'm really one very lucky guy, who have found you finally!"

I snickered. "Yes! Don't you feel blessed, that I'm a resourceful, full- packaged girl?"

"Yes, I'm blessed, you are indeed my answer to my prayer too!"

He cuddled more of my curled body, into his arms, to give me another warm hug of his. Then he fondled my upper and lower back, rapidly with his hand, then ran his long fingers into my curls, to caress my scalp with smooth circular strokes. His such caresses, are unknown to me, yet my feeling is familiar one, they not only composed my trembling emotions of agony, but side by side something surfaced out too, a ruckus of deep down wild passions once again. It is a very tenuous moment for me, in due course of time, he became so impetuous, that he started stroking the contours of my face with his thumb, brushing them with swift strokes, and then he stroked my lips with his thumb, then he began thrusting them, and kept on doing this, for so long, till my lips became apart in gasping delight...his furnace like hot breaths fell on my face, and his eyes started changing their color...they turned smoky for a passionate fire. All this, is making me, heedless like him, to do something rueful at that moment, but to escape from this captivity of untamed wildness. I cautioned him in my throaty voice..."Now, let me go. Shefali and Mira will be in a shock, if they caught me in our love act, in our secret love cove, with their master like this!"

"Will they? Then how about adding a dash of spice, in our secret love? How about allowing this master to 'K' you now? Huh?"

"No you can't, not until we stamped that seal on our pact. I trust you, but that doesn't mean, I'm a total nitwit."

"Oh really! Mini, nobody can knock you down for sure. Go then, bring Tia along, before something shocking really does happen here, in our cove. And Mini, I love you, so so much."

"I love you very very much too, but I'm famished, so do you and Tia, so we love to have our dinner so so much, very very much as well!" With that our fountain of hilarity tinkled then.

It's for the second time that I'm having my meal with Tia and him, together. During our course of the meal, we chatted, laughed, pulled each others leg to make fun at each other.

We enjoyed our food, most of all, the feeling that we belong to each each other! It's one of the best time we are having in our lives. A curious Tia said during our tête-à-tête. "*Ma*, do I have to eat all the vegetables, and have to drink milk as well, when you will be my real *Ma*?!"

"Yes, I'm afraid so, you have to, no matter how difficult it will be, for you!

It will give you stimulants, just how Popeye used to get his, by eating his spinach? Tia, I know you will think *Ma* is being hard on you, but you have to love and respect your *Baba*, the privileges you are given dear. There are so many under-privileged ones out there, who for a bite of morsel, do very regrettable things, dear! Please respect God's love and blessings sweetie.

I'm not scolding you at all, it's my hard core experience of life, which is talking, and I want to share this to my dear daughter. Okay, dear, now tell me are you angry at me? Will you make your *Baba* and *Ma* very happy, by eating a lot, resting a lot, playing a lot, and by faring well in the school?!"

"Yes, I will! I'm not angry. I know all about under-privileged ones, many NGO's come to our school, for student's contributions. I know all that stuff *Ma*. I will try my best to be your good daughter!"

"Really?! My dear daughter. Oh! My Tia, you made so happy! How you have become all grown up? Oh, how time flies? Tia come here sweetie, hug me, and let me kiss your cheek too."

"Mini, why are you kissing her?!" He was witnessing our bond for so long, but suddenly breaking his silence, he interrupted me, to flabbergast!

"What happened? Did I do something wrong here? Why you are looking at me, like that?!"

"Because you have fulfilled your duty as a mother, but how about me??"

"Ah! You are still brooding on that thing, really Debobroto… Tia, let's go to your room, to wash hands, and say Goodnight to *Baba*. I'm going to tuck you in, after that I will clear a few things here. Okay?"

"*Ma*…I love you!" She hung her tiny arms around my neck, by clasping them lovingly.

"I love you too, so how about a piggy back ride to your room. Hop on my back, and let's go then. Where my princess Tia would like to go, to her magical fairy land?!"

"Yes…*Baba* goodnight!" From my back she chimed, her father gave a happy nod before wishing her too. "Yes, Goodnight my teddy, sleep tight!"

We went outside the room while leaving her pouting father there, for my reluctant kiss to him…I helped her to change into her night clothes, to brush her teeth. While I'm tucking her in, she fell asleep instantly, so except for the night light, I switched off the all the lights…Then I ran downstairs to call Mira and Shefali for them to help me, to clear out all the dinner things from his room. We placed the poufs and the table back to their original place, and capped off my errand…I gave Debobroto his medicines, and all those, I did systematically like a machine, and about to switch off the lamp in the room also…when my diamond locket peeped out from my T-shirt to swing forward, I put it back in again, while doing that, I saw his eyes, motioning me to sit beside him on the bed. I sat at the edge, on the foot of the bed, while being wary, as he looked suddenly strange, in the feeble light of the lamp!

"What is it, Debobroto? Are you feeling really sick? Is the

sickness has relapsed? Please tell me!" A panic gripped me to learn the cause. "No silly! I'm all good."

"Then, what is it? Did I say to Tia something revolting, to upset you? I'm so sorry for that, I'm always the preachy type, she is your daughter too, please intervene from now on also to mend my mistakes!"

"Why you say so? You haven't said anything wrong or provocative. You love her wholeheartedly. I know, you will do what's best for her, too!"

"Then, what is it? You are okay, and what I said to Tia, that's been okay too. Then, what's left there? I can't quite follow you."

"Come near, to follow me."

"What? Why?" I distanced myself a little farther from him.

"Let me look at your diamond Neckpiece."

"Oh, that! You seriously scared me just now."

"Did I, to my Ninja?"

" Yes... You did!"

" Who gave you that?"

"My *Ma*, at my nineteenth birthday."

"You still miss your Parents a lot. Don't you?"

"Yes, a whole lot. Other than that, what else can I do? Now go to sleep. It's getting rather late, right? SOS me, through your mobile, if you need anything. My mobile and my eyes will be switched on, for that." I smiled at him, but he is not in his convincing mood, of leaving me at all. I sunk in my sea of confusions, as he keeps staring real hard at me with his midnight dark cool gaze. "Debobroto is something wrong? Do you regret now, that we are getting married? Is all that's about?!"

"No! I will die without you!"

"Then... What are you meditating on, so much??"

" YOU!"

"Me??! Why??"

"I don't know Mini, but I feel so heavenly seeing you by my side. I want you to stay like that, all the time. Your absence even if it is for a fraction of a moment, yet it kills me. Every single thing you have done for me and Tia, moved my heart so much, that without your presence, it's getting to me unbearable even to breathe."

"Oh, that! What's there to worry about? When I'm all yours." "Is it? Then how about giving me a 'K'?!"

"I should have known about my blabber mouth, and the thing that's haunting your mind so much!" For constancy for that whim, his eyes twinkled, and I sighed for his insistence. Only to pacify his sick body, I gave a soft kiss, with the full pressure of my lips on his cheek. "Now go to sleep. You had your Goodnight kiss, just now!"

"But I'm an adult, that was only a chaste kiss and not stimulating enough for me, to become a Popeye!"

"You are awful. Look, if you still do this, I promise you, I will go away, in the morning. Do you want that?!"

"You know, what I want? Come here, give me a kiss, like a good girl, this will not blemish your morals. It's alright if you kiss, please come closer to me...demonstration of love is also a way to define love, Mini!"

He became so adamant about this, that he sat up in the bed with whatever strength he has! And claimed my one upper arm, while placing his other arm around me, he pulled me to his chest area, his inflexible grips seized me real hard! All this happened so fast, that I didn't get enough time to escape from his shackle of love. Then he leaned over my face, his lips touched mine slightly, almost like brushing…At first, he kissed slightly so not to scare me, but no matter how slight it is, that collided touch of ours, leashed out a wild beast of passion into him…Slowly he pushed my lips back, and gave few short, quick kisses on my lips, one by one. Then his lips pushed back again on mine tenderly, and they just remained there for a long time, for a long kiss. It is such a long and intense kiss, that it has drawn out my whole breath, and then, his mouth started getting more and more demanding with its passionate smooching, and due to that, little muffled sounds escaped from my throat, that must have excited him, because his demanding lips, continued getting so hard over mine, that my whole breath is sucked out by him. I tried to free them, but he controlled them, so fiercely, that I became really afraid of his, enraptured supremacy on me. And then he bit my bottom lip by a very slight pressure of his teeth, it felt, as if I'm stung with a bee sting. That's the very point of my resistance, I pushed my hand against his chest hard, to release myself from his grip! I became successful in doing that also. I took gasps of air. My angry self for his sudden, coarse behavior ignored the sweet aftertaste of his kissing, which lingered on my tingling lips. Through my uneven breathing, I scorned at him in odium.

"Why you behaved like a brute, all of a sudden? Why did you do that to me?! What are you trying to do? Have you had any idea? I'm going away for sure tomorrow, and I won't come here, even if you SOS me!" I became nonplussed at his rude attitude!

And he looked sheepish, his apology reasoned his act. "I'm so sorry Mini. I lost my head in your love. But I'm not a brute. It was just one long and sweet kiss from your lover. Please don't leave me. Your hugs are so soft and enchanting, but your lips are more sweet and delicate, that I felt an enraptured feeling. As if being in an euphoria, Mini! I will not bother you, anymore. It's my promise. Okay? Alright, from now on, if you want to come here, come only with Mira?"

"Yes, that's the wisest thing to do."

"Mini, are you really angry? But believe me, I will not repeat this, till our wedding night. I promise. You looked so poignant while remembering your forlorn days, that my heart became restless, and to balm your painful bruises, I did that..." He is right, every time he touches me, my pain, my unsettling nerves and my disquiet of heart, all becomes calm. Yet I snapped, to conceal my recent receptive pleasure. "So that's why you lent your lips to me? Did I ask for that service?"

"So did you like my touch of lips? Or am I such a bad kisser, that my Mini is angry at me?!"

"How do I know? It was my first time. Beside kissing, you were nibbling me. I'm going away...I will come back with Mira, if you need anything. Goodnight then."

"Mini, don't go, being angry. I did wrong, but it was, only an expression of pure love, not lust. Please believe me. And that was just a pressure of my teeth."

"Let me refresh your memory. I told you earlier, and I'm telling you now, I despise being toyed around, and I'm not your plaything. You remember that, and for now go to sleep. You need a rest too."

"Yes, I remember, what you have told me, I will try to remember that in future too. So does my Mini will forgive me? Is there any hope of reconciling? Will she marry me, when she doesn't have any commitment denial syndrome?!" He looked so cute, in apprehension of losing me, in a dark guilt, that I had to suppress a smile. "I will sleep on it!"

He laughed at that even in his guilt-ridden eyes. "Goodnight then, my lovely-tender-honey-coated lips of the Mini." Teases of his are not going to replace his twinges of guilt, I know.

You are simply impossible. Now why did you say that? I will never set a foot again here, not till I become your wedded bride. I'm a head strong girl, nobody can bend my decisions." This I sworn with a disdain, before descending the stairs. I returned to my old room to sleep. But in the middle of the night, I jerked my sleepy head, to check if there are any SOS calls of him, time to time, even after what have happened there…by dawn, I found myself sleeping. I jumped out from the bed for a new day, and then touched my first kissed lips, stung, swollen lips. Surprisingly, that sweet feeling is still lingering on them, a beautiful feeling of my first kiss! It's Sunday morning, I gave him and Tia their respective breakfasts, and all the time Mira was with me, in his room, like a lady-in-waiting. After the breakfast, the doctor came to certify his perfect health and condition, and advised him that by Monday morning he will be well enough to join his office.

In my relieved and rejoiced self, I thanked God once again. And before the doctor, Shefali, Mira, me, and Tia could go to our separate ways, he popped out his concerned inquiry. I wonder, why his sincere looks, looked so playful all of a sudden? I guessed it right, he and his teases. "Doctor, am I good enough to go to the restroom? To downstairs, and so on?"

"Yes, Debobroto. You are perfectly well, and capable do everything...even you can go to your gym for some light exercises, if you want."

"Hmm...That means, I'm well enough to marry too, in next to next week." His eyes twinkled in waggishness. "What?? Really?! So my boy is marrying. Yes, you can marry, and have stacks of kids too! You have my blessing and the certification for that. As you are one of the finest healthy boy, with perfect, disciplined body, I have ever seen in my entire medical life. But tell me, who is the lucky lady?!" Now the mischievous pair of that elderly doctor threw me a slanting glance with a hunch.

Debobroto's frenzy talks of future joys, carried on. "Well, the lucky lady for this lucky boy, is Miss Minisha Ganguli, who is standing right here, beside all of us, and blushing like a new bride!"

I wish then, to teleport myself out from there into another world for a few moments, he really does have a knack to abash me! The goose bumps ran all over me, due to his declaration of our upcoming marriage ceremony like that, right in front of all! I touched my cheeks, for that much talked about blush, and yes, my cheeks are hot! I'm blushing hard after all. Though I'm a little bit of angry, but a whole lot elated too, for his sudden mischief. And I know this deliberate action of his, just to team up with his acquaintances against me, so if in the near future, in some way, I refused his proposal, I will be prosecuted by them, in return. Mira, Shefali, the doctor, all congratulated me, and they looked so happy, and the trio of them cried in unison. "What took you so long? We knew it all along! Oh! We are so happy for you! You deserve this happiness!"

Then both Shefali and Mira hugged me, and I hugged them back with all my enraptured smiles, and latter showered his blessings to both of us, and I touched his feet, because he indeed seems to me like my elderly uncle. And during this recess, Tia is in such an euphoria, that she hopped and danced like anything, for a quite a long time. "Wowy! I'm going to attend *Ma* and *Baba's* wedding! *Ma* will stay with us forever, and we will go for picnics in an amusement park for every Sunday."

All, except Tia and me, left the room. "Tia, let's go from here, for your over-excited and over-thrilled *Baba* to have a rest." We were ready to prance our happy feet forward, when he requested me. "Mini, could you come back here, after leaving Tia in her room, it's rather urgent!"

But my silence said nothing in response to that, to punish him a little on his yester night's exploit, so he can introspect, before trying out any more of such dared acts. I left Tia, with her favorite teddy and her choicest of storybooks, and a jar of assorted cookies, with a glass chocolate milkshake to go by it, for her second round of refreshments, while she will amuse herself with books and play. With feeble steps, I rushed foolishly to oblige her father's rather urgent, SOS call! I tapped at the door and left the door wide open for a purpose, and he grinned at my mock test of self-defense. "Yes, what is it?"

"Mini, you are still angry, I reckon?"

"For what?!"

"For everything, answer me please! Have you forgiven me, for the last night?"

"Did I slapped you hard across your face, or clenched my claws on your cheeks for yester night, to show my contempt at your indecent felony?!"

"What??! Noo! You haven't done those. I didn't noticed any kind of abhorrence, in your behavior either?"

"So! You got your answer now."

"Oh! So that means you are not angry at me anymore. But wait a minute, then if you could, you would have done this to me, in real anger, without any hesitation, without any qualms at your conscience!" He just guffawed at my remark.

"Yes, I'm a wild cat, then it's no surprise to you. But tell me one thing. Do you really love me, or it's just a marriage of convenience, for your K...'s and future S...'s?!"

"What?!" He hooted again in humor. "So you are practically boiling mad because of that. Didn't I love you then, without touching you even? And I love you whole heartedly now. I'm marrying for our heart's convenience, and to show my appreciative love, I did all those demonstrations. They are the chapters from the subject named love. Are they not? Are you going to back off? Are you skeptical about our marriage?!"

"Don't worry, I'm not a coward. Our marriage plans are not going to be foil up, but do remember this, I'm marrying for Tia only, and for my once love Debobroto. Not for this present identical twin brother of his."I curled my lips to show me audaciousness.

"Pooh Mini, really! But at least, you are marrying with your once sunshine boy, I'm relieved to hear that. But tell me. Is he as handsome as this present twin brother, of his? And have enough prowess and valor in love making, *haan*?!"

"You are, too much!" I stomped my foot. "I will be back to call for lunch, when my naughty and healthy macho man, will be hungry enough, to concentrate on the food, and not on other S-rated substitutes." I could hear his peals of laughs still, echoing outside the corridor.

During lunchtime, at the dining table, I announced my decision of heading off to lodge by this evening, as I have an office work from tomorrow on. When everything is back to its rosiness and normalcy. Tia looked disheartened, he dejected, but he kept that to himself. I simply engaged myself in the task of picking up fish bones, for the former, when I noticed his constant eyeing on my lips. I pressed my anticipated lips hard to command them from any intoxicated desires. Its very difficult to remain calm, due to his pricking gazes at me. To change the subject into something else. I asked Tia, if there is anything amiss in her *Baba,* and she shook her head. But I insisted. "Look carefully dear, why it seems to me, that his eyes are squinted at one particular direction, all of a sudden?!"

It made her curious and she went close to her *Baba* to inspect both of his eyes. "*Ma,* they are alright." Her honest scrutiny replied.

"Are they?!" At this point, my suppressed laughter escaped from my mouth. Those resonating amuse, irked him, he pretended to challenge me as a revenge, for being caught up red-handed during his act of drooling.

"Tia, tell your *Ma,* that this squinty eyes have some surprise for her, a return gift for what she has done for us! It seems only after a couple of weeks later, she will set foot here, so to make up for the absence, and to commemorate on our jubilation, I will sing for her and she will honor me, by joining in, I will be deeply obliged!" He bowed slightly at me like some lord...

That came as a great surprise, his singing! It's the sweetest gift of all! I didn't have any inkling of his talent! Debobroto strummed his acoustic guitar strings with perfect tune, while singing melodiously with such perfect pitch, that my acoustic simply danced in enchantment! To lead his love song concert, he sang first...

*I'm not a perfect person,*
*There's many thing I wish I didn't do,*
*But I continue learning,*
*I never meant to do those things to you,*
*And so I have to say before I go,*
*That I just want you to know,*
*I've found a reason for me,*
*To change who I used to be,*
*A reason to start over new,*
*And the reason is you…*

Then the song *Runaway* then *I'm yours* then he sang *Marry you*, his musical recital stayed on, like some beautiful play list…Step by step, he depicted the rendition of his heart, through his beautiful euphony, keeping in sync the rhythm of his flirtatious side…from how he has faults, but his feelings for me has budded, shaped, that's why he placed that in his pure heart, how my name is simply etched on it…and now is imprinted on his lips! Naughty, naughty man! Then he supplicated again for my hand in marriage, and for my love…Through my euphonious euphoria for his musical endearments, I acknowledged his toast of song request.

And we have chosen that our first love-duet, of my first love symphony which has perked up his heart strings! *You are my sunshine, my only sunshine….You make me happy when skies are gray….Please don't take my sunshine away…..*

And lovely Tia, danced in our love tune, in melody of our joy, and the guitar chords corded our tune of heart, which wants to vocalize our feelings…Finally we relaxed into our truce smiles after concluding a musical journey.

I hugged Tia and kissed her profusely on her cheeks, the parting time is very painful I know. Yet I have to do what's important, while keeping my head together. "Call me as much you want, and tell your *Baba* to eat well, and take care of himself, and you, very well. I'm just an SOS call away from my lodge, whenever you need me…and tell your father, if he changes his mind, he can call me too." We both hugged in an agreement.

Debobroto pulled my hand from there, and pinned me into a corner of the wall before requesting Tia to leave us alone. "Run along to Mira, I have something urgent to talk to, with your *Ma*, before she goes away!" She obeyed her *Baba*. Then he turned to face me, while becoming tentative in his emotions. "Mini, you are not going but you are taking my sunshine…and listen, please take care of yourself too, we fatigued you, a hell lot, and be safe! And thanks for loving us, so much. Call me, anytime, every now and then, otherwise I will barge into your lodge gate with a bulldozer, and will scream at top of my voice, on how you have left me, as an estranged husband!"

That alarmed me, post hearing his impish remark. I know his extremes, he is capable of doing anything with his innovative ideas, simply to meet me. "Oh! Don't do that, please, I will call for sure. I have to stay there for another week?" "So, to seal this deal, how about giving me a S rated K…? To this squinty eyes, and to thank me, for my return gift as well?" His face came closer, to bend closer over my lips, and cupping my face with his hands, he nudged his nose against mine, his lips moved on my parted ones, while brushing them seductively, to catch them, and to see how much more, my lips are going to resist these attempts of temptation? The disobedient ones are already getting ready to approve his pleading of kissing them, the remembrance of earlier sedation in the sensation of his love has enticed them.

"Noo...please don't...don't over exert your weak nerves please." I placed my hand to his cheek slightly, to still his seduction. But on the contrary, he grabbed my hand. "So how about 'K' ing this wild claw of yours, to timid it, from its future spirited acts?"

Without waiting for my permission, he kissed my back of the hand. Then one by one, my fingers, and it's tips, then my hollow of the palm, with his amatory kisses, and then picking my other hand, he did the same! I'm so besotted by this, as they have created a racket of tantalizing sensations into my whole body. I felt as if I'm consumed by a fire of strong passion! But somehow I jerked my hands off, from his passionate spell, and literally ran for cover to my lodge, while leaving my love in his repository of heart....While leaving his floating impish remark, behind me. "Mini, I will twirl the pasta, the way you have said, do remember that, for getting your kisses!"

Post reaching to my place, I simply entranced into my love-struck fantasy world, to feel his lingering love touches once again, which are along with me, and for that I took my first noon nap, to have my sweet reverie about him!

\*\*\*\*\*\*\*\*\*\*\*\*\*\*\*\*\*\*\*\*\*\*\*\*\*\*\*

# Chapter Twelve: Marital Bliss

Almost rest of the evening passed away and night approached, in the due course of our phone call! Reason? My and Tia's futile attempts to talk properly! Due to her *Baba*'s repeated interruptions into our calls! Seeing no other way out, we had to end our call abruptly. We have been persuaded to do that even when we didn't want to. Yet she and I, fell asleep with some re-assurance and comfort, because we are at least being connected through the phone. That call, has shortened our distance, and something else also as well, my eye candy Debobroto's sweet and naughty text message to me instead of calling!

I'm up for Monday, and ready for my work...Reaching there, I'm being called up by my Boss in her cabin, in the middle of my work? As being expected, my impish Debobroto came there to publicly announce our marriage date, to her and among my office colleagues!

As perceived I'm attacked by her series of blatant envy. She seems to be thunder bolted by my sudden fortunate situation! "Minisha! What's this? Why didn't you tell me this before?! How did it happen?? Don't tell me, it happened at the party? Yes, the way you were looking!? I knew it, you are going to snare someone rich there! I knew all along you are going to hit a jackpot, the minute I became aware of yours and Mr.

Mukherjee's acquaintance! It's just unbelievable! Well, I'm happy anyhow, hope Mr. Mukherhjee will make you happy too, and allow you to work for us, and will continue his kindness to us!"

My humbleness stammered despite of those artless, tart remarks. " I... I... Yes Ma'am... It's unexpected. Thank you... No, I will stay here to work. Now, I must go...I left something at my desk rather urgent. Please excuse me." If I could box his ears for creating such din to my office, then I would've done that? I glared at him for subjugating me with this rude shock, but he simply flashed his sweet smiles...And he remained there for a brunch, because a pressing Mrs. Guha wanted to flaunt her convivial side to him, to impress him, for more contracts.

Later in the evening at the office gate I'm choked up with Congratulatory wishes by my colleagues, after office hour. I somehow managed to escape, from the overcrowded envious glares of the fellow office girls and rest of others too, who are equally stunned as how could an intern is marrying a man of business, reputation, wealth, and looks...All their earlier efforts to attract attention during the party when seems to be in vain! Their failures glared at me with such intensity, that they are enough to scorch me, and kill me! I have to jump out from there in the street, and when I saw the culprit, who created this mayhem, waving at me and grinning along while leaning on his car, and this gesture of his, made all of them who are out there even more jealous!

I flared up! On the contrary, ignoring the milieu, he admired my flushed cheeks, blowing curls in the breeze, U neck sleeveless tank top which I wore with a flimsy, see through shrug, to cover my shoulders, my little cropped up Jegging with gladiator sandals...smitten by all of me, he smiled sweetly even when I snarled at him, due to his daze of my loveliness!

"What are you doing here? Do you know, how your news has burned my office? I was hardly able to keep myself alive there!"

"Really Mini, I did that?! But what I should do? As being your would-be husband, is it fair to hide, from those gossipers?! So I'm here to pick you up? And tomorrow, we will go to the marriage registrar office, to put up our marriage registration notice! Come, get in!"

"Where's your driver?!"

"I'm driving. I don't want him to intrude in our intimate moments."

"What? You need more intimacy? Didn't you have enough of it, in your house?" He grinned from ear to ear and explained himself. "Get in, we have so much to do. Besides Mini, it's not safe to travel around alone, before the marriage. I'm experienced, listen to me please. So from now on, I will pick you up and drop you off as well, to your office, to your lodge. You will have to be with me for every preparation, when both of us don't have our parents or relations either, to do all this stuff. When there is so much to do and only a few days left in our hands?"

I complied with him, as every word of his rang true, we are in time constraint, indeed, as only a week left for the ceremony. I felt ashamed for my earlier glares and scowls to him, when he is being so sweet and caring to me all the while. I blamed my wariness. Honestly, there is another motive. I want to rescue myself from the glares of my office mates. Pondering, my compatible self sat inside the car. "Yes, alright! I think you are right, when your hands will be on the steering wheel all the time. So I think, I'm quite safe!"

"What? Oh my God! What you think of me?"

"A first rate, flirt and pervert!"

"What? Mini, you will be kissed for this. But tell me, why you are like a model today? Do you by any chance want to go on a date with your squinty eyed boyfriend?"

"You betcha! Just for SA!"

"You mean Sex Appeal, Mini! Really for me, you did this?"

"Tell your high adrenaline hormones to take a rest, it simply means-Super Admiration!" This remark of mine is enough to aerate his bawdiness in open air, he seems to be in a real mood for that, so he quizzed me while keeping his smug for his expert knowledge, and mastery over techniques, in this field. "*Accha* Mini, you love fruits, but I betcha, you never have tasted this exceptional fruit, ever before!?"

"Which one?! I have tasted everything. Is it some exotic one? Of which, I'm totally unaware of?"

"Yes! It's very exotic one, and it's been called the *forbidden fruit*. Just wait till I make you so used to it, that you will forget all other fruits of your basket."

"My dear Debobroto got a doctorate in Ribald-rated talks. On a second thought, I'm regretting now my decision to be with you, in this car?"

"Oh come on! This is such a harmless talk, and when we are just few days away from all this, Mini!"

"Seriously! Tell me something, as now I'm getting surer and surer, about this. Were you by any chance an ex-playboy before your marriage?"

"What wild accusations you are hurling at me now?"

"I'm having a hunch...You sure did have tons of girlfriends?"

"No! I didn't have tons, but I did have one steady girl."

"What? I knew it, some lover of yours is going to ambush me. How steady, you were with her?"

"Oh, it's just a boyhood crush, and it lasted less than a year, and so many solitary years passed after that, before I got married!"

I sulked knowing this secret. "Was she very pretty, your ex-GF?"

"Yes, she was. But not like my Mini...you are much prettier than anyone else, you are one of a kind!"

"I think you should pull over. I'm getting out."

"What happened?! Are you still brooding on that? She must have been married by now and had children of her own! Oh! Stop being so childish. Now tell me. Why only the male colleagues were congratulating you, not females?"

"That's called office camaraderie, but as the girls were drooling on you, and resentful enough to dig their clenched claws at me. So it's hard to tell, about them!"

"I should tame them. What you say? When your claws are defenseless now. But still...why you are in your western thingies?"

"Has there been a dress code? Let me enjoy my remaining Bachelorette days, and for your kind information, I'm fully-clothed top to bottom. So, what's wrong in it?"

"Hey, sorry! I'm your feminist would-be husband here. I didn't mean that way, to ruffle you up, you are absolutely decently clothed. But Mini by any chance are you regretting on marrying me? You are so young and I'm older than you, and besides with a child?"

"No, Debobroto! We have our banters, but that doesn't mean I'm regretting anything? Honestly I love you dearly, and simply adore Tia! You two, are my life! Please, don't ever think of that. If I really care to marry a young boy, I should have done that long ago. I didn't do that because, whomever were around, all were hollow, in their characters."

"I'm so relieved to know that. Okay, I will call you every night regarding our tight schedules? After office, we have to go to so many places."

"Alright! How's Tia? She's in school now? What you are going to tell her *Didai*? Why are you driving again? When you are not fit enough, and on top of all you have become my chauffeur. Have you had your lunch? How about some coffee?"

"Easy Mini, everything has been just fine, and Tia is with me, and yes, she went to the school. I told her *Didai* and *Dadu*, both everything, about me and my daughter's happiness, which lies with you, they gave their consent to our marriage! Even if it's *Babai* who had persuaded his wife!"

"Really?! That's a stupendous news, an eighth wonder of the world! Oh! your *Babai* really loves us! Like your *Mamoni*, who dotes you and Tia, very much!"

"Yes. Isn't that it? Don't worry, someday she will dote you too, no one can remain aloof from your charm of sweetness."

"You mean from my concocting food which has black magic as she thinks?"

"True!" He cried in amuse. "Debobroto, why you love me, an ordinary pauper? When thousands of rich, pretty, smart girls are in queue for you?"

"Because I'm a pauper in my heart, and you are rich on that. You are my chosen SA, from that long long queue! Happy now?"

"Oh! Don't make me cry honestly, drive quietly. But oh! From where have you learnt to sing and strum like that?" My reverence appreciated his talent, as I didn't know he have such flair in music. "Ah, that! It's not self-taught but from the private coaching...I used to be the lead singer of my college band!"

"Oh! You are such a superb, wonderful, full packaged person. I'm so so lucky to have you, so how about sparing an autograph, my rock star, to this drooling fan of yours!" I looked at him starry eyed, and that pleased him, through his waggishness, he said. "Am I?! And you want an autograph too. Hmm...So how about me, kissing your fan's lips? Are you game?"

"Ah seriously! You should keep a distance from your obsession of K's for a while now, because when I will finish kissing, you will never want to be kissed by anyone else. So for the time being have patience, and put a lasso around your libido, before a ride of your S's, my libidinous cowboy!"

"From where have you learnt all this? Don't tell me, Mini? You don't sneak peek into those? Didja?"

"What, those?"

"Those movies?!"

"Which ones...you meant, mushy-mushy ones?! "

"No, beyond that. I meant adult movies. What do you know about them?"

"Of course! I know about their existence, but I didn't have the time, or an inclination to sneak peek at them, when my hands were full of my hell!"

"Thank God for that! You are such a curious kid, I became worried."

"Really? You are worried? Look, who's talking? What you have done to me? Didn't you addicted me with your K's and with your S'holic talks?"

"Really Mini, I have done that, but you looked so beautiful in your Sari that I lost control!"

"Where's that snap, let me look at it? Oh! You have edited it."

"No, I didn't."

"Then, why I looked so pretty?"

"Because you are a very photogenic and pretty lady. Oh! Mini, I wish, I could meet you, when I was eighteen. Where were you? And why didn't you searched for me?"

"Oh! Debobroto, I was here only...but at that time I was just eight years old. How could an innocent child playing the doll house with her friends, could jostle into the crazy crowd of college fan girls, to make a way through, for that famous rock star of the band? Tell me?"

"You are right Mini, you were just a little kid then...But we get along so well like BFF's, of the same age, so like-minded, that I keep forgetting that we do have a age gap of one decade between us. Well then, how about having a cuppa coffee with this rock star date? I'm feeling rather tired, and if you don't mind, can we stop for a short refreshment? Huh Mini?"

He looked so ardent and super cute with his request, that I didn't have a heart to say a no, to him, when he is up recently from his illness. And he wearied himself out the entire day, leaving his business, simply for me…"I'm so sorry, I tired you out like that, when you are not fit enough to drive. I'm really sorry. Alright…Could you stop at some Chinese or Thai restaurant? It's my treat this time. Let's have Momo with our belly full, it's not wise to have your coffee on an empty stomach. Okay? I reckon, steamed food is not going to harm you, at all. What you say?"

I proposed my earnestness. He pondered before agreeing. That made me so fearful, I thought that I have dared with something which have hurt him. But I should have known him better, he and his jest by now.

"So no pasta for me. Alright, suits me fine then, as you are, who is paying, and not me! But let me warn you, that I'm opting for an expensive one. How about that?!" He sallied his demand to trap me into his impishness. "Don't worry about that. I will pay the bill definitely, will not allow them to force you on washing the dishes, I promise, even if by any chance there is some shortage in the bill payment. I can't even imagine that, not in your present condition at least!" I outsmarted his impish remark.

"What?! So if I'm supposed to be fit, then you will not be bothered even to glance back, before running off to the back exit!" We are into our peals of laughter once again, while enjoying our drive.

As promised he have chosen the most expensive, yet quite an exquisite restaurant. During our sumptuous amount of *Momo*, I noted how his amused eyes are admiring my Queenie way to handle them, with my chopsticks and napkin, my self-consciousness mulled over it, before placing my query to him. "What?! Am I putting you to a shame by my piggy style of eating?"

"No, Mini. You are real Queenie, and you have refinement while eating, and you will never put me into a shame even if you will eat like a pig, I know that. Understand?"

I smiled faintly at him, while squeaking a reply. "Thanks a bunch, now let's get going then."

"Alright! But first let me see your snaps of Queenie days. I'm your soon to be husband, it's my command! What you used to say then, to those people, when they puts you off with something?" I know why he is doing this, just to lighten up the emotional environment, so the reminder of my Queenie style of eating, doesn't thrust me into an abyss of bitter and hurtful memories. He is so affable, sweet, and understanding, that I handed him my phone quietly to empathize with his kindness. "Oh, nothing lewd. Just-*How gross!*" I laughed at my teen silliness, and his laugh allied with me.

"Really? You were bit like a cheerleader girlie type then. Alright, let's see, hmm...oh...my...oh...oh dear God...now what's this Mini?! After seeing this, my adrenaline is sure going to rush! Well Mini, I will not let you go away tonight, not till the morning, not after this snap! Till I K...you, and have S... with you, in my own doctorate way, and for that even if we need to take some protection, I'm willing to do that!"

He is getting lucid on that hidden desire, after sliding the pictures on my mobile, I have experienced how obstinate he was, on kissing me? All those irrational compulsive actions of his, are enough to steam me! I snapped to confront him in my sharpest tone. "Now, what type of smutty talk is this?? What snap?!"

Then I realized, about my much discussed snap, the one he is indicating at, it was during my eighteenth year's seaside holiday time, when my college friend clicked that for me. I was in my one piece, decent halter-neck bikini, my leg part was covered with a sarong too, except a bit of creamy shapely leg was visible, through the slit of that wrapped garment. Ah! And a rather apparent bosom valley peering from that too, in light!

"What I'm going to do?" I floundered, and in my ultimate inhibition, I realized how alluring I must have been looking at that time, with my curls blowing in the sea breeze beside looking akin to bikini clad featured girls of some TV series. That's enough to lure him into a temptation! "Oh Debobroto! That's my mistake, I have completely forgotten about that. What should I do now? Please don't be like that, please stop that. You can't be serious. Are you tempted really? Please tell me that, I beg of you!"

My pleadings of heart, who relies on him blindly, are getting tearful for his sudden keen on a rude motive. My tears moved him, and he is abashed about his sudden salacious intent, he remarked honestly. "Sorry Mini! That was simply a joke, nothing else. I went overboard and overreacted in teasing you mindlessly. I promise you, you are safe from me. Believe me, please. I'm not an indecent character, I love, and respect you, a lot! I won't do anything without your consent, especially anything dishonorable, trust me! But you look like a water nymph. Oh Mini! Why you are so beautiful and fascinating to the eye?"

"I don't know about that really, but ask your reflection that too. Why you are so handsome and charming to the eye?" We smiled warmly at each other as the clouds of doubt which are hovering over us, are cleared away...And when we are about to go, then I handed him the takeaway box of *Momos* for Tia, for her to relish. "What's that?" He looked baffled.

"Oh, seriously! That's for Tia. Is it humane of us to enjoy our fullest, while the child is getting deprived of that little bit of enjoyment?"

"Mini! you are so thoughtful like always, and for that, I feel so proud of you. Let's go...and thank you for giving me a lovely time. It has been a real nice treat with someone really nice. You are a congenial and compassionate person, Mini. Thank you for being like that." I flattered a teary smile, I'm loving the way he is complimenting me.

"Oh! You do have a knack to melt someone. You are very congenial and compassionate too, Debobroto! "

"Really Mini! I melted you, thank you. I know about my *Sweet-heart*." He alluded on the later part of his sentence, to make me his felt emotion with a twinkle of a wink, with a crafting of sweet, lop-sided smile (his hallmark one) he jested then. "That's good then! As there is no *how gross* waiting for me?" I laughed a little while shaking my curly head to deny any such appreciation which is waiting for him. "Okay Mini, let's hit the road. Shall we?"

We must be in the middle of our journey to way back home, when he asked me eagerly. "Mini, who took that photo?"

"Oh, that! That was my girlfriend's boyfriend Vikas." My that one simple answer, impaled an unease into him, and his journey of a thorough query, begun from then on! "What?! Who?! How could he dare doing that?!

Why?! For heaven's name, answer me?"

"Why you are being like this?! Why there are so many question marks in your remark?! Are you by anyway cross-questioning me?! Seriously, we were just friends, were into our college trip...there were so many girl and boy students along with us, wearing the beach outfit like me, alongside at the beach with our teachers, who were present. As that happened to be a co-ed college, so didn't that obvious, my girlfriend had a boyfriend? And when she requested him to take the snap so fervently, after that I took theirs too, while they stood close. What was the harm in it?"

"What co-ed? Why didn't you tell me that at first?! What happened after that?? I want to know every single detail! Do you understand?! The bottom of the truth, the whole story? Mini! I will catch you, if you try to lie or hide anything from me, just remember that!"

Like some disciplinarian guardian, like some investigator, he probed, with his interrogations to me, thinking me as his unruly ward? His boasting of being a feminist masculine, just evaporated then? But my honest heart and a fiery temper are ready to match his probe. "What a chauvinistic remark was that?! A girl can't have a simple, pure college trip with her college mates, like other normal girls at her age? What's that supposed to mean?! We girls returned to our separate rooms in our all girls quarter, with our lady class teacher, after enjoying there a little bit with others. Why should I lie or hide anything when there is nothing for you to discover? What do you mean, should supposed to happen there, tell me honestly?!" I looked so ruffled up with his behavior, when I'm a naiveté on the referred subject, that he let it pass for me then.

Shamefaced, he replied. "Oh Mini! You are so beautiful that I lost my head twice now. I'm sorry for suspecting, a naive, un-spoilt, angelic Mini! Deep down fear of losing you, is still there. Please forgive me!"

He looked so earnest in his remorse, that I have decided to let it pass too, for his sake. Yet chided him, while sniffing a whiff of his suspicion. "Oh really? You are acting just like a suspecting, jealous husband here? Why you? You! How could you even think of that? Seriously, it is not sinister, dark, and polluted always in co-ed colleges, it sometimes rather filled with healthy friendships too. Oh, seriously! You should trust me, you know even my strict parents didn't asked a single thing? You are going to be punished by me, for suspecting me like that!"

"Yes, punish me. I'm sorry, please forgive me, even when I have witnessed your first-hand illiteracy on this particular subject. I should have figured out that how inexperienced you are, in this field!"

"What I'm an illiterate and you a doctorate? Seriously, wait, till I delve into my womanhood instinctive, you will be knocked down by me for sure!"

"What?! I'm waiting for that, for you to knock me down, Mini honestly." He twinkled lasciviously at my thrown innuendo, I blushed like a fool.

"What?? Oh dear God! You've such a dirty mind. How gross!!"

We both laughed heartily at that, at our lifeline, our banters continued like this, throughout our rest of the car drive...I don't know how or when, the time has been flown away. During all this entire week, it felt like we were flowing in a rhythm of a ticking clock only. Along with Debobroto, I had to submerge deeply into the load of tasks, of planning and preparing for our matrimony rituals...from going to a marriage registrar's office, to taking an appointment of the certified *Purohit*; from booking the banquet resort, a wedding planner to a caterer; we have done all those for our civil and court marriage, and then for reception purposes. Amid this we have finished our shopping also, and bought a whole lot of things, and he practically bought almost a departmental store for me, and Tia! Because he reasoned, that he wants to replenish my wasted shopping years. He kept his honorable promise, like a true gentleman, he didn't touch me for once, not even my finger, nor he talked to me in his usual ribald ways, his fuel for teasing his one and only, Mini!

With Tia, Mira, and Shefali by my side, I celebrated our Bachelorette party!

In my old room, where Debobroto is not allowed to set a foot even, in our gaiety, for being a male! That teased his curiosity on our *Single girls party*, for that he paced back and forth restlessly in his room, I could hear his apparent footsteps from the above, while the party is in full swing. I never had such a splendid time before, we noshed oodles of goodies, saw a fun movie, jived in our lively dances, karaoke along with foot tapping numbers. Then tiresome we, retired to our own rooms, with an elated heart! For the final time, I settled on the bed of my old room, until the time will come for me to shift upstairs so to be with my Debobroto, before old Minisha can be replaced by a new one! This was my last day, as being a bachelorette also, on this earth year!

This time we are married for real, not like the puerile way we solemnized our ritual earlier, by our three times calling game... my paranoid Debobroto has been in such a worry, about losing me, that he insisted, us to be married two times! Our auspicious marriage date has fallen on the 26th of May!

First we have been married in the eyes of law, through our registry marriage, at the court's marriage registrar office, to be a legally husband and wife. Then we are married in a traditional Bengali ritual, for our civil marriage, in a banquet resort…While sacred priests chanted out the sacred *mantras*, while the sacred sound of conch blowing and ululation pervaded there, we involved ourselves into seven vows, taken for each other by circumambulating around the sacred fire of *Saat Pak* ceremony. We tied our nuptial knot through it, to become socially, a husband and wife. Now, we are officially a man and a wife, one body, one soul, in the eyes of God, law, and society… he is one of the splendid looking Bengali groom anyone can ever laid their eyes on, one in a million, in his head gear of *Sholar Topor, silk Panjabi, Garoder* shawl, and silk *Dhooti,* as his wedding attire, and I, his pretty Bengali bride, clad in with a B*enarasi* sari, *Sholar mukut* on my head, *Shankha, Pala,* (conch and coral bangles worn by bride while getting married) and *Shonar bolloy* (gold Bangles) in my wrists, and vermilion on the parting of my hair, which my husband has put, with a full authority and love!

On the day of our reception, we both sat in our high chairs as a chief guest husband, as a chief guest wife, this time, his formal exquisite styled attire of tuxedo suit, is adorning him, and my *Jamewar* pink sari equally does the justice of adornment. Our Tia, is sitting pretty and lovely in a purple *Benarasi,* a specially cut Sari for children, like a princess by our side… Many people thronged to commemorate in our jubilated day, from his friends, his office subordinates, his business associates to my office colleagues. Shefali, Mira, guards, Babulal, Romon*da,* the doctor, Mrs. Guha, everyone… Yet in that crowd of guests, yet to that percussion of the rejoicing; we, three quintessentially commemorated between ourselves, our exhilarated joys, in our reclusive world of paradise!

When he laughed and whispered in my ear, his implication. "Mini, now there is no scope for you either to run away, or to desert me! We are legally and socially bound into a marriage, into a lifetime commitment. I'm your Sunshine husband, you are my Sunshine wife! I have simply enough power to prosecute you, if I don't get enough quota of my K's and S's from now on."

I embarked my opinion keeping in sync with his tease. "Okay! I will thenprosecute you back, if you escape from me without having any!"

"Really Mini?!" His exhilaration exclaimed. *"Hoon.* You betcha!" I threw a simper at him.

An amaze ambushed us! Mr. and Mrs. Banerjee attended our wedding reception, which we haven't anticipated at all! And latter promised me that she will try to forgive me! Debobroto and I, touched their feets, and both, blessed us full-heartedly! My tears of joy knows no bound, for that wonder, specially when she welcomed me in my man's home, during *Bou Boron* ceremony (reception of a new bride) as being Debobroto's mother, with complete ritual and ululation, while Mira blew the conch!

I didn't once believed myself, that I would be married one day with a man, I love! My early curse of poignancy of being lonely, of being single, has been broken by the warm presence of Debobroto's love. Yes, he is my harbinger of blessing! Who would have imagined, that I will be in this master bedroom, to share my life with him, to share our conjugal bliss, our wedding night, by being his wife, while waiting for him desperately, like this?! It is my one of unbelievable dream come true, I pinched myself hard for that...I must have been dozing off on the window seat beside that starlit sky, during my gazing of the stars, while I thanked my parents, and God, for their benediction. In this due course of time, I have persisted for Tia being with me, but her *Didai* scolded me to reason that, before being a mother,

I'm Debobroto's wife, and that I should make my first and primary priority, in life. As tonight is our first night, so Tia should be in her room only. I should think of my husband and his needs too. I bowed down to what she has said, when she is like my *Mamoni*! It made me so emotional, that I hugged her for the first time, voluntarily. So seeing me complying with her, she further advised me in her rarity, in her sweet-tone?

"Alright Minisha! *Pagol Meye* (silly girl) listen to me...you are like my daughter Shamita, and from now on I will think that she has come back to me once again, in the form of you Remember this child, I'm trusting you to become a good mother and a good wife. Your *Babai* and mine's blessings are with you, for always, now, we must get going to our house...

It's my other daughter's house, and their parents can't stay long here, it's against society's wishes."

She kissed my cheek, and tears rolled down from her eyes, as if she is giving me a *Bidai* (farewell) as a mother, I cried my heart too, and hugged her once more. Her bitterness seemed to be evaporating, and I'm entering into her heart slowly and softly. I could percept that.

"Oh *Mamoni*! Thank you. You are an angel. I will not disappoint you. I promise you that from my heart, if I do something wrong, then scold me, like you always do." She smiled at me sweetly, before leaving me, with my new family, so I can commence a new journey of life, a new phase with them. I kissed a good night to weary Tia and tucked her into a sleep. I stroked her head gently and kissed her, and then returned to my room, and placed that picture of three of us, clicked with him, at the amusement park. Our sunny smiles, framed into a teakwood wooden frame, so it can remain framed for infinity. I put that on his bedside table, to face his sunny side. Our present life picture, just the way he desired it to be. I kept my promise! All those, I did during the interlude period of my dozing off.

When I opened my blinking eyes, I saw Debobroto, my prince charming scooping me up from the seat, to carry me in his arms, and then he placed me on the bed, so gently, with a fear that he might crush a fragile flower.

"Mini! Are you really feeling sleepy?" He sounded desperate, yet he felt sorry, in disturbing my slumber like that, so I teased him in return.

"*Hoon* very. Why?!"

"What? Have you forgotten that it's our first night, of being together?!"

"Ah! Yes! I remember now." I pulled his leg once again, after seeing his bewildered face. His astonish made him more cute and handsome.

"What? Then why don't you change into something comfy, when a heavy Sari makes you itchy?"

"Hmm...you think so. Alright, when you are my husband, I will do what you wish for."

"Really Mini? You will listen to me?"Nodding my head I climbed down from the bed, touched his feet before leaving. He is so astounded by my recent behavior, so he asked. "Mini, why you did that?!"

"Well, you are my husband and older than me, so it's my duty, being a dutiful wife, call me an old fashioned, but you can't take away this authority from me ever. In every morning, I will touch your feet, and you will have to bless me too generously, without being a stingy one, understand?!"

"Alright, I will bless you, but right now, I have a delicious blessing in my mind, to give you, so come back quickly here for that, understand?!"

"*Hoon,* understood!"

I rushed to the restroom to change my bridal attire. When I noticed something beautiful and soft, hanging on the hook? A baby pink, low-cut, full length night negligee, in silk. A very sensuous one with two thin strips crossing over the shoulder, with lace works all the way around the neckline, and it fitted me to a T. To my utter disbelief, I'm looking like an incredibly amorous beauty, more like a seductress, moreover, my cleavage area together with a conspicuous pair of bosoms are displayed, even tight peaks, under that sheer soft material! I blushed hard at my reflection! I know now why he was so resolute on my changing of clothes, as he wanted me to try this out...he must have remembered my bikini clad snap while buying this, naughtiness was on his mind then, I thought. To punish his impishness and to tease him further. I decided to keep the negligee worn by me under wraps. I covered myself with a thick bathrobe, I have thrown it over my shoulder. After concealing his gift of love, I fastened the robe's belt around, and went outside looking all unaware and unsuspecting...He looked so disappointed and flustered at my hideous robe, that he questioned me with a longing voice. "Mini, why all of a sudden you are wearing that?? You have not found out anything else there?"

"What?? Oh, this was hanging on the hook. Why? Is there suppose to be something else too, that I should find there?!" My self-pretense answered him through my innocent eyes.

This baffled him so much, that he mulled over that thing's non-existence by ruffling his hair, it's getting difficult to suppress my mischievous laughter, in front of my cute husband. "Now, do what your wife says, go and change into something comfy too."

"What? Oh yes!"

Moments later, he came out wearing his boxer shorts and my Sunshine T-shirt, looking like a cute boy, and that very sight is enough for me, to burst into roars of laughter. I rolled down on my bed, my body shaking with rib-tickling laughs. "Hold on Mini! Why you are so hysteric? Stop it, I'm your husband, I'm commanding you. You ask for it. Come here, for the punishment of your disobedience, and let me see, what you are hiding inside your robe. It's getting very suspicious by now, your sudden liking to a thick robe at this summer time."

He peeked inside the robe. "Caught ya! Aha! There's my gift, now let me look at it, please."

I clutched my Robe ends desperately, but he tickled me very hard, and it is getting difficult for me to stay still...so I relented. "I give up, alright take a peek-a-boo then!"

I slipped down the robe, and there I'm, with my night slip on, into the light, with my curls spreading around my shoulders, and few locks came forward to my face, few are adorning my cleavage, he is so bewitched by the sight, of my new found ravishing, seductive, and curvaceous beauty, that he gaped his mouth in open! He growled in an enchanted passion. "Oh Mini! Come to me, or I will prosecute you." He crouched on top of me, to lean over me, and then he caught my two hands in his captive imprisonment. "Mini, my sweet wife...now tell me, how this cowboy should act with his libido?"

I blushed crimson red and I veiled my eyes with my lush lashes, to escape from his piercing and burning gaze. He playfully fired away his passionate suggestions to me, through my imitative phrases of love. "Do you want a side-way, or a half-way, or a full-way, or an ultimate way of my love, to you!"

"Debobroto! In every way, if you please, as you are so determined to love me in any way!" I fired away my straight-lace quip too, amid my inhibition. We snickered in our mischief of hilarity.

At first he kissed on my neck slightly, then kisses are continued pouring, on my soft skin lavishly while he is cuddling me, so this is called 'necking' I thought. I totally sunk into the lovely sensations of sparks created by his friction of lips... then a hoarse and husky voice urged…"You are so lovely Mini! I'm afraid, I will lose my control tonight, so don't be scared of me dear. Trust me and follow me along, like some dance movements, follow with the flow of my love movements. Trust me and follow me, my love."

I nodded at him in my rapt smile, while permitting, and surrendering my body and soul, to become one with him, and pleaded with my imploring eyes to guide me, to teach me, about love-making...Post, getting my approval to consummate the marriage, he slid his arms behind my back, with master hands fondled there with rapid strokes, then they became fierce...he kneaded the back as if the passion has broken loose. Slowly, he put both his hands on my bosoms, squeezing them slightly, a passionate cry torn out from my throat, like a mate call, this aroused him. He started kissing my cheeks, eyes, nose, ears, my cleavage, without lifting his hands from them. The grip instead became tighter on them in return, they seemed to swell up more by his ecstatic touches. Then he smooched furiously my lips by his carnal desire…as if it is a spontaneous reaction, I lifted my arm to run my hand through his luxuriant hair, and pulled his head closer and closer to taste his lips more. I, with equal desire, responded to his wild kisses, with my well matched lips, while following his every movement. We are into each others lips with such demanding passions, that I wonder, how I could do that, who taught me to do that? Finally, somehow I know instinctively, that it is the time, and the sign for me, to begin my first love making lesson of which I've been waiting for so long. He have flamed my awakening desires. With his swift and skilled hands he splayed my thighs gently before stroking, to expose my lower beauty, then he slid his hand behind my lower back to lift my bottom up so my lower part can meet his erected front part. After entering into my soft area, he guided me, how helping him in thrusting and pushing of his love shoves. He continued shoving in my soft lower area with his hard and throbbing member with each sensory, thrusting pushes off, in and out motion, its force and pace are increasing too, with each passing of time. Those penetrating moves are getting deep down there, while pushing in and out, over and over. My lower part is not remained hidden anymore, is not remained untouched anymore.

I lost my chastity there and then! I moaned in sweet delights while he grunted in an equal emotion, as if a challenge have commenced...The battle of the softness against the hardness, it is so tender and sweet at the beginning, but later, it started becoming passionate and wild, with its quickening pace and shallow thrusts, so fierce, that he pulled my legs to hook them up to his behind, he carried on pulling my bottom from behind to make it move along, with his thrusting movements. It is such an ecstatic moment for me, that I moaned loud for his recent overpowering love, strength over me, and he became so primal in love-making, devouring me with such wildness all of a sudden, that perspiration broke into my whole body. I drenched in sweat, and my curls became all wet, because of this experience of exquisite consuming passion, and on account of his heavy weight over me, besides the constant flames on his heated aroused body, those explosive love frictions altogether, simply melted me, in his fire of passionate love! It is too much for me to bear. He carried on in his fierce love-making and it lasted for a long period of time, before he can reach for his climax. Before his arousal can go limp, he gave few more of his languid thrusts into inside, then his exhausting body collapsed over me to rest into a deep sleep… It's the crack of dawn, my sleepy eyes recalled our first love making night, our consummation of marriage! I could not believe myself still the fact, that we actually made love together, with such wild and scorching fire of passion,how we have shared a bed being a life partner, how we became one to share our feelings, now will be going to share our life! After kissing his neck slightly, which I coined as my AM kissing, I rested my head on his arms to nestle into his side-way embrace…Mine and his clothes have been discarded off on the bed, they are, all crushed and crumpled, looking like an evidence of our passionate act, we are sleeping in our *Au naturel,* in our nature's given clothing. I slipped from his strong arm, quickly put on my cast-offs before sleeping again, before his naughtiness can be wide awake!

I was in my sleep when I felt tingling frictions in my leg. Debobroto have entangled his legs over mine during my sleeping duration, with his toe, rubbing my calf, to stroke briskly on the skin, and side by side his animated front arousal trying to entice me, through the barrier of my thin material of the negligee. He is seducing me, I can witness that through my gap of sleepy eyes, his passionate eyes flamed. He groaned while rubbing his body against me, in back and forth moves. "Oh Mini! How about having another round! Huh?"

"*Uuhnu*, no, please not now, I'm feeling sleepy. We need our rest when it's almost morning, let's shut our eyes for the sleep, into our embrace."

"Okay! I'm an obedient husband, but promise me, you will pay your tax, otherwise will be penalized by me, for your non-payment of overdue love tax?"

"Alright." Before falling into sleep, he kissed me on my lips, passionately, then crushed me into his arms again, we are so close that not a breeze could pass through our body. Resting my head on his chest, I slept peacefully when he put his arms around, till the morning.

After waking up in the morning, my love-filled being took it's pandiculation in a marital bliss. I caressed him affectionately by my adoring glances. I slipped out from his tight clasp while making sure, his slumber is not stirred.

Quickly taking a shower, I cladded in a cotton Sari. The sprinkling warm water has soothed my body, it was aching due my last night's maiden experience of love! It's time to check my Tia. I have my duty as Mother beside being a Wife, as well. I dried my hair with a towel. Thought, if I turn to a hair dryer for this purpose, then it will be time consuming for me...I let my wet curls, the way they are to dry naturally. Into the process of settling my Sari pleats into evenness, I'm being grabbed by my husband from behind, he made a way through my Sari, to slip his hands into it, to grab my waist area. I can see from the mirror, the reflection of his bright glances which are affixed into my delightful sight, how they are enjoying the touch of my soft skin. I sparkled my sweet smiles at him, to my love-struck romancer through the mirror. "Oh! You are awake. Good morning, Debobroto! Let me touch your feet." But holding my hand, he placed that on his chest, before kissing it. Then cupping my chin, he lifted it to his eye level. "Mini not there, but right into my arms. Oh! You are looking so ethereal beauty, with enchanting wet curls, that I feel like drowning into your pending tax, right now!"

"Don't be so naughty. I must go to Tia, please. It's her breakfast and school time. I love to dote her also?"

"Okay, go, but not before my tonic K...I'm feeling sick again!"

"Ah! Really!" I kissed him on his cheek.

"No...not there, here." He put his finger on his lips, I touched them slightly there with my lips, but he grabbed me around to give me hug, and started smooching my bottom lip.

"*Uhn.*" I freed my lips from his. "Now please, it's getting late. I have to prepare breakfast, now go freshen up....you will be late for the office."

I managed to mumble in my heavy breathing, he replied in his panting. "Alright! But I will go tomorrow. I'm not leaving my lovely bride, all alone here…Mini, I love you so much... that was a very beautiful and lovely night together, and you were so delicate, my well sculpted soft beauty, and were so sweet like honey, at our love-making. Oh! Mini, I'm not exaggerating. Will you believe me?! If I tell you this, that last night was the one and only beautiful experience I ever had, since the past!"

He confided his sooth of heart to inhibit me, he does have the knack to open up bluntly. Hot blushes appeared on my cheeks after the recollection of the last night, but still I replied to him in my steady voice. "Really! So I'm a good learner then?"

"Yes, you are, and you will soon going to get an 'A' from me, but for that you have to work very hard. There is still lots to learn!" He winked at me naughtily, a lopsided naughty grin played on his face. "But tell me, am I a good master too?" He boasted on his caliber, while looking smug. "Yes, you are like a Dean. I have to immune myself from your love lessons in the future. But can you have a pity on this student, by giving her some concessions at least? You charge rather skyrocketed fees!" We both snickered, before he could go to the washroom.

From there, I went to Tia's room. She was wide awake, waiting for me to help her get ready. Whilst she showered. I straightened out her bed and tidied up the room, checked the contents of her school bag. She came bright and shining. I straightened out her school uniform too...brushed her hair gently to make two pony tails with expert hands, while I was tying her school ribbons into bows, when she requested me with something fervently. "*Ma*, don't quit your job, please. All my friend's mothers are career women, I also want to boast about it, that my *Ma* is a career woman...I want someone to take inspiration from."

"Really, sweetie? Then I will not quit, and work with perseverance for my Tia! But I will return home at the near-about six thirty after work, you will be back at three from your school. How will you manage those three and half hour alone? For that time being, you have to be alone with Mira and Shefali? What am I going to do? Do you want a nanny?"

"No-oo...I don't want any nanny. I'm used to be with Mira and Shefali from earlier, so I don't mind, if they mind me, and of your being late from office that's alright, my friend's mom also arrives home at this hour too." "Oh! You are such a good and brave girl... Please help your *Ma* to become one too, a real good mother for my Tia, help me dearie!"

"I will do that. I want to become just like you, you are my role model *Ma*. Even I'm just a little girl, still I know, how you have strive in your life, keeping your head high to become something." Her sagacious words overwhelmed me, such a little and innocent girl, yet so wise and smart. Such tender-heart and understanding one, that she is ready to sacrifice her happiness, to adjust her lifestyle just for her mother's career. I hugged her, sealing the pact between us. At that time someone else also joined in, into our hugged bodies, it is her *Baba*, and his arms are wrapping us into a big family hug. Together we stayed like that for a while. When all of a sudden, he became so curious about our chit-chat. "So what secret, my two lovely ladies has hatched, between themselves?"

"Nothing at all, Tia wants me to continue my work."

"Alright! I have no objection to that, then work for me."

But Tia protested loudly. "No *Baba*... I prefer *Ma* to stay in her current office with her independent feet on, without depending on anybody else. I will not mind if she returns late, and that's final!"

Our little princess stamped her ruling over us, and we both parents smiled satisfactorily at each other, while swelling with pride for our responsible and understanding little grown-up girl! I became so proud that I kissed her on both the cheeks, and she giggled harder.

"Alright Tia! Your *Ma* will build an empire for you to inherit. Okay?!"

"What if you fail, then?" He challenged me with a smirk on his face, his questioning brow arched up to tease me.

"Then Tia will inherit, my salary!" I challenged him back with my quip. And three of us, laughed at this bright idea.

He, Tia, and I, all of us breakfasted, heartily, amid our loud plans and hilarious chatters. I waved for so long at Tia's car, which is heading for the school. I waved cheerfully at my own Sunshine daughter, even after it's been long gone, faded out of my sight!

I must be deeply engaged in my kitchen work, that I didn't notice when Debobroto is leaning against the doorway. "Minisha! Where you have put that file?...Oh! Mira, Shefali, I want to ask you a favor. Can you two manage for a week without your *Boudimoni* in kitchen, until she finishes her office leave, as I don't want my new bride getting overworked. Will you do this favor for your *Dada*?!" They gave an approved nod at him, to each other a mischievous knowing smile, for his, this asked favor. It's so embarrassing for me to stay there, I followed him out, he just pulled my hand and released the grip only after reaching into our room. He even bolted the door securely after that my miff simply exploded. "Ooh! What you have done? So humiliating, you look like a possessive husband, hurling innuendos out there?"

"Do I? Well, it suits me fine then."

"Now, what's this about a file?"

"Yes, an important and confidential file, I need to consult, it's called Love Tax! Now pay me with full penalty. Why you only love Tia a lot, but not her *Baba* a whole lot?!" He pouted.

"Now! In this broad daylight?!"

"Why your eyes are rounded like that? You are my new bride, I'm your groom. Just imagine, if we have supposedly gone to our honeymoon, then didn't we would have done the same?"

"What?! All day and night along? What about the sight seeing?"

"You want sight seeing, then how about going to a lover's cruise, with only two of us as a company?"

"Leaving Tia all alone here? Are you out of your mind? Talk some sense!"

It seems to me that he wants to relish a sensual banter, that's why he suggested something impossible. "Hmm, that can wait. But how about a long and never ending drive?"

"Well, that's alright then, along with Tia, we can go to our long drive every Sunday, to that amusement park, or to some other nice places. How about that?"

"How can you be so dense, all of a sudden, I didn't mean a car drive?"

"Then what? I didn't get you, what you are indicating at now?"

"Silly! I'm talking about my craving drive for that juicy fruit... We will take ride into each other without any lasso around to our untamed carnal desires. How about that?! Or I will become your chauffeur in driving our desire car, for that long-long S drive?"

"Dear lord! What R-rated words? Why you are being so naughty, all of a sudden? What has gotten into you? As you have missed 'Your morning win, that's why you want to have an afternoon spin'?"

"Mini, you sure know how to write a jingle. Now come sit by my side." He patted on the side of the bed where he sat. "Listen, you are going to be a great mother to Tia, and just perfect love and life partner, for me! Undoubtedly. But don't you want me to compliment you, through my appreciative love deeds? How about that?!"

Without giving me any notice of his action, he pulled my hand, so gently I can sit on the bed, I can settle down. Grabbing me from behind, gently parted away my curls from the shoulder while putting them at a side, before kissing on it. Then he placed his chin on it, before kissing my column of the neck, with his tender kisses...I became numb to this tantalizing sensation, which are enticing me, that without flinching, I passively accorded to him, while he is in his process of caressing me, touching me, even in his next move of dare! He removed the end of my sari...Unclasped the back hooks of my blouse, with the quickness of his hands, that piece of garment simply slipped off, while sliding off from my shoulders, like my sari edge. Then he unfastened my top under garment too, it exposed my bosoms and from behind, he cupped my tingling parts due to this sensuous grip, a passionate, soft sound escaped from my throat...That instigated his desire more, that he flipped me around, so I could fall over his chest, then he rolled over me, taking me along with him, while I'm being placed under him, so I can lie there on my back, stretched. With swift hands, he removed his T-shirt, and his well-chiseled chest is exposed to me, to make me more aroused, then he made a lunge over me, brushed his tight chest peaks against my soft mounts into a rhythmic stroke. It seems that both his, and mine, are kissing each other like that. By this time he is fully turned on, in a peak, for that ultimate step...Finally, his aroused voice, murmured his seductive endearment to me, they are gushing out from his sensuous mouth, to express his dark eye's desire, which have turned into pewter color. The intoxicated effects can be felt in his hot, uneven breath as well, which are scorching my face with carnal desire. "So now, how about having a brunch of high-cal love? My lovely sunshine wife, come, let's have some hanky-panky! Oh Mini, you are so beautiful darling, being blessed with such curves, that you are just like a sculpted marble figurine to me! Oh Mini...you are a drug for me. I'm getting Mini-holic...Why you are so lovely, inside out? I'm so lucky to have you...your skin is so petal smooth, so creamy soft... your enormous eyes beckoning me to drown in them, like your sweet lips, they are pleading me, to sink into them..." Hot, seductive words of his flattery, flattered his need to love. With that, he bent over my lips, to kiss them fiercely, he showered a downpour of soft kisses on my whole body. On my shoulders, neck, eyelids, ears, nose, cheeks, chin, lips, my recess of bosoms, before kissing my belly. His grazing lips are tingling and lingering all over me, making it impossible for me, not to moan in a sweet delight. My receptive twisted body of extreme pleasure is getting beyond my control, it wants to surrender when his canoodling foreplay, thrust me into this?

"Ohh...I want to be Debobroto-holic too, yes please, yes!" My candor opened out. He understood my plea, so we can journey together along with our yes-manship of desires. He conferred with my wish. "Ohh...Mini, yes, I will....for you!"

At that time he splayed the part between my knee, while slightly brushing the thigh with his thumb, without wasting a single moment further on, he quickly slid his arm reach for my bottom, and for few moments fondled them, then they are grappled by him, to raise up my lower part to collide with his hedonistic front, he entered it languidly inside to put a deep and long strokes of back and forth thrusts, he moved on and on, while carrying my uplifted back and bottom along with it, by his hands. I paired into his tender love thrusting movements by encircling my one arm around his back, so that my body can be pressed close and with other hand, I ran my fingers through his thick hair, while fastening my raising legs around his behind, the way he have taught me last night...I'm a good learner! My raised legs together, hooked his behind, so I can aid him aptly, in his more shallower and faster love moves. Both ours, his and mine sensual parts are having passionate pleasures individually, yet keeping in sync in with one love. It carried on for a long, time, till we can conquer our love victory, till we can reach to our apex moment. All the while, our whole bodies bathed into each others tingling closeness, sensory feelings, and that's how, we have made love together again…It felt so wonderful and tender, as how our bodies whetted in our famished passion and love this time round also. We fell into each others arms languorously, to have a love nap.

After quite a while I woke up, to smile tenderly at my Debobroto, while he is still asleep with his parted lips, I snuggled close into his loving and warm embrace, while burying my head to his neck, to smell his tantalizing masculine scent. I lay there for a moment more, so I can transport a warm flying smile, full of love and care, to my darling daughter Tia! I slipped past from his arms like I did in the morning, without stirring him up at all, to shower and put myself into a fresh Sari…I smiled at my previous crisp one there, it is now crumbled into a ball, balled up by my beloved husband, for his drive. I snickered at his earlier love puns, he is just the perfect match for me. After I changed into my Kota silk sari, and gathered my fountain of curly hair to knot into a bulky bun, by securing that with a gold clasp which Debobroto have gifted me as my wedding present. I stroked on it lovingly, at my husband's fetish for my hair. *"He is so romantic really!"* I blushed. I have to rush to the kitchen also, along with my inhibition and afterglow of love, for Tia and his refreshments, for their peckish self's sake, even if I'm defying his wishes by doing this! Mira and Shefali looked astonished, but I hushed them for my secret surprise to him, as lunch is ready, so I got ample time for my cuisine making. It's quarter to twelve in the afternoon, already. I thought of preparing some *Momos* for Tia and his snacks, and to commemorate that *Momo* day, which we both have spent together earlier. I went upstairs to see if he is awake? It's past one already, and he is sleeping like a log. Tiptoeing to his side, to sit gently beside him while crouching over his sleeping side carefully. I gave a little to kiss on his tempting and velvety parted lips...I kissed him for so long...my lips to his lips...my mouth to his mouth. I relished his sweetness and lusciousness of lips. In fact, I'm doing this to seduce him for his awakening so he can love me once more, once again...I must be occupied with my kissing that I failed to percept his wakefulness, his locking of lips on mine...We are being like a perfect lip-catching partners, with perfect kiss-steps. Heaving in heavy breaths, we separated our captive's lips.

"Caught ya! Who's this girl, stealing kisses from this sleeping prince?" I tinkled in my laugh at his teasing remark. "Oh! Mini, you are here to have another S... round? Then come, kiss me more properly!"

To comply my husband's wish, I kissed him right on his lips once more with same intense passion. To provoke him utmost in his irresistible arousal for me. I kissed him for so long, by my one long seductive kiss. For that my mouth caved in for a deep down exploration, of his mouth's. Fires sparked between us. And to give a signature of passion on his lips, I bit his bottom lip gently and tenderly, the way he did that night, like a caress from my teeth. He groaned in pleasure.

"Oh...*uuhnn*...Mini, you are such a seductress in kissing. Let's have a quick one, then, alright, come quickly, come."

"I'm here to wake my Prince for his lunch?"

"No, I want you to be my lunch... Why you knotted your hair, why you did that?"

"Many hours have past since your breakfast, have something please, and remember, you yourself have bought this gold clasp. Don't you want me to try this out, your love gift? Do I look a hideous?"

He groaned in such enrapture, that he pulled me into his arms. "No, you are more sensuous with your exposed slender neck and with your sculpted back, and that front deep area is getting more highlighted, which my eyes always longs to see, those are much more well defined now, for me to love you more!"

"But Shefali has cooked a lunch for us, have some please."

"I will not have any. I will only eat what you will cook." "Ah! But you don't want me to do that, still I defied you, to make some *Momos*. Do you like to have those now?" "Perhaps later, but right now let me taste my *Momo* Queenie first." I giggled in naughtiness. "Okay! Taste me as much as you want, but a very quick one, as only one and half hour hardly left, for Tia's arrival from the school?"

"Don't worry, I'm your fast lover... I'm going to make a world record on that!" Before I can climb into the bed, to join him in acclaiming his world record fame, with quick hands, I cast off all my clothes, to place them on the sofa chair beside the bed, I did that without any shyness. I stripped before my loving husband, to stand in bare nakedness, and why I feel inhibited, when he and I, are one body and one soul. I gave him a coquettish smile, and then loosened up my hair, so it can spread like a silk fountain of curls, over my sculpted body...My whole being perked up with such flirtatiousness, with such arousal to seduce him for my amatory desires...

I must be at my peak of arousal, and he in his bewitchment, looked at my amorous beauty, at my body language which

I'm using to woo him, my unspoken craves of need. "Mini! You look like a water nymph, come here fast my darling, my nymph. Mini, come hastily... I can't wait any longer." He seized me, with his grabbing hands, pulled me underneath him, swooping down over me, he sizzled me by his scorching kisses on my cheeks, lips, forehead, ears, earlobes, nose, eyes, neck, shoulder area, throat, bosoms and then cupping them gave a gentle squeeze, then kissing again on them softly, one by one. That act of his, swooned me in my potent bodily want, to satiate that, I moaned loud. "Oh! Debobroto please love me, please make-love fast-please-to me..." "Mini, yes, I will, just hold on sweetheart."

He fondled my whole body with his hands, kissed all the tasted parts once again, cupping my bosoms, he started again on my lips, again and again by his pounding sweet, lovely kissing of mouth to mouth. And then with a very daring version of mouth kissing of his, which he gave it to me! He bent to grab my bare back into a tight clasp, I clutched his bare back too, then he inserted his pushes. He is pushing, shoving, stroking, thrusting deeply, and intensely, his penetrating moves, which are motioned in such a rhythm, in such a swift passionate speed, that I purred out cries, of the content pleasure...Then after that, when our ultimate peak of delight is over... He flattened over me into a collapse. His exhausted hard body weighing down on my soft body... and that's our second love making the round for today...I'm really amazed at my dared act of love, my way of seduction, so that he can feel the taste of my love, he can drown in the never ending feeling to taste me, I, in a same way to be tasted by him. What an addictive feeling, my sweet and passionate lover Debobroto have given me...that I have become a love-holic for him for my entire life? I called him out of his sleep. "Hey! Please wake up, go shower and change into some fresh clothes... It's time for you to have really something...till then, I will catch my sleep okay." He concurred and after a while came fully clothed and showered. Fresh and bright, looking so super cute and dashing.

"Mini, come on...wake up. It's your time too."I wrapped the coverlet to my bare bod, with a coy smile, ran to the restroom, before grabbing my things which I have stripped off with such seductiveness...and his sweet touches lingered while I showered...

In a while I brought a heavy tray of *Momos* and two flasks of orange and black grape juice. Mira helped me to hand them, one by one, from outside of the door, with an intention of not to invade in our privacy. I respected her, for that consideration! We indulged in our delicious *Momo* lunch, those tasted heavenly, especially because someone delicious like my Debobroto is there by my side. He is loving it to the core, and according to him, it tastes far better than the restaurant, he preferred the ambience of our bed room's sitting nook with his convivial and lovely wife, but he is getting rather intrigued about my sussing out the recipe of *Momo*...and that, with chopsticks Tia can pick fish bones too. As I want her to learn how to pick fish bones. "Really?! You could do that with them?"

"Yes, I will show you."

"I'm really amazed, how you have learnt so many things, who taught you?

Or maybe you are born with it!"

"Well, thank you. Even if I'm not born with it, but when you say like this, it seems to me that, it's the real truth." He grinned at my flattery in his dazed eyes, he must be in his trance still, as how his love have reciprocated and married him, how after drenching into the sweet love, she is sitting beside him now, it must be a dream to him still. "Mini, wish I could be in a time machine, and can go back to the past, when my Mini was eighteen, just to be her boyfriend! That can't be possible, I know. Oh! I love you so much. Alright, let's do something. Why don't you join my club to practice your aerobics and swimming? We can swim together, like a beach boy and a bikini girl? How about that?!"

"Okay, let's. But on one condition, Tia will join too, the children's section to learn her swimming lessons. Girls at her age usually start taking the classes to become a good swimmer. That will be just great for her fitness. Who knows, one day, she will become a swimming champ? How about that? Let's tag her along with us?"

"Oh Mini...you are so good, alright, it's a deal. What as a father, I never have thought of, which you simply considered that for Tia. Thank you so much sweetheart!" He hugged me with tenderness.

"Alright...alright, Tia is my daughter, I'm her mother. So it's my heart's duty to be thoughtful. But Debobroto tell me one thing, are you really happy in your teens?"

"Yes! Very. I was my parent's only child, and my mother pampered me a lot...Do you believe me, if I tell you this, she was just like you?! The way you think about us, the way you care for us, the way you cook for us!?"

"Really! Oh, I didn't know that. It's such a great honor. Thank you so much, dear. You think, I do have such qualities. I'm skilled enough for that, thank you for thinking me like that!" I hugged him, with happy tears flowing down my cheeks. "Yes...do you know why? Because we are made for each other, have the same wavelength."

"Debobroto, we do have like-mindedness, like soul mates. That's why, I want to know something? Were you honestly smitten by me, at the first sight?!"

"Yes... Indeed, so much so, that I was ready to do that thing right there!"

"What??! Oh! That's why you were so charming to me, but I thought that feeling came, after my bikini photo?"

"No, my heart took the initiative to make you mine, but that snap stirred some raw passions inside. You were so fairy looking at the first day, that I didn't know you have a sultry side hidden, as well."

"I didn't know. I looked like that. Can I confide into something, even I thought the same, at the first sight?!"

"What?! I didn't believe it?"

"Debobrato, I don't know what exact feeling that was, my naivety then, made me inexpressive now." I asked him then which always hovered over my mind. "Um...can you tell me something?!"

"*Hoon.*" He gazed at me in intrigue. "Actually, it inspired me to cook for you and Tia. You looked so pitiable that day, when I came to your house. You had your dinner, but still attacked to those cookies and hot cocoa, like someone famished, who hadn't eaten for days. I thought of you being some eccentric. That picture of yours just mapped in my brain. But I haven't seen you doing that again? What happened exactly?!"

"You happened!"

"What?! But I didn't eat your share of dinner? Then why?" I blinked hard innocently at his laughing face. "Mini, I was unable to sleep that night because your beauty haunted me.

I turned and tossed in my bed for so long. Thought glucose would at least sedate me into a sleep. So was eating something sugary, rather than having a fitful sleep. But what happened instead? You appeared there, all beautiful with your night dress on, to torment me even more!"

"I didn't come there on purpose, came to refill my water carafe. You looked so cold and remote, that I didn't realize what was going on in your mind?"

"Yes, you were unaware, but I was coping hard, to control my inner bases with the greatest difficulty."

"Really? Oh my God! You were so naughty then. You burnt so much sugar, for me?"

"Mini you are something. You are my one sassy girl...Then how about giving me, that latest seductive kiss...You are getting so good at it, that I can't possibly going to undermine you anymore, you surely have knocked me down!" He bent over my lips to taste my mouth. "Ah! Wait! The sauce is smeared on your lips, let me wipe it off with the napkin first, then kiss."

"No...there is another how gross method to do that. Use your 'T' for that." "My goodness! What a titillated idea? Noo... wash your mouth, if you want to have that kiss." "*Uhnnu.*" His adamant self simply wiped off his mouth, with the corner of my Sari end. "Now time for that, sweet dessert." He fondled my back with such rapacity, pulled my mouth with so much yearn under his, expeditiously, that before I can know anything, he already have coveted my lips, for that mouth to mouth kissing!

I co-partnered with him too by fondling his back, to simply dive my lips deep down into his mouth, for my craved kissing!

*****************************

# Epilogue: Heaven on Earth

Tia returned from the school. We had our lunch with her, with *Momos* once again. All that love making famished, our bodies it seems...While dazzling around with each other, we finished our meal...For the usual noon nap, a tired Tia along with me and him, went to her room. Her happiness knows no bounds, as her parent's presence are with her, she laughed in an effervesce. I stroked her head, sitting by her side, while he intently studied us from the sofa chair, with his pair of black, attentive eyes. I decided to speak out a candor, regarding a matter of significance, which is troubling me.

"Debobroto, after a couple of days, Tia's summer vacations are going to start. What should we do about it? We can't leave the child by herself, with Mira and Shefali around? Though I trust them, undoubtedly, but still as a Parent, we should chalk out something? We both will be out, all day for work, only by evening we will return. Do you think, we really could go for a holiday trip during this summer, three of us, somewhere?!"

"No! Mini we can't. I will be busy, these coming months, it's only during Tia's Autumn break, I think, at the time of *Durga Pujo*, I can spare some free time."

"Oh! What we should do then?!"

"Mini, we can send Tia to her *Didai's* place, as she is waiting with so much expectation for her granddaughter to spend this vacation. I can't break her heart."

"You think so, alright then. I know how she misses Tia so much." I inquired for my daughter's honest say before taking any decision, when it's her holiday. "Tia would you like to go there, in this summer vacation, tell me dear?!"

"Yes, I will go in *Dadu* and *Didai's* house, I know they love me, but on one condition, *Ma!*"

"What is it sweetie?"

"You will go there with me, to spend my holidays...You will drive me there, and from there you can go to the office regularly. I can't stay there without you."

"Yes, Tia, your *Ma* can't stay without you either. I just hope, your *Didai* doesn't refuse our plan, or show any objection of my staying there? What do you think Debobroto?!"

He looked crestfallen at the idea. "Well, Mini! What about me, then how am I suppose to stay without...?!"

"Yes, you are right, you will miss Tia a lot. We have to think of something else, then. But what?"

Hearing his and Tia's distress, I started churning my brain to think something to appease his and her suffering. I didn't know, his actual anguish and perspective is going to be different, far from what I have concluded. "Yes, I will miss Tia, but at present, I'm talking about you. I'm not going to agree. I can't possibly stay without you not even for a second. These two months will be like a century for me, it will be my death Mini. I have an idea, which will save the candle from burning from both the ends. We will simply invite her *Didai* here to spend the duration of vacation. It's high time, she should spend some time here. I hope, she will not mind, as now she has a soft corner for you. As for Tia's *Dadu*, he usually goes to visit his younger brother, at this time of year... So that's settled then."

Tia and I, whooped with joy at Debobroto's superb engineered plan, after learning about the resolution of the problem, she fell into a sleep, with so much content. Our serene hearts kissed her sleepy forehead, we sneaked out of the room softly, while closing the door behind quietly. In our room, Debobroto unraveled his further elaborated plans. "And Mini, I will buy a car for you, so you can drive it to the office, for your ongoing and off-going purposes. How about it? In case of emergency, you could go to Tia's school without disturbing the servants, or their allotted car! How about a test drive tomorrow? If you like...You can drop this honey bunch of yours, to his office, or pick him up for back home. You will save so much time in travel, could return much earlier for Tia too!"

His exuding deepest concerns overwhelmed me, it seems to be an excellent viewpoint of his, regarding Tia's benefit. Above all, for which my heart is touched, on what his benevolent heart has thought. He planned this only for my safety, in my roundabout travels. I acceded at his endorsed idea.

"Oh Debobroto! You can't hide this any longer. I caught this from your compassionate heart. Why you love me so much? Tell me? Why your Mini?" I hugged him in contentment, while resting my head on his chest in serenity.

"What is it Mini? What you have caught from my heart, my love for you?"

"Yes, your selfless, unconditional love for me, you are doing this only for me, so I could travel safely. Didn't that you planned?"

"Yes Mini! You caught me."

He made our embrace much warmer in love. But it's my time to endorse my suggestion. "I'm taking this on one condition, that you will lend me the entire amount, which you are going to spend on the car payment. Alright? Because I intended to return back every spent amount through my installment with an interest, every month. How about that Debobroto?"

"Now your husband has become a loan shark? When everything is all yours, as a right of a wife, then why you want to do that?!"

"Yes, dear, I know that, but I want to do this as an independent woman, and for the sake of Tia, to take an inspiration. I promised her, I can't simply break her heart!"

"Alright Mini, that's why I love my considerate, self-reliant and strong-willed Minisha. But I have a condition. I want only love as an interest in your installment payouts at my beck and call, otherwise this loan shark will charge you double love payment."

I snickered at my naughty and sweet creditor, he too at his beloved debtor, once again we melted in our warmth of love hug.

"Debobroto, it's near about time for evening fare, let me make something for Tia and you, please *Shona* (honey) in the meantime, check your emails or your phone calls, to keep a tab on your work. How about that? I will be back shortly."

"Mini! Did you know, what impossible thing you have done?!" His eyes danced with full mischief.

"What??! Tell me, what is it?" My agog asked.

"You called me *Shona*! You have given me, my pet name! From now on, you are going to call me by that, when we will be intimate. That's an order!" While putting his arms around my waist, pulling me closer, he urged, while uttering those words, he kissed me on my lips, between the interval of his each and every word.

I blushed hard in inhibition, bit my lip for error. "Oh, that! It just slipped out from my mouth!" I placed a playful punch on his chest, and laughed in shyness while lowering my eyes. "Alright, that's a deal then, I will call you that, now do what I have told you to, alright my *Shona*!"

He chortled at my shyness, kissed me again, full on my lips, by leveling up my chin to his face. He hinted something playfully, through his invented pun. "Mini, we have to pipe down our love noises, while we will be in our love act, because Tia's *Didai* has sharp pricked ears. Do you have any idea what will happen, while we will be at our interactive intercourse?!"

"What? Ah! You are such a naughty one." I cackled in mirth, before pointing out in my serious tone. "But Debobroto, are you going to be so busy these past months, that you will arrive late? So only Sundays, we can have you? How Tia and I, then suppose to spend our time without you?"

"Yes! Mini. It will be hard for me, but don't worry, I will be back by seven, every evening. Oh! Mini, all day without you in office. I'm shivering with a fright, at the thought of it. You are right, at least we can have our Sundays. We will go together with Tia somewhere then."

"Yes, we should do that, we can't deprive her, from her much deserved affection of parents, let's do that honestly."

Nodding our heads to concord, we both remained lost in each

other, in our blessed and soothing arms for a while, before losing ourselves actually in our chaotic, routine life.

"Okay! *Ebar amay chharo* (let me go now). I have loads to do, really Debobroto."

"Not until you call me *Shona*, three times, while kissing me on my lips, uttering each syllable. Until then, *aami kintu tomay sohoje chharchhi na* (I will not let you get away so easily)."

"Ah! Really!....*Shona*…" I uttered that word, then kissed his lip, likewise repeated the process for three times, then only I got my freedom from the love clasp, of my Prince Charming.

I made *Mysore Pak* for them in the evening, along with other savories. Tia is having her *Pak*, but Debobroto looked confused and downcast as well.

"What is it Debobroto...is it that bad? Tia, is it so bad?" I queried around with anxiety about my sweet dish. She shook her head. "No *Ma*! It's fantastic...it's *Daroon*! (Awesome) "

"Yes Mini...it's excellent, but can I use my hand to eat this? I don't think, I'm good at it with chopsticks, like the way you are, while eating your dessert?"

"Ah! You are always in your humor, I said that figuratively, yes, you can... I'm using mine too, see like Tia, and eating by hand has it's own charm, it's world's most civilized way of eating etiquette, I'm proud of my Indian style of eating. So without any hesitation, simply go on."

We did have a royal fete…then we three went to our bedroom, to open all the unopened gifts and presents, given at the time of our marriage, we are having such a fantastic time in our guessing and playing game of 'Who has given, what Gift?' It's been decided that the best guesser will win points and the scorer of the high points, will get a surprise gift!

Debobroto quipped amid this. "I know what to give your *Ma*, Tia, if she wins, she really loves to have that!" He grinned waggishly at his insinuation.

"I know, what your *Baba* wants by now, I'm good at giving return gifts too, Tia." I quipped while grinning in return. "And Tia, will have our love as a gift." I concluded that, while stroking her head tenderly. Three of us shrieked in our bubbly laughs!

Then suddenly, he confessed his sincere love for us, ripped open his beautiful heart for us to see the depth of his love, he has. "Mini, I love you so much. You are so wonderful wife beyond anyone's dream, and Tia, your *Baba* loves you too much. You are such a splendid daughter, that any father could be proud of. I simply love my marvelous family very much. I think, my home and my family, is my heaven on earth!"

Emotional tears came to my eyes for his sweet and simple confession, that encouraged me, to put my sincere side of love before them. "*Ma* adores Tia and her *Baba*, both, very much. You people have changed my entire topsy-turvy life into something meaningful, filled it with so much love, that I couldn't ask for more! No more blessing I can ask from the God. And yes,

I already got my gifts -The gift of my Sunshine-husband and Sunshine-daughter. So I thank my Sunshine-family, my heartfelt thanks for giving me immense sunny love and happiness. I pray and thank God, my *Baba* and *Ma*, my *Baba*-in-law and my *Ma*-in-law, from the bottom of my heart, for giving their blessings to our Sunshine-life! I pray once again for this sunniness of ours to stay forever, for one another in our heart and home!"

They became elated with this thankfulness filled prayer, that their brimming emotions embraced them. They are able to comprehend the true essence of my love for them. To give a seal on that prayer, we three, gave a hug to each other, we simply snuggled ourselves, into our one big Sunshine-family embrace! I pondered on those true words of Debobroto once again, of my *Shona's*...Yes, this is our heaven on earth indeed! How my feet had been meandering for years in my dessert like life, in search of an oasis love.

Seeing my perseverance, my harsh destiny for once pitied upon me, blessed me with my desired oasis, in the form of my adorable husband and daughter, and their love! I'm the richest and happiest one in this entire universe! I have my infinite Sunshine love with me!

I wish to narrate about our **fortitude, and indescribable love beyond words,** more often. For now taking a momentary repose, till I unfold my next narrative. Trust this Minisha, she is not keeping this in abeyance!

### THE END